WAYWARD VOYAGE

WAYWARD VOYAGE

ANNA M HOLMES

The Book Guild Ltd

First published in Great Britain in 2021 by
The Book Guild Ltd
9 Priory Business Park
Wistow Road, Kibworth
Leicestershire, LE8 0RX
Freephone: 0800 999 2982
www.bookguild.co.uk
Email: info@bookguild.co.uk
Twitter: @bookguild

Typeset in 12pt Adobe Jenson Pro

Printed and bound by CPI Group (UK) Ltd, Croydon, CR0 4YY

ISBN 978 1913551 728

British Library Cataloguing in Publication Data.
A catalogue record for this book is available from the British Library.

To all women who are
adventurous at heart and in deed.

PROLOGUE

Spanish Town, Jamaica
November 1720

MILITARY DRUMS AND FIFE NOTES SLICED THE morning air. Anne jumped onto a bench under the high window, gripped the iron bars and peered out.

An Admiralty Marshal, ceremonial silver oar in hand, marched into view, head erect, a fifer and two drummers keeping step. She spat as far as she could. A futile gesture that fell short, but she didn't care about the pompous-looking official, it was those following she was impatient to see.

She yelled above the drums, 'Godspeed! Godspeed!'

A man's voice reached her. 'We go to the devil if he'll take us.'

Let the devil take him.

A second voice responded, 'And God be with you, lass.'

These weren't the ones she wanted. Perhaps he wasn't there? They were moving too fast, the Marshal already passing out of sight… Yes! He was at the rear, head bowed, wrists lashed together. Standing on tiptoes, she pressed her face as far as she could between the bars and shouted, 'You!'

His head jerked up and twisted to face her.

'If you'd fought like a man you wouldn't have to die like a dog!'

He smiled and gave a quick shake of his head. Smiled! She had more to say – words she had rehearsed over and over the past days and nights when sleep wouldn't come, but it was too late. Craning her neck, she watched till they were out of sight, listening to the footsteps and fife and drums fade. The gates thudded shut but still she could hear the drums – faintly – then not at all.

Resting her forehead against the wall she waited for her breath to steady.

'I won't be next.' Her words emerged as a croak. She cleared her throat and spoke forcefully. 'I'll not die.'

'Anne...'

Anne turned to meet the gaze of the woman sitting slumped against their cell wall in blood-encrusted seaman's clothes.

She stared into the raddled face.

'Neither of us are going to die. You hear me?'

She was not ready to die and could not bear to think of what was unfolding beyond the gates.

PART ONE

1704 – 1716

To America

So good luck to those people and safe may they land
They're leaving their country for a far distant strand.
They're leaving old Ireland no longer can stay
And thousands are sailing to Amerikay.

CHORUS, TRADITIONAL SONG

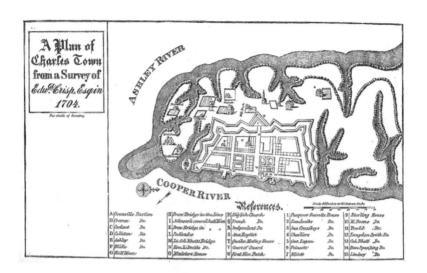

Charles Town and surroundings, South Carolina

1

WITH HER NEW WOOLLEN CLOAK WRAPPED AGAINST A biting spring wind, Anne raised herself on tiptoe and peeped over the handrail of the *William and Mary*. They glided along Cobh's long estuary on the outgoing tide, passing green hills dotted with white cottages, smoke curling from chimneys. Aged six, she had never been on any boat, let alone something this size. 'A brigantine,' Pa said.

Other family groups were making the journey and some big girls, too young to be alone, Ma thought. Most of the passengers were men who looked younger than Pa, some no more than big boys. She tugged the sleeve of a shivering man next to her.

'You'd best fetch your jacket, don't you think?'

He looked down, sneering. 'Little bitch.'

She drew back, seeking refuge with Pa. 'Why are they hugging themselves and why is that man sad?'

He cocked his head. 'That scrawny young fella. Perhaps he's keeping his jacket for best, don't ye think? And that one over there with the patched-up jacket, he must've lost his buttons and didn't have time to find them, he was so busy packing.'

'Ma can sew them on for him.'

'For sure, but don't go asking him about his buttons, there's a good girl... Dear heart, how would you feel if you sailed away and never saw your friends or your brothers and sisters or your ma and pa again? Or your home?'

'I don't have brothers and sisters. And they'll just have to find a new home.'

'That's true.' Pa ruffled her hair, and she raced off to explore.

On the open sea Anne watched sailors balancing on foot ropes under thick wooden poles – the yards – that extended from both masts high above her. On deck sailors worked, hand over hand, pulling on dangling ropes. As they pulled, massive sheets of sailcloth unfurled, until hauling on different ropes – ropes she learnt had particular names – made the yards swing around and a sagging sail snap and stretch tight. Soon the *William and Mary* was fully dressed.

The tarred rigging ropes were called shrouds, but she scoffed when Pa said, 'If all this rope y'see about you was laid out it would stretch along the road from Kinsale to Cork and a good way back again. What d'ye say to that?'

She didn't dare call him a liar.

The rigging she liked best had a special name – ratlines – and if sailors could climb these spiderweb ladders, so could she. She clambered onto a rail and tested her feet on the ropes, facing directly into the wind, eyes watering. Clinging on, she looked up at the sky, then down into the white-tipped waves. Before she was ready to come down she was plucked off by a passing sailor; next time she was determined to go higher.

Spending time below deck didn't interest her. The smell of stale bilge water was only the beginning; within a day a sharp smell of vomit filled the air. If they opened the hatch to let in air, sea spray came in. She had to jump about to keep warm, flapping her cloak to try and dry it.

Ma took to bed with a queasy stomach. They were lucky, they had a pallet of straw to sleep on; others didn't. Anne tried to help by hauling the stinky leather bucket up the steep ladder and emptying it over the side. Somehow she managed to spill Ma's sick over her dress, making her gag and cry a little. When an older boy scoffed, she felt ashamed.

'Pa, I want my breeches. Open up the trunk, I know where to find them.'

'Your breeches? Sure they don't bring back bad memories?'

Ma had made them and cut her hair short, so she could pretend to be a boy and study in Pa's office in his effort to "get some schooling into that skull of yours".

That hadn't lasted long. The lady Pa was married to had stormed in and made a big fuss. Soon after Pa decided to take her and Ma away.

Balling up her discarded dress, Anne foraged in the trunk for her breeches and didn't take them off for the rest of the voyage. When her shoes were soaked she kicked them off, so her feet turned blue and her toes became covered in chilblains.

She learned new words: heads, mizzen mast, bowsprit. And others tripped off her tongue: puke and shit. If Pa or Ma minded, they didn't say.

One big storm marked the voyage. Fear was as catching as seasickness. Trying to keep to her feet, she pushed her way through the huddled crowds on the 'tween deck.

'Pa, Pa, hold on to me!' He reached out and hugged her.

'Oh, dear heart, I couldn't find you! I'm so sorry.'

His voice sounded shaky as he pressed her cheek against his rough wool jacket.

'Make it stop. Tell the Captain to make this stop!'

'He'll be doing all he can. Maybe God can help. Whisper to him, he might hear.'

She screwed up her eyes but didn't know what to say. In any case, she doubted God would know her as Ma had never taken her to church.

Waves crashed over the deck and cascaded through the broken hatch; the anchor thudded against the hull; the shuddering *William and Mary* plunged into valleys of water and bucked backwards, so everyone screamed. She rode out the storm gripping to Pa's jacket.

Once it ended, she gave it no more thought.

Her playmates started as a group of nine, but shrank to seven. The first death was a boy she didn't like much, but the second, a girl named Lizzy, had been kind, helping her stand up to older bullies. She hadn't liked watching Lizzy's sobbing parents carry her body in a stitched-up sheet. She hadn't liked watching Captain Browne read some words from the Bible, or seeing Lizzy lowered over the side and bobbing along before sinking. This was the second time she cried, fingers pressed to her ears, screaming and screaming.

'Pa, I don't want to die, I don't want to go into the sea.'

'Ah, child, no fear of that, you're as fit as a flea. But your ma isn't well. Will you help me look after her?'

Ma? She pushed out of her mind a picture of Ma's bare feet disappearing over the rail.

Eleven more people died, some before the big storm, and soon afterwards a baby she couldn't be sad about because it had cried and cried and wasn't a real person yet. Then the sailor with the squinty eye wasn't there, and she felt sorry she had poked her tongue out and called him names.

Ma continued to be grey-faced and sweaty, and she couldn't stop shivering. She always managed to alert Pa to help her squat over the bucket that had become her toilet. Everyone could see, and no one cared. A young man with no one to help him shitted his bed. Anne saw no reason for him to cry, but she felt sorry when his stinking straw pallet had to be thrown away and he slept on bare boards. He died within days, and she watched with steely eyes, determined this would not happen to her.

One day Ma turned away from the wall, opened her eyes and smiled. Anne jumped on the pallet next to her.

'Look!' She opened her mouth wide.

Ma reached out to stroke her cheek. 'Ah, darling girl, you've lost another tooth.'

'Pa says new ones will grow.'

Stories spilled out: who had won a game of chase, how many rungs up the ratlines she had climbed.

'I got to eight, and—'

'You mustn't—'

'Captain Browne chased me. I went higher but he grabbed my foot.'

'Anne!'

'Then he threw me backwards over his shoulder like a sack of potatoes and climbed down. He said if I did it again he'd lock me up with the rats.'

'Anne, prom—'

'Ma, it's all right. He said I could join his crew when I'm older, and I said I'd think about it.'

Satisfied Ma would live, she joined her friends.

She had given up trying to pick lice off her clothes and hair and resigned herself to itching day and night. When a sore bump under her arm began to weep pus, she was embarrassed to find herself crying again. Pa wiped away her tears. At home he used to shave every day but now he had a dirty beard. He laid her hand on his cheek.

'I've got one under here too and—' He leant closer and whispered, patting his backside. 'Another down here. I can't sit down.'

She laughed, just a little.

'You're such a brave girl, I'm so proud of you. It won't be long now.'

But more days and weeks passed.

One day she watched four boys wearing only their breeches swinging from the ratlines. Anne could feel the boiling sun on the back of her neck and her shirt was sweaty so she stripped it off and clambered up to join them. Her hands were calloused like the sailors', and she could hang on swinging and making whooping noises like the creatures called monkeys they had told her about. As she swung she wrapped her legs around one boy trying to pull him off.

'Anne! Get down.'

Pa glared up at her, Ma by his side. He had shaved and they wore their best clothes.

'Mary, I'll not have her going ashore like this.'

Pa grabbed her leg and she fell into his arms.

'Look at you, naked as a savage, filthy and scabby all over.' Pa sighed.

She yowled when Ma dragged a comb through her salt-encrusted hair. She protested when her outgrown shoes were jammed on her feet. She squirmed when Ma laced her dress, but at least it had been washed and didn't stink of sick.

At the rail she squeezed in front of Pa and Ma to get a good view.

The *William and Mary* glided into the estuary with just the jib catching enough wind for the helmsman to steer. She knew the names of things now. Ahead were low sand dunes and strange tall trees with spiky leaves, and the call of birds were unfamiliar.

'So still... Empty... So humid... Nothing like home, William.' Ma sounded anxious.

'It'll be fine – just fine.' Pa always said that.

They slid past low swamp and brown creeks surrounded by reeds. Pa pointed out three shaven-headed brown-skinned men sitting in a canoe with fishing nets. One stood, a spear poised to strike a fish, naked except for a bit of cloth around his private parts. Ma gasped, and Pa cleared his throat, mumbling, 'Well, well.' Anne wondered if she would be allowed to run around naked in this new land.

Charles Town, where they'd come to live, came in view.

'It's tiny...' Ma's fingers clutched Anne's shoulder.

Ma was right. It was a small settlement with half-built defensive walls edging the water and lots of forest behind.

'You'd think they'd station a man-of-war here,' Pa said to Ma.

There was nothing like that that Anne could see. Nothing much at all really.

Passengers began hauling trunks up as sailors dropped anchor, so Anne kept out of the way and watched small boats leaving the quayside to collect them. She counted six, then began counting the rowers. She stared at them to make sure before rushing off to find Ma to share her discovery.

'Look at the men rowing. Look at their faces. They're inky black!'

Ma's fingers gripped tighter than before. Anne wriggled away, impatient to be ashore.

For all that this land was strange, William didn't regret leaving Ireland – or Europe – as that distant place seemed to be tearing itself apart with land wars in the Netherlands and sea battles in Spanish waters.

The population of Charles Town, tucked into the point between the Ashley and Cooper Rivers, was tinier than he had expected – well below three thousand white settlers and as many blacks. There were taverns aplenty and a church or meeting house on every corner to satisfy all persuasions, whether Church of England or one of the Dissenter congregations such as Quaker, Methodist, Baptist. There was no tolerance for Catholics, so Mary would just have to adapt to this. Popish doctrine was too close to Spanish sovereignty – and the Spanish were themselves too close for comfort: south along the coast in Florida.

Taverns were the best place to pick up gossip and advice and William favoured the White Horse on the waterfront. The easy camaraderie reminded him of his first weeks at school as a new boy: survivors like to boast and create a frisson of danger for newcomers. At the White Horse he listened to stories of attacks and heard of men sliced and battered. One tough-looking fellow had just returned from such an encounter. He'd taken up arms and joined with the militia and Creek Indians to attack and destroy Catholic missions on Spanish territory. Carolina wanted to discourage their better-established Spanish neighbours from spreading the Roman Catholic faith far and wide to the Indian tribes. During the recent excursion, buildings had been razed, dozens killed, and hundreds of Indians – who had sided with the Spanish – enslaved.

'That priest, he put up a decent fight. Reckon he'd put the fear of God into those Apalachees barricaded in the church along with him and women and kids. We tried to smoke 'em out, but arrows came flying. My word, they are accurate, make no mistake. I didn't expect to make it back home.'

The fellow rolled up his breeches to show a nasty-looking arrow wound on his thigh.

'Well, turns out our God was on our side and the Popish God didn't save 'em. It was a messy business, though we didn't mean to harm the women and children, I swear to you...'

The fighting fellow chuckled and winked at William. 'Brought some souvenirs home: four Indian bucks. Selling at a good price. Interested?'

'Don't waste your money, stay clear of 'em!' The unmistakeable tones of an Ulsterman joined the conversation. 'First chance they get, they'll leg it into the interior back to their people. You'd be wiser putting your money into Africans. Where're they going to go? Can't swim home.'

Each man in the tavern had stories to tell about the recent smallpox epidemic: of family members dead, or neighbouring houses where no one survived. Then there was fever that caused skin to turn yellow and vomit to turn black. Nearly two hundred citizens of this small town had died from that, including many of the town's leaders.

While the ravages of fevers and plagues that could sweep through a community were known to William, earthquakes were something else entirely.

'Just like being at sea. You feel the boards under your feet rolling and swaying. Scariest thing ever! We grabbed the baby and legged it!'

William, wide-eyed, listened to this Charles Town inhabitant tell his tale and could only exclaim, 'Is that a fact?'

Each man tried to describe the sound and fury of a hurricane, give advice about the best variety of crops, and sturdiest building methods to withstand the winds and deluges that sometimes swept inland.

William's head was spinning. Danger lurked at every corner it seemed, yet people took things in their stride, or left to seek a better life elsewhere if they believed such a place existed outside heaven. Back in Cork, Captain Browne had spoken in such glowing terms of Carolina, and William decided the name of his vessel, the *William and Mary*, was a good portent. William was here now: here in the heat and dust, the downpours and thunderstorms, and pestered by mosquitoes. He must make this his home, as he knew another ocean voyage was beyond him.

William found people hell bent on making the most of their lives, however long or short they might be. You only had to stand still at the wharves and look about you to know what drove this colony. Commerce. Tightly controlled commerce.

Charles Town's sheltered harbour formed one point in a formidable trading triangle. Exports of deer skin traded with Indians in the forested interior; rice from the growing number of plantations carved out from cypress swamps along the many waterways meandering through the coastal low country; timber from the forests and cleared swamps; navy supplies – tar and pitch extracted from the abundant pine trees. All this bountiful produce was packed and shipped to England or English colonies, aboard English ships. The ships themselves were crafted in England from their colonies' timbers and sailed right back to this side of the world loaded with linens and all manner of things their young colonies had not yet managed to create for themselves. The third sea leg of this trading triangle was what provided the engine for Carolina: enslaved black labour from the African West Coast. Slaves to be sold as chattel property.

To get on in this colony meant buying into its way of life. He brushed aside the uncomfortable truth that the Irish had suffered under the yoke of English oppression for centuries and he was about to do the same to others. On the sea voyage, apart from seasickness and fever, Mary had been afflicted by a different kind of nausea and had confided she was with child. He had a growing family to care for and meant to purchase land and slaves to work it.

2

HOME WAS A PLANTATION ALONG A MUDDY CREEK OFF the Ashley River. A German man Pa had met in the White Horse had owned it and Pa thought that once his wife and son had died Mr Schneider had lost heart. When she wasn't busy looking after Billy, her little brother, Ma did the bookkeeping. Pa learned about rice planting and hired a white overseer, though it seemed to Anne that Otto, Samuel and Abba, and other slaves they'd bought from Mr Schneider, knew how rice planting was done and didn't need anyone minding them in the fields.

Phoebe didn't need anyone to mind her either. She was easily as tall and broad as Pa and fiercely ruled the cook-house and vegetable garden, a turban of coloured cloth atop a shiny black face. Anne couldn't say she was scared of Phoebe, but Phoebe might swat her with a dishcloth if Anne got in the way when she was cooking.

As often as she could, she visited the Croomes'. Their plantation bordered her own but was much bigger and their house was much grander with a long sweeping driveway. Emily was her chief playmate, but Richar, who was older than she was, looked forward to her visits too. A broad smile lit up his face whenever he saw her. Richard knew he could count on her to play games he couldn't entice his sister to join in with. The skills Richard was acquiring at his fencing lessons in Charles Town were like a magnet. She handled Richard's long-bladed rapier with envy, though Mrs Croome soon took it from her, and she and Richard played with long wooden sticks.

'Thrust, Anne! Put me out of action!' Richard proved a willing target. She tried but it wasn't so easy when someone jumped about. 'Ah ha, got you!' Richard's stick-rapier found its mark in her stomach and she yelped and doubled over, winded.

Mrs Croome rushed up to them mid-fight, her hands fluttering. 'Poor Anne. Richard, stop now! Anne doesn't want to play these rough games, and besides, it's not seemly.' She turned to Anne with startled eyes. 'My goodness. Are you hurt, dear? Emily, fetch a cool drink for your guest.'

As Emily trotted off, Anne seethed. Of course, she wanted to play, of course, she wasn't hurt, not enough to make a fuss about, so she and Richard practised in the barn, well away from Mrs Croome and unconcerned about the blacks who fetched or returned harnesses, tools and farm implements. Here Anne honed her fencing skills. Sometimes Richard would mimic his mother's fluting voice: 'My goodness, Anne, this isn't seemly!' setting her off into peals of laughter.

One day Anne persuaded Richard to bring his rapier into the barn and let her have a go. She thrust it into a stack of straw, expelling a satisfying, 'Ha!' as she lunged. Then she tried some slicing actions. When Richard asked for his sword back she refused.

'Catch me!' She ran off, heading up a ladder into the loft brandishing his sword.

'Get down, it's dangerous!'

'Make me.' She goaded him.

He chased her but she warded him off, eyes wild with the thrill of her power over him. She had a real sword in her hand and could kill him in an instant!

'Give it back!' Richard's face turned red.

She jumped off the ladder towards him; he swerved; she flailed about, slashing. The rapier struck a glancing blow on a metal plough, flew from her hand in a high arc, landing with a clatter. Richard picked it up, inspected it for damage and walked out without saying a word. They didn't see each other for some weeks and Richard never offered her his real sword again.

Twice a year Trader Mac called by their plantation. He always wore buckskin leggings, which Anne admired, and on cool days he'd wear a long soft skin jacket. In spring he'd be heading inland, his mules packed with metal hoes and kettles – many bought from Tomboy, one of their blacks, who had a smelter behind his hut. Mac would return in autumn with dozens of deer hides bound for warehouses at Charles Town's quayside. During summer, he'd told Anne, he lived with a Catawbas woman and they had a bunch of kids. She loved hearing stories of Indian villages Mac had visited: the games children played; what they wore; how tribal women made important decisions along with the men. It was fascinating to learn that the kind of life she lived was not the only life that might be lived. And it was Mac who had helped name her foal. 'How about Shotek?' he had suggested. 'Means sky in Chickasaw.'

When the time came, Anne helped geld Shotek. She stroked his head whispering to keep him calm while keeping an eye on what was happening at his other end. She hated to see him hurt, but as Otto and Samuel held the bound horse,

O'Neil, their new overseer, worked quickly. When it was over he wiped his bloodied knife on a cloth, eyeing her. 'You weren't girly about it.' She glanced at the pink globular balls discarded on the ground. 'No. Has to be done,' she told him, and turned back to stroking Shotek's head.

No one knew much of O'Neil's past. He'd spent some years in the mountains of Virginia – he'd said as much, but not more. Anne knew all about leprechauns from Ma's tales and wondered if O'Neil was of this breed of men. He and Ma were the same height – Anne was nearly as tall as them both – and he walked with a rolling gait on bandy legs. Apart from his size and the look of him, which he couldn't do much about, he had a disgusting habit of chewing tobacco and spitting gobs out. A habit, Pa said, he could curb if he wished. Worse still, he seemed to deliberately aim for her feet.

'He's a bogtrotting Irishman if ever you saw one.' Pa would shake his head when telling his family of another of O'Neil's stubborn habits.

'You hired him, Pa. Why don't you get rid of him?'

'Not so easy to find white men these days.' So O'Neil stayed.

One day, after Anne had helped O'Neil with the horses, she trailed after him to the bench outside his hut. She squatted at a distance and watched as he carved a cow-horn for his gunpowder. He had lovingly polished it, and began carving some picture taking shape in his mind. Whenever she tried to look over his shoulder he'd stop.

'Can't be having you watchin'...'

She backed off and waited to be shown where he had got to.

Bit by bit a picture emerged of mountains. She thought they were very realistic and told him so. He nodded and seemed pleased enough but wouldn't say, or didn't know, what would be in the foreground. Eventually an image of a man riding a horse took shape. When he offered it for her inspection she studied it. The horse's head wasn't quite right, and the man looked a bit squat, a little like O'Neil, but she bit back any criticism and decided to compliment him.

'I couldn't do this, you're really clever. When I'm old enough, I'd like one with a picture of me and Shotek.' She hoped this might encourage him to make another and gift it to her, but as weeks passed she never spotted him crafting another such horn, and so far no gift had come her way.

O'Neil provided meat for their table and his own. He cooked for himself in his small log cabin at the back of the house, near the cook-house and vegetable garden which were Phoebe's domain. He would shoot anything that moved: raccoons, rabbits, squirrels, possums and bigger prey. Whenever she spotted him sitting on his bench cleaning his flintlock she knew he was about to set off. She felt indignant Pa allowed such a horrible little man to ride such a magnificent beast as Farran, but Pa was adamant.

'I can't withhold those privileges from O'Neil – it wouldn't be fair. I've let other overseers ride Farran till they got their own horse. Besides, we all benefit from his kill, don't we?'

They watched O'Neil return one day: flintlock slung across one shoulder, powder horn across the other, and his kill, a raccoon and several squirrels, dangling from Farran's rump. Froth streamed from the horse's mouth, but O'Neil had his answer ready for her father's sharp criticism.

'Had to run hard for home, Mr Cormac. Damned Indians near ambushed me.'

'Again? Same thing happened last time. Should we be worried?'

'Don't think they'll trouble us. But it's true, no lies. Had to skedaddle. Turned around in m' saddle and I got one. Bang!

Right through the chest. Had to push him hard, in and out trees. It's a mercy I'm back at all.'

As they watched O'Neil walk Farran back to the field, Pa grumbled, 'For sure, there are plenty of Indians out there, but why O'Neil always comes across a hostile bunch, the Lord only knows. That damned bogtrotting Irishman. Sometimes I'm sorry I hired him. I know he loves the horses, but it's a hard love, I think.'

Anne believed O'Neil needed to be at the centre of some small adventure to spice up his life. Returning from these trips was the only time she heard him string more than a few words together. She didn't like O'Neil, but she didn't condemn him. She too could imagine flying through the forest paths on Shotek; but she would never allow O'Neil to mount her boy. Ever.

While Anne waited for Shotek to grow big enough to ride so she could explore the land around her, the waterways were on her doorstep.

'Taking Catfish downriver tomorrow. Want to go?' Pa knew what her answer would be.

Their flatboat had got its name after the day she flew up the garden from the creek dragging a small wheeled trolley containing a massive catfish she'd helped land. She'd run towards the house, hollering, 'Pa, Ma, Phoebe, look what I caught!'

On these trips transporting barrels of rice downriver to Charles Town's merchants and coming back home with supplies she would help sail. Their brown tributary creek and Ashley River were teeming with fish. They would put out lines and nets to catch perch, bass and on occasion net another catfish which would set her shrieking and sweating with effort. People weren't the only predators on the waterways:

herons and egrets stood patient and alert in the shallow water, and snakebirds with long necks swam and dived. Ducks swam between the reeds, and the sounds of migrating birds filled the air during winter months. She would gut fish they caught, throwing innards into the river, where she watched birds and fish fight over the free meal. Back home she offered her catch to Phoebe to cook, while the others took their catch to share with their community in the slave huts.

The seasons dictated the rhythm of plantation life. Her life. Anne accepted this as a given and gave it no more consideration than night following day.

3

WILLIAM'S SLAVES WORKED HOUR AFTER HOUR, DAY after day, threshing and pounding in deep wooden mortars with heavy pestles. Each barrel held twenty bushels, and there were many barrels to fill. It had been a good harvest and now he needed to prepare his rice for shipping; to get his crop to England as quickly as possible, as only then would he get paid and he could complete his payments for Samuel and two others of his slaves. He was not unaware of the irony, but this was the way of commerce and his slaves were part of the circulation of cash.

For days Samuel, a fit and healthy black man in his thirties, had been grumbling. 'Master, let me do fences. I'm good at chopping...'

'No, not today, Samuel. Today you pound with the women. Get to it.'

Maybe Samuel thought working with an axe or sawing timber a more masculine occupation, or maybe the man was shirking. William suspected Samuel could complete a hundred rails quicker than he could pound seven mortars of rice, allowing himself more time to tend to his garden and hogs. The exact measurement of allotted daily tasks was not to be tampered with. Some things were more sacred than the holy word of God, and this system was one of them.

When O'Neil reported Samuel was falling behind in his work this had to be challenged. William had tried to reason with Samuel, then had taken away a privilege, and when this didn't work he had ordered O'Neil to confiscate one of Samuel's own crops which he intended to sell at market.

One day O'Neil came to William, sporting a bloody head.

'That nigger should be lynched. Struck me with hoe... Near killed me.'

No black could ever strike a white man, and certainly his slaves had never shown the slightest indication of being violent. William wanted to dampen things down.

'Well, perhaps not so close. Perhaps it's not so bad as—'

'Would ye take his side? Are ye telling me that you'd—?'

'No, no, no. Rest assured he'll be punished.'

'A whipping then. I'll see to it.' O'Neil grunted, satisfied.

'Yes, a whipping, but I'll do it myself.'

O'Neil's face screwed up. 'That's my duty.'

William shook his head and dismissed the grumbling O'Neil. William had little appetite for the day-to-day running of his plantation but less for O'Neil.

He had found O'Neil staggering out of a tavern on the Charles Town waterfront. Servants were increasingly hard to find, and William knew he was scraping the bottom of the barrel. William did not altogether trust O'Neil and would not yet empower him to carry out punishments. All the same, he was happy to have another white man on the property. He knew how vulnerable they were with so many blacks around them and Indian tribes more and more dissatisfied.

When William told his family of the upcoming punishment he was surprised at Anne's outrage. 'Don't do it, Pa!'

'I have to, and you need to understand, this is the law. Why, when I was at the Cork assizes, representing some fella at the county court before we left Ireland, I saw a felon sentenced to be whipped for stealing a horse, then he was to be transported to Virginia.'

'Who cares about the law and courts in Ireland? I like Samuel.' Anne's face was red with pent-up fury. 'Don't bother with the law. You can do what you want. It's your plantation.'

'I must. If any of us do wrong things, there are consequences. And you will witness this. One day you'll own your own—'

'Hah!' Anne stalked off. She had no answer. This was her life as much as it was his own and she'd have to get used to it.

William practised on a carcass of a hog to perfect his strokes. He analysed the skin after each stroke to see the effect it had; what force was needed to merely raise welts; what to break open skin; how much effort it took to cut to the bone.

Even as his wrists were bound to the whipping post by a smirking O'Neil, Samuel remained indignant and unrepentant. 'Master... I not lazy... Master!'

Eight black faces huddled together in silent witness. William had made all his slaves turn out, apart from the little ones. Anne, Mary and Billy stood further away on the porch of the house, Billy gripping Mary's skirt. Mary and Anne had not wanted to watch, but he had insisted. Anne stood, arms crossed and scowling. William tried to show a neutral face to his family to demonstrate he was not doing this in anger.

'Pa! I won't talk to you again. Ever!' Anne's voice cut through the air, cutting into his concentration.

He could not listen to her or distract himself. He focused on the moment and getting it right. He judged his distance and angle, raised his right arm, then unfurled the long whip with a resounding crack on Samuel's bare back.

Samuel gasped. He craned his head towards William, sweat beading his forehead, eyes wide in shock.

'Master... Master! I do it, I do it!'

'Pa, I hate you!' William caught a glimpse of Anne's skirt disappearing around the side of the house. Anne's words cut him deeply. She had a full vocabulary of spicy cuss words and a sharp tongue, but she had never uttered words of hate to him, and never anything in front of his slaves. This would not do! He'd deal with her later. And where had Billy gone? Only Mary stood on the porch, white-faced, her arms stiffly to her side.

He had to do this; must assert his authority. Samuel wasn't the only one sweating.

After the second stroke he paused once more, took a breath and out of the corner of his eye noticed Billy amongst the huddled group of slaves and saw his son hand in hand with Ebo. Damnation. He had not wanted Ebo watching his father humiliated like this. He raised his arm a third time.

It wasn't a vicious lashing, William hadn't the stomach for that, but three licks of the whip left ugly welts. This would give a powerful warning to the rest of them. Negotiation with his slaves was by far the best means of control – all the planters were agreed on that. Why physically harm them when they had to work? The punishment all slaves really feared was to be sent back for auction. Who knew what their next master might be like? Who could tell how far away they would be transplanted, torn from family and friends? Who knew if they could reach a ready market for their own small assets, built up over their years of enslavement?

William acknowledged the early days had been different. Then he had worked with his slaves. Side by side, knee-deep in swamp water, with heaven only knew what creatures lurking beneath, they had cut back cypress and drained swamps to extend his fields. He had sweated and experienced fever along with the rest of them. His body had hardened from his years of toil and his heart had hardened accordingly.

After Samuel's whipping William sought absolution in prayer. He tried not to feel guilty. These were his chattels, his slaves to do with as he wished, but he was not a violent man. He offered a prayer for the well-being of all his family, including his slaves. Next, he found a bottle of rum, which he found more effective at settling his soul. Mary went to their bedroom, and Billy stared at him as only a small child can. William had not seen Anne and understood this wound between them would require time to heal. He had taught her to be just, but also to face up to the occasionally brutal new world of theirs.

Stepping out onto his porch William raised a glass of rum with a shaking hand. The sun, hanging low in the winter sky, lent his property a rosy hue. Before him, at the end of the long path, to the right was his slave quarter: wattle and daub round huts with thatched roofs and garden plots nearby; to the left, separated by a drainage ditch, his rice fields stretching outwards for acres and acres. Ahead, at the creek, a small jetty with Catfish tied up. Behind his house lay pasture and yet-to-be-cleared forest, and to the right a gate led to a dusty road.

His house was not nearly as grand as some of those gracing the waterways of the low country. It was a simple two-storey home: a long central passage downstairs with airy rooms either side, two bedrooms above and the cook-house separate. Schneider, the previous owner, had not tried to screen the house behind trees or fancy gardens, telling William, 'I am a plain man. Why vood I want to hide away from my work?'

At this moment, William wished he could be a little more shielded from the angry eyes of his blacks, but on the whole he felt satisfied with the setup of his plantation. He had made improvements to the house and his newly painted residence could always be extended... All in good time.

From his porch William observed Abba carrying a wooden pail into the hut she shared with Samuel and Ebo. No doubt she would wash the wounds, apply balm and listen to Samuel's cusses. And no doubt Ebo would be convinced he, William, was a red-faced monster out to get him too.

William knew Billy had far too close a relationship with his blacks. He and Ebo were inseparable and his son spoke more Gullah than English. And as for Anne, he could see no sign in the eleven-year-old girl of the fine lady he hoped would emerge miraculously like a butterfly to take her place in society. And Mary was little help in shaping their daughter; her confidence had not yet blossomed. He sighed.

The rum produced a satisfactory internal glow, and he inhaled the delicious smell drifting from the cook-house: a shellfish boil, his favourite supper, which he had insisted Phoebe prepare. William began to regain his composure.

4

If Ma criticised her or fell into the trap of comparing her with politer girls of their acquaintance, Anne had her retorts ready. 'You were nothing but a servant girl – Pa's servant!' 'You had me, and you and Pa weren't even married!' 'You'll never be a fine lady yourself!' Unkind words just burst from her mouth before she could stop them. She expected Pa to punish her, but it never happened, and Anne could only surmise that Ma didn't tell tales.

High winds and driving rain were relentlessly battering them. Having been cooped up inside for days, Anne stalked the house, ready to pick a fight. Ma looked up cautiously, her needle poised above a new shirt she was sewing for Billy.

'Will you help me? Or how about sewing a new shift for yourself?'

Anne groaned. Ever since she was small, when Ma had forced her to make an embroidered sampler, she had hated any kind of needlework.

'Not now, maybe later...'

'All right.' Ma smiled. 'This seems a good time to learn a dance or two.'

It was a statement, but a tentative one, Ma's eyes beseeching her to be accommodating. All the neighbourhood girls were excited when the next social occasion offered itself, but Anne hadn't been keen on learning to dance, chiefly because she didn't think she would be good at it. Her long legs would surely get in a tangle and people would laugh at her ungainly efforts. With only herself and Ma in the room, this seemed a good time to make a fool of herself, and she didn't have anything better to do. She sighed and shrugged pointedly. 'All right, if you want.'

Ma quickly put aside her sewing and jumped up before she changed her mind. 'Let's start with a dance I remember. I loved this as a girl.'

Ma lifted up her skirt so Anne could see her feet and taught her some bouncy steps. Ma hummed a favourite Irish reel and the two of them held hands and bounded up and down the room.

This was all right. Better than all right. Why on earth had she been wary? She shouted for Billy. They needed more people and he would have to do for now. Anne laughed, watching Billy hold hands with Ma jigging about and kicking his feet out.

Pa paused at the doorway, drawn in by the laughing and singing. 'Well now, I have a fleet-footed family, I see. Have ye taught them the de Coverley or just one of your clod-hopping Irish country dances?'

'Clod-hopping indeed. They're the best. These dances and tunes lift the soul.' Ma's face looked flushed and happy.

Pa rubbed hands together and came into the room. 'Come now, let's learn the Roger de Coverley together... Stand over there, Anne, next to your Ma, and Billy, come here by me...

You greet your partner with a curtsey or a bow... Just so...
Now, we take some skips forward... That's the way now...'

Anne skipped first towards Pa, then to Billy, then back
again, and hand in hand with Pa she galloped down a line of
imaginary people, Pa trying to sing at the same time, Billy and
Ma clapping and beating time with their feet.

'Tone it down, dear heart. You'll spin any young fellow
you're partnering off his feet if you go at this rate.' Pa was pink-
faced and puffing.

'Look up, Anne, look up. Your feet know what they're doing.
And stand up straight. You are doing well.' Ma sounded proud.

Anne clapped and tapped her foot while Pa swung Ma
around. He lifted his knees and pretended to be clumsy and
stamp on her feet. 'You see, Mary, if I hadn't rescued you, you'd
have been stuck with that clod-hopper of a fella you told me
was sweet on you when you were sixteen.'

Ma's eyes sparkled, her face flushed, and Anne couldn't
remember seeing her look so happy. And Anne felt happy
too: loud and laughing and enjoying this moment with her
family. She grabbed Billy and the two of them swung each
other around faster and faster. Before she knew it, they had
somehow knocked Ma's special ornament off its little table,
smashing it, so their dancing lesson came to a halt.

Soon afterwards Ma had another child in her belly, so between
this and coming down with fever, Ma was hardly ever well –
certainly not well enough to dance. There had been another
child on the way a year earlier, but it came too early and Anne
wasn't sure if the dead half-baby had been a boy or a girl. Ma
hadn't talked about it and she hadn't asked.

This time Ma gave birth to another boy but couldn't feed
him, and Phoebe and Abba rushed about to neighbouring
plantations to find a black woman to nurse him.

Anne tiptoed up to her parents' bedroom door; Pa sat by the bed reading out loud to Ma. Ma's freckles were the only colour on her shrunken cheeks, and she fingered her rosary beads. Ma's eyes flickered towards her and she smiled. Anne decided what she wanted to say could wait.

Waking next morning she couldn't smell coffee or the comforting smell of hominy; couldn't hear Phoebe's heavy footfall in the house, nor her voice calling her for breakfast. She couldn't hear Pa's voice outside, giving instructions to O'Neil. Walking softly across the upstairs landing, guided by the sound of sobbing, Anne pushed open her parents' bedroom door. Her breath was sucked from her. Pa and Phoebe, both openly weeping, were struggling to clothe Ma in her best dress, her thin body floppy and her skin a waxy white.

Phoebe caught her eye. 'You comin' in? Say goodbye to your Ma?'

'Ah, Anne, I didn't want to wake you,' Pa choked.

Anne stood in the doorway, unable to step into the room to confront this terrible thing. Whispered words – they must be hers: 'Ma can't be dead... not yet... not yet.' She wanted to tell Ma things. Uppermost in her mind she wanted to say sorry for the mean things she'd said. She wanted to tell Ma she loved her. When had she last said so? She couldn't remember.

New thoughts, selfish thoughts, flooded into her mind and would not stop. She did not want to take on the burden of running the household, doing all the accounts: something her mother had done without complaining and with some pride. And Billy? Would she be expected to look after him, and the new baby? They hadn't even settled on a name for him. Anne knew nothing of raising babies. She had seen how Beth, a girl of her acquaintance, had become old before her time taking on family responsibilities after her mother died; a girl who had been full of life became a domestic drudge. Tears of sorrow and self-pity flowed down Anne's cheeks.

'Pa...' She spoke softly, still reluctant to go closer.

Pa stood and took a step towards her. 'Come here, child.'

Anne took tentative steps towards the bed but could not face touching Ma's cold skin.

She fled to the only thing that could provide comfort: Shotek. O'Neil had judged him old enough to ride, and Anne rode him as she loved best: bareback, Indian-style, her thighs gripping his warm flanks. She drove him hard, leaping water courses and dikes, spoiling rice crops in her blind determination to get away. She headed away from the plantation, past the swamps and fields and enclosure, heading for the trees at full gallop, her face hard, hair streaming behind her.

She'd witnessed death often enough, and before her own time came she resolved to live life fully. She would drive herself forward just as now she drove Shotek and take life at a gallop.

In spring, Trader Mac passed through. 'Sorry to hear about your ma, Anne. You must miss her.' She bit her lip and nodded. Mac was silent a moment then offered: 'If you're allowed, why don't you ride with me tomorrow? If you want to, that is.' He laughed, hearing her sharp intake of breath. 'I take it that's a yes. I'll make sure you turn back in plenty of time to reach home before sundown. Perhaps your pa can spare one of the blacks to come with you.'

Anne raced to the house, yelling, 'Pa! Pa!', scaring everyone into thinking there had been an accident. He hummed and ha'ed in the annoying way he had, then agreed on condition that O'Neil accompany them; he would promote one of his blacks as overseer for the day.

'O'Neil! He'll spoil it,' she begged, but Pa insisted.

'Him, or not at all.'

They set out at sunrise. For hours they rode along Indian trails – paths through wetlands close to home – before travelling into unknown territory where the land became drier. She had to be patient, riding at a walking pace with Mac leading his mules packed high with goods he intended to trade, including liquor. This was another reason he stopped by their plantation on his journeys inland. Somewhere nearby he was doing business with someone with a still, turning out gut-wrenching hooch.

'Sure, it's illegal, but they have to catch me first. Damn rules and regulations. Don't see nuthin' wrong with trading stuff folks want.' Mac had been indignant when Pa had queried the wisdom of this.

On the trail Mac stopped when they met others: white and Indian hunters; traders. If they shared a language or part-language they swapped news. What's the hunting like? Which Indian village, or tribe, has fallen out with another? Has fever been reported? All this informed where he went.

Mac talked about the forest plants they passed: which she could eat and which to avoid. She knew a lot already. Phoebe often charged her with gathering fruit and berries in season: mulberries, persimmons, cranberries, chestnuts and hickories. The land had an abundance of things to eat. Mac pointed out trees whose bark made good tea, and small leafy chickweed you could chew. He warned her about pokeweed berries, "'less you want to kill y'self".

'And Anne, we're not likely to see the stuff right now, but you should know about pennyroyal and cotton root in case you get in the family way and—'

'You shut y' damn mouth, Mac!'

Anne turned to see O'Neil's face screwed up in fury. 'You've no cause to be talking with the girl about such things. Ain't right!'

'That so?' Mac digested O'Neil's words. 'Don't see the harm in it.'

'No one has the right to interfere with God's will. Any rate, this ain't your business.'

'God's will, you say. Well, that's a matter of opinion. I know many a fine woman, Indian, black or white, who might disagree. No need to get riled up.'

Anne decided she would ask Phoebe if she were curious about such a thing. Since Ma had died, who else might she ask?

When the sun dipped behind the trees Mac said, 'Well now, figure it's time you two headed home.'

'Not yet. Keep going a little longer. O'Neil and I can ride fast.' Anne turned to O'Neil for confirmation and he grinned. 'Sure can!' For the first time she actually liked him.

They continued a while longer till Mac stopped again. He cocked his hat and indicated there would be no further debate, so Anne and O'Neil turned their horses for home. It had been a wonderful day and she couldn't wait to go again, but not with O'Neil. Next time she'd go alone.

With her father in Charles Town on business and O'Neil out in the fields, Anne picked her morning. She still hadn't saved enough to buy buckskin trousers, so she wore leggings she had fashioned herself, and took her sheathed hunting knife, a small horse whip and provisions for the day slung in a canvas bag over her shoulder. As she led Shotek out of his enclosure she encountered Phoebe collecting eggs. She hadn't reckoned on Phoebe.

'So, Missy Anne, where you goin'?'

'Just to visit Emily and Richard.' She often visited her neighbours. Nothing unusual.

Phoebe looked her up and down. 'Umm um. Dressed like that, with ya hunting knife? Doesn't Mrs Croome feed ya?'

Phoebe couldn't challenge her directly, but Anne was never in any doubt about what was on her mind: chin jutting, narrowed eyes looking down her nose. Anne retorted with a tart, 'Mind your own business.'

Phoebe didn't flinch. 'Your Pa know?'

Rather than lie outright, Anne ignored her and mounted Shotek.

For hours she rode the forest trails, talking to Shotek, nodding and saying, 'Good day,' to the occasional trader or hunter she came across. She did not get lost and set off home the way she had come, singing softly.

Shotek flicked his head. A man stood in the trail blocking her path and she instinctively pulled on the reins. He cut a rough figure, with an unkempt beard, a torn jacket, no boots, feet bound with rags. Likely a mountain man.

She had her knife but the one tucked in his belt was considerably bigger. Between the man's hairy beard his lips stretched into a grin to reveal brown teeth. He jerked his chin upwards. 'Get off.'

The man inched forward, a lustful look in his eyes – not for her – for Shotek.

'He's a beauty... and you're a perty little thing.' His beady eyes rose to meet hers and he sensed her indecision. 'Don't try! If you give him up without a fight, I won't hurt ya. I'm done with the sea, I'm heading inland. Ya can help me or hinder me. Your choice, girly.'

Anne dug her heels into Shotek, whipped his flank, and charged. The man lunged at Shotek's bridle and with the other hand grabbed her ankle in a strong grip and tugged. She clutched Shotek's mane. Shotek reared, and she and the horse screamed.

With a thud she landed hard, winded, and Shotek bolted. The man hovered over her breathing hard; his forehead was etched with grime, his teeth stained with tobacco juice and he stank. Her throat constricted in a dry retch.

'Y' should've given him up and walked away. This is your fault: brought this on y'rself.'

He unsheathed his knife… He meant to kill her! Breathe… Breathe… Instead, holding his knife to her throat with one hand he removed hers with the other, tossed it away, then fumbled with his breeches and withdrew his cock, swollen and held like a weapon. It shocked her. Tears welled up. The idea of having this thing in her body revolted her. She yelled, kicked out, and twisted away.

Play wrestling with Billy was easy – she always won – and Richard good-naturedly gave in. This man did not give in. He pinned her to the ground with an iron grip: his arms and hands strong from years of hauling rope and sail. Stones dug into her back. His face hovered above hers, and she almost gagged with his stink as he whispered, 'It won't hurt a bit.' He ripped off her leggings and whispered again, 'Won't hurt a bit, girly, just be still.'

Pain shot through her and she gasped. She turned her head to see Shotek standing at a distance, ears back, pawing the ground. All through her ordeal she fixed her gaze on her beloved horse.

Done, the man grunted and knelt back, for a moment relaxed and vulnerable. Instantly, Anne rolled aside and clawed her way towards his knife. Her hand grasped the handle even as his ham-sized hand closed on her ankle and dragged her back.

Swivelling and jackknifing her body, she slashed out. The blade sliced his outer right thigh, blood seeping through his breeches. He cursed, his grip loosening. The second stab entered his groin. Too shocked to do more than grunt, the man tried to stagger to his feet. No! With her long thin legs she took a flying kick at his chest, toppling him backward. Expertly, she slashed her knife across his throat as she had done many times when hunting rabbits and other small creatures in the fields near home.

As blood pumped out of his throat he gurgled; surprised eyes locked on hers. Over. He would never tell others of this outrageous act; would never hurt another girl. She flung his knife as far away as she could.

Getting him off the trail proved difficult. He was heavy and she had no rope to make use of Shotek's strength to haul him, so she rolled him over and over, kicking his body away from the track, leaving a trail of blood. She tugged his legs, then his arms, and rolled him again. Satisfied, she covered his body with branches. He wasn't out of sight, but you'd have to look hard to see him.

With her boot she scuffed soil, leaves and stones over the bloodstains. It would have to do; these trails were not empty places, and she did not want anyone to see her. She hauled herself into the saddle, wiped tears and snot from her face with the back of a sleeve, and pushed Shotek into a canter.

O'Neil saw her riding into the field. Damn him. She had waited till sundown and taken a back track into the plantation in the hope of sneaking in undetected.

O'Neil whistled. 'A bear catch ya?' He looked genuinely concerned as he took in her dishevelled hair, bloodied clothes and ripped leggings.

'Nah. I found a dead deer – practised skinning it.'

He laughed and laughed before ambling away.

Every stitch of clothing she had worn and every item she had with her that day she ritually destroyed. She carted wood to make a bonfire and waited till the fire blazed. Piece by piece everything was consigned to the fierce flames and reduced to ashes. The things which couldn't be burnt, her knife and whip, she broke and buried. She scoured her body as if to remove the top layers of skin, and cut her hair short, wanting to be rid of that too.

It hurt to walk and over the following weeks she rarely went out. Phoebe knew there had been no visit to the Croomes', and Anne suspected she wasn't as gullible as O'Neil, but she said nothing, and Pa just seemed bemused at her new hairstyle.

She knew she was old enough to bear a child. But how would she know if one had been started? With Ma dead, who could she ask? This was like the time, six months earlier, when she felt blood trickling down her inside thigh. Anne had waited a day, and when the bleeding didn't stop she had to ask someone, so she hung around Abba and Samuel's garden, waiting for Abba to come in from the fields. The first day Abba had come home bone-weary, Anne didn't know what to say, but the second day Abba got the hint.

'What is it, Missy Anne? You wan' me for summin'?'

Anne had found herself nervous. This was personal and Abba was her slave. She could only nod. Abba sat down on her step then patted the space next to her.

Anne had taken comfort from the sweaty warm smell of the young woman and eventually managed to get her story out.

'It's jus' your moon bleedin'. Comes 'round every month. You's a woman now. You c'n have a baby. No one tell you 'bout this?' Abba had looked puzzled.

No, they had not! Who would? For all of Anne's knowledge about horses and cattle breeding – no one had gone into details.

'Get some rags and pin 'em to a belt 'round your waist under your shift.'

A hazy memory of women washing bloody strips of rag on their sea voyage from Ireland came to her. Why on earth hadn't Ma told her then and there, and be done with it? Or maybe Ma had said something, but she hadn't listened. It was too long ago to recall.

Anne fretted until she was certain no baby had resulted from the assault and no missing mariner had been reported murdered. He had probably jumped ship, and there were too many deaths and killings going on for anyone to care. She fantasised about a bear snuffling through the leaves, discovering his body and feasting on the carcass, and hoped this would happen.

If sex was like that, Anne didn't want any of it. She suspected it needn't be as brutal; Pa would never have behaved in such an ungentlemanly way, nor would Ma's frail body have withstood such a violent act. But maybe all men turned into brutes, even her father, and her mother had meekly submitted. Whatever the case, she was determined no man would ever force himself on her again.

5

JACK RACKHAM FOUND HIMSELF FLAT ON HIS BACK looking up at the sky, his nose clogged with blood and his ears full of dust, and what were bound to be loud Spanish curses, though he couldn't understand the language. Didn't the damn fellow know they weren't at war now?

He raised a hand tentatively to explore his nose, flinched and offered fresh curses in English. His nose was literally out of joint, and he momentarily wondered if this would affect his chances with the ladies.

As Jack picked himself up and dusted off his clothes his assailant placed an arm proprietorially around the waist of the handsome woman he had had such high hopes of. It could have been worse – he could have met with the large knife tucked in the fellow's belt. Jack needed to arm himself and get some practice in, and learning some Spanish wouldn't go amiss to avoid unnecessary misunderstandings.

He'd learnt a few things these past hours since he had landed: chiefly, that Cuban women weren't ugly. He could put that lie to rest. In fact, many of the women he'd seen were much to his liking. While this encounter had not worked out, he felt confident another would.

News of peace between England, Spain and France trickled down slowly to those not involved in the war. Jack had been at a small dock on one of the Chesapeake's numerous waterways, helping load hogsheads of tobacco, when this momentous news reached him. He was signed up with a merchant vessel carrying barrels of salted fish from Newfoundland, and they were topping up their cargo in Virginia before continuing to Jamaica.

With the war ended they'd no longer have to worry about losing valuable cargoes – or vessels – to French and Spanish privateers. Vessels he was on had been chased and attacked on numerous occasions. Although he himself had never been harmed, his mind imagined all sorts of atrocities.

Within a day of leaving Virginia, heading south, it became clear to Jack that something troubled his captain: he seemed preoccupied and out of sorts. By the time they were cruising along the Florida coast the man was deeply agitated, dropping hints that the end of the war was playing on his mind.

'Captain. Are you worried about attacks? You think there might be Spanish privateers about that haven't heard the good news?'

'No, no, not at all, Rackham.' His captain sucked his teeth. 'But maybe this peace deal means places that have been off-limits are now open to us. Wouldn't you say?'

'Maybe.' Jack hadn't thought about it.

'In a matter of days we'll be cruising near Cuba. Do you suppose they'll allow us to drop anchor at Havana? If we wished to make this small detour... A friendly call.'

'Captain?' Jack couldn't follow his train of thought.

'Assuming we didn't mind adding a few more days to our cruise. You'd have no objection, would you, Rackham?'

Jack could only shrug.

'You see,' the captain continued, 'I've heard two opinions of the women in Cuba, and I'd like to find out the truth of the matter. Some say they're as ugly as sin, others say they are glorious to behold.' He scratched his chin, pondering what appeared to be the greatest mystery on earth. Jack didn't know what to say. His captain had seemed a rational man until this moment – not a man who might risk his entire cargo through one foolhardy investigation.

Following his tentative exploration of the subject with Jack, the captain opened his mind to the seven other crew members.

'Are you curious to find out? I'll not force you – I've no intention of risking lives to investigate the matter. If you say no I'll not raise the subject again.'

Jack and the rest of the crew found they were curious, and they weren't the ones risking the cargo.

They turned towards Cuba sailing towards the solid fortress guarding the mouth of Havana's harbour. When they weren't fired on, they passed cautiously through the narrow entrance, and still, when no one shot at them, they anchored and ventured ashore.

In the seven years he had been at sea criss-crossing the Atlantic, sometimes taking in the African coast as well as the Americas, Jack had become an experienced seaman, and an experienced man of the world. Little fazed him. He'd learnt to handle ships in all weathers and deal with volatile men. Usually. Storms had a way of passing, as did disputes if you waited long enough. Jack was measured, not one of those hot-heads whose temper would flare as if touched by a fuse, and ships were small worlds so best to get on with your companions.

Women were another matter. He saw no point in hanging back when he would only be in port for brief periods, so his courtships were direct and to the point.

This first encounter in Havana had been unfortunate. In his haste to bed the woman he had made some errors of judgement.

From the age of ten Jack had worked, plying the Thames in small boats. All the boys and men he'd known worked at the docks or went to sea. Aged fourteen or thereabouts, he played with his brother Hal, two years younger than him, roaming the east London streets making nuisances of themselves, but sometimes his body behaved in unexpected ways and he found himself looking at girls and women. Summer was best, when they weren't bundled up in layers of woollen clothes. He would stare at softly curving outlines under cotton blouses and fantasise about things that didn't seem right.

More of his evenings were spent wandering the Wapping waterfront, not yet ready to join the men or approach a girl he might fancy. Hanging around pub doorways, a tankard of ale in his hand, he'd listen to merchant seamen tell tales of places they had been to, and naval men – as often as not maimed – talk of battles they had fought. Why risk dying for the Queen, who didn't seem to care about these old fighters and surely wouldn't care about him either? Listening to stories gave him plenty of time to eye up whores. Initially their frank stares embarrassed him, and he'd imagined they were mocking the worn clothes he was fast growing out of.

They began to tease him, saying things like, 'If I charged for being looked at, I'd be rich.' One night a woman whose tightly laced bodice pushed up massive breasts sauntered towards him, swinging her hips. 'Hello, darlin'. You lost? Don't know your way home? How about you come with me?' She flashed her breast and licked her lips. Others nearby giggled, egging her on. Jack grinned, almost tempted to walk up to her. Almost. He turned away, confused, and an old whore collared him. She must have been at least thirty or forty. She pressed her face close to his.

'You've been sniffing around long enough. Got any money? Price of a drink?'

Her breath reeked of gin. He drew back and took in her lined face and clouded eyes, wanting to run; no, wanting to stay.

'Sure you got money?' She leant in closer.

He nodded and let himself be led away to a back alley.

She raised her skirt, and he didn't have to think things through; his cock knew exactly what to do and it was easy. The whore earned the price of a drink in seconds. He didn't even speak to her but tidied himself in embarrassment, tossed her a coin and fled.

This fumble marked the end of his boyhood. It hadn't been like his fantasies, but it had been a start. He wanted women he would choose; wanted to taste life, explore the world.

He sailed out of the Thames estuary on a merchantman heading to Virginia. To larboard, he passed Canvey Island, to starboard familiar Kent landmarks: the mouth of the River Medway and the Isle of Sheppey. Beyond the Isle of Thanet, at the eastern most edge of Kent, the gleaming White Cliffs of Dover were his last sight of England. He'd promised his mother he would stay out of trouble; a promise he had found impossible to keep.

Sailing from the Spanish island, all the crew agreed with their captain that Cuban women had certain charms – and yes, they assured him, they had ample evidence to prove this vital matter. Jack's captain rubbed his hands, beaming. 'Good, good. I'm delighted.'

'And yourself, sir? Did you satisfy yourself on the matter?' One of Jack's crewmates posed this question, to which his captain chuckled and nodded.

Jack wasn't so sure about this and doubted he had allowed himself time for pleasures of the flesh. Jack had watched him darting in and out of warehouses like a bee to flowers. Boats had been active too, rowing out to their vessel and returning time and again with hogsheads of tobacco Jack had recently helped load in Virginia. The captain must have negotiated a good price from the Spanish. He would have to cook the books or cover his tracks in some other way before arriving at Jamaica, where the English port authorities would pore over every detail.

'Wily old bastard,' Jack whispered in admiration, and considered whether he too might profit by some crafty trading here and there. He would keep a sharp eye out for fresh opportunities now the war had ended.

6

'Good shot!'

Richard's voice rang out behind her as Anne ran ahead through the lush spring pasture. She'd tied her hair back, a wide-brimmed leather hat shaded her eyes, and she wore her favourite hunting clothes: her treasured buckskin trousers and a loose cotton shirt. A musket hung from a shoulder.

She reached the twitching hare. It had been a good shot! Unsheathing her knife, she expertly slit its throat, putting it beyond any suffering she had caused.

Richard arrived, panting slightly from the run, and leant on his musket. He had the sturdy physique of his father. He grinned at her with a mixture of pride and uncertainty, and she suspected he might be beginning to share his mother's views that her activities were unseemly.

'Getting good at this. The best shot in the district, I should think.'

'The district? Hell no, why not the whole county?' She could afford to boast a little.

Richard picked up the bloodied animal by its back legs, and the two of them ambled to where their horses quietly grazed. Anne enjoyed Richard's company. She could talk with him without minding her words, and they enjoyed challenging each other. This time she had shot three hares to his one, but it wasn't always the case.

Shotek raised his head at her approach. Richard picked up the other hares lying on the grass and began lashing them together: three for her, and one for him.

Anne held up her hand. 'No, you take it. Two each.'

'You sure? You shot them.'

'Take them – give them to one of your blacks.' That's what she meant to do with hers: give them to Abba for her pot.

They lashed the hares to their saddles and Anne mounted first, digging her heels into Shotek's flank. 'Race you to the boundary!'

'Hey! What happened to a fair start?'

The rhythmic sound of Shotek's thumping hooves and the swish of long grass filled her ears. Her hat dangled from its straps, her hair flew free, the wind in her face. Anne glanced behind to see Richard catching up. She knew he would. He rode a strong fourteen-hander, and it could fly. She jumped one ditch, speeding on towards the boundary between their two properties, Shotek's head stretching, ears back, mane rippling. She, a young woman, could control this powerful animal, and if she did something wrong, she might go flying and likely die. She couldn't imagine anything more thrilling. Richard was on her tail and they took the ditch together, both of them whooping and laughing, before slowing their horses to a walk.

'Reckon I won, for all that I was behind you. I think I nosed ahead at the end.'

She snorted. 'Hah! I don't think so!'

'You never do. You never admit you're wrong. A bad loser, that's what you are.' Richard good-naturedly poked her with his whip.

'I am not!' Everyone said the same: Billy, even Phoebe dared to call her Mistress Stubborn sometimes.

'You can argue all you like,' Richard teased. 'Others will back me up, I'm sure of it.'

They reached the path where their ways separated, so she turned Shotek homeward with a casual wave. 'See you soon.'

'Anne!' She turned in her saddle to see Richard's amused face. 'Saturday, right?'

'Yes, yes of course!' She was momentarily embarrassed; the occasion had slipped her mind. Richard would be twenty-one and his family were holding a party.

'Ma's been organising it a long time. Don't you dare forget!'

'Yes, I know. We're looking forward to it.' She made a conscious effort to say cordial words as she waved once more over her shoulder, shouting, 'See you Saturday,' and continued walking Shotek homeward, conscious of Richard's gaze.

Saying she was looking forward to his party wasn't an outright lie, but the upcoming social event didn't consume her as it did the other girls her age. She felt slightly uneasy, which was why she put it to the back of her mind. For years Richard had been her closest companion. They had duelled with wooden swords and wrestled fiercely, neither of them willing to concede; now he was, in the whispered words of women in neighbouring plantations, "a good catch". He was wealthy, good-looking enough, and above all else, kind. Still, the prospect of a party made her anxious. She did not want anyone thinking she meant to "catch" Richard, but at the same time she didn't want to lose him to one of the simpering girls who circled him after church.

The previous Sunday after service, Anne had gathered under the trees with the other girls and listened as their excitement reached a new pitch: what dress each was wearing; how much cleavage would be appropriate to show; how each would dress their hair, and what colour ribbons they favoured. On and on. Anne had little to contribute to the conversation and found herself at the margin of the gaggle of girls. Ma had never been a fashionable sort, and with Ma long dead, she had no older woman to help her navigate the sometimes perplexing journey to womanhood. She had no idea about latest fashions, and it had not crossed her mind to look through the journals Pa sometimes ordered from London.

She kicked Shotek with more force than necessary and galloped for home, passing their field hands, bending, sowing rice seed, standing, heeling it in with a bare foot and moving on a step. She glanced at Ebo, no longer given a child's privilege, doing this back-breaking, monotonous work beside his mother, Abba, and rode on. Dismounting at Abba and Samuel's hut, she dropped the hares on their doorstep and found a sack to cover them. They'd know where they came from.

Taking a detour, she walked Shotek past the family burial ground where Tomboy had made iron fencing to surround the site under a large oak tree. A wooden cross bearing the name Mary Cormac along with the date of her death marked Ma's grave, with the two dead babies buried next to her. This was a place she rarely visited. Anne turned her back on the three family graves and rode Shotek towards the house, dismounted and dropped the reins, noticing O'Neil approach.

'O'Neil! Here, deal with him for me.'

'Can't a fella come in for food?' He scowled at her. Anne knew she should look after Shotek, but she wasn't in the mood.

Hearing her arrive, Pa came out to the porch to greet her. 'I was wondering where you were, I need you to help with Billy. Anyway, you shouldn't be gallivanting off by yourself. It's not safe.'

'I was with Richard.'

His face brightened. 'Good, good. That's different, then. But promise me you'll take care, mmm? You'd think after the years we've been here, things would be more settled, but it never is, and the forest trails are no place to be alone. Promise me?'

'Don't fuss, I can look after myself.'

That wasn't quite true. Pa was thinking of Indians, but she shuddered, remembering her rape by the mariner. She brushed passed him, dropped her musket and hat on the porch bench, and strode through the door. 'Phoebe! I'm starving!' Food would cheer her up.

For some reason Anne had seemed agitated before Richard's party. Anything William said seemed to be wrong.

When they arrived at the Croomes' Anne immediately fortified herself with a glass or two of punch, and he fought the urge to interfere. He couldn't help but notice she had become loud and animated and hoped this wasn't too unladylike. Whatever others may think, she appeared to be happy, and this made him happy too. He helped himself to a drink and sought out his friends.

As he chatted he spotted Anne galloping energetically through a reel, hand in hand with her dancing partner. His eyesight was deteriorating – he should do something about it – and he couldn't keep up with the offspring of his acquaintances. Boys and girls had shot up and become manly or womanly. He searched his mind to put a name to the face of the young fellow. He knew most of the grown boys, as they all had to take part in military practice. Whoever he was, Anne had not been short of dancing partners, Richard most particularly.

The fiddler finished his tune, and the young women were escorted off the dance floor by their partners. William excused himself and made his way through the crowded room to say hello to the young folk.

'Compliments, Miss Emily – you look a picture of loveliness today.' He took her hand and kissed it. He could always find a turn of phrase to charm the ladies, even at his age. Emily blushed and dropped a small curtsey. 'Why, Mr Cormac, thank you.'

William's eyes rested on the chest of another young woman, her fresh young bosom rising above her bodice like two yeasty buns. He looked away guiltily. Goodness, how these girls had grown! He was pleased to see Beth Cunningham looked well; she deserved a good time, poor girl, so many responsibilities.

And Anne? He appraised her dispassionately. His daughter looked fair, very fair indeed. Amongst the simpering, fan-fluttering young women dressed in their finery, Anne held her own. She'd grown tall, perhaps a bit on the slender side, but she had this from her mother. He wouldn't call her pretty exactly, but striking, yes, striking was an apt word, with her light brown hair and candid eyes. His admiration for his daughter was cut short as her unguarded laugh rang through the room and she didn't bother to cover her mouth. He sighed. Whatever Anne was, or was not, she had an energy about her he admired. Thankfully she enjoyed dancing – this was one feminine skill she had mastered.

The Croomes hadn't spared the pennies for their beloved son. He watched Anne and Richard prance up and down the line with a great deal less finesse than other couples. William sipped his drink, his eyes still on Anne and Richard as they swung each other around with gusto, broad grins on their faces. He sighed again. He should stop worrying about her.

'William! Join us if you will.'

He made his way towards a group of men smoking and drinking at the edge of the room.

'William.' Dan Cunningham, one of his neighbours, caught his eye. 'We were agreeing, it seems more dangerous now, even with the war well and truly over.'

'It's all those damned mariners out of work now the navy doesn't need them,' Robert Croome weighed in. 'They're turning pirate in ever greater numbers, and what's being done? Nothing at all, while some of those in power like to line their pockets.'

Croome was bitter. He had lost a great deal of rice after the merchant vessel transporting it had been raided at sea. Croome had been unlucky, but it could have happened to any of them. He spoke with strong conviction. 'That damn Trott should've been lynched at the time. How dare a man that considers himself a gentleman stoop so low? Now look what's come of it.'

A decade earlier, Nicholas Trott, then governor in the Bahamas, had accepted an inducement, a massive fortune in fact, to harbour the pirate Henry Avery. Now Benjamin Hornigold, the new pirate kingpin, was using the Bahamas as his base, and it had been one of his gang who had attacked the vessel carrying Croome's goods.

Up till now pirates had been tolerated. Charles Town people wanted to be left alone to do things their own way, even illegal trafficking with pirates. If goods were being sold at a low price, why question where they came from? And pirates' money spent ashore was just as good as anyone's.

Consequently Spanish and French coins circulated along with English money, and it didn't seem to matter. Now things had gone too far – pirates were spotting opportunities and grabbing them with both hands.

With each incoming vessel they waited anxiously for news from the West Indies. That place was a mess and, consequently, in Virginia and Carolina they were suffering. Each vessel carrying their precious goods away to England, or to English colonies south of Florida, was vulnerable to attack. The sea routes were their only connection to the rest of the world, and their Carolina coastline, with its inlets and shallow waterways, provided an open invitation for small vessels to hide, preying on passing shipping.

Piracy had become a hot topic and Hornigold's name came up time after time. It was all second-hand news, from traders, ship's captains, mariners and goggle-eyed passengers, but a picture was building of a thriving racketing trade on the seas, supported in no small way by public servants holding high office.

Croome continued, 'And what are the leaders of our fair colonies doing about it?' It was a rhetorical question and he didn't wait for input from others. 'I'll tell you what—'

'Printing money!' William jumped in to turn the conversation. This caused bitter laughter. Their Carolina pound was now worth three to one against British sterling and heading south. This devaluation hurt their pockets badly with their tied-in trading deals with England.

Laura Croome tapped her husband's arm. 'Robert, I hope you gentlemen aren't going to talk business all evening. We ladies would welcome a dance.'

'If you insist, Laura.'

'Gentlemen.' Her eyes swept over them all. 'Your wives await you. Dan and William, let me see, who can we find for you both?'

'No, no, thank you Laura.' William hurriedly refused her offer, not meaning to be palmed off with some dried-up old biddy. He would enjoy circulating the room to find a suitable lady to dance with. His ambitions went no further. After Mary died he had grieved, but another marriage had little appeal, and Anne and Billy would have to get by with only his guidance.

After one dance he found himself partnering Laura Croome, who seemed to have crept up at his side and smiled invitingly at him, so of course he had to be gallant. He complimented her on the party, and as he promenaded her, she leant closer and whispered, 'It would be a good match.'

'Mmm?' What could she mean?

She nodded towards their children. Richard was standing close to Anne, leaning forward, talking into her ear. The music and chatter were loud so Richard would need to do this, wouldn't he, just to be heard? William sighed; of course this wasn't the reason for their intimacy. 'All in good time, Laura.'

'William! They aren't children. Anne's nearly eighteen. I know Richard's fond of her. And I am too, for all she's a wild wee thing at times. And she's not so little any more...'

'Indeed, she's not.'

'She has spirit and I admire it in her. And marriage will tame her, I know it for a fact.' Laura Croome looked a little wistful.

William's mind raced. Everything he did now was for the future of his children. His creditors were paid off and all his slaves were owned outright, so from now on whatever he generated from his plantation was purely profit. The Assembly had had the sense to reject an English statute demanding property be entailed; he could leave his property to whom he wished. But must he lose his daughter so soon?

As they danced, William warmed to the picture forming in his mind. Anne would become his neighbour, hardly any distance at all, and she would be well provided for, which had always been his ambition. He smiled at the woman he now hoped would become Anne's mother-in-law and she smiled back.

7

A LITTLE MORE THAN A MONTH AFTER RICHARD'S party Anne came flying up to him, shrieking, 'Didn't we tell him not to go? Didn't we warn him? Everyone's dying, Pa!'

So William learnt that Mac, who had been part of the warp and weft of their lives for years, had died. The Yamasees were killing off the traders one by one, and Mac had not been spared. William shuddered. At least he had been spared the protracted torture meted out to Nairne, a government agent, sent to negotiate. He had taken a week to die as his body burnt, lit fuses placed into slits all over his skin.

Concerns about abuses between traders and Indian tribes had been escalating for years, and this had exploded into out-and-out confrontation. William knew Mac had been as keen to make a sharp deal as the next man, but he also trusted Mac had not been as vicious or unscrupulous as some. He had passed through their plantation just before Richard's party, and William had urged him not to travel into the interior, but Mac had been stubborn.

'I'll not be put off. I was in this line of work long 'fore all those out-of-work good-for-nothin's decided to take up the trade. They're the ones to blame for over-hunting of stock and supplying too much liquor and not treating 'em good. I always treat 'em good.'

William knew Mac traded in liquor, but clearly he didn't see the harm in it. He also knew Mac had respected the tribes – in his own way. Well, Mac was dead now.

Through the summer, William waited anxiously as mile after mile of valuable plantation land was torched by irate Indians. Dry grasses blazed, fanned by strong winds and sometimes he could see the smoke from his own land.

William armed his blacks properly – something he had never done before – and O'Neil undertook basic drill with them all, including Billy and Ebo. Tomboy turned out rudimentary spears for the women, and all of them carried knives. Here was a strange turnaround. In recent years William and his fellow white planters had fretted about potential slave uprisings now their numbers were so high, but the flip side was they now needed their slaves fighting on their side.

Throughout the summer Billy practised with a musket, and William knew Anne kept a knife under her pillow. Good for her! At a time like this he was delighted he had such a practical daughter. During the daylight hours Anne went about the house and yard with a sheathed knife hanging from her belt, and if she went further afield, even within the boundary of their plantation, she armed herself with her musket. He would only allow her and Richard to ride out together if they needed meat for the table, and then only in a large group. Safety in numbers.

Rarely did they go out and rarely did they receive visitors, but still the rhythm of the work on the plantation continued.

Most of the Indian rampaging died out, but every so often a random attack occurred; you could never be sure where it might happen.

As autumn turned to winter William had less concern about his pasture as it was too wet to burn, but his livestock could be slaughtered, and his homestead torched. His main concern was naturally for his family – scalping and other such atrocities were still taking place – but he felt as prepared as he could be and would not be cowed by this latest challenge.

Gunshots woke her, along with O'Neil's cries and high-pitched squeals of terrified horses. Anne swung her feet out of bed, hearing Pa's and Billy's shouts inside the house, shouts from the slave quarter and clanging pots. No time for shoes or light; just grab her knife.

'Pa! Billy!' Wearing only her nightdress she rushed downstairs and onto the porch.

A burning torch bobbed towards her from the direction of the slave huts. For a split second Anne believed Indians were about to burn the house, but she remembered this was part of the drill. Someone kept a fire alight through the night; this must be one of her people.

Panicking horses snorted and whinnied. She raced around the back of the house towards the horse enclosure, a quarter moon the only light. O'Neil's voice: yelling, begging, cursing.

They were to be massacred! She hesitated, heart racing, uncertain what to do, which way to run. The sound of galloping hooves and the victorious whoops of Indian warriors filled her ears.

'Shotek!' She screamed and sped on.

At the field no large dark shapes of horses or soft snorts greeted her; through the broken fence she saw the enclosure was empty except for Samuel bending over something.

She twisted her head, searching for what belonged to her. Screeching 'Shotek!', she raced after the disappearing horses.

Abba caught up with her, tugging her arm. 'Don' look, Missy Anne, don' look!'

Abba gripped her harder, repeating her warning. Pa was by her side now, and Billy and a group of blacks, everyone jabbering with fright.

Samuel stood holding a hatchet. 'They done it, Master. They done it.'

It? It? What was Samuel talking about?

O'Neil's body lay a short distance from Samuel's feet. Even in the dim light she could tell his skull had been cleaved open. She moved closer to Abba, who appeared calm; she herself was trembling, teeth rattling.

'What happened, Samuel?' Pa's voice was steady.

'Got here quick, Master. They was takin' the horses. O'Neil, he was tryin' to stop 'em. He weren't going to let 'em go. He hung on, then they done this. I couldn't...' Samuel dropped the hatchet.

'All right, Samuel,' Pa reassured him. 'Poor O'Neil. He loved the horses; we all know that. It's a terrible thing that's happened. Is everyone else accounted for? Everyone else all right?' Pa looked around and took out a kerchief to wipe his brow. 'It looks like the rest of us are spared tonight, and there's no burning. We can offer a prayer for our delivery if this is the worst of it. It's a shame about the horses, but we can restock.'

A sour taste rose in Anne's throat. She turned and retched and retched. Restock! She could never replace Shotek. The one thing she truly loved was lost. She stared at the empty dark enclosure where Pa stooped over O'Neil's body. Shotek was gone, and she felt hollowed out.

Abba was at her side. 'It's done, Missy Anne. All done now. Goat's dead.'

Anne felt faint. She had no idea what Abba was talking about.

Richard and Mr Croome rode over as soon as word reached them. While Pa received Mr Croome inside, Anne sat on the porch, wrapped in a blanket, shivering in the chill morning air. Richard sat next to her, his arm lightly around her shoulders.

'Anne, I know how much Shotek meant to you, but be glad he's alive. Those Indians love their horses and he'll be fine, I'm sure of it.'

This gave her little comfort right now.

'And I don't want you staying here. Ma wants you to come over to us for a spell... You can share Emily's room – she's offered. I... we all want to know you're safe.'

She remained silent; head bowed as he squeezed her shoulder.

'Anne? Will you do it for us?' Richard lifted her chin and looked in her eyes. 'Will you do this for me?'

His eyes were tender and full of affection. She knew he cared for her, but... There was always a "but".

She shook her head. 'I don't think they'll be back – they got what they wanted.'

She was determined to stay at her own home; needed time to think.

Richard nodded, not pressing her further, and she took comfort from his presence.

With the start of the new year Anne's life settled back into routine, and there had been no more raids nearby. Pa bought more horses she could ride whenever she wanted, but she had little interest. Abba went around singing and cheerful in her work as her stomach swelled: this would be Samuel's child. Abba must have made use of Mac's herbs when O'Neil didn't leave her alone. She understood. Richard visited more and more, and they had taken to walking out together after church. She understood this too. She was growing up; being courted.

8

THE DEW DROP INN PROVIDED A ONE-STOP SHOP FOR seamen, Jack included. It was one of many taverns that had sprouted along the Kingston waterfront following the devastating hurricane three years earlier. Before that, an earthquake had swallowed up Port Royal across the harbour, forcing people to abandon that settlement.

The Inn's name conjured images of a snug English village pub, but not a drop of refinement could be squeezed from this haven for boozing and carousing. After her husband's death Betsy had taken over running the tavern and explored her business skills by opening a gambling house with billiard and card tables, dice and shuffleboard games. Still feeling there was untapped potential for emptying pockets, Betsy began employing girls to whore for her. Jack teased Betsy about her pink curtains with frills and flounces; there was nothing genteel about this big, raw-boned woman who kept a stout baton hanging from a belt around her waist.

Betsy's customers knew the Dew Drop Inn, or the Dropsy as Jack referred to it, as a place to gather, drink, gamble and rent one of the back-room beds. These two rooms were banned to weary travellers; the beds were solely for fucking one of Betsy's girls, none of whom were aged more than twenty and some with barely developed breasts. Once Jack had felt Betsy's baton across his backside, and her powerful arms had yanked him out of bed for daring to fall asleep while she was losing money.

Jack had recently left Cuba – his base for the past two years – on the cruise that had landed him in Jamaica, and whatever he had earned by way of looted goods was flowing out to Betsy.

Jack was at the Dew Drop when a lively conversation about a hurricane caught his attention. His hand paused in its exploratory journey up the thigh of the girl perched on his knee as he looked at two seamen who'd rushed in, faces animated, spreading news.

He shoved the girl off his lap, puzzled. 'The entire convoy? Every damned ship? How's that possible?'

'The devil take me if I tell a lie. Smashed to bits, all of it.' One of the tale-tellers crossed his chest.

'There's loads still there, spread out for miles.' The other news-bringer jiggled about; a grin spread ear to ear.

Pressing forward, Jack crowded in with other jabbering seamen all of them eager to know the same thing: how in all creation could the entire Spanish treasure fleet sink? How could all those massive galleons be overcome? Then questions turned to, 'Why? When? Who?' Why hadn't the convoy sought shelter from the storm? Why had they set off in the first place? When exactly did this happen? Who told you? Questions rained down on the visitors.

Jack could hardly take in such a preposterous tale, so he rushed out to seek more reliable tongues and men with better brains. But it had happened, if the newly delivered Boston journal passing from hand to hand was to be believed, and it was an even more spectacular catastrophe than he had first understood. Never before had anything of this magnitude happened. Jack could feel his face shaping into a comical mask of surprise: eyes wide, jaw slack.

For several years the Spanish had hoarded treasure in the West Indies and Spanish Main, not daring to risk attacks from British privateers on the sea voyage back to Europe. But now the war had ended, the Spanish Crown was desperate to replenish its coffers from its dominions. A convoy of twelve heavily laden armed galleons and smaller support vessels had left Havana stuffed full of gold and silver ingots, coins, jewels, china, pearls, precious silks – all manner of treasure along with regular trading goods and brazilwood.

An early season hurricane had battered the convoy. Skies had turned black, giant waves and ferocious winds had smashed masts, shredded sails and driven ten massive vessels on to reefs and shores along the Florida coast, splintering ships, spilling treasure and dumping more than a thousand corpses onto the beach. Another thousand or so men had survived the ordeal and were attempting to salvage the treasure and ward off those who would seek to plunder it. One vessel in the convoy had been lost at sea and one had made it to safety, initially unaware of the fate that had befallen the rest. It had been this single remaining vessel that had raised the alarm.

Jack shuddered. He had enough imagination and years at sea to know what those final hours and minutes would have been like for the men; then his thoughts turned to the disgorged cargoes. Here, by all accounts, was treasure worth several million pesos. Jack imagined every man in the world would be tempted to set sail for this treasure, whether or not they'd ever laid eyes on the sea. This once-in-a-lifetime chance would drive them crazy with desire.

'Damnation!' He cursed at his bad luck. Better to have stayed in Cuba or Nassau, even though he hated the place; in fact anywhere in the north-east of the Indies would be better than Jamaica. This wrecking had happened four months ago, so surely the Spanish would have reclaimed most of the treasure by now.

Jack elbowed his way through the group of frenzied men at the waterfront, seeking news of vessels and captains. He cursed again. The only vessel of any consequence among the dozens riding at anchor was an English naval frigate; the captain being waylaid, his sleeves tugged by men desperate to have his ear.

'C'mon, Captain, what d' you say? You'll get more bending down to pick some coins off the sand than a lifetime of slaving your guts out for King 'n country.'

'And no risk, Cap'n. No fucking enemy – just riches.'

The captain pulled free and addressed the seaman cajoling him and the dozens of others pushing and shoving.

"Fraid not, though I can see the temptation. Governor Hamilton has similar views to you, you might like to know, but it's not ours to take. We're not at war with Spain now, and I have a duty to uphold the peace. We signed a treaty and—'

'Damn the treaty!' 'Who cares?' Jack joined the outcry. Loot was loot and finders' keepers.

As the captain climbed into his waiting longboat he called back, 'If any of you need some honest work, I need crew. Oddly enough, some of my men have disappeared.' He indicated empty seats and the men gathered on shore took a step back as if in one body. 'No takers?' The captain sneered and signalled to his rowers to pull away.

Looking at the scowling faces of the rowers, Jack speculated the captain might find himself short of a few more men before the day ended. The naval frigate had dropped anchor far out into the harbour to discourage deserters swimming ashore. Betsy and all the other brothel owners had sent boatload after boatload of girls out. This would keep the men from thinking with their brains until it was time to up anchor. Even so, with the knowledge of the treasure out there, Jack was certain some would find a way to jump ship.

Taking the King's shilling had no appeal for Jack. He'd been a merchant seaman for years before slipping into the life of a rover. He couldn't even say how it had happened, but bit by bit he had taken bigger gambles and now operated on the wrong side of the law. Right now, he'd settle for any seaworthy vessel that could be fitted out and any captain to lead her.

Two days later Captain Henry Jennings stood on a box on the quayside, the better to be seen by hundreds of seamen anxious to hear his plans. Jennings had recently brought his brig the *Basheba* into port, and Jack understood he had met with Governor Hamilton.

Jennings held up his hands for quiet. 'No panic, gentlemen. The Spanish are rather short of vessels.' This raised a cheer. 'It's taking them time to make return trips to Havana, or other Spanish havens. I am reliably informed that although much has been retrieved, there's much still there.' A massive cheer followed, and Jennings raised his arms high, rallying them all. 'Let them do the hard work. Let them kill themselves diving for it. What do you say? Are you in?'

The roar was deafening. Yes, they were in!

Jack pushed and shoved and before long had his few moments with Jennings. He had sailed under the man a few times and considered him decent; Jack had got by well enough on the proceeds. When he'd spent his money on booze and women he'd taken to sea again. Easy come, easy go.

Jennings greeted Jack warmly. 'Ah, Rackham. I knew, if you were about town, you'd be in for the cruise.'

Jennings extended his hand and they shook.

'So, Captain – how do we stand with it? Is my neck on the line?' Jack wanted to be clear about this delicate but crucial point.

'Hamilton's up for a slice himself, so he's promised a letter of marque. We'll operate under that.' And with this assurance Jennings turned to the next man seeking to sign up.

This satisfied Jack. If Governor Hamilton gave them any scrap of documentation to validate the questionable legality of the enterprise, it would save them from the gallows. A fine line divided privateering and pirating, but Hamilton would be the one to face the questions if the law came asking – and let's face it, he was the law.

A steady stream of willing men presented themselves to join the crew. Jack had come across many of these sea dogs who roved the trade routes living off the proceeds of others' toil and, like feral dogs, they had their packs. Jack belonged to Jennings's gang, as did Charles Vane, another who signed up on the *Basheba*.

Jack and Vane had run into each other from time to time at the inns and brothels strung like pearls around the safe harbours favoured by pirates throughout the Indies. Vane was ambitious and made no secret of his desire to lead his own gang. For this reason, Jack made every effort to keep on his good side, if he had one. Vane was a potential source of future employment, should things not work out with Jennings. Roving gangs were fluid and men free to change allegiance if a leader proved incompetent. Now both he and Vane were in Kingston, both enthusiastic about Jennings's venture, and doing all they could to fit out the *Basheba* to hasten their departure.

Fully provisioned, fitted with great guns, with eighty armed men aboard, the *Basheba* set sail accompanied by the *Eagle* carrying nearly a hundred men, all of them hungry for adventure. As they beat their way north towards the low-lying Florida coast, giving Cuba a wide berth, Jack said a silent farewell to the Spanish island he had called home the past two years. He had a strong suspicion an English mariner might not be welcome after plundering Spanish treasure. Pity. He liked Cuba. He'd kept a low profile, based in a small cove on the south of the island and visiting Havana from time to time – a town much to his liking. English settlements in the Indies weren't a patch on the Spanish ones. Jack could speak a smattering of Spanish, and by and large got on well with Spanish people, chiefly Rosario, his *encantadora dama*. He had left Rosario with their new-born child. He had enjoyed being a family man for a time, but it didn't sit easily with life at sea. Jack silently mouthed a farewell: '*Adiós. Dios te bendiga.*'

Sailing along the featureless Florida coast, the devastation became clear. Skulls and rib cages of large animals, broken masts and hulls, iron fixings and cannon balls: all manner of evidence of the calamity lay strewn along the narrow beach. Shredded strips of sail and rope festooned low-lying trees and shrubs, while the tops of tall palm trees dangled at an angle, trunks shattered by the force of the storm.

That night, campfires flickered in the distance. Time to reef sails. Time to drop anchors. Time to check arms. Time to lower boats.

In pitch dark, Jack put his back into his oars. He wore dark colours and had blackened his face with charcoal, as had the others. Some had muskets slung over their shoulders, though Jack considered these cumbersome. He had two charged pistols tucked in his belt along with a dagger. Chief among his weapons was his cutlass. A cutlass never ran out of ammunition. So far those who had suffered at his hands had been violent drunken men, picking a fight or unhappy to have lost at dice or cards. Crews of the merchant ships and coastal vessels he had helped capture were mostly sensible men and submitted without a fight. On the rare occasions they were opposed, Jennings, or whichever captain he was under at the time, would urge his men, 'First crew aboard gets the pick of their weapons!' And there were always men mad enough or drunk enough to take the gamble of being first over the side onto a prize. Some died in that suicidal rush, sometimes crushed between vessels or shot. Better to be second crew over, less risk as far as Jack was concerned: you kept your life and still received a reasonable share of the prize.

High breakers roared as they ploughed through. Jack's boat and two more lurched forward on a wave and scraped the sandy shoreline. He leaped into the thigh-high surf.

A shot rang out from a Spanish sentry. They had been spotted. Jennings gave his order. 'Surprise is out of the question, so we'll announce ourselves.'

As they marched several men began to beat drums, and Jack and dozens of others let out booming whoops and war cries. He had no idea what defensive forces would greet them or if there would be anything of value to pick over.

At dawn they reached the edge of the Spanish encampment of makeshift shelters built from broken wood and canvas sails. A lone soldier approached, waving a scrap of white sailcloth above his head. Behind him, fifty or so ragged men gathered around the dying embers of fires, arms dangling or raised above heads. This staggered Jack. There would be no resistance.

The peacemaker walked towards Jennings. 'Admiral Francisco Salmond.' The Spanish commander's gaze took in Jennings's smart uniform and the hotchpotch of armed seamen gathered in force behind him with drummers beating a tattoo. 'Are we at war again? Excuse me, we are a little isolated here.'

'Indeed not, sir.' Jennings, ever the gentleman, bowed. 'Captain Jennings. No, sir, not at war, not in the least, but we are here to relieve you of your wealth.'

'I see. But I cannot allow it. It belongs to His Majesty King Philip, our gracious Catholic king of Spain.'

'He'll be a disappointed man then!' some cock behind Jack shouted, and they all joined in raucous laughter. 'We're here to collect it for you. Didn't you get the message?' This from another in his gang of plunderers. Jennings raised his hand to hush them.

'Well, Admiral, you see I have men with me.' Jennings's eye took in the depleted group guarding the camp. 'Reason says we are a stronger force than you. Will you have your men die for this?' Admiral Salmond knew little could be gained by stalling, but history would judge him badly if he didn't attempt to defend this extraordinary quantity of wealth belonging to his Crown, so he tried to bargain, and when this didn't work he tried to fob off Jennings with a bribe.

Jennings shook his head. 'No, sir, but your men will vouch you've done your duty. We mean to have it all.'

At Jennings's signal, Jack moved forward with the rest of them. There was no resistance and Salmond retreated to sit on an upturned box and watch helplessly. Jack felt some sympathy for the man.

For months these Spanish wretches had barely survived, with little to eat or drink. Those who could swim had braved the surf and dived in deep water where the broken hulls of the *Capitan* and *Almiranta* could be seen. This was where the bulk of the treasure lay. Some ships had broken up on shore while others were lost at sea. A great deal of treasure had already made its way south to Havana, but much more waited, stored neatly on the beach.

Jennings whipped away canvas covers to reveal chests and boxes. A grin spread over his face. Sullen Spanish sailors walked them to nearby dunes and pointed. Jennings couldn't contain his glee and kept up a steady stream of rousing encouragements.

'Dig, men. Dig, and don't overlook a fucking thing!'

With spades and bare hands Jack and all the men dug into the dunes to drag out chests and boxes and barrels, and larger items wrapped in sailcloth. Jack helped roll a heavy cask back to the growing pile of loot, and with considerable difficulty hoisted it upright. He forced the lid open. No wonder it was so damned heavy. He plunged his hands into the cask and tossed a silver ingot to the man behind him. Others dug deep into a pile of gold and silver ingots and silver coins. One danced a jig, yelling in jubilation as he twirled a string of pearls above his head; another whirled a silver candlestick. They were intoxicated.

A shot rang out.

Vane, his pistol pointed into the air. 'The next shot strikes flesh. Get on with it. Play your games later. Shift this fucking stuff!'

He was Jennings's enforcer, and there was nothing Vane enjoyed more than to maim a man and plead it had been done for good reason.

Jack did get on with it. Rolling casks and barrels, partly emptying heavy trunks the better to manoeuvre them;

pushing and dragging looted goods up improvised wooden ramps to lift them into boats threatening to sink under the weight; rowing out to their anchored vessels; with nets, ropes and tackle they hoisted and stowed their booty on the *Basheba* and *Eagle*.

Trip after trip, day after day.

Jack found a length of what had been exquisitely embroidered Chinese silk, its delicate stitching ruined by seawater, scoured by jagged shells and sand. He wrapped it around his head and shoulders to ward off the hundreds of mosquitoes settling on his sweat-drenched body to suck his blood. He could only slake his own thirst in pools of brackish water. It was exhausting, but gathering this once-in-a-lifetime treasure trove drove them on. His share of the booty would be small, but even so it would set him up for a good while to come.

There could be no pretence that they were privateers, and Jack doubted Hamilton's letter of marque would hold up in an Admiralty Court. But who could stop them? Who could enforce the peace treaty with France and Spain? Jack laughed out loud at the absurdity of it.

No turning back. He'd join Jennings, Hornigold, Blackbeard, Vane and the rest of them to fight out turf wars, and may the best man win.

9

Anne left Samuel and Otto loading supplies onto Catfish ready for the journey home. With time to fill she meandered along Charles Town's quayside, side-stepping barrels being rolled towards waiting boats and onward to anchored ships bound for England. Beyond the White Horse the sound of rowdy laughter coming through the open door of what Pa called a spit-and-sawdust alehouse drew her attention. She paused at the open door.

Seamen sat around a table, thumping their fists, chanting, 'Twenty-one... Twen-ty... Nine-teen...' One called out encouragingly, 'C'mon, don't let me down.'

All eyes were on a young man, drunkenly balancing full tankards of ale on outstretched open palms, with a third tankard balanced precariously on his head, while balancing on one leg. He had a friendly freckled face, coppery curly hair, rough callused hands with ragged nails. The countdown continued. 'Thir-teen... Twelve...' The fellow rocked unsteadily his gaze fixed resolutely on a point ahead.

From the threshold, Anne laughed. 'And a wager from me: a shilling if you do it!' She tossed a coin to one of the seamen, who snapped his hand deftly catching it. And the balancing seaman might have done it, but he became aware of her, and before the countdown reached six all was lost. Tankards crashed to the floor and Anne leapt back, ale splashing her skirt. Cries followed: 'That's not fair!' 'She put him off!' Men laughed away their losses, while others divided coins to share.

One of the seamen beckoned. 'I'll not take your money, though by rights it's mine, but join us if you've a mind for our company.' He indicated a jug of ale on the table.

Such places were not for well-brought-up young women. She glanced back along the quayside and estimated it would be some time before Otto and Samuel were ready to leave.

'Why not?' She lifted her skirt, stepped over the threshold and looked confidently at the gathered group. The young seaman made room for her next to him on a bench.

'Next time luckier, eh? I'm James, by the way.'

She accepted a tankard and raised it to her lips. Pa need never know what she'd been up to. 'So,' she smiled at James, 'what brings you here?'

'Loading the coming days. Heading south to the Indies with supplies. After that we take on sugar and head back to England... So the cap'n says.'

'You like it, at sea?'

'I just go where the work is.' He shrugged.

'That's it?' Anne frowned. 'I remember when I was a little girl voyaging from Ireland. I loved to climb the ratlines and feel the wind in my face and—'

'Who has time for that!' James scoffed. It was her turn to shrug.

An older seaman winked at her. 'There's a freedom out

there, unlike anything else. Once you've tasted life at sea, there's no other way...'

Anne absorbed his words.

As she sat drinking with the rough seamen, she liked that they accepted her so readily, didn't have expectations, though to be fair they didn't know a thing about her.

'Missy Anne!' She looked up to see Samuel hovering by the door. Leaving her drink unfinished she left with a brief, 'Bye,' and James raised a hand casually in farewell. She wagged her finger at Samuel, grinning, 'Don't tell Pa!' then ran to where Otto waited to cast off Catfish.

Two days after her meeting with the mariners she was indoors idly flicking through a journal. At the sound of an approaching horse Anne went to the porch, where she found Richard tethering his horse.

'Glad to find you in.' He grinned.

Richard politely refused Phoebe's offer of refreshments and Phoebe left, closing the door. He picked up an open journal. 'Anything interesting?'

'Pa wanted me to find out about furniture...'

She and Richard talked about latest designs for some minutes, which proved hard going as neither of them knew much. They moved on to the price of grain, which he knew a great deal about but did not interest her. The conversation ground to a halt, then Richard stood and cleared his throat.

'This is difficult but, well, we've known each other a long time, and you know how much you mean to me—'

'We're best friends—'

'More than that. Come on, Anne, much more. I want to ask—'

'No, no, don't spoil it!'

Before she knew it Richard was kneeling beside her and taken her hands in his. Oh no. Not this. She froze in her chair as Richard looked deeply into her eyes and spoke kindly.

'Spoil it? Why should I spoil it? I want to marry you. You must know? Please say you will.'

This boy, this man, she had known for years was her dearest friend, and yet, and yet... She jumped to her feet. 'I don't know. Please. I need time...'

He also sprang up. 'Of course you do. Of course...'

The two of them, who had rolled together in the dirt, inflicted all manner of bruises on each other's shins and shared confidences, now found themselves facing each other, tongues unable to form words that had come so easily in the past. She could feel her cheeks glowing and saw perspiration on Richard's brow; they were each as embarrassed as the other.

After a long, long moment Richard cleared his throat and tried once more. 'I love you, Anne.' He laughed and expelled a whoop. 'There! I've spoken the words. Can't take them back now. There's a burden off my mind!'

And it looked like it was. Richard grinned and lightly punched her arm, looking relaxed like the boy she'd always known. But her own burden felt a good deal heavier. Richard loved her. This made her feel warm, comfortable, but she didn't feel ready.

Richard took her hands in his again; stood close.

The door opened, and Pa was before them. They hadn't heard him arriving.

Richard jumped back. 'I'd best be going.' He acknowledged her father. 'Good to see you, sir.'

Pa looked flustered too. 'No, no – no rush, now. Stay awhile.'

Oh, this was so awkward! Anne wished they were both out of the room. She felt stifled and longed to flee and howl into the wind.

Richard paused at the door. 'Anne?'

She forced a smile, tried to relax the muscles in her neck and control her hands from flapping at her side.

'May I call again in a few days?' Richard was politeness personified.

She nodded automatically; listened to Richard's footsteps retreating and Phoebe seeing him out. Through the window she watched him ride away, and turned to her father, his eyes on her. He knew, of course.

Pa cleared his throat. 'He cares for ye. I know—'

'Pa! Let's not talk about it.' Talking about feelings like this with Pa was embarrassing.

'Hear me out now. Please.' He settled and patted the seat beside him, but she paced restlessly from window to table and back again. 'He's a good match; a sensible lad; got his head screwed on the right way, you know.' Pa laughed and tried to lighten her mood. 'Who else would put up with your nonsense, mmm? It's everything I could wish—'

'Pa. No!' She put her hands to her ears but could still hear him.

'Just imagine. You'd be set up very nicely over there and Billy could take over this place in due course. It would be wonderful. We'd be neighbours—'

'Stop, stop! I don't want this. Any of it.' Panic was rising just as surely as vomit had done when she realised Shotek had been taken.

Pa looked perplexed. 'Dear heart. What on earth do you mean?'

'I don't know… I don't know… I'm not sure I love Richard – not in that way. And living here, running a plantation—'

'My child!' Pa looked relieved she had no bigger objection.

Anne could feel Pa willing her to conform. Perhaps he had forgotten his own past: his affair with Ma when she was his servant resulting in her own birth; leaving his wife; leaving Ireland itself, persuaded by the pamphlet promising Carolina as a land of opportunity. Pa often joked that if he'd known what it was really like he might not have been so keen.

'Pa. You took a risk with Ma and me... coming here—'

'A long time ago...' Pa flapped his hands, pushing the past away.

'I don't want to spend Sundays choosing which set of china to put on the table, or what dress patterns to choose, and—'

'Heavens above, it'll be a privilege to do such things and not have to labour!'

'—and children. I don't want any—'

'Ah, that's a woman's lot in life. Laura and Robert are thinking of building another house—'

'You've talked about this with Mr and Mrs Croome? About me?'

'Well...'

Anne was no longer jealous of any of her friends. Let one of them marry Richard. She was certain she could not make Richard happy, as year on year her discontent would surely grow. She craved something else; something less predictable. Something bigger than the life around her. Something that would not tie her to land, husband, children.

Soon after Richard's proposal Anne found a reason to return to Charles Town while James's vessel remained in the harbour. They fooled about and joked, and she drank more than she was accustomed to at home. Her booming voice could hold its own with the men around the table, and she felt released from the constrictions of her usual social circle. They parted with his cheery, 'I'll buy you a drink next time – maybe in a year or two... unless you want to come with me?' And her equally offhand, 'I might just do that.'

The day after this second meeting with James, Richard again asked her to marry him. Again she demurred, again she saw his pain.

'Anne, what more can I say to make you say yes?' Richard pressed her hand as if to imprint his wishes into her skin. 'The plantation's doing well – very well. You wouldn't have to worry about money. We'd go on much as we always have done. We get on so well together, and don't deny it.'

She begged to be given a few more days.

A fierce argument with Pa followed. Pa threatened he'd not give her a penny of his money if she was so ungrateful for the chances being given her. He'd often teased her about such things when she'd misbehaved but now he sounded serious.

Her thoughts turned to James. Might he help? She longed to be far away: at sea recapturing her six-year-old self, voyaging from grey-skied Cork to unknown Carolina. Pa had come with nothing and made a life for them all. If he could do it here, she could do it in her own way.

That evening, Anne paced and paced, determined not to have her life mapped out. She picked up a sheet of paper and pen and began to write. 'Dear Pa…' She could still use those words. 'I'm going away and don't know if I'll be back.' What else to say? 'Please try to understand…' What else? '…and tell Richard I'm so sorry. Tell him I need to go.'

As she placed what she knew was an inadequate note on Pa's desk, she doubted neither he nor Richard would understand.

It took all night and all her resolve to sail Catfish along their creek to where it joined the Ashley River, and all the way to Charles Town. The darkness held no terror, and she was comforted by the chorus of cicadas and frogs, but she cursed time and again as she found herself in shallows or too close to banks. It had been challenging but she focused on the task of sailing; escaping.

Reaching Charles Town at dawn, she sailed out to the merchant ship she knew James to be on, shouting up to a watchman to fetch him. He returned to the rail, rubbing sleep from his eyes.

'Take me with you. I want to come. I don't care where!' She sounded as desperate as she felt.

'Now? With us?' James leaned over the rail, eyeing her bobbing unsteadily below.

'Yes, now. With you. I want to leave. You said I could.'

'In jest. I said it as a jest.'

'Dare you.' She locked eyes with him.

Keeping Catfish upright was a struggle and if it tipped she would lose her bag with her few valuable possessions: her gunpowder horn that had been O'Neil's, and her hunting knife. She couldn't lay claim to the money and pistol. These she had taken from her father's drawer: stolen, she supposed.

'Well? What do you say?' Anne willed James to say "yes".

James turned away, shouting, 'Captain!', and before long a middle-aged craggy-faced man was at James's side. She could hear their whispered conversation, then the captain raised his voice. 'If she's coming – if you want her to – you'll have to get married. I'll not carry a single woman on board. Be clear about that.'

'Married?' Anne was taken aback. This was going faster than she, or James, had expected. He looked just as shocked as she felt.

James laughed. 'Marriage, heh? What d'you say? I'll wager a shilling… Dare you!'

She hadn't bargained for this. After all, she had been twisting and snaking away from Richard for months to avoid just such a thing, and she cared for Richard a great deal, could even admit she loved him. She hardly knew this man. James was nothing to her. Nothing. Just a means to escape.

James shrugged and turned to go. 'See you next time… Maybe.'

'No. Wait! Wait!'

James turned back. 'If you want to come, you'll have to take me.' He spread his arms wide, mocking her. 'Think of me as part of the bargain.'

She took a deep breath. 'Well, why not?' Her chin jutted in defiance, but there was no one to talk her out of such a crazy act.

'You've got till midday.' The captain shook his head in disbelief as James clambered down to join her and others gathered at the rails, hooting with laughter.

The first minister they found at the Church of England church house dismissed them, so they hurried to another church house and knocked urgently at the door. They were told the Lutheran pastor could be found at the church, so they raced to find him.

'Would you please, please marry us! James is leaving on the outgoing tide and we want to marry before he goes.' Anne's face reflected as much urgency as her words.

Anne knew this wouldn't be the first time the pastor had conducted a rapid service, deciding it better for a man and woman to be married prior to a hasty tumble in bed before the man set off to sea. She did not tell the pastor she intended to leave too. After a brief ceremony, she and James sped back to the quayside hand in hand, shrieking with the silliness of it all.

Pa or Billy would guess she'd headed to Charles Town, but it would take some hours to travel by horse along the rough roads, even at a gallop. No one could catch her!

She left Catfish tied up and persuaded the first man they saw with a small boat to row them out. As Anne settled she noticed an open upper window at the White Horse and a woman leaning out, shaking a blanket.

'Quick, remind me, James – where're we heading?'

'Nassau, New Providence Island in the Bahamas, then on to Jamaica. So I'm told.'

Anne hollered and waved to attract the woman's attention. 'When you see him, tell Pa, tell Mr Cormac, I'm off to seek my fortune in Jamaica, or maybe New Providence. Tell him I think New Providence is a lovely name. Be sure to tell him!'

As James's merchantman sailed beyond Sullivan's Island she cupped her hands in the shape of a boat, held them in front of her mouth and blew, allowing her cupped hands to bob away from to the length of her arms, just as Pa had done in Ireland, tempting her across the Atlantic by rolling the sweet-sounding name of Carolina around his tongue, saying, 'Carolina… It's a pretty name, don't you think? Shall we have an adventure?'

Well, Pa must have had his dreams, and she did too. And New Providence was a lovely name. Full of promise. Her heart quickened.

PART TWO

1716 – 1719

To The Bahamas

Hell is empty and all the devils are here.

THE TEMPEST

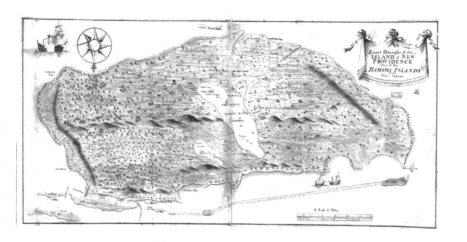

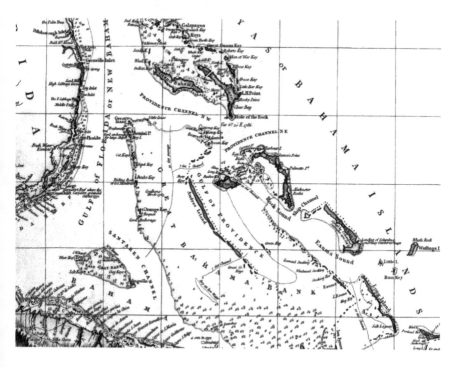

New Providence Island. The Bahamas

10

As they sailed south along the Florida coast Anne discovered she and James had little in common. James had no more prospects than any other uneducated seaman, and he told her more than once, 'You're more stubborn than a damn mule!' and mockingly called her "Mistress High-and-Mighty".

Sharing a hammock had been the subject of their first argument – she had refused point blank to do that – so they'd reached an agreement that she could keep her body to herself until they were at the first port of call: New Providence.

New Providence Island in the Bahamas conjured images of bounty and beauty. They were nearing the entrance to Nassau harbour and her spirits soared. She admired a well-trimmed sloop, the *Benjamin*, heading out to sea. A sailor on James's weather-beaten merchantman leant on the rails next to her and whistled.

'She's a sleek little lady. Look at her lines. She's made for speed, this one, and dressed pretty too. Someone loves her.'

And the *Benjamin* did look splendid: freshly painted, polished and buffed with ten guns mounted on her sides, stern and bow, her deck crowded with men. This vessel clearly belonged to someone who had done well for himself. Anne decided Nassau must be a prosperous kind of place.

The stench reached her first. She recognised the sickly-sweet smell of rotting flesh along with other indeterminable foul smells, so turned to face seaward filling her lungs with less pungent air. Her unease grew as they entered the harbour and looked for safe anchorage among the multitude of sunken and burnt-out hulls poking out of the water. The land itself offered little comfort. Beyond Nassau's beachfront, semi-permanent shacks and hovels were strung along the coast from the eastern reach of the settlement to the crumbling fort at the western edge. Here was no orderly quayside and wharves as in Charles Town – just a beach to haul boats up onto. And on the beach hundreds of ramshackle shelters made from driftwood or broken planks supporting flapping sailcloth walls and palm-leaf roofs. And men: hundreds of rough-looking men.

Everywhere Anne looked she saw unkempt men, lounging on the beach swigging liquor or squatting around fires poking at skewered roasting meat. Those on their feet were dismantling broken boats to construct new shelters. As she took in the scene, she could detect the cause of the stench: heaps of festering animal skins and carcasses.

No amount of repeating the words "New Providence" could magic away the reality of the place. She felt sick to the pit of her stomach. Thank goodness James's captain only intended to offload supplies; she hoped Jamaica would prove more inviting.

She sought out James. 'Is this where you meant to bring me? To "do it" with me? At this stink hole?'

James's face turned pink as nearby seamen sniggered. 'It's just for a few days. The captain doesn't want to be here much either.'

'Can't be quick enough.' Her sharp words reflecting her dismay.

'Look, Mistress High-and-Mighty – remember whose idea it was to come?' She turned away with a flick of her head, but James grabbed her shoulder. 'Look at me!'

Tight-lipped, she hoped her face did not betray her anxiety.

'You chose this, I just helped you out, remember? Fine by me, and I have no objection to being married… Leastwise, I don't think I do, but what would I know since we haven't, as you put it, "done it". No, I've no objection – as long as there's somethin' in it for me.'

She lifted her chin. 'I've decided to stay on board – it'll be safer here.'

'Oh no! We're both going ashore whether you like it or not.' James gripped her arm. 'I'm planning on finding a room some—'

'A room!' She snorted. 'I can't even see anything resembling a house. No, I'm staying put. I'll not camp out on the beach.'

'If needs be, we'll sleep there. That's where we'll finally be husband and wife. I don't give a shit. I've waited long enough.'

She yelled at him, horrified at the very idea of men leering at them through broken planks or gaping sailcloth, and James yelled back at her to take the first passage home, which of course she wouldn't. She couldn't. Not until she had explored whatever she had set out for. Not until she could return victorious. She was stuck with James, her husband, a man she barely knew.

'How about this – just for tonight? Can't afford more.' James was elated. He had paid a high price for a room above

one of the taverns on the beachfront. The place was obviously
a brothel, but better here than out on the beach with the
dregs of mankind. James had only secured the room when he
told the hard-faced scrawny woman owner they were newly
married. This raised a cheer, with one fellow joking, 'The first
wedding here for years, perhaps ever. Drinks are on us!'

Anne accepted refill after refill, before following James up
a rickety staircase and putting her bag down by the equally
rickety bed with a lumpy mattress.

This would be her first night with her husband, with the
sounds of carousing men and women rising through the gaps
in the floorboards and hundreds more men partying hard on
the beach. So be it. She determined to face this squarely. James
was right – she had brought it on herself.

She dropped down on the mattress and managed to laugh.
'This will do well enough, Mr Bonny!'

'Pleased to see the scowl's left your face – thought it was
stuck on for good.' James looked relieved.

'Race you!' She kicked off her shoes.

Naked, James threw himself next to her on the stained
mattress. She had been anxious about this moment, worried
she would be reminded of her forest ordeal, but that man
had rotted away long ago, while James was very much alive.
Anne slapped his bare backside and he tickled her, making her
shriek. This would be all right and would help pass the time
they had to remain in this stink hole. She hoped this coupling
wouldn't start a baby – this was something she needed to find
out how to avoid.

She lay awake with James's knees fitting snugly into
the back of her own, listening to his even breathing, while
outside a man on the beach sang a sentimental ballad and
others joined in the chorus: a tale of a seaman parting from
his lover.

'…I remember one night, a drizzling rain, round my heart I felt an aching pain… fare thee well, my honey, fare thee well…'

Towards dawn the third drunken rendition of 'The Ballad of Captain Kidd' drifted up to her through the glassless window. Clearly this was a favourite.

'…I'd a Bible in my hand, as I sailed, as I sailed, and I sunk it in the sand, as I sailed as I sailed …Oh m' name is Captain Kidd, as I sailed as I sailed…'

Finally she slept.

Her next argument with James occurred that afternoon.

'Anne, listen. I've been talking to the fellows on the beach – those who know Hornigold, he's the main man, y'know – Benjamin Hornigold – we saw his flagship as we arrived.'

She wouldn't forget the *Benjamin* in a hurry. So, this is what a pirate captain kept for himself. 'What of it?'

James looked sheepish. 'I've been thinking. Maybe I should try my luck here. Those that've come back from the Spanish wrecks with Jennings are doing well.'

'What? …What d'you mean? We're sailing to Jamaica!' This didn't make sense.

'You just have to look at what they're bringing in – it's crazy money for some of them, and they don't work too hard, so they say—'

'Joining them? You've had nothing good to say about them. They're thieves, they'd cut your throat – or you'd be hanged if the law catches you!' This was a fact. Even the last choruses of 'The Ballad of Captain Kidd' ended in his execution; she'd heard that song sung over and over during the night.

'Not all of 'em are bad – I've been asking around. I'd steer clear of a man called Blackbeard, but other captains, they know what they're about. So I'm told.'

Anne discovered the human flotsam and jetsam washed up on Nassau's single stretch of beach were seamen, traders and pirates camped out alongside unemployed logwood cutters ejected from Spanish-held territories. All hoping for a turn in their fortunes.

She had taken little interest in world affairs and knew only that the war with Spain and France had ended. But with the end of the war, employment opportunities for mariners had dried up. Her sense of geography hadn't extended far beyond her home: church, neighbours, Charles Town and the small web-like radius of trails spanning outwards from home where she could ride for the day and still be back by nightfall. And as to history – the least said about that the better. She regretted her lack of inquisitiveness, and not having made use of the Croomes' extensive library.

For two days she argued with James until, with a jolt, reality hit her. The small amount of money she had brought with her had disappeared; Nassau prices were a great deal higher than in Charles Town as virtually everything had to be brought in. They needed to earn their way here, or anywhere else for that matter, or they'd starve.

James was right; she had instigated this, so she would lie in the bed she had made for herself, including literally lying in bed with James.

'All right then. We'll give it a go, and if it doesn't work out we'll move on.'

'It's a deal.' James spat on his hand and they shook.

11

AMONG THE JUMBLE OF RUINED SILKS AND BROCADES strewn at the Spanish Wrecks site, Jack had found a sad-looking roll of red striped calico. The sturdy cotton had withstood its dunking in the sea, so he'd kept it for himself and when he arrived back in Kingston he had one of Betsy's girls make snug breeches for him for land and cut-off trousers for sea.

Jack wasn't as tall or as broad-shouldered as his father had been in his prime, but he considered he cut quite a figure with his long wavy dark hair, his beard trimmed short, the best hats he could find, a well-cut jacket and now distinctive red breeches showing off his shapely legs. He meant to stand out amongst the rest of the rabble.

Before long, the wrecks lured Jack back to the Florida coast. This time three vessels set sail from Jamaica with Jennings in command on the *Basheba*. They arrived to find English vessels circling like vultures around carcasses. All of them jostled, argued and fought over the small pickings that could be retrieved from the seabed in deeper waters without bursting the lungs of the divers they'd brought with them. While the divers were at their work Jack spent hours on a beach sorting through ammunition and keeping thieving hands off their loot.

Someone whistled. 'Who's the pretty boy then? Hey, Rackham! Red-arse!'

Vane flapped his arms, making shrieking sounds like a parrot. Vane was part of the crew of the *Discovery* – one of the vessels under Jennings's overall command.

Jack wouldn't rise to the bait. 'Ah, you'd like your own?' He struck a pose.

'Do I want to look like a bloody parrot?' Vane snorted and shot him a dismissive look. Men nearby hooted with laughter.

In the following days Vane, and others keen to toady up to him, greeted Jack with, 'Hey, Parrot!' It diverted them, and he could laugh with them. Life at sea had brought him into contact with all manner of broken men whose only satisfaction in life seemed to be to make another man's life more miserable than their own, but this banter was good-natured. Jack found himself dubbed "Parrot" for a time, till it became a joke amongst them vying to give him a fitting nickname. "Red Jack", "Red Butt" and "Red Shanks" did the rounds, and before long he wasn't plain "Jack" but "Calico Jack". He liked the galloping rhythm.

New clothes, new name and money in his pocket.

Jack returned to Kingston and became a fixture at the Dropsy. Within weeks he discovered one of Betsy's whores, or most likely some of them, had left him with more than just a memory of a good time.

'I know just the doctor for you. He'll sort you. That's where I send my girls when the occasion arises.'

Jack followed Betsy's advice and visited the doctor. Jack had him pegged as a quack if ever there was one. The man treated him unceremoniously with a lime and molasses concoction squirted up his cock and firmly told him he should refrain from "engagements of a sexual nature" for some time. The penetration of the metal nozzle made Jack's eyes water, and he hoped three doses would be adequate. Soon after, he left word where he could be found and set off for one of the remoter parts of the Bahamas.

Eleuthera was away from temptation but, oh, he found life dull! The long narrow island was sparsely inhabited by farmers eking out a life on scrubby patches of cleared land, while others plied the coastal waters, if they could afford such luxuries as a vessel. Jack found himself barely tolerated; farmers had harsh words for him but still accepted his coin. It riled them to have to trade with the likes of him.

Before long Vane arrived, looking for him and others to round up. While Jack had been hanging out in Kingston snoozing, boozing and performing blanket hornpipes with Betsy's girls, then whiling away time in Eleuthera, Vane had been busy. He had captured a brigantine with a cargo of slaves en route from the Guinea coast to Barbados. He'd sold the slaves and renamed the vessel the *Ranger*. With its weather deck flush, stripped of its forecastle and quarterdeck and fitted with twelve guns, the vessel was fighting fit, as was her captain.

Vane dropped anchor and rowed ashore to be greeted by a motley group of men curious to hear his news and his plans. Jack had nothing to do, so better to be at sea and off this dreary strip of land. Although he didn't much like Vane, Jack sensed he was on the way up, so best hitch a ride.

Following this cruise with Vane – which hadn't gone too badly – they finished up in Nassau. Jack squatted on the *Ranger*'s deck, dividing the valuables into piles according to ship's articles, while around him men pressed in watching like hawks to ensure he didn't short-change them. This vital process had to be completed before they went their ways.

Coins of different currencies, trinkets, knives and goods that could be sold on, all manner of things they had pillaged over recent weeks, were spread out on deck. Jack emptied a leather pouch containing pieces of eight, adding them to the growing piles.

'That ain't right. That ain't right at all,' a disgruntled seaman challenged him. 'There was more when we took it from *la Garza*. It ain't all here and I should know – I was with Vane.'

'He's right, Calico. The pouch had more. We opened it – didn't count, but more than what's here now, I swear to it.' This from another disgruntled man, standing hands on hips, daring him to challenge his version of the truth.

Jack sat back on his heels, surveying the fidgeting, defiant men surrounding him, and his eyes rested on Vane, staring him down. God damn the man! The words formed in Jack's brain, but he said nothing as his eyes slid away. It was Jack's role as quartermaster to look after anything they pillaged. Did they think he had kept stuff back, or did they suspect Vane? He remembered the *la Garza* – a small Spanish trader they had intercepted off Hispaniola. He had made a log of everything they took, and his log showed only nine pieces of eight, all of which were accounted for on deck.

'Are you sure?' Jack played for time and once again glanced at Vane. Jack recalled Vane had pistol-whipped the Spanish captain and taken charge of the valuables before handing them over for Jack's safekeeping.

'I gave you the money. Remember?' Vane's right hand rested lightly on his cutlass hilt.

Jack eased himself up and eyed Vane. 'You gave me the pouch and I logged everything in it. What you gave me is all accounted for.'

Clearing vessels taken at sea were chaotic times: men heaving heavy goods from vessel to vessel, often in heavy seas; storing and lashing goods safely. After this Jack would make an inventory of everything, keeping valuables locked away.

Jack addressed the crew. 'I've no reason to steal from you, and if you doubt me, search my possessions. Go on. Go ahead.'

He knew they didn't doubt him, but he could see eyes darting in Vane's direction.

Vane kept his hand hovering near his cutlass and planted his legs wide, head thrust forward. 'You cockroaches want to search my cabin too? Think I'm holding something back?'

No one answered.

'Well? Tell me!' Vane barked his challenge then strode towards the seaman who had voiced his suspicion. 'It ain't all there.' Vane mimicked the man. 'You sure about that? You challenging me? You'd challenge your captain, would you? And this, when you are about to go ashore with your pockets full. What's it to be?'

The other men were drawing back, leaving Vane and the glowering seaman facing each other, noses no more than six inches apart.

'So? What's it to be?' Again, Vane's question was met by silence.

Jack edged closer to the two belligerent men, neither in the mood to back down, both shifting their stance, eyes locked.

'Listen. Here's my plan.' Jack carefully nudged the suspicious seaman back and stepped into the gap, hoping he sounded reasonable. 'Let's get this divided and get ashore. I promise the best hotchpotch cook-up you've had in months. Turtles, fowl, sheep, whatever you damn well fancy throwing in the pot – that'll be on me.' Jack turned and placed his hand on Vane's shoulder. 'And the captain's treating us all to his kill-devil rum. Right, Charles?'

Jack raised an eyebrow at Vane, willing the man to back down. Vane grunted his acknowledgement and shrugged off Jack's hand.

Jack wanted to be done with this cruise, go ashore and celebrate, though he might pass on the kill-devil rum: gunpowder mixed with rum distilled into flasks. This drink created quite a kick, and from past experience gave him gut-ache for days.

12

.

'WELL, NOT EXACTLY... THERE'S A SORT-OF GOVERNOR here... but he can't do nothin'' Charlotte laughingly replied to Anne's question about who was in charge.

Charlotte, a tiny, skinny, hard-faced mixed-race woman, ran the tavern she had stayed in on her first night in Nassau. The following nights she and James had slept on the beach, and this would not do. The place was dangerous, and she could not survive without James's protection. She had seen how the men eyed her. These men had been attracted to Nassau like flies to rotting corpses; most of them had been away from female company for years at a time, working at remote logging camps or away at sea. All of them were wild men with ideas of being free from society's laws.

Anne tidied herself up and set off in the burning morning sun along a dusty track to find the house of the man "sort-of" in charge: Governor Thomas Walker. He could advise how she and James might thrive. She knew when she had found his place, as it was the only well-built dwelling she had come across. Mr Walker's house was freshly painted, set within a well-tended garden filled with flowering shrubs, shady trees and alive with birdsong. She had no idea what to ask him, but she needed advice. There must be some work James could do.

At her knock, a middle-aged black woman opened the door slightly. She enquired, 'Is Mr Walker home?'

The woman held the door ajar. 'Are you alone?'

Anne nodded. The woman frowned but didn't open the door wider. Anne repeated her question and the woman replied, 'Yes, he's here.'

'Please tell your master I'd like to meet with him or arrange a time if it's not convenient.' Anne meant to sound courteous but firm.

'And your name is…?'

'Anne Bonny. Tell him, Mrs Bonny.'

The woman smiled. 'Good morning, Mrs Bonny, and may I ask why you wish to see Mr Walker? Perhaps I can help you instead?'

Anne frowned. This woman, who spoke very well, did not know her place. 'Just tell him we're new arrivals.' Her answer was curt.

'I'll see if my husband can receive you.' And with this the woman disappeared.

This black woman was the governor's wife? Back home, in Carolina, she had grown aware some men used their women slaves and servants badly – there was enough evidence of that – and her eyes had been opened to Abba's plight. But here a black woman held a position of power as the top official's wife! Inside, she could hear children. She made a mental adjustment.

Mrs Walker ushered her into an airy study lined with books, the windows wide open, allowing a slight breeze. Mr Walker sat at a large desk spread with samples of dried plants, leaves, flowers and stacks of paper held in place by stones to stop them blowing away. He rose to greet her, removed his spectacles and gestured to his work.

'I'm making the most of my time here – so much of interest to collect and document if you are in the slightest bit curious about the bounties of nature… Please.' He ushered her to a chair. 'Sarah, dear.' He turned to his wife. 'I'm sure our guest would like some refreshment.'

Anne longed for a cool drink but hardly dared look at the woman she had assumed to be a slave, or at best a servant.

'What can I get you?' Mrs Walker spoke kindly. 'We've lovely fruits if I can tempt you, or refreshing herbal teas from our garden?' Anne mumbled and nodded. She would accept whatever this unusual couple thought fit to offer.

'Now, what can I do for you?' Mr Walker leant his backside against his desk.

'What is there here for honest people? Those who don't take to pirating?' She meant to find this out and bring her answer to James.

Mr Walker smiled. 'What indeed! Don't be fooled by the activities you find me doing.' He glanced back at the table. 'It takes my mind off my duties.' He fixed her with a piercing look. 'Honest people, you say? We need such people more than ever, but daily it's a losing battle.' He pulled up a chair and faced her. 'Settlers… farmers… here and on Eleuthera. If your husband, and you, wish to go in that direction I can grant you land and get you started. In fact, we have places ready to walk straight onto, to pick up where others have left off.'

Her heart sank. These would be the plots of land and tumbledown shacks she had passed, many of them abandoned. And these so-called settlers would be the broken-looking men and women and snotty-nosed children she had asked directions from. To Anne they looked like poor whites coming for supplies in Charles Town before disappearing for a year or so into the depths of the Carolina interior, or little better than the swamp vagrants she had heard described eking out a living in isolated North Carolina waterways. Even Phoebe looked down on them. She couldn't think what to say.

'What does your husband do, Mrs Bonny, and you yourself? Do you have a competency, a flair for something, we may put to good use?'

'He's a seaman, and I... Well, my father owned a plantation outside Charles Town just off the Ashley. I didn't have to consider work.' She knew her father's plantation was modest, but Mr Walker needn't know. She felt her back stiffening and knew she sounded proud and had no right to be. Not any longer.

'Ah, we may have common acquaintances, I know many good families in Charles Town, but we'll leave that discussion for another day. And your husband – is he an officer or does he own a merchant vessel?'

She shook her head. 'No, no, nothing like that.'

'Well, Mrs Bonny, if your husband is to be at sea, perhaps you intend to offer our society more genteel gifts? Are you skilled in needlework?' She shook her head. 'Or music? We have a much-loved but very out-of-tune harpsichord, and unfortunately the excellent tutor our children had died recently. Fever. He's sadly missed.'

She shook her head again and mumbled, 'I'm sorry, no.'

Mr Walker paused before continuing. 'Or perhaps you have an eye for drawing or watercolour? My good wife has a fine hand for illustration and is helping me with my documentation of the flora.' He picked up a sheet of paper to show a carefully sketched and labelled illustration of foliage.

Anne was beginning to panic. What could she claim to be good at? Not scholarship, and she couldn't sew a straight seam to save her soul. Or spin or weave. Nor play an instrument or sing. Anne realised she knew next to nothing about cooking – that had been Phoebe's work. Worse still, she didn't know the first thing about farming, even though this was the source of her family's wealth. Their slaves worked in the fields! She could feel her armpits prickling with sweat and did not know what to answer. Swordsmanship? Riding? Shooting? Hunting? All were true enough, but they seemed inappropriate answers.

Mr Walker continued, more cautious now. 'Or possibly you are inclined to the spiritual? We no longer have a church, but we do have a preacher who does his best on Sundays: Anglican, of course. We have a small gathering here at the house, you and your husband would be most welcome to attend, and I know our preacher would value help with the children to run a Sunday school.'

'No, no… I'm sorry…' She sensed he was confused as to why she had visited but was too polite to ask directly.

Mr Walker started on a new tack. 'So what draws men here?' He did not expect an answer but continued with his soliloquy. 'Pirating. Smuggling. Arms dealing. That's what brings men to these islands. Honest options are limited, but they are possible – I want to stress this. Over the years, men have survived taking what they can scavenge from wrecks or selling ambergris, but there is little left of that, I'm afraid. Some turn to logging, others to fishing, birding and turtling. The thing is they take from the land and the sea, Mrs Bonny. Do you understand me? They take what God has provided and do not give back, so they are destroying the very bounty they feed off. Labour is required to make a success of any enterprise, albeit by slaves or servants in your home country, but here it is the white men and women along with freed blacks from Barbados who must labour.'

Anne mumbled her agreement, not really keeping up with Mr Walker's train of thought; feeling out of her depth.

'We need people who are not afraid of honest work. We have some merchants and farmers here, but the men I see arriving daily do not want to labour – they want to take from the land and the sea, and from others. Especially from others. I do my utmost to discourage pirating and free trade, but it's a losing battle. I sincerely hope your husband will not be tempted by such a life. There are honest ways a man might make his living, and I will do everything to help you and your husband.'

Mr Walker stared candidly, and Anne felt a fresh blush rise before she had controlled the last. Mrs Walker returned holding a tray bearing a plate of diced fruit and cups of steaming greenish liquid. Anne smiled in relief that the conversation with the "sort-of" governor had ended. She thanked Mrs Walker and thought, perhaps in time, she could make a friend of her – despite the fact she was a black woman.

Mr and Mrs Walker expressed shock her husband had allowed her to venture out alone, so Thomas, their eldest son, whom she judged to be a little older than herself, accompanied her back to Nassau, armed with a pistol. She did not tell him she carried a pistol and a knife concealed in her bag, nor that she had not considered it necessary to consult with James before setting out today, but as Thomas regaled her with recent stories of pillage and – he coughed discreetly with an "excuse me, ma'am" – of rape and murder, and told her of Hornigold's recent threat to kill his father, she began seriously to heed how little her life counted for.

Some days after her visit to Governor Walker a series of blasts from beyond the harbour entrance alerted those on land to expect a new arrival. What vessel warranted such a signal?

Anne and James, along with hundreds of others, crowded onto the narrow beach, waiting anxiously to see what would appear.

'I'm not waiting around to find out.' One grumbling man turned tail before heading to the safety of the forest. Others fearful of another Spanish raid did the same. Anne hesitated: should she wait or run? Curiosity aroused, she and James stayed, but she took the precaution of preparing her pistol.

Three large vessels, bristling with guns, sailed into the harbour. Not Spanish nor the French – as evident from the flags on the masts. The *Basheba*, along with two other captured naval vessels, had arrived home. Cheers and whistles erupted. 'Look at the prizes Jennings has got himself!' 'What a fucking fleet!' 'Fit to fight the King.'

Jennings was up there jostling with Hornigold to be top dog in this pirate society, and each of them had his gang. Anne watched the ships drop anchor and those on shore – men desperate to be taken on as crew, men aspiring to this life – crow and brag as if this were their own success. Men rushed into the water to haul up Jennings's boat; to be the first to slap him on the back.

Charlotte, along with a group of her girls, joined Anne. 'Looks like we're in for a busy time, ladies. We can expect hundreds of gentlemen callers.' Charlotte frowned, and Anne could sense her brain ticking, calculating the logistics and money. 'I'll have to set a stricter time limit.' Charlotte might be happy, but none of her girls looked too enthusiastic.

Charlotte squeezed Anne's arm. 'Sure I can't tempt you, honey? I do have some married ladies, y'know, though Lord knows what became of their husbands.'

Anne hastily withdrew her arm and scowled. 'I'll not spread my legs for any of these dogs. You make that clear to any who ask. You tell them, if I see their prick anywhere near me, they'll feel more than a prick from my knife!'

Charlotte cackled. 'You're settlin' in quickly to our ways. I'll be sure to give them your message.' Charlotte linked arms with Anne and tugged her forward to join the jostling throng of men.

Casks were rowed ashore, rolled along the beach and prised open. Jennings's crew of two hundred or so men joined hundreds already camped out and everyone drank their fill of fine madeira and rich rum. Anne watched groups of men slink off to Charlotte's and return a short while later to continue drinking and singing the night away.

Sometime in the middle of the night, as a fellow with a fine voice sang about bold Robin Hood, Anne sat on the sand with James's arm draped across her shoulder and another man's arm around her waist. They were all enjoying the party, swaying to the rhythm of the song, and she belted out the refrain:

'Derry down! Hey! Derry, derry down!'

While Robin Hood had robbed the bishop of his gold in the song, in real life it was Jennings who had been doing the stealing – a great deal of it.

Anne turned to James and kissed him deeply and drunkenly, determined to embrace the life she had chosen. 'If you're going to join this bunch, or any of them, then you'd better be good at it. Make a success of it, James. Make me proud. Make us rich, make us stinking rich!'

James laughed and kissed her back. 'Damn right I will.'

Over the coming days Jennings's men ferried booty across the harbour to Hog Island, to divide the spoils along with weapons taken from the captured naval vessels. All manner of goods Jennings didn't want to keep for his own use were brought ashore to sell.

For days the waterfront market was busier, more varied and more robust than Charles Town's market had ever been. Men were knifed and killed for deals gone sour or trying to protect newly purchased goods. The shacks on the beach provided little security from thieving hands reaching between gaps in the planks as drunken seamen slept. It was evident to Anne that loyalty to brethren of the sea only went so far.

Anne began her new life in earnest. She hustled and haggled with the arms dealers, securing a decent-enough pistol for James, then her money ran out. She had nothing left to jingle in her purse, but she considered it an investment. Seeing Hornigold's and Jennings's magnificent flagships and their evident success had set the bar high.

James found a place in one or other of the roving gangs, but he did not become rich. He needed more determination in Anne's view, but when she said as much he did not take it kindly. While Anne's ambition for her husband remained unfulfilled, she and James scavenged and hoped for better times. She carried her pistol and her hunting knife tucked in her belt. Men understood Mrs Bonny was not to be mucked with, affording her more respect than they gave to the girls and young women working for Charlotte and other brothel keepers.

Anne did not visit Mrs Walker as she meant to. The social gap between them widened, and, the colour of her skin notwithstanding, Anne sensed herself no longer fit company for the governor's wife. In any case the Walker family were not there for long. Again, Hornigold threatened to kill the governor along with his son Thomas, and the family fled to the safety of Carolina. Meanwhile Nassau was under the rule of volatile pirates who didn't give a damn for anything – not even their own lives. Hornigold, intent on ruling the roost, nightly pitched his gang against Jennings's or Vane's. The beach had never been safe, and now became a theatre for bloody turf battles. Any semblance of law in the Bahamas had ended and Anne was right there.

13

THE SIGN OF THE THREE TRADE HORSES SWUNG IN the early morning breeze as Mary Read wrapped her shawl around her head and closed the door. Lifting her bag containing a few personal belongings, including her dead husband's clothes and tobacco pipe, she set off walking in the direction of Rotterdam.

Mary was in her mid-twenties when she walked away from the inn at a crossroads near Breda, in the low Countries. Most of the locals knew her as the wife of the landlord serving ale and meals, but this had not been the only life she knew.

Portsmouth on the south coast of England had been her home town – a place where just about everyone relied on the comings and goings of ships for employment. Aged twelve, she decided the navy offered better prospects and a better wage than being a servant. An indoor life of servitude had no appeal. With her hair cut short and wearing boy's clothes, Mary began her life at sea, signed on the muster book as Mark Read. It had not proved difficult to pass herself off as a youth. She kept to herself, and on the rare occasions she washed her body or her clothes, she disappeared to the depths of the hold.

She spent years serving on warships, learning everything there was to know about fighting at sea. She had run up and down ladders as a powder monkey, carrying powder magazines to the gunners; assisted surgeons on the blood-slicked floor of the orlop deck as they amputated limbs, bound wounds and left the badly injured to die: gunners, officers and anyone unlucky enough to find their skin proved a fragile shield. She learnt to handle ropes, till her hands were hard and calloused; she knew all the lines and rigging and could bring any ship up to full sail in no time at all. When she left the navy, she emerged a sturdy young woman and someone who could be relied on to work resolutely hour after hour.

Brutal hand-to-hand fighting skills had been learnt on the battlefields of Flanders as a soldier with an English foot regiment. She credited an experienced soldier from the north of England with her survival – him and good luck. After she had dragged the wounded soldier from a muddy battlefield he had shown his gratitude by training her in combat tactics, chiefly with blades and knives, and urged her to "keep a cool head and live another day". What she lacked in brawn she made up in brains. She learnt to fight tactically, and emerged from many skirmishes, battle-hardened and "a canny wee fighter", as her grateful colleague put it.

Above all else Mary learnt no one noticed she was a woman. While serving in the navy she had spent some weeks on a hospital vessel in their convoy when a gash on her thigh turned septic. Those attending her barely looked at her or her wound. She had waited anxiously, caring less if she died than that they discovered her to be a female, as she would have been immediately discharged with no salary.

Throughout her days as cabin boy, able seaman and foot soldier Mary had dressed and acted as a man, adopting the voice and mannerisms of the men about her. This had been her life before her brief marriage to another former soldier in her Flanders regiment. The few years she had helped him run the inn on the outskirts of Breda was the only period she'd lived in circumstances outsiders might consider normal for a woman.

But with the end of the war and the Treaty of Utrecht, soldiers, their chief customers, had drifted away. Now, following her husband's death, it was time to move on.

Mary meant to go to sea again, and she knew that once she reached port, she would be competing with hundreds of out-of-work soldiers and sailors, many of them maimed, all jostling to be noticed.

As she trudged northwards, doubts troubled her. She could do the physical work required, but could she continue to pass for a youth? Several years earlier her breasts had been firm and small, her shoulders and arm muscles iron-hard and her hips narrow. Now, after years ashore and a baby born and buried, her body had softened. Binding her breasts tight to her chest and wearing her husband's clothes would be a start, but her lack of facial hair could not be explained away. She planned to keep her head down and quietly go about the work required of her. Needs must, as her mother had impressed on her.

She could not afford to be scared by what the future might hold, so she approached this new challenge as she always had, going doggedly about her life with as much courage as she could muster. And she had plenty of courage; there were many who would testify to this. She buoyed herself up with this knowledge as she trudged on, huddled against a sudden downpour, lifting her sodden skirt above the muddy road.

A forest of masts rose from the Rotterdam waterfront: homeward-bound English merchantmen, on their final port of call; Dutch East India Company ships heading to or from the Spice Islands and their dominions in the East Indies; Dutch slavers setting off to West Africa; traders bound for the Americas. The quayside was a frenzy of activity, with bales of fabrics, crated china and indigo slabs offloaded from India, barrels of herring from Newfoundland's rich fishing grounds, sacks of cloves from Spice Islands and hogsheads of sugar from the Indies. Ships preparing to leave were provisioning and loading their cargoes.

Now dressed in her husband's clothes, Mary studied recruiting posters lining the walls of the taverns, all of them with information about types of vessels, destinations, captains and crews required. Everyone appeared preoccupied with their own business and gave her no more than a casual glance. A Dutch trader was due to leave, taking out supplies to Batavia and planning a return trip laden with peppers, nutmeg and other goods from the East Indies. She made her way to the recruiting desk.

'*Ervaring?*' The fellow with a droopy moustache matching his droopy eyes barely glanced at her.

'Topman...'

That got his attention. '*Ja? ...geen gelul?*'

Mary nodded. She was an experienced topman, prepared to climb the rigging to the very top of the masts and out along the yards at dizzying heights to furl or unfurl sails in all weather. No one but an idiot or desperate man would lie to a recruiter about such skills; once at sea, they'd soon be found out when they were put to the test or would likely plunge to their deaths from a great height.

'*Ja, ik heb... um... veel ervaring...*' She deliberately spoke Dutch haltingly.

'*Engels?*'

'*Ja.*' She bobbed her head again. Pretending not to speak much Dutch would allow her to keep her own company – if she was taken on board.

The Dutchman looked her over with a practised eye. She was well-fed, fit and had no obvious ailment, unlike many of those surrounding her. He grunted and turned the muster book to face her. She signed, 'Mark Read.'

With her watchkeeping duty over, before heading down to her hammock, Mary took out her pipe and cut a wedge of tobacco. Puffing contentedly, she leant on the leeward rail as grey early-morning light seeped above the eastern horizon. She mumbled, 'Morning,' to a fellow emerging for the change of watch. He grunted, '*Goedemorgen,*' grabbed hold of the rigging, swung onto the rail downwind from her and spread his legs. A stream of piss arced into the air a yard away from her face. Mary smiled in the certain knowledge she had become one of the men again. She knocked the wooden rail for luck.

14

A NEW RHYTHM MARKED ANNE'S LIFE, NO LONGER measured by the annual planting and harvesting of rice by her father's slaves but by what could be harvested from the sea with her own hands. The Bahamian waters, more than the land itself, provided sustenance as it had done for hundreds of venturers before them. Anne and James crewed small vessels hustling to harvest, scavenge and trade. Abundant turtles thrived in the shallow seas, yielding flesh, shells and oil; salt was panned from southern islands; goods were salvaged from wrecks and sold on. They had enough to get by on, as James frequently told her, and she played her part working alongside him. She had little choice in the matter.

She kept well away from the beach these days. It was a transient place for transient men: somewhere to divide looted goods, eat, drink, fuck and move on. She had witnessed enough brawls with head-butting and eye-gouging, ending with limbs sliced, skulls fractured and as often as not a dead body to be disposed of. These gangs – Hornigold's, Jennings's, Vane's,

Blackbeard's and the rest of them – carved out their territory and carved up each other. James was not as committed to the causes of freedom at all costs and free-for-all plunder, but this life drew him in from time to time. So, they got by.

As soon as Anne found herself pregnant, she did everything she could to end it. Charlotte's remedy of "as much gin as you can handle sittin' in a tub of scaldin' water as hot as you can handle" hadn't worked. Twice she had sat, drunk and stewing, her face puce and dripping with sweat. Charlotte had clicked her tongue. 'Sorry to hear that – it mostly works for my girls, and they have plenty need of it. Bad luck. You've got a strong womb.'

Next, Anne sought out a black woman known for her bush medicines and came away with bunches of herbs and leaves which she pounded and boiled. The concoctions made her dizzy or vomit, but still her belly swelled. She kept her efforts to abort her baby from James, who accepted the arrival of a child as inevitable, but was otherwise indifferent to the coming birth, mirroring her indifference to him. They had weathered their first eighteen months of married life and she was counting.

With the baby coming they needed a more settled life. After a hurricane laid waste to the town of tents and ramshackle huts that was Nassau, those with carpentry skills were in great demand and could charge what they liked. New, more substantial houses were being erected in the hope that these would withstand the fierce gales and hurricanes they had come to expect.

'How about we move onto one of the abandoned plots?' This was James's suggestion.

Harvesting from the sea was one thing, but eking out a meagre living from the thin soils of the island was quite another. Earlier, hopeful settlers had renamed the island New Providence, but in Anne's opinion this optimism was misplaced. When James showed her the shack and patch of barren land he had in mind – one of the places she had been so dismissive about – she could not bite back her indignation. 'Would you have me work like a field hand with dirt under my nails day and night?'

'What else are you going to do? Tell me? A reasonable question, isn't it?'

She had no answer as she surveyed the tumbledown house, nor did she have a solution two days later when they were sheltering at Charlotte's tavern-come-brothel after a downpour had sent them rushing for cover.

'So, what do you want to do – unless you want to work here?' James gestured about him.

Standing at Charlotte's, hair plastered to her head and sodden dress clinging to her swollen belly, Anne agreed to James's plan. Acknowledging that the baby would come into the world in a few months and that James was right in other ways too did not give her comfort.

Was this the bigger life she had sought? Setting up home in a shack with a husband she tolerated but did not love, looking after a baby she did not want and scraping a living from the soil? It seemed impossible to make headway.

With the help of carpenters, they built a house for themselves, marginally better than O'Neil's hut near Phoebe's cook-house, and definitely bigger and more comfortable than Samuel and Abba's meagre hut. But the memory of Phoebe's and Samuel's crops put her own efforts to shame. For all that she planted seeds, watered and waited and willed the soil to yield something edible, she found her cheeks burning with fury when James returned home saying, 'Let's see what progress has been made, hey?' The idea of being judged by her efforts to grow crops wound her up. He had no idea why she was so touchy when he said, 'It's pitiful a grown woman can't tease some green out of the soil.' She gratefully harvested lemons and oranges from trees planted by earlier Spanish settlers.

Her baby thrived in her womb. She seemed to be good at growing a baby despite her efforts to do otherwise. In the sweltering heat of late summer, with James away, she was fearful of being alone when the time came, so she set herself up in a Nassau lodging house. Peggy, one of Charlotte's girls who had given birth herself, offered to assist.

Anne lay propped in bed, the skin of her belly stretched tight. Low, gravelly moaning sounds forced their way up through her throat, while between her thighs the baby tore her, pushing its way into the world. It hurt! The unimaginable pain of it. Between her shrieks and panting she begged, 'Do something… Do something, why can't you!'

Peggy didn't have a clue what to do, but the baby girl arrived, nevertheless. Peggy severed the cord with a none-too-clean pair of shears, lifted the baby from between her quivering thighs and placed her between bloated breasts.

With shaking hands Anne accepted her daughter into her arms and wiped the blood and mucus from her face and coppery hair. One more push and the bloody, meaty afterbirth expelled itself from her body, its membranes, veins and tubes looking like a slaughtered animal. This was precisely how she felt: cut open and dissected with her guts spilling out.

'I need to get back soon, if you don't need me no more.' Peggy offered Anne a glass of water, which she accepted with shaking hands. 'I'll send someone to check on you. First I'll get rid of this.' Peggy jerked her head towards the afterbirth.

Anne lay still, dimly aware of Peggy wiping between her legs, removing the soiled sheet from under her and wrapping up the afterbirth to take away. She felt numb, all emotions emptied along with the baby she had ejected. Instinctively she helped her tiny daughter's mouth find a nipple. Between the slatted wooden blinds, motes of dust floated in shafts of sunlight and voices drifted in – an argument between two men. One swore, 'I'll rip the fuckin' eyes from ya lying face!' and the other retaliated with some promised action equal if not greater. She closed her eyes and her ears to the world.

Drifting into a fitful sleep, she decided she did not want this to happen again. Where was the fun in any of it? She had probably enjoyed having sex with James at the time of this child's conception, but she hadn't enjoyed carrying the baby, feeling sick and dizzy and seeing her body swell and become ungainly, and no one in their right mind could say they enjoyed birthing a child. Drowsily she considered the argument she'd heard outside the window and weighed the relative pain and inconvenience of having an eye ripped out and giving birth. A final conscious thought passed through her brain before an exhausted sleep claimed her: never again.

Anne learnt to sew a, more or less, straight seam because of the baby she named Nancy. The small child needed clothing and James proved a surprising teacher. Years at sea had taught him self-reliance: sewing pants and shirts, mending sails and nets. While Anne tried to teach him to read and write, which he showed little aptitude for, he schooled her in some necessary domestic skills. Enough to get by. It was James who added flourishing touches to their joint sewing efforts, and once she returned home to find him delicately embroidering tiny flowers around the hem of a small dress. He looked up sheepishly, no longer indifferent to the baby. Nancy had claimed a big place in his heart.

When he was home, Anne put meals on the table – that was her job – but she found James didn't mind cooking, though his efforts were as basic as hers. More than once Anne wished she had learnt from Phoebe. She missed the food from her childhood: the comfort of hominy, the sharp tastes of shrimp and grits, Phoebe's peanut and sweet potato soup, and how she prepared pork. She had taken it all for granted. She recalled the taste but had no idea how to recreate those dishes, and now with Nancy to look after she had little energy or interest in further domestic chores.

One evening, as James prepared food and she nursed Nancy, he said, 'You know, I wouldn't mind giving up the sea, if I could manage to farm a patch of land and keep thieving hands off our crops and animals. I really wouldn't mind, you know.'

'Give up the life? Why would you? You're only starting out. You can work your way up – you could have your own vessel – your own crew!'

'C'mon. You think I've got it in me to do that? To even want to?'

'Yes, why not?' She was horrified. James was to be her means to the bigger life, which was getting further and further away, just like the lure of a rainbow's coloured lights, always in the distance, always out of reach. Again, she appealed to him: 'Well? Why not?'

James took his time to answer, stoking the fire and stirring the stew. 'You wanted this life for me – and I'm doing it and getting by well enough—'

'Well enough! You call this well enough!' Nancy yowled in protest as Anne pulled her off her breast. 'Look at us. I swear we're no better than the rest of the white trash in these—'

'You wanted to come, Mistress High-and-Mighty! Face your life, Anne. This is it!'

James always said the same, and always she sensed her inadequacy for the role she had carved out for herself. She thrust Nancy into his arms.

'But this needn't be it. There can be more.' Hadn't she flung those words, or similar words to her father? Was she bound to be disappointed by the men in her life? Were they right? Was life made up of small inconsequential things? She could have been mistress of a wealthy plantation, but she had rejected life with Richard as too confining, too predictable; now she found herself living in little more than a hovel with a child, married to an uneducated seaman of limited ambition.

Anne could hardly breathe for the anger filling her as she glared at her husband jiggling a howling baby over his shoulder, the bubbling stew forgotten for the moment.

James spoke loudly over Nancy's howls. 'I tell you; I don't think this is going to last. There's going to be some massive bust-up before long – mark my words.'

He did not mean their marriage; he meant the lives of all those living in Nassau.

'Oh, Mr Walker's back, by the way. The whole family.' James reached out one arm to stir the stew, jiggling Nancy in the other.

This surprised her. For whatever reasons drove him, the governor and his family had returned from exile in Charles Town and once again taken up residence in their ransacked property. She suspected they wouldn't have found many books left – paper made excellent fire starters – and she wondered if the out-of-tune harpsichord had become kindling. She also wondered at Mr Walker's perseverance. What could he hope to achieve? For all that she loathed the squalor and the rough edges of this place, she had come to appreciate the lack of barriers, the freedom to consider anything possible. She did not wish to heed James's words of doom. A bigger life could be achieved, if only she could find the way to it.

15

Vane leered at the captain of the vessel Jack had helped capture. 'A toast, before we release you. To your governor.'

'Of Virginia?' The captain spoke nervously.

'Where else? That's where you've come from, isn't it?' Vane raised his glass. 'Lieutenant Colonel Spotswood. Fuck the governor!'

Vane always liked a show. So they raised their glasses and cursed the governor of Virginia, then Vane turned his attention to Carolina. 'And fuck Governor Johnson!'

Unbeknown to Johnson and his Assembly, they had been playing host to Vane and Jack – and the rest of them on the *Ranger* – for some weeks as they sailed in and out of creeks and inlets of the Carolinas pouncing on vessels. 'Yep, fuck Johnson and that judge of his – Judge Trot!'

Jack toasted heartily, 'Fuck Judge Trot!'

They had learnt four pirates had been hanged at Charles Town: local men making a nuisance of themselves. Neither

Jack nor Vane knew or cared about those unfortunates, but it sent a clear message to the rest of them.

Now came Vane's favourite toast. 'And damnation to King George, and may he roast in hell!' Vane filled his glass and tossed the fiery liquid down his throat without pause. During any serious drinking bout, and there were many, Vane always included a curse on the King. He had long run out of inventive epithets, and all his men were beyond shock at anything in life, so it was only the captain of the sloop they had seized whose face flushed scarlet at this insult to His Majesty.

'You're rogues! Rogues – all of you!' The captain of the captured vessel spluttered and could think of no stronger words for them, nor could he bring himself to join in such a blasphemous and treasonous toast, but Jack could play along with Vane. He lifted his glass. 'Damn the King!'

They offloaded what they wanted and handed back to the captain his considerably lighter vessel.

Sailing south along the American coast they saw nothing worth taking, and Jack was impatient to be done with this cruise. They needed a prize, a decent one, and they could all go ashore and go their separate ways. The Windward passage was a busy shipping lane so here they would surely find vessels to prey on.

Between Cuba and Hispaniola the lookout cried the longed-for words: 'Sail ahead! Looks promising!'

The square-rigged frigate was far in the distance and Jack couldn't tell what she was. Orders to trim sails and prepare arms resounded. As they drew closer the prey raised her jibs and spanker till she was fully rigged, meaning to out-race and outmanoeuvre them. On board the *Ranger* more canvas was unfurled, and with Vane's signature flag hoisted, the chase commenced. Their purpose could not be clearer.

Vane gloated. 'We'll take her – take her for ourselves and expand my fleet. She looks like a vessel fit for any purpose. Fucking perfect! Prepare for action!'

Jack grinned. He was happy – they all were. What merchant captain would be mad enough to face them? It hadn't happened yet, and this was surely a merchant vessel... wasn't it?

'Vane!' Jack had his spyglass out and he spoke sharply. He could make out a white fleur-de-lis flag flying alongside other emblems. 'Shit. She's a French fighter!'

Vane cursed and grabbed the spyglass to see for himself. Within minutes the frigate had swung about, gunports open, and carriage guns let loose a volley of fire, smoke filling the distance between them.

'Fuck me!' Jack stepped back in surprise. In her haste to fire, the French frigate had missed, but following rounds would not. These were professional fighters.

Men urged Vane, 'Take her on, Cap'n.' 'Let's give it a go!'

A decision had to be made. Now. Vane turned to Jack. 'What d'ya say?'

'I say we can take her.' All the men heard him, but his tone was neutral, cautious. He knew the men wanted action, as did he, but he didn't want to lead them to slaughter.

Vane hesitated as his men pressed in, urging him to chase down the prize.

'No... No. Veer away! Veer away!' Vane yelled the order. He was captain and he had made his decision. He would save his vessel and his skin. This shocked Jack. Since when had Vane ever backed off from a fight?

'What?' 'No way!' 'Fucking coward!' 'We've a right to decide!' The men were furious.

Vane yelled louder, his finger jabbing. 'Captain's orders! My right – I have the power to decide! Veer away, I tell ya!'

Orders rang out and men scampered.

As the French man-of-war blasted a second and third round, the *Ranger* slowly turned, offering her stern.

The *Ranger* was safe from pounding cannon fire, but Jack's heart pounded in his chest. Vane, the man they all feared, himself included if he were honest, had backed down, backed away from fighting a prize worth taking. This shocked the entire company and it changed everything. Vane no longer commanded the men's respect. They no longer feared him or would do his bidding. It was all but over for him.

That night Jack did the rounds. He needed to be sure; the men trusted him enough to have voted for him as quartermaster, but would they take the next step? As dawn broke he stood on deck with the gathered men, Vane amongst them. He let his eyes slide off Vane and picked a friendlier face. Now or never.

'You have the right to elect your captain. We're all here for the same thing – to win prizes and make what we can of things. What happened yesterday wasn't what we wanted. Not what we expect from a captain.'

Jack could feel Vane's eyes boring into him. He turned to face him squarely. 'We should've attacked! I was for it. You heard me!'

Shouts of agreement greeted him. Yes, he had spoken up in favour of an attack; no one disputed it. Jack grabbed the rigging and leapt onto the rails of the *Ranger*. Vane was not the only one who could create a sense of theatre.

'I'm putting myself to you. Do you vote me for captain?' Jack's voice boomed out.

'Calico Jack for captain!' 'Aye, I'm with you!' Hand after hand was raised.

He hadn't got the vote of the entire company, but there was enough. He gratefully watched his old mates George and Dick raise their hands. Those two would stick with him through thick and thin.

The deed was done. Jack commanded the *Ranger*, and they'd record the vote and change of command on the copy of ship's articles. Now he needed to get Vane off the vessel. His vessel. Thankfully they still had a captured sloop accompanying them, so he could set Vane and his bunch of supporters off in it with supplies.

Vane sauntered over, no longer a dangerous man now all his weapons had been removed. 'So this is it then, you red-arsed bastard. Didn't think I needed to keep an eye on you. Very coolly done, cocksucker!' Vane spoke quietly.

Vane could not hide his fury, but Jack sensed an underlying respect for how he had been outmanoeuvred. This was after all what their game was about: winning and losing. Jack had won this game and he felt great.

16

THE FIRST BLAST OF CANNON FIRE WAS UNREMARKABLE, and Anne barely paused, expecting it would be a vessel announcing itself at the harbour entrance. After the second, third and fourth rounds fired in quick succession she knew something must be wrong. She gathered up Nancy, covered her ginger hair with a bonnet to protect her fair skin and strapped her to her back with a long piece of fabric wrapped in the way Abba had carried Ebo as a baby: a sensible way to carry a child and leave your hands free. Grabbing her knife and pistol, she set off along the track towards town, passing ditches alive with mosquitoes. She judged the continued firing must be from the fort and broke into a jog, Nancy bouncing up and down, secured in the small of her back.

The Union Jack had been removed some time ago, and now a black flag fluttered atop the fort: a plain black square, not specific to any pirate commander, proclaiming Nassau as pirate territory. Pirates were firing repeatedly at an armed vessel anchored in the far west of the harbour. Nassau had received an unexpected visitor who would not be deterred.

Anne joined hundreds of men and dozens of women at the shore, all of them curious but cautious. At the base of the fort, one man shielded his eyes against the sun, yelling to those on the ramparts. 'Vane! You hear me? Hold off, you idiot. Let's at least see what they want!'

So it was Vane up there, blasting off some rounds.

Vane had arrived back in town having been turfed off his own vessel by Jack Rackham, a man she had heard about but never met. After this incident Vane had captured a heavily armed French brigantine with a hold packed with valuable cargo, including brandy and wine. She had been one of his black market customers.

From the rooftop Vane responded to the call for caution. 'Fuck 'em! While I'm here, any visitor that flies an official flag 'n wears an official-looking jacket on his back and official-lookin' hat on his head's not welcome. I'll not put up with any interference to my rule.'

His rule? Anne scoffed. He didn't have Hornigold's brains, only pent-up rage, which was always shooting off in new directions, and right now his shooting was directed at the anchored vessel and the uniformed officers she could see aboard.

'Vane. For Christ's sake. Hold your fire!' The man at the base of the fort wasn't giving up.

'Nah. This can't be anything good – be sure of it.'

Vane ordered another round of shot directed into the harbour. Their visitor held fire, though her gunports were open with great guns rolled out and aimed at the fort.

More men yelled at Vane to stop, but he ignored them.

Yes, Vane would do this. Anne had had words with him when he'd assumed hers to be a body for hire, propositioning her with a leering, 'How much for one fuck... How much for two?'

She had drawn her hunting knife, saying, 'You're as pissed as a skunk, and I doubt you could get it up.' He'd sniggered, and in an instant had disarmed her, sending her knife spinning from her hand, and had her pinned to the wall, his own knife to her throat. 'Not so drunk, cunt.' Others had come to her rescue, pulling Vane away. 'Leave off, she's James Bonny's missus.' He had grunted, groped her between her thighs and shambled away, mumbling, 'Lucky James then.' Anne had bitten back a retort, thinking James might not agree as she was reluctant to risk becoming pregnant again.

Atop the fort Vane eventually tired of wasting ammunition. Sensing a ceasing of hostilities, the anchored vessel lowered a longboat and a group of men rowed towards shore. Anne wasn't sure if they were courageous or foolhardy. A uniformed man in the boat waved his hat, perhaps as a form of greeting, or to show he was not holding a weapon, while in his other hand he clutched a sheaf of papers high in the air.

Men and women in the crowd speculated. 'You think the King's dead?' 'Could be... Could be...' 'Nah, maybe we're at war again...'

Anne climbed onto the back of a wagon for a better view and spotted Captain Jennings on the beach, king of his territory, with hundreds of armed men beside him ready to receive their guest. Vane strode towards Jennings, curiosity having got the better of him.

A young uniformed man stepped ashore to find himself immediately surrounded. If he was daunted by his welcome, he hid it well.

'Captain John Bennett.' He spoke loudly and waved his hat at those still on top of the fort. 'Thank you, gentlemen, for holding fire. I am instructed by my father, Colonel John Bennett, Lieutenant Governor of Bermuda, to deliver a message from his gracious Majesty, King George.'

At the mention of the King, Anne thought the captain might be run through with a sword as men pressed forward booing and hissing. Jennings held up his hand, urging them back. 'You've chosen to land on a Republic of Pirates, Captain Bennett. We don't hold with anything the King says. In any case it's bound to be bad news.'

'Gentleman, I do indeed bring news – but excellent news. I am here to offer the King's most gracious pardon. His Majesty's offering an amnesty to those who turn their back on pirating!' Captain Bennett grinned at the surprised faces staring at him and held aloft a bundle of leaflets.

'It's a trap!' 'Damn the King!' 'How can we trust this man?' These and other concerns and insults filled the air.

'If this is a trap, I'll be the one to kill you.' Jennings asserted his authority, his pistol pointed at Bennett's head. 'If you offer a pardon to any of my men only to capture them and string them up, I swear I'll kill you.'

'Kill him now! Kill the bastard!' Vane's suggestion, it seemed to Anne, was shared by the majority, but Jennings lowered his pistol, shouted for quiet and thrust the men away. Boxes were found, and Jennings invited their guest to sit. Anne could not hear their conversation; only Vane's bellowing reached her as he waved his pistol in the air. 'I'll kill any of ya who give yourselves up for this bullshit pardon!'

'Gentleman!' Captain Bennett tried again. 'Accept this from me now or face the consequences when your new governor arrives. Governor Rogers is a man on a mission. A man of great resolve.'

A new governor? A fresh buzz went through the crowd at that news.

Nancy, awake and hungry, yowled in her ear. Anne could no longer hear anything so sought the shade of Charlotte's to see to her daughter's needs.

News reached her soon enough. A man rushed in yelling to anyone that would listen, 'Jennings is going to go with Bennett to Bermuda, along with a couple of others keen to surrender... plan to come back and tell the rest of us how they got on. Make sure there's no tricks or anything...'

Fools, Anne decided. Men who would plunder and kill one day were the next day prepared to turn themselves in. Why would they give in so easily? Anne doubted there were enough lawful jobs out there if they gave up their lives as sea rovers. She snatched a leaflet from another seaman who had come in for a drink, frowning as she continued to suckle Nancy and read the proclamation. Maybe James was right. Maybe change was in the air. It made her uneasy.

Anne headed back to the beach, cradling Nancy in her arms. Mr Walker had just arrived and clearly felt it safe enough to enter the fray. He pushed through the cluster of men to shake Bennett's hand.

'Welcome, sir. This is most welcome news, I assure you.'

Walker pumped Captain Bennett's hand as if to shake it lose from his sleeve as the men exchanged pleasantries. Anne was amazed at Mr Walker's resilience. The fact he had stayed on the island at all was astounding, and now he stood shoulder to shoulder with those who might take it upon themselves to try and kill him again.

Captain Bennett spoke loudly. 'You'll find me in my cabin, ready to record your names. This is your chance to become the honest men you once were.'

A flotilla of small boats accompanied Captain Bennett away from shore, some heading to his vessel, others to Jennings's and Hornigold's sloops, each full of men ready to surrender. Anne watched a Union Jack once again hoisted up the flagpole, the black flag banished from sight, then turned away from the beachfront and headed home to ponder this turn of events.

By the time James returned from sea four weeks later, the black flag flew high over Nassau again. Anne was scathing of the men who had flocked to Captain Bennett to cleanse their souls, as they might seek absolution from a priest, only to revert to their old ways. The beach continued to be littered with bottles, stinking hides, carcasses and campfires. Pirates remained in control of their Republic. Nothing had changed.

Anne gave a leaflet to James and helped him read.

'Pity I wasn't here.'

'What? You'd have signed yourself?'

'Would you have me face the gallows? Is this how you want to get rid of me?'

Anne wasn't quick enough with her denial and she was aware of his reproachful look. Of course she didn't want such a fate for him, but life at sea need not end at the gallows – not if you were smart enough... She looked away guiltily. James was exactly the kind of man, an ordinary man, who would be caught while Vane and other bolder men escaped justice.

Anne said candidly, 'I don't want you to come to any harm. How could you think so? Besides, if you died what would become of me?'

'And Nancy,' James added.

'Of course – Nancy too.'

Yes, there was always Nancy to think about. This small child who gave James such pleasure was, against her will, beginning to burrow into her own heart. Anne felt trapped.

17

One early evening in late July, Governor Woodes Rogers's fleet arrived in New Providence. The *Delicia*, a solid 460-ton merchant ship riding low in the water, was armed with great guns, but principally this capacious ship held hundreds of settlers. Good sturdy Protestant stock: Germans, Swiss, Dutch and some English. These farmers, skilled craftsmen, teachers and preachers, men and women alike, could, Woodes believed, be relied on to set the moral tone of the recharged colony. Deep in the *Delicia's* hold lay a cargo of cattle, hogs and other stock, along with farm implements and seeds and many other practical necessities.

Accompanying the *Delicia* were the *Shark*, *Buck*, HMS *Rose* and HMS *Milford*. These armed vessels held troops to uphold the law and deter those who sought to undermine it.

Locked safely in his sea chest, Woodes had his commission as Captain-General and Governor-in-Chief and Captain of the Independent Company of Foot: his official titles and roles. He had further copies of His Majesty's Act of Grace – the royal pardon – and had found room to store religious brochures from the Society for Promoting Christian Knowledge.

The *Delicia* lay beyond the western stretch of the harbour while Woodes sent the *Rose* and *Shark* ahead to prepare the way. He strode the deck restlessly, longing to be ashore, every so often raising his spyglass to look about him at his new territory. Through the harbour entrance he had a partial view. He could see dozens of vessels anchored, some clearly trading vessels and some armed, including the *Katherine*, a French sloop, flying its colours. It puzzled him why this might be here. Other vessels were beyond any useful purpose, being half submerged or burnt to the waterline.

He sought out Captain Gale, the *Delicia's* commander, began talking through preparations to land, when the boom of cannon blast took them by surprise. He instinctively looked towards the shore expecting it had come from the fort.

'A welcome. Excellent! Perhaps we can assume it is safe to proceed, Captain Gale.'

'Or perhaps not, sir. Look.'

The tell-tale sign of smoke rose from the *Katherine*.

'Ah, it's not as I thought... What of Whitney?'

Woodes felt suddenly anxious for the well-being of the captain of the *Rose* who he had sent ahead. Through his spyglass Woodes watched Whitney being rowed toward the *Katherine*, where men on deck were gesticulating. Shortly after, Whitney continued towards shore and Woodes relaxed a little. All must be well. He busied himself with final preparations to land while he waited for Whitney's return and explanation.

Some hours later, by the light of a waxing moon, Whitney's boat approached. Woodes, impatient to hear the captain's report, could barely wait for him to climb aboard before interrogating him.

'Well, Captain Whitney, you've survived your first foray into the hornet's nest. What news, man, and why was the *Rose* fired at?'

Whitney saluted him. 'Sir. Charles Vane sends his greeting. He says he intends to use his utmost endeavour to burn all our vessels tonight. We are forewarned.'

'Does he, indeed. So Vane's got his hands on the French vessel.'

Woodes had hoped for a more promising start, but immediately his mind switched tack. 'As to burning us – idle threats. We have him boxed in. He can't escape.' His eyes gleamed with the challenge. 'Is this the welcome I can expect from all of them, Captain Whitney?'

'It's not as bad as you may suppose, and in fact, I can report the majority are ready for change.'

Woodes allowed himself a small smile. 'Are the hornets – Vane excepted – losing their desire to sting, perhaps?'

'I've spoken to some leaders of the gangs, least those who would dare to be seen meeting with me. I would judge there is discontent among them. Some I spoke to seem to be honest enough men, given half a chance to be so, although—'

'Let's hope you're right,' Woodes couldn't help interjecting.

'There's nothing much for them to do here apart from pirating.'

'We mean to change that.'

'You'll find a welcome, sir, I've been guaranteed as much.'

Woodes smiled in relief. 'I'm sure Vane's threat is sheer bravado. Return to your ship, Captain Whitney. Let's gather ourselves and plan for an official arrival in the morning.'

Late in the evening, Woodes could hear distant "huzzahs" carried on the wind from the other vessels in his convoy. He and Captain Gale had already presided over the gathering of the *Delicia*'s company with prayers and a toast to King George. Their own "huzzahs" carried out to sea on a stiff offshore breeze, but he hoped some of their rejoicing and toasts reached the ears of Vane and his men.

Seafaring and trade was in Woodes's very marrow. Years earlier he had served his maritime and mercantile apprenticeship: accompanied his father on regular trips to Newfoundland, travelling home to Bristol with holds full of salted cod. Then he turned his attention to exploration and privateering, successfully leading a convoy of ships circumnavigating the world – one of the first to do so – discovering much that was new. He had spent years and years away at sea and now his mission was to expel those pirates who stubbornly refused to be dislodged.

For the past two years Woodes had researched all there was to find out about the Bahamas. He had sought out enterprising merchants and ship owners; listened to the views of the East India Company directors; sounded out financiers; read letters to and reports from the Trade and Plantations Committee.

Next he sought an audience with Josiah Burchett, Secretary to the Admiralty. Burchett had seen extensive service at sea and Woodes needed his support for any proposed mission. Burchett had also known and admired Admiral Whetstone, Woodes's deceased father-in-law; the connection paved the way for a meeting.

Once ushered into the Admiralty office he found Burchett studying a scale model of a frigate displayed on a cabinet, and the blueprints held down by paperweights at the side.

'What do you think of her?' Burchett beckoned him.

Woodes inspected the model and blueprints as they talked over this latest design. Both men knew a thing or two about how the slightest innovation could improve the speed or manoeuvrability of a vessel, and prove to be the difference between life and death, survival and sinking.

'The West Indies then.' Burchett indicated a plush chair the other side of his mahogany desk. 'You need to be aware we currently have four warships and two armed sloops out there – and we're talking two thousand miles of ocean east to west and a little less north to south. The area is vast. And the estimate of seven hundred islands doesn't do justice to the place. So, what are the odds, Captain Rogers, of our few ships achieving anything?'

Burchett's eyes drilled into his so Woodes answered cautiously. 'No doubt you have calculated what you need to patrol the region?'

Burchett laughed harshly. 'Give me a hundred ships and hundred times as many men and this might be effective, but it's pure fantasy. It's all well and good staking our claims and colouring maps, but holding on to territory...' Burchett paused and shrugged. 'However, let's not be downhearted before we start. Tell me, what are your ideas?'

Woodes rested his hands on his cane and leant forward in his chair. 'I want hundreds of settlers to do honest God-fearing work; I intend to take out hundreds of livestock, and critically – this is where I need your backing – I'll need armed warships and trained soldiers. Will you press my case with the King? He might listen to you...'

Burchett smiled. 'I'll see what I can do. We know how tight-fisted our monarch is when it comes to spending money on England.'

With his efforts to eradicate pirates in Madagascar, Woodes had hoped the Bible would be the way to turn men to the path of righteousness. He had taken hundreds of religious pamphlets, distributing them to errant pirates, but had achieved little. He concluded salvation must be by the law of the land – British law – guided by the good Lord above, but administered by men on earth.

Woodes was ready to be the man to take on the pirates.

In his cabin on the *Delicia*, Woodes wrote up his journal and fell into a deep sleep.

A massive explosion sent shockwaves through the water. He was on his feet, fumbling for his cane and out on the quarterdeck in an instant. A huge bonfire lit up the night sky. He allowed himself to relax: the pirates must be celebrating his arrival. He shook the sleep from his brain, looked again, and his ears and eyes woke to new sounds and sights as he recalled Vane's threat.

An exploding fireship lit up the sky as it drifted with the outgoing tide straight for the anchored *Rose* and the *Shark*. With the intense heat, the carriage guns had exploded, catapulting metal shards skyward.

On board the *Rose*, the vessel nearest him, Woodes could make out distant figures hacking away at the anchor cable, and first one jib then another was raised. Slowly, oh so slowly, the *Rose* turned, allowing a slight breeze to catch her sails and the crew manoeuvred the vessel out of the path of the inferno. It was like a nightmare where everything is in slow motion; Woodes could only grip the handrail and watch helplessly.

A second, even bigger explosion ripped through the fireship, sending shards of burning wood and sailcloth high into the air. The breached gunpowder store was adding to the spectacle, but it was one he could have done without. Woodes prayed the *Rose* could avoid the burning debris falling from the sky.

'Vane. Damn the audacity of the man!' Woodes spoke softly, not wanting to alarm those surrounding him, huddled in their sleeping clothes.

'Sweet Jesus, sir.' 'Are we to be roasted?' 'Up anchor, I beg you!' Anxious faces appealed to him.

His officers stood alert, eyes turning from him to Captain Gale and back again, waiting for an order. Gale and he were confident the *Delicia* was safe, but Woodes willed the sails of his endangered vessels to fill enough to escape the inferno. He turned to those assembled on deck and rubbed his hands, determined to underplay the moment.

'This is an unexpected welcome, to be sure. But we're safe – no need to move our anchorage – the bonfire sent to greet us will burn to the waterline shortly and won't trouble us. Enjoy the sight while it lasts, ladies and gentlemen, there won't be another like it in the future.'

The settlers he had tempted out to this new life did not look reassured. Perhaps another rousing talk would be needed before they went ashore, and perhaps he would send a bigger party ashore tomorrow: a heavily armed party. In fact, thinking on it, he might delay his official entrance a day or so to steady nerves.

Woodes watched grim-eyed until he was certain both the *Shark* and the *Rose* were out of harm's way and turned his thoughts to punishment.

Blast this audacious act! But the man couldn't escape as they had the harbour entrance covered. At dawn he would send a party out to capture Vane and others responsible for this little show. Bringing Vane in would be a spectacular way to commence his governance.

Two days later, preparing to go ashore, Woodes shaved carefully around his scarred jaw. Seeing his reflection during this daily grooming ritual would return him to the sea battle with the Spanish galleon, some years earlier, when a musket ball had ripped through his cheek, smashing part of his jaw along with some teeth. And soon after his left heel had been shattered by splintering wood when a cannon ball hit the deck, resulting in a limp and the use of a walking cane. He was sanguine about these injuries, received in service of his country. He brushed down his dress uniform, a little musty after being stored these past weeks, but the buttons were polished, and his shoes buffed. He, and his uniform, would have to pass muster.

Out on deck Woodes stood with a group of settlers clustered behind him as the *Delicia* was piloted through Nassau's wide western harbour mouth. Massive chunks of charred wood from the fireship bobbed in the sea around them, not yet dissipated on the tides. Ahead lay the narrow strait between the eastern end of Hog Island and New Providence mainland. He eyed the eastern passage and pressed his lips together. Charles Vane had eluded him. Vane had escaped on the *Katherine* after making his feelings so apparent. Whitney had started to give chase in a longboat, but Vane had raised his flag, fired at them and taunted them before disappearing the far side of Hog Island through the narrow shallow eastern opening. Woodes had been disappointed but pragmatic: at least the man was not ashore to stir up strife and hadn't killed any of his own men – that would have been a bad start. Securing the eastern entrance to the harbour to control that escape route jumped high up his list of priorities.

As the *Delicia* glided towards her anchoring position, Woodes turned his gaze larboard towards the flat barren sandy expanse of Hog Island covered in low-lying scrub and palm trees, then turned portside. Nassau, the place which was to be his new home, revealed itself fully.

'Is this the town, Governor Rogers?'

He turned to the middle-aged woman dressed in a simple brown cotton frock with a plain white cap covering her hair.

'Indeed, ma'am. I don't think there is more hiding from us.'

'It looks as if it would be best to pull it down and start again.'

'Oh come, come. But if this is the case, then we will do so.' Woodes gave a hearty laugh. He must keep everyone's spirits up, and imbue them all with a sense of purpose, but as he gazed out at Nassau he was inclined to agree with the woman.

Nassau, named in honour of King William of Orange-Nassau, had been an orderly planned town with properly constructed houses, a church and fort. Now the place was little better than a shanty town. And as to the fort... Woodes took out his spyglass for better inspection... he doubted many, if any, of the original twenty-eight cannons were in situ. He could see cracked walls. One well-aimed round shot from the *Delicia* might bring the structure tumbling down.

As he was rowed ashore, a series of shots boomed out from the *Rose* and *Milford*'s guns, but this pomp could not smother the reality of the place.

A decent-sized welcoming party waited on the beach, and he identified Thomas Walker with his wife next to him. He watched Mrs Walker tuck her hand into her husband's arm, saw him lean sideways to whisper to her and saw her easy laugh. He felt a pang of envy and would have loved to have his own wife at his side, but she had elected to stay in England, their marriage all but over. He looked away from this small intimacy and concentrated on the others. He could only guess which among the group were upright citizens and which were the pirate gang leaders Whitney had met with. None of them had signs hung around their necks saying "pirate", and all of them were conventionally dressed.

After being handed out of the beached longboat he would have given the world to be able to stride out without the aid of a walking cane, believing his limping gait might compromise the dignified and authoritative first impression he wished to convey.

'Sir. We heartily welcome you and look forward to becoming acquainted.' Thomas Walker stepped forward, gave a small bow and grasped Woodes's hand. 'My wife, Sarah.'

His own wife's name. Another Sarah then. Woodes smiled as Mrs Walker beamed at him and dropped a curtsey.

'Governor.' Whitney saluted him. 'These here are the men I told you about, ready to stand by you.'

Woodes nodded to the two men who presented themselves. If they owned silk scarves, embroidered waistcoats and other such exotic attire, they were keeping them out of sight and were dressed in orthodox fashion, looking like wealthy merchants.

'Benjamin Hornigold.' Woodes eyed the middle-aged man, introducing himself.

'John Cockram.' Woodes took in the younger former pirate leader dipping his head.

Soldiers held aloft the Union Jack while the steady beat of military drums announced his presence. Escorted by his officers, and a good show of armed troops, Woodes's procession made its way along a cleared pathway between rough shelters pitched on the beach with uncouth-looking seamen nonchalantly sitting in the shade or stretched on the sand reluctant to budge.

Piles of animal hides and bones lay abandoned on the beach along with broken bottles and pottery. He had noticed the vile odour from afar; at close quarters it was overpowering. As he swatted away flies he wondered what kind of society could be so indifferent to this. Woodes was sorely tempted to withdraw his ceremonial sword and skewer one of several rats he could see. It amused him to think on it.

When they reached the weed-strewn parade ground Woodes turned to Walker, Hornigold and Cockram. 'Well, gentlemen. I extend an invitation to join me above.' He indicated the roof of the fort. 'I take it the stairs haven't fallen away?'

The staircase proved to be intact, but once on the roof Woodes could only see one nine-pounder cannon in place amongst the broken parapets. He raised his eyebrows to indicate the empty spaces, and Hornigold read his thoughts.

'They've long gone – and Vane stripped out the last bit of iron when he saw you arriving.'

'Ah, possibly it was the one fired at Captain Whitney when he gave chase.'

'Possibly… In fact, probably. It was definitely in working order when it left here.' Hornigold grinned.

Woodes gave Hornigold a piercing look. 'I hope we shall be on friendly terms.'

Hornigold gave a slight smile. 'I share the same hope – wholeheartedly.'

'We all do.' Mr Walker nodded. 'New beginnings, eh, Governor Rogers, we will put the past behind us?' Walker's gaze took in Hornigold, his erstwhile tormentor.

Woodes looked about. 'I had best position myself by the one remaining cannon. I'll read the King's proclamation from that vantage point.'

While he waited for his officers to arrange themselves and the Union Jack behind him, Woodes scrutinised those below on the parade ground. He estimated upward of two hundred people were gathering with more arriving by the minute, curious to see and hear what the drums and flag portended.

He could tell which men, with red-baked leathery faces, were farmers and which were seamen as easily as he could distinguish a cow from a horse. Seamen were a breed apart, with strong upper bodies, arms hung well away from their sides, a rolling gait and distinctive clothing. Many of these seamen below wore an array of clothes likely pilfered from vessels and in all probability from dead men. The farmers wore rough cotton trousers and shirts and broad-brimmed woven hats. Some in the crowd appeared more prosperous, men and women alike; they must be merchants. He counted upward of twenty children and was pleased to see a younger generation taking root. His gaze took in the fifty or more barefoot negroes and Indians from these parts. Of the white women among the crowd, he picked out the weather-beaten faces of farmers and fisherwomen, while others, their cheeks rouged and wearing low-cut tightly laced bodices, had all the markings of harlots.

Captain Gale led a rousing, 'Three cheers for our new governor! Huzzah!'

As dozens of battered and torn hats rose in the air and answering, 'Huzzahs!' soared even higher, Woodes smiled in satisfaction. He had arrived.

18

NANCY WAS A CONTENTED AND HEALTHY CHILD, AND
as her character revealed itself Anne found words of
endearment tripping off her tongue – 'Petal' or 'Precious' –
and she would entertain Nancy with songs and rhymes. Anne
had grown to care deeply for her small daughter with her mop
of ginger hair, delighting in each new development: sitting,
crawling, pulling herself to stand. Then one day Nancy woke
with cheeks bright red and skin burning with fever.

Anne flew to seek help from neighbours, sat with her child
on her lap and bathed her face, willing her to get better. She
kept vigil, a candle burning through the night, attentive to the
little girl's every breath. Nancy would not drink, so Anne lay
propped in bed, offering her the comfort of her breast. She had
no milk left, but suckling comforted them both, and she could
feel Nancy's burning cheek against her cooler breast. Towards
dawn even the effort of sucking became too much, and Anne
felt her child's mouth drop away and heard her breath become
shallower and shallower until it stopped altogether.

In her garden Anne selected a spot to bury Nancy – a place she could see from a window. She attacked the hard soil with a pickaxe, then with a spade she dug and dug till her hands were blistered. She dressed her tiny limp daughter in her best dress, wrapped her in a sheet and buried her along with her favourite toy: a soft doll, its face embroidered with coloured wool, floppy limbs and body stuffed with thistledown. This had been James's offering to their daughter, and he had delighted in making it for her, stitch by stitch, carefully considering its features and colours. Nancy had been inseparable from the toy, crawling around the room, dragging it everywhere, never settling at night without it clutched to her chest.

Anne mourned her small child and took comfort in knowing Nancy remained close to the house and close to her. Here was proof, if it were needed, there was no joy in loving something only for it to be snatched away. With Nancy dead, Anne's heart ached more than she could bear, and she determined never to love anyone so much again.

Within days Anne became ill. She had experienced fevers before but nothing like this. Her body shook so hard her teeth rattled. The cotton sheet she lay on became soaked with sweat and her hair fell lankly either side of her cheeks. She could not keep down water, light ale or any brew offered to her. She would sip something only to bend over double and gasp as lightning-sharp cramps gripped her gut, followed by an urgent need to empty her bowels. Blinding headaches made it painful to raise herself.

Who would mourn for her if she died? James might, barely, but James wasn't here. He had accepted pardon from Governor Rogers and was on a merchant vessel somewhere out at sea.

Thank goodness for Charlotte. She insisted, 'You're comin' back to mine whether you like it or not, 'cos I can't keep trekking back 'n forth to keep an eye on you.'

Anne's neighbour hitched a cart to an old farm nag and trundled her along the bumpy track into Nassau, where Charlotte's girls carried her to a small room, little more than a cupboard, off Charlotte's noisy kitchen.

'Can't give up one of my top rooms for you, but I can keep an eye on you here seeing you haven't got Simple Simon at home to look after ya.'

'Who? What?' Anne was confused.

'That husband of yours.'

Anne let Charlotte settle her on a makeshift bed with clean, fresh-smelling sheets and it felt good.

'You remember Megan, the little Welsh girl?'

'Vaguely...'

'Sat with her till she died. Drifted off easily. And Katy, with the ginger hair – you'll recall her?'

'I don't think...'

'She suffered, sad to say. Pitiful.'

Charlotte plumped the pillow and cheerfully added, 'Don't fear, I won't leave you alone!'

But Charlotte wasn't required to dispose of her body. In time she drew back towards the world of the living, her body emaciated and eyes deep pools in her shrunken face. As she recuperated, Anne got to know Charlotte and learnt a little of her background.

'I'm from Barbados, and before that my people came from God only know where. All I know is I'm bits of this and bits of that... Some Arawak chucked in... Some distant grannie was a slave set free by a Portuguese master. That's as much as I know.' Charlotte leant in close confidentially. 'Tell you somethin' – there's been a whole lot of white men, Dutch or Portuguese or English, who have poked the black and brown women in my family.' Charlotte laughed. 'Tell you something else: none of them ever poked me for free! Now I have my own business, so when men poke my girls it's on my terms. Sometimes I turn away one of those sons of bitches and give him an earful, just to keep the spirits of my ancestral grannies happy.' She roared with laughter.

Anne appreciated the story and began to appreciate the teller of the tale.

Eventually she recovered enough to return home – to a small house holding nothing for her, and to a husband whom Charlotte had taken to calling Simple Simon, unfairly Anne thought, but then Charlotte rarely had kind words for any man.

Anne was resting when James returned. She heard his footsteps, the door opening and the soft thud of his canvas bag dropping to the floor. She opened her eyes to meet her husband's gaze.

'Where's Nancy?' James looked puzzled as he searched the empty room.

Why hadn't he asked about her first? Anne's heart contracted and for a moment she could not answer.

'Where's Nancy?' James spoke more urgently.

Little by little dry whispered words and half-sentences were pulled from her. She told him how fast it had happened, then he asked what she had done to save Nancy. That hurt. She had done everything she could. Everything. She told him about the doll and told him where he'd find her grave.

James went outside. She could hear weeping and knew he would be kneeling by the fresh mound of soil. The following day he made a small wooden memorial for Nancy carved with flowers and her name branded on it, then he planted it on her grave.

She and James said little to each other for some days but as she recovered she turned to James, all her bitterness and disappointments bubbling up. 'And what about me? I nearly died, and you weren't here.'

'I can't be two places – either here or at sea. I've got to earn a living.'

'A living? Is this what you call it? Better to have stayed with Vane, or any of the others.'

'We agreed. You agreed with me, I should accept the pardon and give up the roving life.'

'Yes, only because you weren't good at it. You'd come back home empty-handed or with just a few coins. And now, what you've brought home from Mr Harmon? Not a lot!' She wanted to wound him and could see this stung.

'Why the hell did you marry me in the first place, huh? Why did you bother? If it hadn't been for Nancy—'

'What? What? You'd have left me? I know you've never really loved me.'

'And have you ever loved me? I sometimes think I'd get more comfort from one of Charlotte's whores, only I don't want to get the clap.'

When they'd exhausted themselves expelling all the hurtful pent-up things they needed to say, they began to console each other with an occasional kind word, and sometime later a tentative touch. One night, in bed, James queried, 'You up for things yet?' and she could answer truthfully: 'Yes.'

Whatever passion they had ever had for each other had long ago been replaced by an easy familiarity, and this bond would have to do. As they lay side by side, James with one hand resting under his head, he said cheerfully, 'We'll have another baby. You'll see, it'll be all right.'

Oh, she hoped not! She prayed this act, this coupling, would not result in a baby. She was done with being a mother and done with being hurt. She meant to guard herself against this thing called love.

19

FULL STOMACHS AND PLENTY TO DRINK, PREFERABLY in the form of hard liquor, made for contented men, but Jack found himself with a crew of eighty with supplies dwindling. Much of the *Ranger*'s hold was taken up with stolen goods, but molasses and sugar weren't much use as daily rations, so Jack turned the *Ranger* towards his recent hideaway at Eleuthera to restock.

News had reached Jack that Rogers had tempted Hornigold to turn over a new leaf and hunt down Vane – and who knew if Rogers had tempted others to become pirate hunters? Jack didn't fancy a confrontation with old comrades. It was a gamble returning to the Bahamas, but George was the best navigator he knew, and could traverse these waterways in his sleep.

Once at Eleuthera Jack knew he was being petty, but he insisted on seeking out the thin, stringy Dutch farmer, the chicken man by both trade and appearance, who had berated him when he had holed up on the island recovering from whatever it was Betsy's girls had gifted him. The Dutchman had sold Jack eggs and chickens, but the transactions never passed without the Dutchman sermonising, calling him good-for-nothing, lazy, debauched. Now Jack meant to show that scrawny peasant a thing or two.

He led a bunch of his men to the shack and the Dutchman rushed out, alerted by the hullaballoo.

'Move a muscle and I'll shoot right through your Adam's apple!'

Jack chuckled at the sight of one of his crew holding a pistol to the chicken farmer's scrawny neck, his Adam's apple working up and down as if to avoid the ball. This was going to be fun. He yahooed and screeched with the rest of his men as they chased dozens of crazed, cackling hens and roosters around the yard, all of them adding to the din.

'Catch the buggers! Dinner tonight!'

'Vervloek je zeilen!'

'Dinner tonight... And tomorrow... and the next day!' Jack spurred on his men.

'Schuim der aarde!'

Tears of mirth trickled down Jack's cheeks as he stared at the spindly-legged Dutchman in his wooden clogs, flapping his arms and cursing rich Dutch curses, or so Jack assumed they were. What he didn't understand he couldn't take offence at.

With a pistol held to the chicken farmer's head they gathered eggs, chased and caught a few dozen hens before running off clutching the fowls by their legs, the dangling birds cackling and flapping. All the while Jack and his thieves cavorted, delighting in the chance to make mischief. It was childish, but they needed the food, and a good laugh every so often raised men's spirits.

He remembered far-off childhood days with his brother Hal, stealing fruit from apple trees grown wild in a church graveyard close to where they lived. They'd told tales of ghosts and goblins and pushed each other to greater misdeeds. He pictured himself dancing on a grave, Hal taunting, 'God will get you! God will get you for this!' As Jack tossed his clutch of squawking hens into a waiting crate, he reasoned God had plenty more evidence stored up against him when the time came, and not just stealing chickens from a dirt-poor farmer.

Eleuthera was duller than ever after Jack led his raiding party to strip small holdings of whatever livestock they could carry back to their anchorage in Rock Sound. Soon the *Ranger* was teeming with hogs and sheep tethered to the rails, with chickens running between legs or perched on the rigging, and decks awash with blood from slaughtered animals and dung and piss from those they were keeping alive.

Cruising among the Leeward Islands, holing up in quiet coves, Jack and his crew drank and gamed their days away, taking small prizes when they could. Many of the men had departed along the way, leaving Jack with a crew of thirty-two.

With supplies running low again, they cruised westward towards Jamaica. Landing here, or anywhere under British-ruled territory, was full of risks. The Bahamas wasn't the only territory with a new boss. In Jamaica Governor Lawes had settled in, and Jack wasn't sure he was as amenable as Governor Hamilton had been. He knew if he were to visit the Dropsy as he intended, he would have to put in at one of the isolated bays and steal into town.

On their approach to Jamaica they spotted and chased down a merchant sloop, the *Kingston*. He'd decided it was time to ditch the *Ranger* for a vessel less well known, and this one looked a good bet. After watching her for hours Jack judged his prey held no surprises, so he put all his crew on display, letting the *Kingston* see what force he had. It was easy. He took the *Kingston* just before she gained the safety of Port Royal harbour. As they offloaded guns and goods from the *Ranger* he knew he was gambling, but it seemed a safe-enough bet. They disabled the mainmast of the *Ranger* and swapped vessels.

Jack waved to the displaced captain who limped towards port on the *Ranger*. He slapped George on the back and laughed. 'We've taken the *Kingston* right under the noses of the good people of Kingston town!'

Before long Jack was laughing from the other side of his mouth as two well-armed privateers set sail from Port Royal at the mouth of the harbour.

'Damn it, George. Is this all the sail we can make?' Jack squinted up at the billowing sheets of canvas calculating the square yardage catching the wind.

'Nothin' more to add that'll help us, and the jib's rotted through.'

'She's like a waddling goose!'

'Think you can do better?' George was resentful. Jack waved him away impatiently. He knew George was doing his best, just as he knew the *Kingston* was weighed down by the cargo she carried and badly needed careening. Her hull, full of attached barnacles and weed, was causing significant drag and they'd found many of her sails to be mildewed. If they'd known all this before they seized her they might not have thought her such a tasty prize.

After jettisoning valuable cargo overboard the *Kingston* remained sluggish. They were in a tight spot, and Jack could only blame himself. Yes, he'd rid himself of the *Ranger* as was prudent, and captured this galley-built sloop, which promised to be an ideal vessel for them once they could sell the remainder of her cargo and give her a good clean. But first they needed to get away.

They were heading for the Isle of Pines, on the south-west coast of Cuba. With its abundance of hidden tree-lined coves they would find an ideal spot to careen the *Kingston* and replenish water. But there was the small matter of the two persistent vessels tailing them.

Under cover of night they changed course only to be disappointed when dawn broke to see two sets of distant sails. The hunter was now being hunted. With George and Dick, his two closest hands, Jack watched the relentless privateers with a sinking heart.

'Yep, Calico, bad luck they were fitted out ready to sail. Worst of luck, I reckon.' Even a pull at his tobacco pipe could not give Dick comfort.

'Bad luck?' Jack had been pondering. 'Or maybe Governor Lawes had the vessels ready and waiting. Ready to pounce.' He didn't like the idea there might be some strategy behind it, some element of planning. 'Every damned place they seem to be after us now.'

'So where to next, Calico? Where do'you reckon we should head?'

Dick looked genuinely concerned and George's reply gave him no comfort. 'To the devil. That's what's next – if we're caught.'

George stalked off to give instructions to the helmsman. The smallest adjustment of the tiller in response to the wind gusts would help them make the best pace.

Jack looked back at the privateers. Within a short time they would be in firing range, and he didn't fancy his chances. He looked ahead at the forested outline of the Isle of Pines, tantalisingly close. There's where they needed to be. This was the answer to Dick's, 'Where next?' He had no longer-term ambition at the moment.

The first gun fired was a warning. The iron ball fell with a resounding splash less than twenty yards from them, but the next one and the one after would reach them.

Jack made his decision, bellowing, 'Abandon ship! Now!'

There was no dignity to their exit. It was a chaotic scramble as the lowered periagua splashed into the water. They took what they could, small portable loot and coins, pushing, shoving and shouting as they shimmied down ladders and ropes and crowded into the wooden canoe.

'Pull! Pull away!'

A dozen hands gripped the oars and heaved, stroke by stroke through the choppy water heading to the land. A second cannon ball threatened to spill them out, and listening to the cracks of musket shots Jack prayed they didn't have good marksmen amongst the pursuing crew.

'Pull... Pull!' He urged them on.

Arms and backs strained against oars. They were finding their rhythm now, cutting through the water. When put to it, periaguas were swift vessels, especially when powered by men seeking to save their skins.

From the safety of the cove, Jack slumped panting over his oar and watched their chasers swarm onto the *Kingston*. This was not a good start to his leadership. Half of his crew had already taken to the forest. They were gone. Jack looked around at the dozen or so men still with him, philosophical about their fix. 'You know, some of the best prizes have been taken with canoes. We're strong, we can row and we can fit a mast. It's all we need. We'll wait for our next bit of luck – wait for a vessel dropping into the cove. Right, men – drag the canoe up and hide it in the trees.'

George and Dick would stay with him and there were one or two of the others he'd welcome, but he didn't care much about the rest. He felt weary of the life he was leading, and contemplated seeking clemency from one or other of the governors in these parts... Jack slapped his own face to rid himself of such a blasphemous thought.

'I just need food in my belly.' He spoke out loud and laughed to shake off his mood. 'So, who's up for hunting?' Jack looked around. 'I'm offering a piece of eight from my share to the first men who can bring home the bacon.'

Rewards always did the trick. He, George and Dick got on with starting a cooking fire on the beach as the others headed off into the trees.

They had no cask of booze to console themselves with, just water from a nearby stream, and worse, no shelter. This was another job to sort out before nightfall.

His gamble on the *Kingston* hadn't paid off, but the next would be sure to work in his favour. And the next, and the one after.

20

FOUR SWEATING SOLDIERS WEDGED A CHISELLED block into the crumbling defences as other soldiers, shirtsleeves rolled up, manoeuvred a cannon into place. Sprawled against a wall offering the best shade were five local men. This was the scene Woodes found when he emerged onto the fort roof to see how repairs were progressing.

The captain in charge straightened, wiped his forehead with the back of his hand and saluted. 'Sir!'

'Where're the others? Where are all your men?' Woodes's rebuke was clear but he owed it to the man to hear his explanation before he reprimanded him.

'This is it, sir.' The captain was unabashed. 'All I could muster today. Upward of eighty dead of fever these past months, and twenty deserters as of yesterday.'

'So many?' Woodes was taken aback. 'Will there be no end to these damn fevers? I'm doing everything I can to clean the air – though clearly not enough.'

He had underestimated how badly illness would affect all of them. It wasn't just his troops diminishing in number. He has suffered two bouts of fever himself since arriving, and more than a hundred of his new settlers had succumbed to the peculiar diseases of the place. Moreover, the cattle they had kept in good health throughout the sea voyage had not adapted to their new home and had similarly died of some ailment or other. He meant to write to the governor of Barbados to seek fresh supplies of hogs and cattle, and he would seek more settlers from London. Maybe fresh European blood might draw the infections permeating the land.

He turned back to his captain, hoping his twisted smile looked encouraging. 'Carry on, Captain – do your best. I mean no criticism.'

His officer glanced disparagingly at the local men lolling in the shade. 'The laziest good-for-nothings you're likely to come across. It takes too much effort on my part to try to organise 'em. You'd think they'd want to help, wouldn't you, sir? It's in everyone's interest.'

'Indeed, one would think so.' Woodes walked over to the work-shy men, two of who had shambled to their feet at his arrival, while the other three, elbows propping up dozy heads, continued to observe the work going on. 'On your feet!' Woodes barked. 'Shame on you. You're a disgrace! I'll return later, and I expect to see progress.'

He knew not to hold his breath. Over the past months he had come to understand something of the character of the community he ruled over. It had required heavy bribes to get them involved in building projects, and then only for short periods. People were content to be idle if they could manage it.

Hundreds of sea rovers had drifted to Nassau as news of the King's pardon spread, and Woodes had enticed some reformed pirates to settle down by offering free plots of land. He had imagined they would jump at this chance to make something of themselves, but most had done little more than some half-hearted hoeing, scratching the surface of the soil and scattering valuable seeds that would surely want for water. What's more, he had seen no evidence of proper houses being built, which was part of the free land deal.

Atop the fort, as Woodes contemplated the difficulties of settling the colony, he gazed at the small craft filling the harbour, the only vessels of note belonging to former pirates. He had sent the *Delicia* out on patrol for what little good it might do, the armed vessels escorting him from England long gone. His eyes were drawn to Hornigold's vessel, and as he gazed at it an idea began to take shape…

The next day he called a meeting on the beach, where there were noticeably fewer men camping out. Some had given up the roving life; others had seized boats and headed out to sea to follow their old ways. Woodes sat on a box under an improvised sun shelter, surrounded by former pirates.

'Gentlemen.' Woodes meant to be courteous with these uncouth men. 'You'll have heard of new threats from the Spanish?' Looking at their faces he could not be sure whether they might even welcome an attack just to be rid of him. 'But this isn't why I'm here.' He paused before continuing. 'I want Vane brought in.'

'Vane?' The name rumbled around him.

After the failed fireship attack Vane had tried to have Woodes assassinated – a botched plan he had heard about well in advance. He had his spies among them, reformed pirates happy to accept extra payment, and Vane had enemies in Nassau as well as supporters. The pirate society remained volatile, and it was touch and go which way men would turn.

Now he had their full attention Woodes continued. 'Vane's been sighted hiding out in Green Turtle Cay off Great Abaco.'

The men around him nodded. They all knew where Vane was, and now they knew he knew, just as they knew Green Turtle Cay was in Bahamian waters.

'I don't want him gathering forces. Bring him in. It would give me pleasure to make an example of him and his crew.'

The seamen glanced at each other. This was something new. Vane was nobody's favourite, but still…

'So, we're to turn hunter for you? Is that what you're after?' A man Woodes didn't know posed the question. 'What's in it for us?' Cockram stood before him, arms crossed.

'You'll be paid for your services and we'll all be free of that hot-head. Surely there's an attraction there?'

Rumbling whispers spread as the men mulled over his proposal. Woodes waited, not at all sure of the wisdom of what he was doing.

'I'll do it.' All eyes turned to Hornigold. 'I'll take my vessel. If you provide supplies I'll lead a party and bring Vane in for you.'

Hornigold? Woodes considered the man who had pushed forward. This former pirate had been responsible for establishing the nest of vipers Woodes was determined to destroy. A man who had threatened to kill Mr Walker, forcing him to flee, was now offering to round up Vane.

Hornigold looked around the gathered men and made light of his offer. 'Must be getting old, lads. Let's do what Governor Rogers wants.'

Woodes locked eyes with Hornigold, weighing him up. Each understood a good leader must time his actions wisely, and Woodes knew Hornigold to be wily.

Woodes nodded. 'Very well.' He extended his hand.

So it would be Hornigold he trusted to go after Vane. Poacher turning gamekeeper. Terms were arranged, and extra promises extracted from Woodes not to press any of them too hard about ownership of goods from before they took the King's pardon. Woodes reiterated his promise: what they had acquired before he arrived was no business of his.

He understood Hornigold's motivation for this venture. Hornigold did not want his former position as pirate kingpin usurped by any man, and certainly not by Vane, in the event that Woodes's tenure as governor came to an unexpected, or sticky, end.

Two weeks had passed since Hornigold's crew had set out in pursuit of Vane, and each day Woodes received yet another account of a merchant who had been harassed at sea or had his vessel stolen from the harbour itself by men keen to seek out Vane – not to capture him but to join him. Woodes feared they might be gathering to strike, with Vane – or perhaps even Hornigold himself – wanting to set himself up as top dog. Doubts plagued him.

Well into the third week, Hornigold's sloop sailed into the harbour along with one of Vane's vessels. Woodes, too impatient to wait for Hornigold to come ashore, rowed out, armed militia accompanying him. He hurried aboard and reached for Hornigold's hand, words tumbling out. 'Well done! So tell me – Vane and how many others…?'

Hornigold sucked his teeth. 'Nine locked up below, but Vane got wind of things. Gave us the slip – sorry, Go'vnor. We've not got Vane's head on a spike for you, but brought you the body, so to speak: nine of his men!' Hornigold chuckled.

Blackbeard had recently been killed and beheaded, but Woodes was not in the mood to jest about Vane. 'Blast the man!' He bit back the words he longed to say, and instead nodded to his militia. 'Escort the prisoners to the *Delicia* and put them in irons.' He turned back to Hornigold, his face set. 'So, tell me. What happened?'

It hadn't been easy finding a dozen upright men to serve on his council, but Woodes was satisfied that the group gathered around his dining room table later that day had the colony's best interests at heart. All of them, including Captain Gale, Thomas Walker and a local man William Fairfax, were keen to weigh in with ideas about what to do next.

'We can't risk waiting to ship them back to England. We must deal with them, the sooner the better. We have the right.' Walker looked at him confidently. 'It will send a clear message that you mean business. This is what you've come to do, after all. You've captured them, now I advise you see it through.'

Woodes frowned. 'I don't have the authority for an Admiralty Court, yet we can't leave the men on the *Delicia*. There are many on the beach who would see it a great victory if they could free them.'

Fairfax spoke. 'Sir, you must act. As Chief Justice I believe I can lawfully act as Judge of the Admiralty. It would be a nonsense we hobble ourselves by picking over the finest clauses of your commission. You were sent on a mission to eradicate these vermin. Let's not stumble at this first hurdle.'

'Hear, hear.' Men thumped the table.

'A trial then.' Woodes nodded. 'A trial here on our own territory.'

'Sir.' Captain Gale sought his attention. 'I suggest you release troops from duty elsewhere to increase guard on the *Delicia*. Let's not tempt fate. I'd hate to see the prisoners sprung.'

Fairfax spoke again. 'I'll prepare myself for the trial, and we'll be needing gallows erected – in the event we find them guilt—'

'I'll oversee that.' Walker jumped in quickly. 'It'll be my pleasure.'

21

NEARLY SIX MONTHS AFTER ARRIVING, WOODES, WITH members of his council and three dozen armed guards, stood at the refurbished ramparts on a fresh morning in early December.

From the rooftop, Woodes looked down at the line of gallows at the base of the fort. He had heard one of the beachside taverns was holding a party in defiance, and thought it would be humiliating if more people attended that than his own show, but in the event a good-sized crowd were gathering below: townspeople come to enjoy the spectacle, and, no doubt, seafaring companions of the men about to swing.

Woodes looked dispassionately at the condemned men led out onto the fort roof. They had all been found guilty, naturally. George, a lad from Dorset who had allowed himself to get caught up in Vane's gang, was shaking uncontrollably. Let him sweat a bit more, Woodes decided.

One by one, the condemned men were helped down the ladders from the ramparts and steered up onto a stage where nine gallows waited.

A young Irishman made a show for the crowd. 'This is to make a liar of my friends who said I'd die with my shoes on. Better luck next time, lads!' He heeled his shoes off, kicked them and they flew towards the crowd. Another condemned man, also Irish and reeling with the drink and his fear, yelled to comrades in the crowd, 'Are you going to stand for this? Rush them! Rush the bastards!'

His soldiers adjusted their muskets on their shoulders and Woodes became conscious of stirring in the crowd below.

The priest stepped towards one drunken condemned fellow who greeted the man of God with a forceful, 'Fuck off. I'll have no more of your singin' 'n prayin'!' The pirate turned desperately to the crowd, shouting, 'C'mon, lads! Me today, but you next time. Cowards, the lot of ye!'

Below, Woodes could see spectators bunching more tightly together, with men at the back pushing and leaning into those in front of them.

'Yes, yes... Do it... Rush them... Rush the bastards!' the condemned man shrieked, hopping from foot to foot in desperation. 'Do it... Fuckin' do it!'

Woodes signalled to his soldiers.

A press of bodies propelled Anne forward, as men and women around her responded to the man's pleas from the gallows, 'Rush them... Rush the bastards!' She stuck out her elbows, yelling, 'Back off!' as shots fired over her head and soldiers on the ground thumped heads and shoulders with the butts of muskets and hilts of swords. This futile attempt to disrupt proceedings was soon quashed, and she pushed her way back to James's side and looked up at the men, nooses around their necks.

She had reluctantly agreed to witness the hangings because James wanted to support Governor Rogers making a show of things, and he had sailed with one of the condemned men, John Auger. Vane, a man she would gladly see swing, had been too clever and she grudgingly admired him for that. Instead Hornigold had delivered a snivelling bunch of underlings.

'Poor John, poor soul.' James shook his head.

Anne took in the miserable man, hands bound behind him. John Auger was older than the others, perhaps as old as her own father. His clothes were filthy, he had not shaved for weeks and his hair hung in strands about his face. It was hard to credit this was the same man she'd seen on the beach boasting and bragging, rounding up men to join him.

'At least he lived the life he wanted and did all right from it while it lasted.' She totally understood how someone could live for the moment, but she didn't admire those not smart enough to succeed.

'But poor bastard.' James shook his head. 'I'm not regretting giving it up, not by a long shot.'

James shouted heartfelt farewells while she silently watched the spectacle unfold: the speeches, the prayers... Enough. She turned abruptly. 'I'm going.'

'Oh no!' James grabbed her arm. 'You stay here and at least offer your prayers and some words of comfort. What would happen if it were me up there?'

And this was the thing: James wanted her there to remind her this could be him swinging if he were tempted to turn pirate again. Would she have the strength to be there for him? To shout to him; to make sure the last thing he saw would be her loving face? Could she imagine providing comfort? Perhaps this was meant as a lesson to her.

James's grip on her arm tightened.

Woodes wanted the drama to move along, but it was not in his hands. He listened as other men spoke their final words.

One fellow, John Auger, said, 'We've a good governor, but a harsh one.'

Woodes silently thanked Auger. These were good words to record for posterity.

Now Woodes meant to make his contribution, his voice carrying clearly in the still morning air. 'Release George Rounsivell.' An astonished cry rose up from the crowd, his troops looked surprised, and George, noose around his neck, had to be held up as his legs buckled under him. 'Free him. I believe him to be a son of loyal parents from Weymouth. Remove his noose!'

Like Pontius Pilate he saved one of the condemned men, but he hoped history wouldn't judge him as harshly as the Bible judged the Roman. As young George blubbed, 'Oh God... thank you, thank you...' Woodes cleared his throat and continued.

'Some weeks ago thirty men were strung up at the battery in Charles Town. Thirty pirates led by a man most of you will have met before: Stede Bonnet. Now, here, under my jurisdiction, nine men have been tried and found guilty of piracy on the high seas... Thirty-nine men hunted down, tried and condemned...'

He paused to let the numbers sink in and recalled the occasion he'd watched *The Tempest* at Drury Lane with his wife at his side. Both he and Prospero presided over tropical islands inhabited by monsters. Prospero had granted freedom to Ariel, just as he was granting freedom to George.

Woodes continued, 'You have a choice – all of you. You can work with me to rid the seas of these rogues, but if you choose not to, the consequences are clear.'

He turned to the condemned men. 'May God have mercy on your souls,' he intoned, and raised his hand.

Soldiers took the reins of four horses, their harnesses attached to ropes looped around sturdy barrels supporting

the gallows platform. At their shouted, 'One... Two... Heave!'
men pulled reins and whipped the horses' rumps. The horses
took the strain, heads craning forward, hooves digging into
the ground; barrels scraped and shifted; the platform tilted.

'I wish I'd been a greater plague to these islands! God da—'
The words were squeezed from the man's throat as he dangled.

Woodes watched in silence as feet thrashed, urine trickled
down legs, faces turned purple, eyes bulged and blood-
thickened tongues protruded. He silently prayed for their
souls.

The priest continued reading from the Bible, addressing
the spectators, the dying men now beyond his reach. 'The
mind of sinful man is death, but the mind controlled by the
Spirit is life and peace; the sinful mind is hostile to God. You,
however, are controlled not by the sinful nature but by the
Spirit...'

The Book of Romans, Woodes seemed to recall.

Fairfax's hand grasped his shoulder, and he was grateful
for his terse, 'That's it then – job done.' He caught Walker's
sympathetic smile.

New Providence Island was not a magical isle, nor did
Woodes have the magical powers Prospero commanded in
Shakespeare's play, but he commanded respect. Order was
being created where there had been none. Perhaps there was a
little magic in that.

'I've seen enough. You'll find me at Charlotte's.' Anne
tugged her arm away from James's grip and turned her back
on the men's dangling bodies.

Charlotte had told her, 'Mine's the other party in town. I'll
be toasting the dead and celebrating the living. I'm not one
to witness the death of my former customers – wouldn't be
fitting.'

Anne swished a broken palm frond back and forth as she made her way along the waterfront, a deep frown on her face, mulling over what Governor Rogers had been blathering on about. The mass hangings in Charles Town would have been a huge occasion and she briefly wondered if her father and Billy, or Richard and others of her acquaintance had attended.

Since Captain Bennett's visit the previous year, there had been one further attempt to deliver the King's pardon, but that too had failed to make any impression. Now, with Governor Rogers in charge, things were much changed. James was in awe of him. It was Governor Rogers this or Governor Rogers that. She was sick of hearing his name and did not share James's enthusiasm. She had grown used to the chaotic life here.

Slurred voices emerged from Charlotte's. Anne tossed away the palm frond and walked in. The atmosphere was festive: people determined to enjoy themselves, enjoy the luxury of breathing, drinking, singing. She needed to be here among them, celebrating life, the moment.

'Here's to poor old Bonnet. Wonder if he wore his dressing gown for the hanging? Never saw him wear anything else. Bless his daft soul.' 'Bonnet!' 'Here's to Bonnet!' Tankards raised again and again.

In one corner, a small group of John Auger's old comrades could barely lift their tankards to their lips and their words were slurred as they toasted him. 'To John, the damned fool for getting caught.' 'Blast Rogers!' 'Aye to that!'

At the far side, the centre of attention, she could see a man leaning back in his chair, his red-trousered legs thrust out on a table. Anne stared. This had to be Jack Rackham – Calico Jack; couldn't be anyone else. She took in his black wavy hair and rugged face with a large nose that looked as if it had been broken at some point in his career. She couldn't recall seeing him before, but perhaps in the past he had just been one of the many men hanging out at the beach waiting for the next thing to happen. Now here he was, holding court. She pushed her way through the noisy crowded room towards his group.

'...So there we were, sailing off Cuba, minding our own business, when this Spanish guard ship, massive guns, sailed into sight escorting an English vessel it'd got hold of.'

Jack paused to check his audience was with him. 'Bugger me if it didn't decide to chase us. We were mightily outgunned, but we knew the coast like the back of our hands – and no better navigator than George here.'

Anne noted a sinewy, slight man, drinking near him. The man called George growled and shrugged at the compliment as Jack continued: 'So we were behind a little island – water too shallow for the Spaniards to follow y'see. They expected to nab us in the morning...'

'And?' An ardent listener pressed forward.

'Ah, gotta take risks!' Jack took his feet off the table, spotted Anne and stared frankly. He probably thought she was one of Charlotte's girls. She snorted. She'd enjoy putting him right if he came sniffing around.

Jack swept the table clear of remnants of a meal then plonked down a bottle and a partly eaten hunk of bread. 'Right. This is us.' He gestured to the bottle. 'And that's the island.' He touched the bread. 'We had a shallow draft vessel, y'see – a blessing considering...'

Anne shoved two men aside who were talking loudly together and blocking her view. She wanted to hear more from Calico Jack. The story itself was dull but the storyteller intrigued her. There was something about the man, with his swagger and confidence.

'...So here's what we did...' Jack threw his head back and laughed.

Anne had almost reached the group when someone else thwarted her, tugging at her sleeve. She jabbed her elbow, turning with a scowl... James!

'Bloody Rackham. Listen to him, so full of himself.' James tugged her again. 'C'mon.'

'No, I want to stay. Let's have a drink. No harm, is there?'

'After what we've seen? I've no appetite to party. I knew those men.'

How could she say she wanted to stay at Charlotte's? More to the point, how could she say she wanted to stay to listen to Calico Jack?

She reluctantly allowed James to lead her through the press of drinkers towards the door. Glancing back, she caught Calico Jack's eye. He winked and grinned and raised the bottle in his hand by way of salutation. Cocky bastard! Still, it excited her. She turned away to hide her confusion. She'd experienced plenty of leering and groping men who had propositioned her these past years, and this man, a little drunk and full of himself, was probably no different from all the others. And yet her heart was beating faster.

His wink and cheerful grin were like a spark to tinder. Something that had been dry for a long, long time waiting to be kindled had been touched. It shocked her, and she didn't know how to account for it. Witnessing men having their necks stretched and their breath squeezed out of them, followed by this life-affirming flirtation, had triggered something.

22

MR HARMON, A MIDDLE-AGED, RUDDY-FACED MERCHANT, held Anne's hand in a firm grip between his sunburnt freckled hands.

'Ah, James, so this is your wife.'

He shook her hand vigorously and gallantly raised her equally sunburnt hand to his lips.

'James has talked a lot about you – very pleased to meet you, Mrs Bonny.'

Anne had rowed out to the anchored *William* with James to see him off on another voyage crewing for Mr Harmon.

'And pleased to meet you, sir.' Anne smiled brightly, squeezing Mr Harmon's hand. 'James speaks very highly of you.'

Mr Harmon guffawed. 'And I think well of your husband! I don't invite any Tom, Dick or Harry to join me on the *William!*' Mr Harmon gazed lovingly around his vessel: a sleek sloop in top-notch condition. 'Had her specially made, you know. Guaranteed best Bermuda cedar. Nothing so durable. I could race anything given the chance, and, more to the point, there're no vessels out there that'll catch me.'

Mr Harmon laughed and turned to James and four other men waiting for his orders. 'Best not delay. Idle hands won't earn our keep, heh?' He doffed his hat to Anne as she climbed into the dinghy, waved farewell to James and rowed back to shore.

She was happy to meet Mr Harmon and it did no harm to flatter him, as he was the man who as often as not provided bread for their table. James had regular work with him, but even so, making an honest living was far from easy. Many men who had accepted the King's pardon were turning back to their old ways, but James was determined he would not be one of them. Earlier, as she and James had walked from their house to the beach, James with his canvas sack slung over his shoulder, they had talked about the future.

'If all goes well, Anne, Mr Harmon promises to increase my duties and my wages, so my prospects are getting better all the time.'

James had looked cheerful and she offered him an encouraging, 'Good! That's good!'

'And Governor Rogers is offering payment to those who give him information – let him know which of the men are turning pirate again – any talk that might be useful to him really. "Intelligence", he calls it.'

'Spy for him?' She had stopped in her tracks.

'Well, not exactly – but I suppose you could say that. But we want him to succeed, don't we?'

Again, she had nodded and mumbled, 'Of course.' She did want to prosper and for James to do well, so she couldn't identify the cause of her unease.

Returning to shore from the *William*, Anne tucked up her dress, jumped out of the dinghy and beached it. Rubbing sand from her feet, she slipped her shoes back on, fingered her drab faded cotton dress and headed towards Charlotte's to see if she needed help. On an impulse before entering, she picked a vibrant red hibiscus flower and tucked it behind her ear. It perked her up and she reasoned a little bit of colour would make the customers more cheerful and inclined to spend money – if they needed any such encouragement.

When James was away at sea Anne often dropped by at Charlotte's for the company, and at other times when a shipload of men arrived, Charlotte would send for her and she would hurry to help serve drinks to the sudden influx of customers.

Today Charlotte's seemed busier than usual, and she noticed Jack Rackham sitting on a bench set against the wall, cuddling up with Dolly. Anne grunted, deciding it was a good job he'd chosen to sit by the wall, as it looked like he needed its support to stay upright. She had spotted him once or twice in the days following the hangings, though never spoken with him, and assumed he'd been back at sea this past month.

James was doing his best to raise them both in society, and her spending time at Charlotte's in the company of pirates wouldn't help the cause. But what he didn't know wouldn't hurt him.

Anne greeted Charlotte. 'Need help?'

Charlotte handed her a large jug of ale and nodded towards a table where a dozen or more seamen gathered, many of them with girls on their laps.

'Whenever is there a day I don't need your help or welcome your company? You can start by taking this over – they've paid.' Charlotte nodded in the other direction. 'Calico Jack arrived back yesterday, and he hasn't budged since. His boys tell me he's come back with his pockets full, and I'm happy to help him empty them.'

Anne delivered the jug to the ever-thirsty seamen. She recognised two of Jack's crew; George was one of them, but she didn't know the name of the other, a bulky man with a large domed head. She paused to chat with Charlotte's regulars. Flirting a little did no harm and encouraged customers to buy another drink. Anne had no problem with this.

While she exchanged banter, she glanced over at Jack Rackham and wondered how he was doing so well for himself. Was he trading honestly? Trading in black market goods? Still pirating? Though surely he couldn't manage to do so under Rogers's nose. Whatever the case, men like him might help James's career.

She decided not to waste the opportunity, so made her way over to where Jack sat and tapped him on the shoulder. 'Charlotte tells me you're doing well for yourself.'

'Does she now?' He squinted at her through bleary eyes. 'Just back from Cuba – catching up with someone I haven't seen in a while.'

She shrugged, incurious about where he'd been or who he'd seen. 'I've a favour to ask.' She saw him trying to focus as he raised an eyebrow at her, so she continued. 'I'd like you to help my husband.'

'Your husband? Who the hell's he?' He looked confused.

'I want to know if you have any – you know – plans.'

He stared at her candidly and Dolly answered instead. 'You're too late. Calico's an honest man now, aren't you?' She looked from him back to Anne and said coyly. 'He must've put enough money aside, I reckon.' She fingered the new silk ribbon around her neck and smiled.

'Yup. Accepted King's pardon. Didn't fancy being strung up. A man's got to know when to move on.' Jack raised his tankard. 'Gov'nor Rogers!' He stretched out a leg and hooked his foot around a stool, pulling it closer. 'C'mon. Join us. Come, sit.' He patted the stool.

She hesitated. Dolly didn't look very welcoming, but Anne didn't care; she had come on business. When she sat Jack leaned towards her.

'Yup, an honest man now, but I'll bear your request in mind.' He reached out and touched the flower in her hair. 'In truth, I'm more inclined to invite you than your husband. A pity, no women allowed at sea.'

Anne brushed his hand away.

'But tell you what, we're at anchor. I can invite you to my cabin – I'll row you out myself!' Jack roared with laughter.

She glared at him. Idiot! He and she both. This had been a foolish idea.

'I'm not one of Charlotte's whores like Dolly here, and you know something else? I shoot pretty well!'

Dolly looked offended. 'You needn't be so haughty – unless you think you're not pretty enough for this work.'

Jack grinned and, reaching out, traced a finger down her neck to the crease of her bosom. 'Oh, she's pretty enough, I'd say.'

Anne stood up hurriedly, her face burning. They were all the same, these men.

For an hour or so she continued to serve drinks, chatting to seamen, asking them what they'd been up to. They were cautious, none of them too keen to say where they'd obtained the coins they passed to her for the next jug of ale or plate of food. All the while she was aware of Jack's eyes on her, but she didn't go near him again. Someone else could fill his tankard – she wouldn't. Hah! She had tried to help James, but he would have to find his own contacts, make his own way. Perhaps Mr Harmon was their best bet after all.

Two days later Anne was at the market. She had sold the baskets of lemons and oranges harvested from her own trees and was picking over supplies to supplement her meagre crops. This new market, set back from the beach, was a more orderly affair than the earlier ramshackle one, and there were no arms dealers to be seen: Governor Rogers had banned them from operating.

As Anne decided what to buy, the sound of trotting horses slowing to a walk drew her attention. This was another change. There were more merchants and farmers who could afford to keep horses, but even so, hearing several together was unusual. While seamen might salivate over a sleek-looking seaworthy vessel, she appraised horses with a practised eye.

Jack Rackham rode at the front of several riders, all of them rowdy and armed. She rather hoped his mount would buck him off right then and there and he would land on his arse in the dust. Serve him right for his insolence. Jack remained on his mount while other men bought liquor and secured flagons to their saddles, then something caught his eye and he dismounted, strolled towards a stall and bought himself a straw hat. He planted it on his head and twirled around to the whistles and laughter of his companions. 'Suits you, Calico!'

As he remounted he spotted her watching him, signalled to his men to wait and walked his horse over, squinting down at her. 'You said you can shoot.'

'Thought you'd have been too drunk to recall.'

'Nope, I remember. Years of practice keeping liquor in my belly and my brain sharp.' He paused, weighing up his words. 'D'you like hunting?'

'Now? With you? Is that where you're going?' She glanced at his companions. 'You sure a woman is allowed?'

Jack grinned. 'Don't think there are any rules. If there are we can always make exceptions.' He paused. 'What's your name?'

'Anne, Anne Bonny.'

'Well then, Mrs Bonny. Are you coming, or are you just full of talk?'

If he had said anything else, she would have turned him down; it was a ridiculous idea, but the challenge connected with her. She hesitated. This wasn't right.

'Calico! Coming?' one of the riders shouted impatiently.

'Well?' Jack kept his eyes on hers and extended his hand, meaning to pull her up behind him. When she didn't move Jack shrugged and began to turn his horse.

'I'll come!' The words leapt from her mouth. 'But I'll not sit behind you. I want my own mount.'

Jack looked put out. 'We've hired the damn things!'

He could see the stubborn look on her face, so he scoured his group of men. 'Charlie! Hop off, will you? Give the lady your horse.'

'What! You plannin' on leaving me behind!' The man called Charlie was indignant.

'Go on, man. Give it up. I paid for the damn thing, didn't I?'

Charlie grumbled but slid out of the saddle. The other men sat silently, their indignation apparent. She heard one of them mumble, 'That's our day fucked.'

Anne could sense many eyes on her: stallholders, shoppers and passers-by. Going hunting with a bunch of former pirates was not the way to enhance her position in Nassau society. She should turn away. There was still time to laugh this off as a jest. Instead she took the bridle from Charlie and stroked the old horse's head. This nag was nothing like Shotek, but she hadn't ridden since those far-off days at home. She turned to the disgruntled man. 'Appreciate this, Charlie. Here, have a drink on me.' She pressed a coin into his hand.

Putting her foot in the stirrup, she mounted and hitched up her dress. 'Lead the way then.'

Soon they were cantering far away from Nassau, past her house, beyond all the houses, into the forested interior. Her hair trailed out behind her and a radiant smile lit up her face as it hadn't in years.

23

IT WAS A GLORIOUS JANUARY DAY, WARM BUT NOT
scorching. Jack lay on his back in the shade of a tree, his new
straw hat over his eyes, birdsong, cicadas and the chatter of
his companions washing over him. He raised his head, peered
under the brim of his hat at three men stripped of their
shirts and shoes, fooling about in the shallows of the lake.
At the sound of shots Jack raised himself onto his elbow and
watched two men practise shooting an improvised target set
against a tree, drunkenly wagering with each other. They were
on the shore of a large inland lake bounded by forest. Empty
flagons and bottles lay strewn around their picnic site with the
remains of a hog roasting on a spit.

Jack stretched and sat up. Mrs Bonny was standing by the
fire where one of his men, turning the roasting hog, held out
a piece of cooked meat to her on the tip of his knife. Juice
dribbled down her chin when she took a bite, then she took a
long slug from a flagon of ale before making her way to where
Dick sat tamping tobacco into his pipe. Dick would soon be

extolling the virtues of "his best Virginian" he kept for special occasions. Before Jack could rescue her she had picked up George's cutlass, weighing it and practising some slashing movements, all the while holding her slab of greasy meat in her other hand.

'I'll have that back if you don't mind!' George jumped to his feet, snatched his cutlass off her and wiped the greasy hilt on his trousers.

'Mrs Bonny?' Jack held out his pistol and indicated the tree with a target. 'You told me you liked shooting... Not the same thing as being a good shot.' He raised an eyebrow. 'Well?'

She squinted. 'You doubt me?'

He shrugged. 'Haven't given it a thought.' This wasn't quite true; he was curious about her, but he didn't mean to let her know.

'Let's have a wager then. Go on?' She stared at him.

George was on his feet now. 'Well, Calico, what you got to wager?'

'How about your pistol?' Anne wiped her hands on the grass, took his pistol from him, weighing it up.

'My pistol? Hell no, I'll not wager that. But you can have my hat.'

Mrs Bonny laughed. 'All right. I could do with a new hat.'

Men wagered a shilling and she goaded them. 'Oh, come on. I'm just a woman, after all. What've you got to lose?'

Mrs Bonny led the way, and they all filed behind, laughing and wagering their coins while she kept on pushing them to increase their bets. She took her stance a fair distance from the tree, prepared the pistol, raised her arm, fired and hit the target.

'Not bad. Not bad at all!' Jack was genuinely impressed. This woman could shoot.

She sauntered towards him, a broad grin on her face, snatching his hat off his head. 'Mine, I think.' She planted it on her head, spinning around in a little victory dance, the men cheering her on. 'And now I'll have your money.'

With the hat turned upside down she gathered coins from those foolish enough to have bet. Hah! Jack laughed. Mrs Bonny had added to their party and she could come again as far as he was concerned.

Soon they saddled their horses and set off at a walking pace through inland tracks back to Nassau. Jack hadn't felt so contented in a long time. Days such as this were what made life worth living. He glanced back to see Mrs Bonny riding side by side with one of his men, her skirt tucked up around her thighs with his – now her – straw hat jammed on her head secured under her chin with a ribbon of woven grass. He chuckled.

Minutes later Mrs Bonny rode up beside him, a broad grin on her face. 'I've enjoyed today, it's been fun. Wanted to tell you that.'

He smiled his agreement and they rode on in silence, their horses plodding methodically homeward. He glanced at her and noticed a frown furrowing her forehead. 'Something on your mind, Mrs Bonny?'

She hesitated then pointed to his cutlass. 'Your men say you're good with that.'

'The best!' He liked to brag – where was the harm?

'How about you teach me?'

He met her level gaze. 'This husband of yours, Mrs Bonny. What would he—?'

'I've done nothing wrong. No one can say I've done anything wrong.'

Her reply was sharp, perhaps convincing herself as well as him.

They rode on in silence, his mind in a turmoil. Nassau was a small town, and there were no more than five hundred people on the entire island. Word was bound to get out about this excursion, and it would be playing with fire to meet up with this woman again – this married woman. And yet. He stole a glance at her. She was vivacious, her eyes candid, and despite himself he was attracted to her.

Jack turned in his saddle to face her. 'All right. Tomorrow. An hour before sunset.'

A radiant smile lit up her face. He felt his offer was worth it just to witness that.

'The eastern beach, it's bound to be quiet there. How about it, Mrs Bonny?'

'Yes!' She whooped, dug her heels into the flank of her mount, bounded into a canter and into a gallop.

First he thought of her horse, hoping the nag wouldn't collapse under the unexpected exertion demanded of it and he'd have to pay the farmer for the loss of his beast; then his thoughts turned to the rider as he watched her retreating back.

Jack signalled to his men and they all kicked their mounts into trots or canters, whatever both riders and horses could manage. He doubted any of them could catch Mrs Bonny; surely she'd wait for them further up the track. He made a mental note never to wager money on her horsemanship.

Next day Jack arrived early and was disappointed to see another fellow at the far end of the bay. When Mrs Bonny arrived, or more to the point, if she turned up, he'd have to take her somewhere else to practise.

He'd had a carpenter knock up two short-bladed wooden cutlasses and had sheepishly put up with the jeers of his men. He felt foolish clutching his two wooden weapons and was in two minds whether to walk back to town.

'Jack!'

'I'll be damned!' He stared at the figure waving at him. 'Well, I'll be damned!'

Mrs Bonny ran towards him, wearing a man's loose-fitting shirt and breeches belted tightly around her waist.

'They're James's. It's easier wearing these.'

'Yes... Absolutely... You're right.' He was taken off guard.

She reached out and took one of the practice cutlasses from him, ran her hand along the slightly curved edge of the wooden blade, and whooped in pleasure.

'Very impressive!' She darted about, slicing the cutlass, jigging up and down. 'C'mon, before the sun goes down!'

So, no chat then. No getting to know each other a little. Pity. 'All right, then. The first thing you need to learn...'

As he began to teach her some of the basics, she talked about playing with wooden swords with a childhood friend, and the time she had a real sabre in her hand. He found she had picked up more than rudimentary skills in swordplay, so this made his role more interesting. She was no beginner, but using a cutlass was different.

He demonstrated the best grip of the hilt to pivot the blade. Over and over he made her repeat quick wrist movements to control her cutlass hand until she groaned with the effort. They practised their stance, moving in and out of striking distance; practised positions of the blade: slashing inside and outside actions, diagonally up and down. He taught her how to guard, point up and point down; made her keep her blade forward and her elbow in. He reinforced the importance of instilling fear in your opponent by yelling. She needed no encouragement and attacked him with increasing force and volume.

'Shall we stop?' Jack didn't want to exhaust her.

'No, no, make the most of the daylight! Come on.'

She poked him in the chest with her cutlass. He was disappointed by her enthusiasm, and would have preferred to talk, but he continued to school her. He taught her how to pivot and change the edge of the blade facing him. Over and over they repeated actions.

'That's enough now!' He threw down his wooden weapon. They were both dripping with sweat, and strands of damp hair fell across her face which she brushed back impatiently.

'Next time I'll tie my hair back.'

'Next time? You want to do this again?' He couldn't hide his surprise.

'I can't learn everything in one lesson, can I?' She appealed to him. 'Besides, James is due back in a week or so.'

Ah, the husband. She obviously cared about the damned man, whoever he was. Jack turned to gaze at the sea. He should walk her back to town, and they could go their own ways. Better still, they should separate here. He could think of lots of things he should say, chief among them, 'No.' But what came out of his mouth was, 'Same time tomorrow?'

Mrs Bonny jumped up and down like a child who'd been given a treat.

24

Face to face, Anne tried to strike Jack's shoulder with her wooden cutlass, but he blocked her time and time again. She ducked aside, but not quickly enough to avoid a direct jab. This was rougher play than anything she had experienced with Richard. Over and over they practised things from the previous day. She was sweating and covered in bruises but loving it.

After some time, Jack dropped down in the sand and patted the space next to him. Sitting beside him, she learnt his vessel was the *Curlew*, a brigantine he had taken as a prize before he sought his pardon. He looked at her sideways. 'Perhaps I can show her to you sometime?' Was he inviting her to cruise with him, or propositioning her? She wasn't sure, but she was impressed. Neither of them cared about the long-ago rightful owner of the *Curlew*. She learnt that one or other of his men took turns sleeping on board to guard it, and he sometimes slept on the vessel himself. Other times he rented a room in town and told her quite pointedly where she could find it. He talked about Cuba, and possibly returning to live there.

'And you?' He turned to her. 'Assuming you don't want to live here forever: what do you want?'

How often had people asked her this, or had she asked herself? She could only shrug.

'Not sure… Not what I'm doing now – that much I know.'

'What then?'

'Something more…' She held her arms wide as if to encompass the realm she imagined.

Jack didn't mock her, or look puzzled, but nodded and smiled. He understood.

'C'mon.' She sprang to her feet, reaching for her practice weapon. It was better to do something physical than grapple with difficult subjects she couldn't articulate.

'No. Enough.' Jack pulled her back to sit and gazed at the darkening sky.

She was disappointed and appealed to him. 'Tomorrow then?'

Jack gave her a long look and spoke cautiously. 'All right, if you want. But now, how about a drink? Charlotte's?'

She shook her head. She would not be so brazen.

The following afternoon, well before sundown, Jack drew a boundary marker in the sand.

'There's not much space – this is about it – and you have to imagine the deck's full of men ready to kill. This is where a short blade comes into its own.'

She imagined herself on a ship's deck fighting at close quarters.

'Get me! Come on, get me!' Jack stretched across the short distance and prodded her in the belly, goading her to attack. Bellowing, she rushed him. She was determined she would get one strike.

'Damn you!' She yelled her frustration, as he deftly evaded her. She wanted to strike him, wanted to win, not ready to concede defeat. With ease Jack disarmed her, and with one arm around her neck, swivelled her around, pinned her back to his chest and raised his wooden blade to her throat.

'What a pity, Mrs Bonny. And it's such a lovely neck.'

Damn him! It had happened so quickly. It irked her that men could so easily overpower her. She jabbed Jack sharply in the ribs with her elbow, retrieved her weapon and challenged him afresh. 'Again! ...I'm ready!'

She angled her body, took small gathering steps till she was in cutting distance of Jack, and began. As their weapons clashed, Jack's face was dripping with sweat, his gaze focused though slightly amused. She did not want this to stop. She wanted to continue. All of it. Every bit of it. Anne stared at his face, her heart thudding, knowing the truth: she wanted Jack.

She froze, her wooden cutlass dangling to her side, shocked by the realisation. Perhaps she'd known all along, if she was being honest... If she'd wished to reflect a little.

'What is it?' Jack looked concerned.

She could not move and just stared at him.

'What's the matter?' Jack reached out to brush the hair from her eyes, and before he could ask again, she launched herself at him, not with her weapon but with her body, her face raised to his, pressing her lips to his. She wasn't sure which of them was more surprised. They stood, arms wrapped around each other, and she tasted the sweat on his mouth as they locked together in a deep kiss.

Jack pushed her back and held her at arms' length. 'Well, Mrs Bonny? Well...'

'You wanted to – I know it.' She meant to keep her dignity – if she could.

'I can't deny it, but as God's my witness' – Jack looked up to the sky – 'it was Mrs Bonny who made the first move.' He reached out and touched her cheek, grinning. 'Or can I call you Anne, now formalities have been thrown to the wind?'

A long, satisfying laugh rose from deep in her belly as he pulled her to him.

Away from the beach, hidden among trees, Anne's first coupling with Jack was a short hard act – all urgency and the need to be done with it – her back pressed to a tree, breeches to her knees. Returning to the beach and, with the sun long set, she lay next to Jack looking at the stars and they talked and talked. None of it made sense. There was James doing his best to make their lives better, yet she was risking everything – everything – being with this womanising former pirate. It was so wrong. But so deliciously right.

Jack turned on his side, head propped on his elbow, and grinned at her.

Before dawn they had a more leisurely fuck, before walking back into town and going their separate ways.

She met Jack a fourth time. Neither of them had come with swordplay in mind, and in any case Jack's wooden cutlass snapped in half, all the excuse they needed before finding shelter among the trees. Anne fleetingly considered that she was no better than Nassau's whores, then put that uncomfortable thought out of her head. She didn't want to think about James either.

25

BAHAMIAN SOCIETY WAS AS ROUGH AS EVER. MEN were returning to the sea weekly, but it wasn't only a pirate resurgence, Woodes feared. Intelligence from captains calling into port suggested the Spanish were mustering forces in their thousands, and he knew Nassau stood no chance of withstanding any attack. Even with both harbour entrances defences operational he didn't have the gunpower, or enough soldiers.

Woodes had written to London with his apprehensions, requesting a man-of-war and professional troops, saying he could not trust the former pirates to keep watch, describing how they were drunk, and derelict in guard duties no matter how much he fined them.

He intended to write to a religious society in London requesting a chaplain. Other colonies in the Indies had benefited, and the Bahamas was more in need than most. Education and the church were fundamental if the right type of settlers were to put down roots and communities to thrive, but he had neither here. In the Leeward Islands they had a college, with money bequeathed by a former governor who had acquired a great deal of wealth thanks to his investments in slaves and sugar plantations. It looked increasingly unlikely that this project in the Bahamas would make him or his co-partners wealthy men, and Woodes could not expect to offer such a bequest at the end of his posting. But having a church and chaplain would be a start; a definite improvement.

He was at his desk, halfway through his letter to the Society for the Promotion of Christian Knowledge, when Jeremy interrupted.

'Sir, Mrs Harmon's here.'

Woodes had recently taken on the young man as his clerk, and while Jeremy was full of enthusiasm and eternally grateful to be entrusted with the responsibilities of running his office, it was like having an unleashed puppy around. Before Woodes could open his mouth to instruct Jeremy to delay his visitor, Mrs Harmon's head appeared around the door.

'I hope I am not too early?' Mrs Harmon's short dumpy body followed, and he indicated the chair across his desk. She dropped into the seat and reached for her fan.

'I've never acquired a taste for this climate, but I bear it as well as I can.' Her fan fluttered near her perspiring face. 'I won't keep you long. We, that is the ladies of the Guild, have something to raise with you.'

Woodes nodded. He knew Mrs Walker and other wives of council members and wives of the more honest merchants in town all belonged to this social circle and he encouraged it. He had spoken with Mrs Harmon on an earlier occasion about the need to uplift fallen women and hoped the Ladies' Guild could take a lead. If this plan could be advanced it might mean fewer whorehouses on the waterfront, or at the very least they could assist some of the young girls he had seen working there: girls no older than his own daughter.

'Excellent! So, you have given my ideas some thought?'
Woodes smiled at Mrs Harmon. 'I take it you have some
kind of a scheme in mind. We might consider resettling
them elsewhere – Carolina, perhaps? What do you
propose?'

'Ah… those poor girls.' Mrs Harmon looked distracted.
'Yes, yes, we talked over your proposal and one or two of the
ladies are keen to further that…'

'Delighted to hear it.' He beamed at her. It would mean
he would have to fund it of course but he felt it to be his
Christian duty.

'But we have another cause that *all* the ladies are behind,
and that's what I want to talk to you about.'

'Oh?' Woodes was heartened to hear this, nodding for her
to continue.

'We have a request.'

'So, what new charitable cause have you in mind? How
can I help?'

'By hosting a ball.' Mrs Harmon beamed.

'A ball!' This took him by surprise. 'Madam, I don't have
my wife with me to host…' This sounded a poor excuse, even
before the words were out of his mouth.

'Oh, no, no. We've talked about that. We are all saddened
your wife is not able to join us – not as yet anyway – but we
hope you will encourage her to voyage out soon…'

Mrs Harmon paused, fanning her face, inviting him to
step in, to say more, but he would not. He did not talk
about his private life with anyone, and certainly not with
Mrs Harmon, who had tried to draw him out on this
subject on several occasions. She could be relied on to talk
frankly with all her acquaintances, divulging all that was
most private. He let a silence settle between them. Mrs
Harmon smiled.

'Captain Rogers, we know how busy you are, so we ladies would take the lead in organising the gathering. You would be host in name only – really you would.'

Woodes sensed his way out. 'Ah well, of course, that might be delightful, but my residence is not suitable – it's far too small.' And this was true enough. His needs were simple, and he did not intend to go in for any kind of elaborate entertainment.

'Yes, that is a slight impediment, but we have that covered. Mrs Walker suggests we use her house. It's much bigger – we could host it there.' Mrs Harmon smiled, sensing victory. 'She suggests if the big glass doors were opened onto the garden the whole affair could spill outside. And they have a lovely garden, as you know. It got into a sad state when they were away, but now they are back it is looking glorious, simply glorious.'

'No, no, madam… this is all too much.'

Mrs Harmon's fan fluttered as she hurried on. 'It need only be a small social gathering, with some musicians. We would like to call it a ball, just to raise the tone and create some excitement and allow us to dress in our finest, but of course it would not be anything as grand as you were used to in London.'

Woodes frowned, feeling trapped by this woman though he acknowledged that she was right, at least in part. Such a social event fitted very well with his ideas of improving the tone of society. He only wished they could do it without involving him. He didn't want to waste more time arguing.

'Very well, Mrs Harmon. Please tell your Guild ladies I will be delighted to host some such event, but I forbid you to call it a ball. I stop short of raising expectations so high, when I can count no more than three or four couples who are of any station in life in our small society.'

He was being generous here. In fact, he could only think of the Walkers who might qualify as "quality", but he had no reason to upset Mrs Harmon by saying so. He smiled at her and continued.

'Let us consider it an occasion to reach out to those we would wish to see elevated. This will swell the ranks a little, and I'll be happy to play my part.'

'I think I understand what you mean.' Mrs Harmon frowned. 'But, whatever we call it, we ladies want an occasion to wear our best gowns and to dance to a small orchestra. We hope you can oblige us?'

Woodes resigned himself to whatever fal-la-la the ladies thought fit and was thankful his crippled foot excused him from dancing a minuet or anything more energetic with Mrs Harmon.

26

JAMES RETURNED HOME FULL OF STORIES, BUT ANNE could not share what she had been up to and resented his presence. The fun had gone out of her life and she didn't know what to do. The day after his return, after unloading cargo from the *William*, James arrived home, his face flushed.

'Anne. Listen to this – it concerns you… both of us.'

Anne waited for the blow to fall.

'There's goin' to be some sort of dance, a fancy social thing, and Mr Harmon's told his wife about you – that you're well-bred and so on – and you're invited. We're both invited.'

Anne dropped into a chair; her legs shaky. He had not found out!

James had an exaggerated sense of her own background; perhaps she had encouraged it. Now he delighted in this token of recognition, this demonstration that it was possible to rise in society.

'I can introduce you to Governor Rogers, if he remembers me, and we'll have to make new clothes. I can afford it and we've got a few weeks, it's not till mid-February.' James was proud of the extra money he had, for things beyond necessities. This too demonstrated progress.

Anne smiled weakly, trying to regain her composure. She had never met Mrs Walker again after her embarrassing visit, but if she went to this dance she would be forced to do so. Perhaps Mrs Walker would no longer remember her? Whatever the case, she needed to look presentable – as fashionable and ladylike as she could.

In the following days she avoided Charlotte's, as she could not bear the thought of seeing Jack, but after a while she couldn't bear not seeing him, so she made her way along the waterfront. He was there all right, with Dolly hovering near. As Jack caught her eye he deliberately drew Dolly onto his lap. Deliberately. She tried not to mind, but sharp stabs of jealousy reached under her ribs as surely as Jack's wooden cutlass had.

She stalked up to him and jerked her head at Dolly. 'Is this little show for me?'

Jack replied coolly. 'Just enjoying myself. Some of us here aren't married.'

She would not rise to the bait, instead asked what he'd been up to, to which he shrugged, and by way of something to say, she told him about her invitation.

Jack sneered. 'I've heard about it. Perhaps this is your future, Mrs Bonny. You can join the Ladies' Guild and help raise the moral tone of the town… might do you some good.'

He laughed loudly and she felt her cheeks heating. Was this a rebuke, implying she was no better than Dolly?

'Well, Mrs Bonny.' Jack smiled mockingly. 'You're the only woman of my acquaintance – for what that's worth – who's received an invitation to Rogers's party, so you should look your best.'

'For what that's worth!' Dolly bridled, as Jack stood up, pushing her off his lap to give his full attention to Anne.

'I can get my hands on some fancy fabric for you, if you want.'

Anne chose mid-blue satin for her gown, and one of Charlotte's girls, a former seamstress, cut and sewed it. When it was finished, she dressed in her finery to show him, because this gown, of a shade to bring out the colour of her blue-grey eyes, was really for him. What was the harm? James need never know. James need never know that she raised her skirt above her knees and danced some silly steps as Jack leant against the wall admiring her. James need never know how she bent forward provocatively, displaying the low cut of her bodice; that Jack kissed her neck and breasts; that Jack picked her up and sat her on a table. James need never know that the skirt was above her waist, her legs wrapped around Jack, drawing him close to her; into her. No, James need never know any of this.

Thank goodness for Charlotte and her upstairs rooms. Thank goodness Charlotte knew how to keep secrets and in any case didn't think much of "Simple Simon". Thank goodness James drank at one of the other taverns…

The Walkers' reception room had been cleared of furniture, allowing enough space to dance to a small orchestra of two fiddles and a harpsichord. Anne spotted Governor Rogers, looking as stiff and unbending as always, with a group of men: uniformed army officers, merchants, sea captains and members of the council. Clusters of well-dressed women, seated or standing, fanned themselves as they chatted. She noticed Mrs Walker amongst them and hoped to avoid her.

Anne hadn't attended such a gathering since Richard's coming-of-age party, and this far exceeded anything James had ever known. He clung to her side, overwhelmed. A servant carrying a tray with glasses of punch came their way, and they both gulped down the sweet beverage. Before long they found themselves with refills. Holding on to glasses, taking occasional sips, gave them something to do. She didn't know these people, so had no one to talk to.

The fiddler announced a dance and immediately an enthusiastic looking military officer was by her side. With a gloved hand to his chest he addressed James.

'Sir, would you be kind enough to allow me to dance with your wife? Please don't disappoint me; we are very short of ladies.' He beamed at her as if she would be granting him a precious gift. 'Will you do me the honour, ma'am?'

She could hardly refuse him and allowed herself to be led onto the dance floor. She was on display and meant to make James proud of her as she danced in the arms of the officer, remembering not to laugh too loudly when he made a little joke at Governor Rogers's expense.

She graciously refused a second dance, helped herself to another drink, joined James, and waved and smiled happily to Mr Harmon as he approached.

'Ah, there you are, James, this is where you're hiding... Mrs Bonny, you look charming this evening.' Mr Harmon gallantly raised her hand and bowed. Anne smiled. She did look fine! Her dress was beautiful, though she could not hide her tanned cheeks and calloused hands. There was only so much she could do to turn herself into a lady.

Mr Harmon continued with his charm offensive. 'I wouldn't let her into the arms of those fine fellows if I were you, James – best dance with your wife yourself. But first, let me introduce you to Governor Rogers... Ah...' Mr Harmon noticed Mr Rogers was deep in conversation with Mr Walker. 'In that case let me introduce you to my wife, and we'll say hello to the governor later.'

'I'll wait here.' James indicated a quiet corner of the room as she allowed Mr Harmon to steer her towards a group of women.

'To tell the truth, Mrs Bonny, it was my wife who insisted you were invited. Absolutely insisted! Though of course I would have been delighted to secure an invitation from the governor myself for you both, don't get me wrong. James is coming along fast – you must be proud of him.' She nodded and mumbled her agreement as Mr Harmon continued doggedly. 'But credit where it's due. Inviting you both was my wife's idea – wouldn't let off nagging me until I'd promised her James had the invitation in his hand. Funny creatures, ladies, I don't pretend to understand you.'

As they approached Mrs Harmon's group, their conversation ceased, and fans began to flutter. All eyes were on her, and she sensed a tension that Mr Harmon seemed oblivious to as he introduced her.

'Now, if you'll excuse me, I'll leave you ladies to become acquainted.' Mr Harmon backed away and made his escape.

Mrs Harmon smiled. 'Delighted to meet you, Mrs Bonny.'

Anne offered her own greeting to Mrs Harmon and caught the eye of Mrs Walker, who smiled and nodded.

'It's good to see you again, Mrs Bonny. I am very pleased you danced with one of our officers. And I see your husband is here.'

'Yes, of course James is here. Would you like me to fetch—?'

'Later, maybe later.' Mrs Walker brushed her offer away. 'You know, I'm sorry you never sought me out again. They were difficult times for us back then, but after our return… Well.' Mrs Walker hesitated. 'It's only recently I've heard of you again.'

Mrs Harmon chuckled. 'Yes, my goodness!' She fluttered her fan rapidly and looked at Anne candidly.

The smile froze on Anne's face. Mrs Harmon leant forward and whispered, 'You cut quite a dash in your husband's clothes – I assume they were his – unless of course they were Rackham's? Cutlasses indeed. So my servant told me.'

What else had he told her? Anne gripped her glass tightly. 'My dear.' Mrs Walker smiled gently. 'Is it appropriate for a married woman? In fact, is it appropriate for anyone to be in that ruffian's company, however innocently? We have your best interests at heart, believe me.'

At heart? Anne's own heart was knocking against her ribs. Had she spent all this time making a fine gown, all these days teaching James some dances in anticipation of an enjoyable evening, when all along there had been an ulterior motive for the invitation?

'Is this your business?' At her sharp words the ladies drew back. Mrs Walker smiled at her again, undeterred.

'Such things do matter here. We understand you are from a good family.' Mrs Walker looked at her companions, who all nodded their agreement. 'We are a small society and we want to help you – before it's too late.'

Anne was mortified. When would people stop telling her what to do and interfering in her life? Was she to be made an example of? Would they proudly "own" her as one of the souls they had saved? Would she be expected to show her repentance? Her cheeks burnt.

Mrs Harmon leant forward and tapped Anne's shoulder with her fan to underline her words. 'Indeed. A little more decorum and discretion. We know there can be temptations when our husbands are abroad, but perhaps some distance, don't you think? We're here to help and advise you. All of us.'

This was too much. The insistent tap, tap, tap of Mrs Harmon's fan felt like hammer blows and Anne could see drops of perspiration on her plump cheeks and the zeal in her eyes. The woman was repulsive.

'Mind your own business!' She pushed Mrs Harmon away.

It was only a small push, but Mrs Harmon was caught off balance, or possibly the shove had more force than she intended. Worse, Anne had momentarily forgotten the glass in her hand. It bounced off Mrs Harmon's chest, spilling the contents on her gown before shattering on the floor. Mrs Harmon yelped and staggered as Mrs Walker and another woman held out their arms to break her fall.

Dancers who had moments earlier tripped up and down the floor were now being escorted to their seats and the musicians were silent. Anne flinched, knowing her voice must have carried in this lull, and without a doubt Mrs Harmon's slumped figure was in full view without swirling dancers to impede people's vision.

Appalled faces stared at her and she was rooted to the spot. Across the room Governor Rogers leant towards Mr Harmon, his hand raised to his mouth, and Mr Harmon spluttered into his drink.

Her eyes darted to James, striding towards her. Anne fled through the open doors to the garden. She would not be introduced to Mr Rogers this evening, just as she would not dance again, with James or anyone else.

James caught up with her as she reached the garden gate. 'How could you, Anne? What possessed you?' He grabbed her arm.

She turned shaking with anger and shame. 'I want nothing to do with those busybodies.'

'But it was Mrs Harmon! What were you thinking? What's going on?'

'You want to know? I'll tell you. Better from my lips than anyone else's.'

As they ran along the track, she told him. She told him a good deal – enough so he could be no doubt what she had been up to. James swung her around and slapped her face. She deserved it, she supposed.

'Sweet Jesus. I never thought you'd whore yourself out as soon as my back was turned!'

'It's not like that. He taught me to fight... And, well... It just happened.'

'Just happened? Nothing *just happens*, Anne. Christ!' James shook her shoulders. 'Don't you ever think about what you're doing? I'm your husband! Doesn't that mean anything to you any more? Did it ever mean anything?'

She tried to twist away from his grasp and felt the sting of his hand as he struck her cheek again.

'Don't you dare slap me!'

'Then answer me, damn it!'

'I don't know... I don't know...'

'What do you want, Anne? Simple question. Simple answer.'

'I don't know!' Perhaps this was no longer true. 'I want ... I want something... Something more.'

She heard his intake of breath and his bitter, 'More than me, you mean.'

Despite the darkness, she could see pain and incomprehension etched on his face, but she could not help him. She knew he had tried his best.

James tried again. 'C'mon, let's go home. It was a mistake to come here, but we can still hold our heads up, can't we? You can apologise to Mrs Harmon. No more of your foolishness—'

'Apologise? Foolishness?' Her head was spinning, but within seconds she knew what she had to do.

'No, no, this isn't what I want. There's got to be something more... something bigger... I can't stand this life!'

She twisted her wedding ring off her finger.

'What're you doing?' James reached out to stop her.

She sprang back out of reach. 'I'm going. I'm leaving!'

Tossing her ring away, she lifted her skirt and fled into the night to the anguished sound of James calling her name over and over. Angry. Pleading. Sad.

He did not chase her. Perhaps he thought she would come to her senses when she calmed down. But she would not be going back.

With a clenched fist she hammered on the door of the lodging house she knew Jack sometimes stayed at, then raced to Charlotte's. But no one had seen him. Breathless, she ran to the beach, holding up her satin gown, demanding of any man she met if he'd seen Jack, until one of the men she had ridden out hunting with pointed to the harbour. 'But I'd wait if I were you.'

She would not wait. She found a small beached boat, leant her back into it, pushing it off the sand till it floated and she was thigh-high in water, the skirt of her gown billowing out. Her fierce anger propelled each stroke of the oars as she rowed away from shore. She clawed her way up the ladder hanging over the side of the *Curlew*, climbed down through the hatch to the between deck, felt her way in darkness towards the stern, then threw open the door of Jack's cabin.

They had a candle burning.

She darted forward and yanked Dolly out of bed by her hair, picked up her discarded dress and threw it at her naked scrawny body.

'Get out! Now!' Her voice was icy.

With her new blue gown hanging sodden and ruined and her hair in wild tangles, she turned narrowed eyes on Jack. 'You left the ladder down – were you in such a hurry? I could've been anyone. I could've crept up and killed you, and right now I'd like to run a blade through your lousy heart.'

She took in his nakedness and could barely control her chattering teeth as she snarled, 'Damn you, Jack Rackham!'

27

Vane prodded a finger at the tatty document laid out on his cabin table next to the pen and ink. 'Sign.'

Mary could barely pick out Vane's ship's articles, the page was so crowded with scrawled names. It seemed Vane had reused articles from an earlier cruise. Some names were crossed out – men who had left, died or perhaps been captured by Hornigold. The ink was still wet on two other names: seamen standing next to her, also reconciled to their fate.

Finding a space she wrote, Mark Read.

Mary was on the *Prince* under Vane's command.

She had been on board a merchantman leaving Barbados bound for England when Vane and his men attacked. Vane pistol-whipped the captain and she witnessed one of her shipmates randomly selected and half throttled. All so pointless. They'd had little money on board and Vane had no means of transferring the dozens of heavy barrels of sugar they were carrying. As he couldn't take much of the cargo he meant to take some of the crew. Some idiot on board told Vane she was a topman, and he wasn't letting her go.

She did not know what she dreaded most: being captured or being discovered. So far during her three years back at sea her disguise had worked. She wore her loose-fitting seaman's attire and kept her breasts bound. She was not unsocial and often the first to volunteer when someone needed help, doing whatever was necessary without fuss. This was her way. She didn't talk much but others talked to her, so she knew just about everything there was to know about her companions, at least as much as they cared to talk about, while they knew next to nothing about Mark, the man she had become so convincingly once again.

Mary stood on the *Prince's* deck with all the rest of the crew as Vane strutted like a rooster, full of himself and his plans.

'We're heading for the Spanish Main, away from prying English. You ready to take prizes? Ready to become the biggest fucking pack of rovers in these waters? Well?'

'Aye, Cap'n.' 'We're with you.' 'We're ready.'

Mary joined the chorus. What choice did she have?

Vane grunted, satisfied. 'After I've built my fleet I'm plannin' on taking back Nassau – getting rid of that fucking man, Rogers. Pity I didn't kill him before... What do y'say?'

A holler of support rose around him. These men wanted to believe they could be in charge. Mary punched the air too. She would blend in with the pack.

During her first week on board she kept her head down, did what was required, all the while considering how and when she might escape. Vane wasn't someone worth fighting and dying for. Better to die trying to get away than during a chase that went sour; or risk getting caught and hanged, or – Mary increasingly realised – being mauled to death by Vane's own hands. He was an unpredictable bastard.

Campbell's unmistakable Glaswegian burr drew her attention, shouting as if to raise the devil. She put aside the ropes she was splicing and pushed through a crowd of men to find two drunken seamen, Campbell and a man called Squires, daggers drawn, circling, jabbing and cursing. Before anyone could decide what to do it was too late. Campbell had Squires tackled to the ground and moments later skewered him through the throat, pinning him neatly to the deck.

Mary grimaced, wondering whether Vane would shoot Campbell himself or if he'd order his quartermaster to do the job. Whatever the case, Campbell was a dead man. He'd signed ship's articles and that was that.

Vane pushed through the crush of men and smirked at Campbell. 'I hope ya think it was worth it?'

Campbell looked up from his bloody victim, his eyes wild. 'Bastard cheated me. Cheated me and now he's paid!' Campbell was still belligerent, but this would wear off as reality set in. Mary felt a pang of sympathy for him.

Vane signalled to the watching men. 'Grab him!'

Mary didn't volunteer, but others stepped forward to tussle with Campbell, who wasn't giving in without a fight. Crouching, his dagger thrust before him, he hollered, 'Take me if you dare, fuckers. Take me!'

It didn't take much for a dozen men to overpower one drunk Scotsman. Within minutes Campbell lay on the deck, hands bound behind him. He was finished fighting and could only curse.

Vane prepared his pistol and stood stony-faced as other men bound the struggling Campbell to the mainmast, the cords in his neck standing out and his eyes bulging as he shrieked, 'Motherfuckers! Aye, motherfuckers – all o' ye!'

Vane cocked his pistol and took aim as Campbell let out a bellowing howl of rage. Vane held his arm steady, protracting the moment as Campbell cursed and cursed. Mary wanted Vane to get on with it, so they could dump Campbell's body overboard and everyone could settle down, but Vane lowered his arm.

'Nah – this is too quick. Set up the tackle to give him a ducking underneath. Hoist him up, let him dangle while ya get it sorted.'

Mary took a steadying breath as someone challenged Vane. 'He's to be shot! That's what the articles say!'

Vane whipped around to face the challenger. 'Just to remind you illiterate dogs the words in ship's articles are "shot, or any other punishment the captain thinks fit". Any... other... punishment. Got it?' Vane's face was inches from the challenger. 'And I see fit to keelhaul this piece of shit. Let this be a lesson to all of ya!'

Campbell had stopped shouting and cursing: his face drained of colour. 'Cap'n. For God's sake, mun, shoot me. Make it quick – I beg ye ta make it quick!'

Vane walked within a foot of Campbell and stared into his pleading eyes. 'I want you to feel the barnacles on ya back. I want you to check out the state of the hull and let us know if it needs a clean. I'm countin' on your report.'

A gob of spit landed on Vane's face – the futile action of a powerless man.

Mary wiped sweating hands on her trousers and appealed to Vane. 'Captain – think again – I'll shoot him if you—'

Vane shoved her away, barking, 'Get to it.'

She knew what needed to be done – in theory. She had not personally participated in such a punishment while serving in the navy and never while serving on merchant ships; that wasn't their way. It was barbaric.

A long length of rope was fetched, and two shipmates, holding one end each, climbed out onto the bowsprit. Dropping the rope over and leaving it slack, they walked back to midships, trailing the rope under the hull. She watched in silence as one end was tied to Campbell's feet where he hung from the larboard yardarm, continuing to yowl and curse, and the other end was run through a block secured on the starboard side. Every so often she glanced at Vane, hoping this was a charade and he would change his mind.

No one spoke, and Campbell had given up bellowing and closed his eyes.

Mary gathered at the starboard side, her eyes on Vane, waiting for his order.

'Pull! Pull, dogs, and remember, if any of you feel like breaking ship's rules...'

Mary pulled hand over hand, with all the power she could, as did her companions. Campbell disappeared over the side. More men rushed to the ropes, heaving and heaving, all the sooner to put Campbell out of his misery. Mary glanced at Vane's face but could not read it at all. Was he enjoying this brutal scene? The man was a sadist.

Minutes passed before Campbell was hauled out – his clothes in shreds and the skin on his back stripped to the bone. He had not survived his ducking and now his corpse hung on display from the yard.

'Leave him there. I'll tell ya when ya can cut him down.' Vane stared impassively.

For days Mary watched the seabirds feast off Campbell's bloodied body. It was only the need to unfurl a sail off that yard that forced Vane to remove the corpse. Only then was it flung overboard with a collective shudder from the crew.

She had no idea how to get away from this crazy man, but she would, then she planned to seek pardon. This life was not for her. Vane and all of them were despicable and deserved to be hanged.

28

Urging her horse to greater speed, Anne galloped along the water's edge, kicking up spray. These small New Providence beaches or inland pathways which ended all too soon at the coast were constricting. Behind, Jack rode at a slow canter, refusing to rise to her challenge when she had dug her heels into her mount, shouting, 'Race you!'

Jack had hired the horses; he was indulging her in all manner of things, and she was soaking it up. After three years of scraping by it was liberating to have money to spend – Jack's money – and there seemed to be no end to it. She was eating well, drinking well and had accepted new clothes. His most precious gift by far was a cutlass, and she practised in all seriousness. Many things had changed in the past four months while she had been sharing a lodging room with Jack.

Anne slowed to a canter and turned to walk her mount back to Jack. She patted her horse's neck as she mulled over the problem that had been on her mind for days.

'I've been thinking. How much am I worth to you?'

'Worth?' Jack looked confused. 'What do you mean? Do you want something?'

'No, not for me. Something we can offer James. I've written to him, you see, asking him to release me from our marriage.'

'What? You want me to pay for you? Buy your way out of your marriage?' Jack laughed. 'You're unbelievable! Can't be done, sweetheart. Anyway, I've little enough money left as it is.'

Anne grunted. Perhaps James would do the decent thing and divorce her without any monetary enticement. Her mind moved on to another topic. They had skirted around the subject of what would happen to those who had taken the King's pardon. Now what? How could they earn a living?

'Has Governor Rogers any further cruises planned?' she asked, though she was not keen on Jack working for him.

Jack shook his head. 'I think his pockets are emptying pretty fast too. He's not been back asking. Anyway, you know I'm not likely to do his bidding. Being harnessed to Rogers doesn't suit me.'

Jack and others who had turned their backs on pirating had accepted privateering commissions from Rogers to seek out Spanish ships. Jack had been on one cruise, but it had barely covered anyone's costs, even Rogers's own.

As they plodded homeward Anne said, as casually as she could, 'Well, perhaps you should take up pirating again.'

She felt his eyes on her and heard his sharp intake of breath.

'You'd have me do that?'

'We need money, don't we?'

Jack reached over and held her reins, bringing them both to a stop. 'You witnessed those poor wretches having their necks stretched by the noose. How did you feel, seeing men die?'

She refused to be drawn.

'Look at me. Look at me, Anne!' Jack waited until she met his gaze. 'Imagine it was me. Would you like to watch me die? Because that's what would happen.'

Hadn't James said the same thing?

'Only if you get caught, Jack!' She had faith in him, in this man of hers. 'Of course, you wouldn't get caught! You're a good fighter and you don't take foolish risks! Some of them deserve to die – they're too stupid, or drunk or brutal. You're not like that. You're too smart to get caught.'

Jack broke the silence as they walked their horses back in the direction of Nassau.

'To tell the truth, I've been thinking about it. Talking with George and Dick.'

So! Anne was not surprised to hear this and found she wasn't upset by the idea. In fact, it excited her. She raised an eyebrow at Jack, inviting him to continue.

'We're all keen – the old life calls, I suppose. Hard to turn your back on it, y'know. But if we do go, I'd miss you. I'd not see much of you.'

'Nonsense!'

'It's not nonsense. I could never set foot in the Bahamas again, not while Rogers is here. I would set you up somewhere else, of course, so we could see each other from time to time. But worst case is we might never see each other again. If I'm taken.'

'Stop this, Jack!' She was riled up by his silly talk. 'I'll not be set up in Cuba, or wherever you want to stable me like one of these horses, so that you can visit and ride every so often. I'll never agree to that.'

'Then what? Might you change your mind about James? Or do you want to go back to your father?'

How could he be so stupid!

'No! Don't you see? Don't you see how it could be for us?'

This time Anne pulled the reins of her horse and leant across to yank Jack to a stop. She would have to spell it out to him.

'I'll come too. I'll come with you!'

There. She'd said it. She'd said the thing that had been burning her brain.

Jack threw back his head and roared.

He was laughing! On a reflex, she leant from her saddle and whipped him none too lightly across his back. He yelped as the whip stung his flesh, and he struggled to restrain his startled horse. It would serve him right if it threw him.

'Don't laugh. Don't you dare laugh. Why do you think I've been practising my weapons? Naturally, I'll come with you.'

'Oh, Anne!' Jack wiped away tears of laughter. 'I love your wild ways. You wouldn't be you otherwise, but that's not possible and you know it.'

'Why not?' Anne could not follow his reasoning.

'Women on board. Can't be done. It's hard enough keeping discipline without having men fighting over a woman.'

'But it wouldn't be like that.'

'It's a fact – it would be – and captain's rights don't extend to having his own woman on board. There're no secrets and we share everything.'

'I'd not be the ship's whore!'

'No.' Jack looked at her squarely. 'No, you would not. I'll cut the balls off any man who so much as touches you whether on land or sea while you're my woman. But sorry, sweetheart, no women aboard and that's that.'

Anne seethed. He had taken to calling her sweetheart, which was charming to a point, but in her mind the word conjured up soft, comforting women and did not fit the woman she had become. She doubted her sweetness and sometimes wondered about her heart: how loving and giving it was, or could be, since she had decided to guard against pain and loss.

But women on board ship. Why not? She could not let this assumption stand.

'What about the navy? They allow wives of officers on board, don't they? They mightn't be listed on the muster books, but they're allowed on voyages.'

'True, but—'

'The bosun's wife, and the carpenter's – I assume the rest of the crew leave those women alone, don't they?'

'Probably they're all old and ugly. Anyway, that's the King's navy. And they aren't provisioned for. I'll not starve, even for your delightful company, my sweet.' Jack laughed again, reached across and chucked her under the chin.

She jerked her head back. 'Jack, listen to me. Just listen.'

'I am listening. I can't even outride you to get away from you. You'd catch me up quick enough and argue me into my grave.'

He would not take her seriously and this made Anne angrier. A ride along the beach that had been so uplifting ended with her returning to Nassau in a black mood.

Some days later, she lay listening to Jack's even breathing as he slept, then lightly, so not to wake him, she rose and in the early light of dawn, began to dress. Satisfied, she quietly picked up his knife, returned to the bed and leaning over his naked body, stroked his cheek with the cool steel blade, drawing it down towards his neck.

He woke, body rigid, eyes wide. Then he relaxed, pushing her arm away. 'What the fuck—'

'This is how I can do it, Jack.'

She stood back so he could take in her full attire: his jacket; red breeches cinched to her waist with a thick belt; hat pulled low. All far too big for her.

'Is this a joke?' Jack spoke cautiously. She could see he longed to laugh but didn't wish to provoke her while she held his knife in her hand. 'The very idea—'

She touched the tip of the blade to his throat to prevent him standing up, determined to make her point, determined to be taken seriously.

'Yes, the very idea. Yes. I've dressed as a boy before. I've told you. When I was a little girl. Ma cut my hair short and made me breeches—'

'Ah yes, your father's failed attempt to keep his secret family from his wife while trying to teach you… don't know which was the most misguided—'

Anne thumped him.

Jack sighed and dropped back in the bed. 'Ship's articles, Anne: no women. You know that. Not even in disguise – on pain of death.'

'But Jack—'

'No! Let this be an end to this crazy idea. It's one thing to risk my neck…' Jack pulled her onto the bed. He tossed away his hat and wrapped her hair around her own neck, tipping her chin upwards. '…but I'll not risk yours, even though that tongue of yours can be infuriating.'

'Goddamn, Jack—'

'And what about the little one?' Jack stroked her belly.

Anne had been distressed to find herself pregnant so soon after meeting Jack, her fun cut short too early. She calculated she was due to deliver in late November or early December but didn't want to think about this inconvenience.

'Goddamn—' She opened her mouth to find a new angle about how to join him at sea when Jack bent over and sucked her tongue into his mouth. Damn him! He unbuckled the belt around her waist, peeling his breeches off her legs, all the while keeping his mouth clamped to hers. He began to tickle her, and she shrieked with stifled laughter. All right, Jack Rackham – best enjoy the fun they were about to have. She climbed astride him. Later she'd think about how to persuade him to her way of thinking.

Loud hammering on the door startled them, followed by a male voice bellowing, 'Open up!'

'Who the devil?' Jack spoke for them both as they sat up. The hammering didn't let up and a second voice commanded the door be opened. Jack pulled on his breeches and she reached her arms and head through her cotton shift. Jack had barely unbolted the door before it burst open and two armed uniformed soldiers strode in.

'What's going on?' Jack stepped back, bewildered.

'Governor's orders.' One of the soldiers eyed him and turned to look squarely at her.

She was angry, not just for her own dignity, standing there in her underclothes, but indignant that Rogers should demand to see Jack in such a rude manner.

'Get out! He hasn't done anything!' She thrust her hands into the chest of the nearest soldier, propelling him back. He caught her arm.

'Not him. You. Governor Rogers wants to see you.'

'Anne?' Jack looked as confused as her. 'What could our delightful governor possibly want with Mrs Bonny?'

The other soldier in the room picked up her dress from the floor.

'This must be yours... Mrs Bonny. You want to put it on before we escort you? Mr Rogers likes to start his working day early, very early, sad to say for the rest of us. No company to tempt him to stay in bed like some lucky folk.'

'I'll come too...' Jack started to pull on his shoes.

'Not you, Rackham. The governor doesn't want to see you – just the lady here.'

The soldier sneered as he stressed the word "lady". She pressed her dress against her body. What in hell's name could Governor Rogers possibly want with her? Her mind raced.

29

WOODES STARED CANDIDLY AT THE YOUNG WOMAN standing in front of him, hair loose and tangled and looking as if she had dressed hastily. This early-morning summons had been deliberate; he had intended to take her off guard, while he, on the other hand, was immaculately dressed and seated behind his polished desk.

Mrs Bonny's arms were folded defensively across her body, her eyes wary. Woodes had a fleeting memory of her dancing with one of his officers and hadn't taken any further notice until her unseemly encounter with Mrs Harmon. That had been shocking behaviour, though after the event Thomas Walker had jokingly referred to it as the "almost-sinking of the galleon we know and love as Mrs Harmon". There was a funny side to it, but it would not do to upset the Harmons or condone Mrs Bonny's behaviour.

And now this fresh outrage.

'Will you take a seat, Mrs Bonny?' He motioned to the chair across from him.

She shook her head, barely moving a muscle. Woodes knew she would be curious to know why he had sent for her, but she appeared determined not to ask, her mouth pressed into a tight purse of displeasure as she stared stonily at him. He met her gaze with an equally stony one of his own, then decided he could not waste time conducting a battle of wills. From his drawer he withdrew a folded letter, opened it and turned it to face her.

'Do you recognise this? Is this your hand?' Woodes watched a flicker of recognition register.

'How did you…?' She bit her lip.

'You don't deny you wrote it?'

'What business is this of yours?' Her anger was palpable.

'I wish it were not my business, but sadly your husband brought it to my attention and it's my duty to take action.'

For a moment she looked surprised, either by the fact that her husband had requested this of him or that he was obliged to act, but she remained silent. Mrs Bonny's conscience did not appear to be pricked nor an apology forthcoming, which had been his hope.

'Mrs Bonny.' His voice took on more authority. 'What wife would petition her husband for a divorce in such a calculated manner?'

Her anger, bubbling below the surface, finally erupted.

'What business is it of yours what I do? You're not my guardian. Why should you care?'

'But I am the guardian of this society. I have that authority, and I will not have a wife seeking to buy herself out of a lawful marriage. It is not decent nor Christian, and your husband assures me you were married in a church. What's more, your actions are sinful – and shameful.'

'Really?' Mrs Bonny unfolded her arms and leant her knuckles on his desk, glowering down. 'I tell you, I'm not ashamed.'

Woodes was shocked at how brazen the woman was. He would not give her the advantage of looking down at him, so he rose to confront her; they stood face to face, leaning across his desk.

'Mrs Bonny, let me be clear with you. I will not suffer insubordination—'

'Insubordination!' She almost spat the word. 'I'm not one of your soldiers.'

'But you are part of this community that I govern. I've a good mind to have you flogged and thrown in jail. And, in case you wonder, I assure you I have the authority.'

He'd recently ordered others to be flogged after discovering a plot to kill him and his senior officers, then hand the colony back to the pirates. Granted, that had been a more serious crime, demonstrating how fragile his governance was.

A sneer spread over Mrs Bonny's face. He could see nothing attractive about her at this moment; her face remained hard and determined, but she said nothing, and he suddenly wanted her out of his office.

'Your incautious behaviour will lead to trouble. Go back to your husband where you belong. It will be for the best, I'm sure of it.'

'You're sure of it, are you? If marriage is so wonderful, where is your wife? Why isn't she here with you?' A look of triumph spread over her face.

How dare she! Clearly rumours were circulating about the state of his own marriage, but he would not be drawn. As he folded the letter he could feel a slight tremor in his hands.

'Let us put this behind us. I have it from your husband that he will accept you back. Go home, and I hope not to see you under such uncivil circumstances again.'

'Oh, don't worry, Governor. You won't. I assure you, you won't.'

She smiled at him; Mrs Bonny finally smiled. Perhaps there was a chink in her armour after all. Perhaps this brief conversation had done some good. As she turned and strode out of his office Woodes thought he detected a slight swell in her belly. If he was right, this would be Rackham's bastard. He was happy to see the back of her.

Mrs Harmon had happily passed on gossip about Mrs Bonny living in sin with Rackham. What would entice a reasonable woman to leave a decent husband to cohabit with a second-rate former pirate he could only guess at. He had met Rackham in the course of his duties, and amongst the seamen hanging around his shores, Rackham was someone he had trusted enough to do business with. But only so far. Rackham's privateering cruise to Cuba under his orders hadn't accomplished much and had only served to further empty his own reserves and make him more nervous about Spanish intentions.

At least Rackham could be grateful both he and the *Curlew* had survived unscathed. Woodes couldn't say the same for Hornigold. After they brought in some of Vane's men the previous year, Woodes had commissioned him to set out against the Spanish, but Hornigold's vessel had been caught in a hurricane. The vessel had been smashed and the crew dead. And George, the young fellow from Dorset he had saved from the gallows, had also come to a watery end on another failed mission. And Jennings: where was he? Woodes calculated Jennings must have enough riches from raiding the Spanish wrecks to last his lifetime and was wisely keeping a low profile somewhere. As to Vane – he had no idea where he might be lurking.

Woodes was always on edge, worried about resurgent pirates and Spanish attacks. Here at Nassau they were sitting ducks, easily picked off by a well-armed fleet. The *Delicia*, stationed in the harbour, badly needed careening, but he dared not remove the only protection the island – indeed the entire Bahamas – had.

His thoughts turned to London. With the arrival of each vessel his heart quickened in anticipation of an official letter, news, acknowledgement of his achievements and his struggles. And each time he was disappointed.

Woodes had chided, writing: *This poor colony should be no more accounted as part of his Britannic Majesty's dominions.* He had requested that Parliament reimburse him for the costs he had met personally for the public good. It did not suit him to be at the receiving end, longing for communication from people who had power over his own happiness, as surely as his wife had waited to hear from him during his many years at sea. Waiting was intolerable.

From attempting to persuade one errant woman to do his bidding, Woodes's mind turned to a more noble person. He took out a sheaf of fresh paper to continue his one-way conversation with those with whom he had a legally recognised partnership.

Woodes let his eye rest on the exquisite marquetry of his table cabinet. It was a thing of beauty and served a practical purpose as somewhere he could store his paper, correspondence, pens and ink. It had been made in Mexico for the Spanish market and was one of the few items he had retained for himself from the Spanish galleon he had conquered several years earlier. Whereas he did not share Spanish taste for Catholic religious artefacts – garish images of saints or elaborate crucifixes – he greatly admired the craftsmanship of Spanish furniture, and this portable table cabinet was his pride and joy. Furthermore, it belonged to him by right. He had been a privateer at the time; this was not looted goods but lawfully his. There was a clear line between piracy and privateering.

He began to write in his distinctive large swooping letters, *Most Gracious Sovereign. We, Your Majesty's most dutiful loyal subjects…*

He would flatter him and appeal to His Majesty's goodness. Surely the King could not ignore the responsibilities of the Crown?

30

JACK COULD DRINK ALL HE LIKED BUT THESE DAYS HIS wings were severely clipped. Anne had been clear, telling him, 'There'll be no more whoring on my watch.' Jack was restless. Once a seaman always a seaman. He wasn't surprised so many men had turned their backs on the amnesty. Like others, Jack had no interest in helping to clear land or drain swamps, or in becoming a farmer. He had no intention of making a long-term investment in the Bahamas. He had rolled his eyes in despair at some stories: former seamen who'd been too damned lazy to milk their cows, so had slaughtered them for their meat for a short-term profit. Such actions were depleting the farm stock as much as fevers. Poor Governor Rogers! Jack felt some sympathy for him.

The past weeks Jack had been preparing: nothing too hasty or obvious, nothing to give Governor Rogers or his spies cause for alarm. He had been making plans, with only Anne, Dick and George taken into his confidence. Dick and George would come with him, and he meant to recruit the rest of his crew nearer the time, some of them on the night of departure itself. He would put the word out, and many would jump at the chance to join him on the *Curlew*. He'd already decided which of them he'd accept and which he'd turn down. He knew the troublemakers amongst them, those who turned to the bottle the minute they woke, or were too quick to reach for a knife to settle an argument. On the other hand, he needed a crew hungry to fight and prepared to die for him and the prizes they sought. There was a fine balance to strike and you couldn't always get it right.

Jack had been revising his ship's articles, which would serve as their guide, and the legal framework that everyone signed up to, so it was vital they were thorough and fair. They would live and die by these rules: clarity about the share of prizes; obeying commands; keeping weapons clean; rules on smoking and gambling; safety around gunpowder. All shipboard life and governance had to be clearly outlined. As captain he was not above the rules; they applied to him as much as the rawest recruit.

What to do about Anne? She wasn't like his Cuban woman. Before he'd met Anne he had sailed back to Cuba hoping to see his *mujer encantador* and their child, and perhaps pick up where he had left off, but he had found her living with someone else and the child absorbed into a new family. He had actually felt very little emotion, though he left on good terms. No doubt his gift of several pieces of eight helped keep relations sweet, though the Cuban woman was no longer his own "sweet woman". Anne had taken that place in his life now, and she was different from any woman he had known.

He had been avoiding James, as he knew James had been threatening to kill him, and Jack didn't fancy a confrontation as in all likelihood it would be James who would end up dead. What would be the point? Jack had never been one to fight unnecessarily. Every death should be warranted, and he had no gripe against James, but James was understandably put out by Anne's desertion. Still, Jack didn't want to spend month after month watching his back waiting for James to get over his anger, so it was no bad thing to up sticks and move on. Now, after Anne's confrontation with Rogers, she insisted they both leave.

But what to do about Anne? It troubled him. He wanted her with him, but it was impossible. Unthinkable. He showed her the articles he was working on. The final clause was the one giving him a massive headache: the one about not allowing women on board. She read the scratched-out and rewritten clause and smiled with what he could only describe as a cunning look on her face.

'Change it.'

'What d'you mean, change it?'

'Just say something like, "Any man that meddles with a woman without her consent shall be killed."'

'But that assumes there might be a woman on board.'

'So? You're always saying a roving life is for anyone? Why not me too?'

'There's never been a crew with a woman on board. The men wouldn't stand for it.'

'That's no reason. What do I care what's happened before? I could make them change their mind. I know I could if I'm given a chance.'

'No! I tell you they wouldn't agree. None of them. George and Dick for starters.'

Anne pulled a face. She had little patience for his old comrades and felt they impeded her. 'Don't sail with them, then. Easy. Get other crew.'

Jack was irritated by her interference in matters that didn't concern her. Would she never let up?

'That's not going to happen. I decide who I take on board.'
Jack watched the frown deepen on her brow, so he tried to
appease her. 'We'll work something out. We'll meet up every
now and again.'

'Hah!' Anne's face reflected her view on that.

Together they came up with the final wording:

*'If at any time you meet with a prudent woman, the man that
meddles with her without her consent shall be put to death.'*

Prudent? Did Anne always show sound judgement? He
was unsure about any of it. The clause avoided the direct
statement there must not be a woman on board, but all the
men would of course assume there could not be. Would not
be. Everyone knew such a thing was impossible. Ship's life was
tough and rough, not fit for any woman. What's more, life was
shared, all of it without exceptions. As captain he couldn't
expect to have the privilege of his own woman, and she could
not be in disguise. Too many people in Nassau knew her, even
if she could concoct something for herself.

The problem haunted Jack, and he could not shake it off as
he continued his clandestine preparations.

He hadn't wanted to set alarm bells ringing with Rogers, so
the *Curlew* remained anchored at Nassau and he hired a pink
to go fishing: just himself, Dick and George. There was an easy
camaraderie between the three of them and Jack was happy
to be at sea again. They could manage the vessel between
them, yet it had a decent cargo capacity, which was vital. On
the surface this seemed a leisurely cruise, sailing in and out of
coves, criss-crossing the shallow waters of the Bahamas and
the islands off Cuba, a towed jolly boat bobbing in the wake
of the pink. But the excursion wasn't just about harvesting sea
supplies. They were gathering intelligence from whomever
they met: fishermen, turtlers, log cutters, traders on the coast

and traders at sea; they hailed them all and passed the time of day with them. It seemed leisurely, but there was a hidden purpose. All three of them were plotting, weighing up their chances and deliberating over the risks.

Dozens of turtles swam in the shallow waters off the Cuban coast and they had driven a dozen more onto the beach.

'Are you out of your mind? Has she turned your head soft like this one's belly?'

George paused and prodded the underside of a loggerhead turtle. He took up the slack in the rope he had hooked around the flippers and continued to drag the beast on its back towards the jolly boat. Other turtles they had levered onto their backs lay feebly flapping their flippers under the hot sun. Had Anne turned his head? Jack didn't like to think so, but George was a taciturn fellow; it was unlike him to speak up.

As George heaved, Jack and Dick pushed the turtle from behind, sliding it on its shell. The damned thing was heavy but, this alongside others they had gathered, would provide them with supplies. They meant to salt the meat and store it in barrels for themselves and sell the shells for which there was a ready market. All of this was easy enough.

But Anne? This was the topic on his mind as they toiled in the heat. His head ached, and it wasn't due to the scorching August sun.

'Well, Calico, the way I see it, you should shack her up somewhere.' Dick put in his penny's worth. 'You've done that before, haven't you? Yep, shack her up. I'll settle for her coming on board for a short while, just to get her away from Nassau. I'll not stand in your way if that's what you want to do. We can drop her off somewhere. She's your woman. Yep, she's your woman, so we can help you out.'

Dick panted and sweated and pitted his weight against the turtle's. Dick's brawny ex-prize fighter's bulk betrayed a soft heart and perhaps a soft brain. Even so Jack knew there was a limit to what he would tolerate and having Anne on board was clearly beyond his limit: beyond both Dick's and George's.

This past week sailing with George and Dick gave him time to talk it over, but neither of his companions would contemplate having her around, at least not for long. They weren't too friendly with her, to put it mildly.

They continued to haul and load their turtles.

'She's a witch, that one. Don't know what you see in her. Got to be one of the bossiest women about – got you twisted round her finger.' George let off steam.

'Rubbish!' Jack was indignant. He was perhaps a little in love with Anne, but he was still his own man. No woman would ever rule him.

George continued, 'Besides, she drives a wedge between us.'

'Yep, not like the old days, Calico.' Dick's eyes took on a faraway look. 'You, George and me, we could do anything…'

They'd met after the cessation of hostilities, sometime in 1714, and later they had all been under Jennings's command and got to know each other. Both Dick and George had voted for him as captain while in Vane's company, and Jack had relied on them during recent cruises. They were dependable and skilled seamen.

"The old days." Jack understood Dick's sentiment. They'd had freedom to rove as they wished, and nothing got in their way: not the law, and certainly not any woman. Now the law was tightening its grip, and he supposed Anne could be said to be tightening hers. Jack sighed. Life was getting complicated and he didn't know how to deal with it.

There was an added problem Jack hadn't shared with George and Dick. They didn't know she was with child. Anne had been upset to discover this, but they enjoyed sex together as often as possible, and he refused point blank to fix a fiddly sheep's gut onto his cock, with ribbons tied around his balls. What man would allow himself to be decked out like this, to suffer such an indignity to his masculinity? Not him! And to be fair, Anne had never requested such a thing. He hoped he could persuade her to stay in Nassau for a while until the baby was born.

Right now, getting the turtle on board their boat was the immediate problem – something taking muscle power and some engineering skills, with a sling and net to hoist the beast up. This much Jack could do; grappling with the "Anne problem" was a bigger challenge than the cumbersome loggerhead about to become ship's supplies.

Days later they dropped off the turtles and fish at Eleuthera for the flesh to be salted and stored, and while in harbour Jack ordered water supplies and other provisions. He was doing all of this out of the immediate gaze of Rogers. By the time intelligence reached Rogers that Calico Jack looked like he was provisioning himself again, he'd be gone.

He was ready. Well, almost.

Even as Jack sailed into Nassau harbour he hadn't settled on a definite plan of what to do with Anne. In any case Anne wasn't one to be told what to do – he'd learnt that lesson in the months they'd been together. She would take a hand in her own destiny.

In Charlotte's kitchen Anne began slicing another chicken. There was no end to appetites in need of satisfying.

'Nah, that's enough. Sit down.' Charlotte took the knife from her, pulled her away from the chopping block and steered her towards a chair.

Sinking back, slipping off first one shoe then the other, Anne allowed the activity of Charlotte's always-busy kitchen to continue without her help. Old Zac, the odd-jobs man, rolled in another cask of ale; two cooks sweated over steaming pots; another woman, up to the elbows in scummy water, swilled dishes; girls hurried in with empty jugs and hastily filled them before heading back to thirsty customers. And always Charlotte. In and out of the kitchen, checking a delivery man or woman was not short-changing her, making sure too much meat hadn't been put into the stew; disappearing back through the dividing door to make sure customers had paid for drinks, meals, girls.

Charlotte pulled up a chair in front of her. 'Here – give them to me.' She patted her lap.

Anne gratefully raised her stockinged feet and rested them on Charlotte's knees.

There was not an ounce of fat on Charlotte's spare body – she never stopped working – and now her knobbly fingers poked and probed the soles of Anne's puffy feet and tenderly stroked her swollen ankles.

'Ah, Charlotte, that's good… Don't stop.'

'Happy to sit for a minute or two.'

While Nancy had been easy to carry, this pregnancy was different, and Anne hated the fact her body did not feel her own; the baby seemed to be in charge. Months earlier Charlotte had asked, 'Pity this has happened so soon. Want to get rid of it?' But this time Anne had refused. Now, she looked beyond the growing rise of her belly to her aching feet and wondered if that had been the right decision.

'How can I expect to be at sea, doing a man's job when I can't stand on my feet more than a few hours helping you out? It's so unfair. There's Jack, free and fancy, having a good time fishing and God only knows what else with those two…'

'Oh, come on, you know that's not the case.' Charlotte pinched her foot lightly.

Anne had wanted to go turtling alongside Jack, but acknowledging she wasn't in any condition to do heavy work she had agreed to stay behind. But she begrudged "those two" – Dick and George – sharing precious time with Jack, fearing they were bound to try to talk him out of including her in their plans. And recently further thoughts had been troubling her; if she couldn't talk to Charlotte, then who?

'You think Jack will still want me? Not throw me over now I'm like this. It's been nearly four weeks since I've seen him, and look at me...'

'Hah!' Charlotte looked more amused than worried. 'Not like you to doubt yourself.' She continued to knead Anne's feet, giving the question some thought. 'I've known that son of a whore some years, and I'd say he cares for you well enough. The thing is, you two suit each other, that's obvious to see, and both of ya give as good you take. Not like Simple Simon – that was never going to last.'

Anne hadn't seen James for ages and assumed he must be off with Mr Harmon. She hoped he would get on with his life – find someone else, someone less demanding. What Charlotte said about her and Jack made sense.

'Yes, we do suit each other, I've never doubted the rightness of it, but, oh Lord, I wish babies didn't get in the way...'

Charlotte tapped the soles of her feet and pushed them off her lap.

'Well, it is on its way, whether you want it or not. My offer stands, you know that. And Calico thinks you should stay here too, you know that as well, just as I know you'll do exactly as you want at the end of the day.'

Charlotte went about her business, and Anne considered her words. Again. Jack wanted her to remain with Charlotte to have their baby, and while it was tempting, knowing she would be cared for, it would be something else to hold her back. And then what? Should she take the child with her? Should she find someone to look after it while she went off with Jack? Anne wasn't having it; it could be born on board the *Curlew* for all she cared. She intended to leave with Jack and would not allow "those two" to talk him out of it.

31

WOODES, AND OTHER GOVERNORS OF ENGLISH colonies, were promising rewards for pirates captured in their respective domains, and the money was not to be sneezed at: a hundred pounds for a pirate commander, forty for an officer, thirty for a lower officer and twenty for a private seaman. This would tempt some to try their hands as pirate hunters, and there were days when he himself could imagine nothing better than to be standing on a quarterdeck commanding his own vessel hunting down those vermin.

Rackham had been the most recent gang leader to forfeit his right to clemency by setting out to rove once more. He would be well out of reach of his jurisdiction by now, more's the pity, but there were many others out there.

Woodes had not presided over further hangings since the memorable day several months into his posting. He had meant that public display to act as a deterrent for ever, but men's memories were short, and to Woodes's dismay, they were turning back to their old lives in ever greater numbers.

The proclamation and offer of rewards had attracted the attention of Captain Price, who had arrived with his own vessel, the *Sea Hawk*. Woodes had met with Price and found him to be a sloppy individual, his jacket buttons missing, but if he got the job done what did it matter? However, Woodes had taken the precaution of involving himself in recruitment. If he couldn't captain a vessel himself, he could ensure the men put forward to Price were the best available from Nassau, though he suspected he'd be scraping the bottom of the barrel.

Jeremy knocked on his door and entered, followed by a group of scruffy seamen.

'These are the men, sir.'

One took off his hat, then replaced it, unsure of protocol. As his eyes went from man to man he recognised James Bonny, who had done some snooping around for him, but he didn't know any of the others.

Jeremy handed Woodes a list of their names and retreated to stand by the door.

'So you're all keen to sign on with Captain Price and see who you can bring in?' Woodes smiled encouragingly.

'We know their ways, and Captain Price is offering a fair share of the prize.'

Woodes turned to the smooth-faced seaman who had spoken. 'And your name is…?'

'Read. Mark Read, sir.'

Woodes glanced down his list of names and nodded. 'You were with Vane—'

'Forced. Not my choice.'

'Might we expect to come across him?'

Read grunted. 'Maybe. He was at the Spanish Main, last I saw. But you might see him first; talked about raising a fleet to take over here again.'

Woodes absorbed the news.

'I take it you, er, gentlemen, have reformed? All of you?' He needed to make sure.

Another fellow spoke up. 'If you mean we've accepted King's pardon, then yes, we have our papers.'

There was a shuffle as each man reached into his jacket. Jeremy interrupted. 'No need. I've looked them over – everything's in order.'

Woodes nodded and turned to James. 'Well, Mr Bonny. Perhaps I shouldn't be surprised you want to bring Rackham in, but I rather hoped you could have put it all behind you.'

'I want to get the bastard!' The words exploded from Bonny's mouth; his face flushed in anger. 'I want to be the one who finds him – and my wife!'

'Your wife?' Woodes could not hide his surprise but said no more.

He continued interviewing the men, enquiring about their backgrounds, probing and questioning. Hugh Jenkins was out; the man was a fixture at the waterside taverns virtually pickled by drink. And he would not contemplate putting forward the fellow with eyes and skin yellowed by fever, who might contaminate the whole crew. In fact, he wanted him out of his office as soon as possible. Woodes crossed out the names of the ones he decided would not be up to the job and handed the revised list back to Jeremy.

'Wait outside and Jeremy will give you the details.'

The seamen retreated, and Woodes beckoned to Jeremy to remain.

'Interesting. It seems that hussy hasn't learnt her lesson and is aboard with Rackham.'

'Mrs Bonny?'

'I just hope she knows what she's letting herself in for; it won't be a flogging she faces if I get hold of her, and she might rue the day she didn't take my advice. What kind of woman would take up this life?'

Most women of his acquaintance looked to better their prospects through a stable marriage with a steady husband who could provide for them, yet this young woman seemed hell bent on destroying herself.

'You will get them, sir. I'm sure of it!' Jeremy spoke enthusiastically and headed out to the waiting seamen. As he closed the door Woodes heard his cheery, 'Right, you lot, here's what's going to happen next.'

Woodes hoped these rough recruits were up to the job. Just as the *Delicia* must stay put guarding the harbour, so he could not leave his post to roam the seas as a pirate hunter. But Price would soon be on his way, and others might come forward to join his band of pirate hunters. Progress of sorts.

32

Mary meant to do her bit to rid the seas of bastards like Vane. Escape had been easy in the end. The *Prince* had been anchored at Roatan, off Honduras, where she had volunteered to replenish water. Once in the forest she'd done a runner. While others were scared witless by creatures in the forest, she wasn't fussed and survived well enough until her luck changed. It wasn't long before other more trustworthy vessels dropped anchor to fill water casks.

Leaning on the rail of the *Sea Hawk*, Mary contentedly pulled on her pipe, the tobacco rough stuff she had inherited from a dead seaman.

Frigate birds and boobies rode the crest of waves, dipping and diving, sometimes surfacing with a catch pinched between their beaks, throwing back their heads and swallowing whole fish. Twice she spotted leaping fish caught in the powerful beaks of seabirds lucky enough to swoop and snap their prey. These birds were also hunters in the vastness of the sea.

She glanced up at gulls hovering in the airstream, and higher still at gathering grey clouds in the cooler December sky. The wind was freshening and there would likely be rain before evening. She welcomed not just the chance of fresh drinking water but the luxury of a wash: hair, body and clothes. As accustomed as she was to shipboard life, she couldn't abide clothes washed in seawater. It wasn't just some feminine concern of hers, though she liked to keep herself cleaner than many of the reeking men around her; it was a practical consideration. Itchy stiff cloth rubbing under armpits, between elbows and behind knees caused rashes, then before you knew it skin had cracked and festered, and tropical heat invited infection.

In anticipation of a downpour, Mary pocketed her pipe and began to construct a water-catcher from a spare sail. Whatever work Captain Price had demanded of them had been done; the *Sea Hawk* was as clean as his unexacting standards required, and none of them offered to do more.

Life under Captain Price's command was reasonable enough, though his success at bringing in pirates and claiming rewards was dismal. For the past weeks they had cruised the waters of the Bahamas and south into the Caribbean Sea but had little to show for their efforts. Every so often they received intelligence from passing vessels and gave chase, only to lose their prey. And they had lost men who had deserted after discovering hunting pirates was not easy. It was like gambling in a gaming room: the odds were against you. Mary intended to stick this out another few weeks then jump ship if something better offered.

'Want a hand?'

James Bonny looked up at her as she secured the final corner of her water-catcher. She nodded and together they went in search of more spare sail. James was one of the easier men to get on with, a decent enough man, but he had a chip on his shoulder as big as a block. He could not put the past behind him and move on, which was an error to her way of thinking. If his wife had left him, there were plenty more women who would have him.

Once or twice Mary had come across James delicately stringing shells together into a fanciful necklace or knotting string into lacy intricate patterns. He'd talked to her then about his small daughter who had died; she could only offer sympathy and kept her own history and grief over a lost child to herself. Once they'd hailed a local trading vessel to receive news and found a family on board; James had given the girl his small gifts. Mary liked this about him. For all his roughness he was one of those men who needed a family to care for.

As others sat drinking, gaming or trailing fishing lines, she and James set about rigging up another canopy, and she let him begin the conversation.

'You think Price knows what he's doing? That we have a chance of bringing any of them in?'

She shrugged. 'Maybe. He learns what he can from each passing vessel. What more can he do?'

'True, but he's not crafty, that's the thing. He should be trying to think like a rover. Y'know, check out inlets and hidden coves and waterways rather than just cruising aimlessly in open seas.' It was James's turn to shrug. 'But I tell you, if we're to bring in Rackham—'

'Or any of them,' she offered quickly.

'Or any of 'em – we'll be lucky, and we'll pocket some coin.'

James began to climb a ratline with the sailcloth in his hand. 'But Rackham – he's the one I want. I should have stuck a knife in him when I had the chance.'

Mary kept silent and let James repeat his story, one she'd heard in various forms these past weeks.

'That bloody man – he turned her head with all his big talk. Anne's no fool. I can't understand why she did it, what she sees in him. And their baby – she must have had it by now. Wonder if it's a boy or a girl.'

James was jealous of his rival, Mary understood this, but from everything she'd heard about his wife – or past wife – she sounded like someone best got rid of.

'Forget about her – she doesn't seem worth it to me. She sounds a selfish bitch from what you've told—'

'No, no! Not really. She can be good fun, and full of spirit, at her best.'

James could criticise his wife, but no one else could. She grunted. 'Fair enough. Still, best not dwell on the past.'

A gust of wind tugged the sailcloth in her hand followed by a sudden drop in temperature. 'Let's get this thing rigged.'

They finished their task in silence and as they climbed down the first heavy drops of rain fell. Tonight, she would go down into the bowels of the vessel where she could be alone and have a thorough wash. She would find sanctuary among the cooped-up animals and ignore the malodorous manure and bilge water. More importantly, Captain Price finding a worthy prize for them was something else to look forward to. That had better happen soon or they were all wasting time.

Mary was on a mission to hunt down pirates.

PART THREE

1720

To Go Roving

My boat's by the tower, my bark's on the bay
Both must be gone by the dawn of the day.
The moon's in her shroud, and to light thee afar
On the deck of the Daring's a love-lighted star.

So, wake, lady, wake, I'm waiting for thee
On this night, or never, my bride thou shalt be.
Wake, lady, wake, I'm waiting for thee
On this night or never my bride thou shalt be.

A hundred shall serve, the best of the brave,
The chief of a thousand shall kneel as thy slave.
And thou shalt reign queen, and our empire shall last
'Til the black flag, by inches, is torn from the mast.

TRADITIONAL SONG

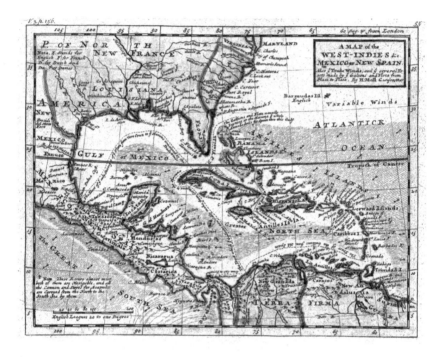

West Indies

33

THE *CURLEW* SWUNG INTO THE WIND, HER MAINSAIL rippling and sagging as she drifted to a standstill, rocking gently in the swell of the bay. Anne watched the ship's boat lowered and two men row towards where she waited on shore. She checked that her wooden box containing weapons and personal belongings was secure, hitched up her seaman's trousers, nervously fingered her short cut hair and angled her broad-brimmed hat over her eyes.

A message in a bottle, in their agreed hiding place, had been the means by which she had communicated with Jack. Weeks passed before Jack had retrieved it and left her a message which she had extracted with shaking hands. This communication had been frustratingly slow but had worked.

Three months earlier Anne had reluctantly complied with Jack's wishes to stay ashore. Towards the end of her pregnancy, Jack set off on the *Curlew*, while she set off for Great Inagua, one of the southernmost islands in the Bahamian chain where Charlotte had some long-lost cousin known for her midwifery skills. Here she would have her child, and here, out of the eye of Rogers, Jack could return for her while the child was cared for by this distant relative till they returned for it. Money talked, and Anne had a pouchful ready for the transaction.

Great Inagua was a desolate place, inhabited by thousands of wetland birds and abundant sea life, but few people. Anne had found the island's animal life, including magnificent flocks of flamingos, far more attractive than the rough men and women living in a small community on the south-west coast. As for Charlotte's long-lost cousin: few remembered her, and she hadn't been seen in years.

Here on this desolate island, Anne gave birth to a boy and immediately passed him to a wet nurse to look after. She did not want to suckle this child nor allow herself to grow to love him, bind her heart to him as had happened with Nancy. Instead she bound her breasts, heavy though they were with milk.

Day after day she worked relentlessly to bring strength back into her body, digging in the salt pans till her hands were hard and calloused and her back and arms ached. With her cutlass she rehearsed the moves Jack had taught her; timed how quickly she could load, shoot and reload her pistol; practised shooting targets at ever increasing distances. And through all this physical activity Anne pushed herself further and further away from her baby, away from the emotional tug of motherhood, in readiness for a life at sea; a life with Jack.

A deal had been struck with Jack, and with Dick and George, who could not be excluded from their scheming. Anne had bargained hard and long with the three of them. On her side she would enter Jack's crew as a youth named Will, a name she'd chosen after her father. If her disguise did not work she would be put ashore at first opportunity and that would be the end of it, and in all likelihood the end of her relationship with Jack. On Jack's part, he knew his crew could vote against him for colluding in this deceit. He could be voted off as captain, losing his command, even risking the *Curlew* being taken from him if the crew turned against him.

Flinty George did not like her, but for Jack's sake had agreed to play along with this elaborate charade. Other than George and Dick, Jack would pick up a fresh crew, who did not know her and might accept her as a youth without question.

She was about to put this to the test.

The rowers barely looked at her as they focused on cutting the best route back to the *Curlew*. Stroke by stroke she drew closer and closer, then reached out and touched the warm hull, took a steadying breath, and climbed the ladder. Jumping onto the deck, she expelled a long sigh.

As the crew worked to bring the *Curlew* around, adjusting the trim of the square sail on the foremast and the gaff-rigged mainsail on the mainmast, none of them showed any interest in her.

'Welcome aboard.' She felt his hand on her shoulder and turned to face Jack. 'Will, isn't it?'

Her heart skipped, but she could do no more than mumble, 'Captain.'

'Come to my cabin later – I'll get you to sign ship's articles.' Jack looked beyond her and yelled, 'Noah!'

'Cap'n?'

Anne turned to see a black fellow approaching.

'Noah here knows you're a landlubber. He's one step ahead of you, joined us recently. He'll show you the ropes. Before you can be any use to us, you've a lot to learn. Knots and splices for starters, then learn the lines.'

This black man was to teach her? Anne bit back a retort as Jack gave her a piercing look. 'Land laws are left behind. Understand? Oh, you'll be sharing Jim's hammock – you're on different watches. Dick'll sort you out.'

Anne stared at Jack's retreating back. This was not the welcome she had imagined from her partner whom she hadn't seen in months.

She helped Noah sort through tangled lengths of cordage, adjusting to the uncomfortable idea of being tutored by him. Out of the way of rushing feet, he taught her a range of knots and hitches and their different purposes. Some were familiar: the bowline and cleat hitches had been in constant use when she'd sailed Catfish or later with James, but there were many more to learn, and she'd have to become adept at the intricate art of splicing cordage if she was going to be a full, useful member of Jack's crew.

Noah spoke softly, in precise English. 'Now this shape.' He demonstrated a figure of eight, and she copied. Anne said little and kept her eyes down as she knotted, untied, then repeated more rapidly. She listened to the men around her joking, making small talk, complaining about the meal Davy had made. So Davy must be the cook. She would find out soon enough, just as she would find out which of them was Jim, her hammock mate.

Anne's stomach tightened as Dick ambled over, but to his credit he didn't blink an eye at her attire and only spoke to introduce another seaman at his side.

'Thomas here's our first mate – he'll sort out your watch duties. Yep, he'll tell you what's what and you'll soon be in the swing of things.' And with this Dick left her to Thomas, a slight man, no taller than herself.

'Jack runs three teams – there are enough of us for that. You're assigned to foremast watch, starting midnight.'

She was about to reach for her box of belongings when Thomas hefted it onto his shoulder as if it weighed nothing at all and gestured for her to follow.

They passed through the gun deck to the crews' quarters. In the confined space of the lower deck pungent odours filled her nostrils: sour sweat with whiffs of stale bilge water and animal dung drifting up from the depths of the hold. In the lantern's dim light Anne could see sleeping men in hammocks, curled on their side or lying on their backs, legs dangling. She calculated that even with a three-watch rotation she could not be guaranteed a hammock; there didn't seem enough of them, which would explain the slumbering bodies she had seen on piles of spare sails out on deck. Sleeping under the stars in fresh air had its attractions, but with any luck she'd be sharing Jack's bed as often as not.

Before long it was time to join her watch, and she threw herself into her new life.

A day later they were cruising past deep inlets and bays of southern Caicos Islands. Jack had not gone out of his way to talk with her, and she was bursting to tell him things and be with him, but he showed no interest in her and she could not read his face. Unresolved tension coiled tightly within her.

'Three periaguas! Bay ahead!' The cry came from the lookout.

As the *Curlew* sailed past a land spit she could see a small fleet of masted fishing canoes in the bay, each with four men aboard.

Jack's assessment was immediate. 'We should take 'em – canoes and tackle, all of it.'

Around her men growled, 'Aye,' and rushed to prepare.

'Shoot wide! Give 'em the message!' Jack shouted his order.

There could be no mistaking the purpose of the *Curlew's* business after musket shots cut through the air – and there could be no mistaking that those in the canoes meant to escape if they could. Fishermen hauled up nets and paddled to shore, digging deep into the water, the three craft fanning out, each aiming for a different part of the coast.

One canoe paddled all the harder for land, but those on the other boats thought better of it and before long were tied up alongside the *Curlew* with eight frightened fishermen on board.

An Irishman in Jack's crew with a hard face held a pistol to one of the fishermen, who flinched and appealed, 'You've got our boats, for Christ's sake. Let us go!' Another said, 'We've no weapons, just knives… gutting fish, y'know.'

The Irishman moved forward with a menacing growl. 'Gutting? Now there's a thought!' He took his own, larger, knife out of his belt raising it menacingly.

'Leave off, Paddy – we've got what we want. Row them to shore.' Jack shoved Paddy aside.

Paddy ran a lingering finger along the edge of his blade and kept his eyes on the fishermen. 'There's a pity – but you're the cap'n.'

The fishermen huddled closer, whispering, uncertain about this volatile Irishman tasked with getting them back to dry land.

'Davy!' The ship's cook shuffled forward at Jack's command. 'Bring up some ale.'

Davy, a small Welshman, blind in his right eye and with a crippled right arm, headed off with others to haul up a cask while Jack interrogated the fishermen. What had they heard of Rogers or the other governors? What other vessels had passed by? Where could they find the nearest fresh water? The sullen fishermen didn't look inclined to do much drinking or talking as Anne, along with Rye and Howie and others she didn't catch the names of, stripped the two canoes of everything of interest, including their catch of turtles and fish.

Late at night she found her chance to slip into Jack's cabin. It was fitted out much as she had seen it before: a built-in cabin bed, table and chairs, and a functional cabinet to keep navigation charts. The cabin was Jack's to sleep in, but ship's business was also done in this small room. When she walked in she found Jack with George poring over a chart spread out on the table. George rose swiftly and stomped out with a surly, 'You'll not be wanting me here.'

Jack stared at her. 'I've waited a long time…' A slow grin spread over his face lighting up his eyes.

The tension drained from her body as she flew across the room, leapt, wrapped her legs around his waist and her arms round his neck, almost unbalancing him. Oh, it felt so good to feel and taste his lips again! She whooped.

Back on her feet, Jack held her at arms' length. 'How are you?' He placed a hand gently on her belly. 'I was so sorry to learn your news, sweetheart. Really sorry.'

Anne's eyes darted away from his caring gaze. Part of the message she had left for Jack in the bottle concerned their baby, saying it was stillborn. It was a terrible thing she had done, and she did not want to think about any of it: her lie to Jack; abandoning the baby itself; the condemnation from the woman she had paid to keep the child for her, saying she would return soon when she had no intention of doing anything of the kind. She had been determined not to allow herself to love this small being and did not want Jack to be burdened either. Sweetheart, Jack's favourite term of endearment for her, felt more and more inappropriate. She pushed Jack's hand away from her belly.

'I'm fine now, really. It's done with and I'm strong again.'

And it was done with. Anne knew she had turned away from any kind of conventional life a woman might reasonably seek. She desperately wanted her new course to spiral outwards into a life of greater adventure, craved this, and only in rare moments of self-doubt pushed away uncomfortable thoughts that her life might be spinning out of control.

Anne met Jack's eyes as he looked at her tenderly. 'Still, it's a pity, Anne. I rather fancied being a father, y'know. We could've returned for the child, when we'd done with the roving life and set up home somewhere.'

'No doubt your time'll come.' She didn't want to dwell on the past and he sensed her reluctance to talk about it, assuming it came from a deep grief. Jack tactfully changed the subject.

'So, an eventful day!' He rubbed his hands and grinned.

'Oh?' She felt genuine surprise. Had it been eventful? The capture of small fry: these small fishing vessels and bits and pieces of tackle? She did not want to dampen his spirits so said no more.

Jack wedged the cabin door shut and turned back. He tossed her hat away, rumpled her short hair, mumbling, 'All gone – such a pity,' then pulled her shirt over her head and began to unwind the long cloth binding her breasts. She twirled around, hastening the release, laughing. It felt wonderful to be free of yet another thing constricting her.

Jack teased, 'Well, my dear Mrs Bonny, I do believe Governor Rogers has seen the back of you for good, so you'll not suffer his lashes on your lovely back. Not if I can help it!' He lightly kissed her shoulder.

Anne's dislike of Rogers had increased to something akin to hatred since she had been marched to his office and he had self-righteously lectured her about her morals and her marriage. She meant to irritate him as much as she could. She wanted to show that damned governor and all the others that they couldn't control her. They could not tell her what to do and how to live her life.

Jack impatiently kicked off his shoes. 'Get out of those blasted trousers.'

She didn't need any encouragement.

Intimate moments with Jack would be few and far between. Too many men about, and they were both far too busy.

Hand over hand Anne worked her way up the ratlines to the mainmast crow's nest, Noah at her heels. She paused halfway up, looked down and her stomach lurched. George had stopped whittling whatever he was carving and was watching her, waiting for her to fail. She would not give him the satisfaction.

'Look up. Jus' look up. First time's bad, then it's easy.' Noah prodded her.

She reached the futtock shrouds, the overhanging ropes set at an angle from the platform where she needed to be. Her legs were trembling, and her breath came in shallow ragged bursts. She had watched men doing this so many times and assumed it would be easy.

'Lean back, trust your arms and legs.' Noah urged her on.

She took a deep steadying breath, reached up and began to climb. For a sickening moment her leather-soled shoe slipped, but her hands and shoulders worked, and she clung on. Noah's calm voice continued behind her, as she hauled herself up to the overhang and onto the lookout platform part-way up the mast. At that moment she appreciated the nerves of the riggers who were sent to the very top in all weather. Sam was one such man in Jack's crew. The man was a bully, but when he wasn't drunk, and even when he was, he could move his bulky frame with great dexterity out along the highest yard ropes.

Standing with Noah on the cramped platform, she squinted out beyond the billowing sails of the *Curlew* to the distant horizon swaying before them. If another vessel had their topsails set she and Noah might spot them first; the *Curlew* was just employing its mainsails so would be less visible to others. The past days they had spotted one potential prey near sunset only to lose her during the night, and everyone was restless for action.

So far Noah had not asked about her background, but she felt curious about him. 'How did you come to this life?'

Noah continued to scan the horizon. 'Bad place...' He jerked his head towards the larboard bow. 'Barbados.'

They were cruising southward on the Atlantic side of the Windward Islands, with Barbados further out into the ocean. She nodded and waited.

'Bad master. Two times ran 'n hid. Master'll kill me if he catch me.'

Anne was certain her father's slaves would not run away. Why would they? He treated them well, to her mind. The way things were done in Barbados must be different – but she was unlikely to find out.

'You could still be hanged – if we're caught.'

Noah paused before answering. 'Cutting cane. Till y' can't stand. Till y' die. You ain't done that for sure. Like the cap'n said, no land rules. I'm free here.' He turned a piercing gaze on her. 'You, me, all the same. I ain't no man's slave.'

Anne looked away. No, she had never been forced to work from sun-up to sundown in intolerable heat; never been branded; felt a whip on her back; or had the threat of mutilation hanging over her for some real or imagined rebellion. Still, the idea that she could be on an equal footing with Noah was unsettling...

Noah returned his gaze to the sea. 'Never know who's huntin' us.' His hand went to his throat and he stuck his tongue out.

Hanging? Anne could not imagine dying; she was too young, too full of life. They were silent for some minutes scanning the horizon, then Noah spoke softly. 'Besides, I owe the cap'n.'

Noah owed Jack. What did he mean? Anne was about to ask him when Noah cupped his hands to his mouth and cried out, 'A sail! A sail! Ship ahead!'

Noah raised his arm pointing to eleven o'clock off their larboard bow. Anne shaded her eyes and could just make out the tiny blur of white against the blue of sea and sky. She cursed herself for not being first to see this; instead it was Noah, an escaped slave, and this didn't seem right.

Below, Jack had his spyglass out. 'Let's intercept her and see what she is.'

George shouted his orders. 'Man the braces! Set the tops'ls!'

Anne moved out of the way as Sam and other riggers pushed past and continued upward. Within minutes they were sidling along the footropes under the top yards, unleashing the sails, while below men hauled on the halyards. Jack was with the helmsman, and George fine-tuned the angle of the yards; the deck was cleared, and anything loose tied down; the fishing canoes they had been towing were hauled from the water and secured to the side of the *Curlew*.

Hours later they were closer. The large galley-rigged ship did not veer away, but with a westerly trade wind pushing her forward, continued a steady course towards the Caribbean Sea. Anne stood near Jack, George and Dick as they passed a spyglass back and forth between them.

'She's low in the water... Looks like a merchantman... I'd say she's easily two hundred tons and looks like she carries eight guns.' Jack passed the glass to Dick.

'I reckon her ensign is Dutch... yup... yup... I'd say for certain she's a Dutch ship. No pennants saying she's commissioned for war.' Dick nodded, satisfied, and passed the glass back to Jack.

Jack raised the glass again and squinted. 'Possibly... I'd say it is... It would make sense she's in these waters. She could be flying false colours, but—'

'Well, Captain?' The words were out of Anne's mouth. Her eyes were on Jack, waiting for his signal, waiting for his words.

'Prepare our own Dutch flag. They may even welcome us. Dick, Thomas, throw water over anyone who's not completely sober. Every man to check weapons and prepare to roll the guns out.'

Anne caught Dick's eye as he said, 'You sure? *All* the men to take up arms?'

'All hands, no exceptions. And keep them out of sight – only ten hands out on deck. We're just a merchant vessel for the time being.'

Anne hurried to retrieve her weapons, her heart racing. The previous day she'd scoured and oiled her pistol and wrapped it in its oiled woollen cloth. It was rust-free and battle-ready. She lined up to collect gunpowder in her horn: the horn O'Neil had carved in those far-off days. With steady hands she prepared cartridges, slotting paper wraps containing a musket ball and powder into a small leather pouch. On Great Inagua she had purchased a small hand-axe from some loggers, which she tucked into her belt along with her knife. Next she collected her precious cutlass, weighed it in her hand and slipped it into the belt hanger. She jiggled about restlessly, not wanting to be confined below deck. Surely there could be no harm in joining Jack.

Out on deck Anne could see they were making good speed against the heavily laden ship they were chasing, closing in, cutting off her line, but still the merchant ship did not change course. She made her way to Jack standing at the bow with Thomas and George, passing the spyglass between them.

Jack frowned at her. 'Told you to stay below.'

'I want to know what's happening.'

George mumbled, 'Trouble,' but Jack didn't send her away; instead he handed her the spyglass.

'Have a look. I don't think they've made up their mind about us, but they've cleared their decks so perhaps mean to fight. Can't be sure of numbers – some might be hiding below deck – but they'd be fools to fight.'

'Time to raise our flag, Cap'n?' Thomas stood ready to act.

Jack raised the spyglass once more to his eye and chuckled. 'I'm looking straight at a fellow with his spyglass trained on us.' He turned to Thomas. 'Shoot across their bow and have someone raise my flag!'

'I'll do it. I'll raise it!' Anne raced to midships. Hand over hand she hoisted Jack's pennant higher and higher up the mainmast till it reached the pinnacle where his signature flag, crossed white cutlasses, a skull above, against a black background, spread and fluttered in the wind. She had dreamt of this moment: being part of Jack's gang.

A boom from their bow swivel gun made her jump. Moving as one, men swarmed up from below, surrounded her, propelling her forward, sucking her into their vortex. Soon they were festooning the ratlines, brandishing cutlasses. She filled her lungs, joining a chorus of deep *whomps* reaching across the sea. This was a show of force: a solid wall of power.

She was no longer an innocent child clinging to the ratlines of the *William and Mary*. She was a woman prepared to fight, to kill if necessary, in defiance of the law.

34

JACK SIGNALLED HIS MEN TO CEASE HOLLERING AND raised his speaking trumpet.

'Ho! Heave-to! Heave-to!'

No response; he yelled again. 'Captain. If you resist there'll be no quarter. Understand? No quarter. Heave-to!'

Within minutes the chase's topsails were backed and Jack smiled in relief. He took up his trumpet and yelled.

'Where from? Where bound?'

An amplified voice with a distinctive Dutch accent reached him. 'Guiana. Bound for Amsterdam.'

'How many aboard?'

'Twenty-eight.'

A good size crew, Jack thought, but not nearly enough to thwart them.

'What're you carrying?'

'Logs, from our forests, bound for our shipyards.'

'And? What else?'

'Sugar and supplies.'

This wouldn't be the whole story. They wouldn't have cruised to South America with an empty ship.

'Before Guiana. Where from?'

He sensed a slight hesitation before the reply came. 'St Eustatius.'

It all made sense. The Dutch West India Company merchantman had done a circuit to West Africa, then across to the Windward Islands to offload a parcel of slaves in Dutch-controlled St Eustatius, before heading to their territories in Guiana to fill their hold with roundwood logs and sugar before the homeward stretch to Europe.

Jack figured he and his crew would not be able to offload much timber mid-ocean, but some would be useful. The sugar they could sell and there'd be much else of value. The biggest question was how many slaves had been sold.

In theory the slave trade was tightly regulated, but the Dutch liked to undercut the English, selling slaves cheaper to French and English living in the West Indies, which the English frequently sold on to the Spanish. Only the English were permitted to sell slaves to the Spanish, as agreed at the end of the war several years earlier, but trade laws were, to Jack, and most merchant captains and traders he knew, made to be circumvented if there was a profit in it. St Eustatius was a tiny island, but sloops and traders from all around, including English and French territories, congregated there to pick up slaves fresh off Dutch ships.

It was just possible this Dutch captain had accepted sugar and molasses from the French islands of Martinique or Guadeloupe in exchange for his slaves, but Jack expected that most transactions were in coins. Hard currency. There was a great shortage of this circulating in the West Indies. He could expect to pick up some Spanish pieces of eight, doubloons and dollars, with maybe some French pistoles and crowns amongst the mix, all of it useful. Jack calculated not all of this money from selling slaves would have been spent in Guiana on timber. Most likely the captain would have some other arrangement, perhaps with timber and sugar suppliers in Guiana awaiting payment from sales in Holland.

Jack picked up his trumpet again. 'Bring all your men out on deck. Put your weapons where we can see them. We're coming aboard.'

It was to be easy then. The *Curlew* carried eleven guns; four mounted upon wheeled wooden carriages on larboard and starboard sides, a mix of four-, six- and nine-pounders, whatever he had been able to lay his hands on; two swivel chase guns were mounted at the bow and another at the stern. For the time being they wouldn't be needed.

Jack scrutinised his men all pumped up and ready to fight, armed with pistols, cutlasses and knives, some with muskets and axes. His eyes rested on Anne. Over the past days he had been astounded no one had discovered her disguise, but seeing her now, dirty, dishevelled and committed to the job at hand, even he would not guess her to be female.

The helmsman eased the *Curlew* to the windward side of their prize, with a plan to board amidships. They had a choppy sea to contend with but nothing they couldn't handle. Jack kept muskets trained on the Dutch captain and his helmsman as grappling irons were thrown across and the vessels lashed together. Within minutes they had boarded, rounded up the nervous crew and begun carrying up goods from below, sorting and stacking rope, spare sail and ship's tackle.

Jack confronted the middle-aged Dutchman, whose stony face betrayed shock and disbelief – and perhaps shame he had surrendered without putting up a fight. The Dutchman stared at him with unveiled contempt.

'And who the devil am I receiving onto my ship?'

If the only resistance the captain offered were some choice words, Jack could handle that. 'Captain John Rackham – Calico Jack if you wish.'

The Dutch captain's lips curled. 'The day these seas are clear of your kind, I'll be a happy man.'

'You say *your kind*, Captain, as if my men and I walk the earth with three legs or two heads. I've yet to meet any man of the sea, or customs officer at any port, who didn't ignore the law for his own gain. You included.'

'What? You're suggesting I am a pirate? Such nonsense!'

'No, but you'll have traded freely with whoever you like if you think you can get away with it…'

A flush spread over the Dutch captain's neck and cheeks. What Jack said hit the mark. Everyone wanted to profit as best they could from whatever enterprise they undertook – and the blasted governments back in Europe were forever imposing new trade restrictions on their American and Indies colonies.

Jack continued. 'I'm a betting man. I bet you'll be long dead before the day comes the seas are free of us.'

The Dutchman leered. 'Let's have a private wager. Unless you mean to kill me yourself, which would be unsporting. My name's Willem van den Oetelaar – remember that – and look out in shipping journals for news of my death. And you – I'll remember your name and will be looking out for it – in the broadsheets. Your trial and execution will be sure to be recorded.'

'Hah! Let's not talk of death. You see we've been generous to you and your men – none harmed… yet. Bring up your brandy and rum; I mean to share a drink with you and learn about your entire cargo, particularly your slaves. Details: how many men, women and children you purchased; if any died during the passage; how many you sold. I want to see bills of lading and learn about your personal investment. If I doubt your words, or if your documents are missing, I'll question your men. Understand?'

Jack had already assessed the tonnage and calculated the human cargo it was capable of carrying. He knew, more or less, what each negro male, female and child would fetch at market if they'd all arrived in reasonable health. While Jack had not had any formal schooling, early in his life he had learnt to calculate in his head: to add, subtract and multiply.

A clamour grew around them from caged chickens dumped on the deck, the entrapped birds flapping and squawking, their clucks soon joined by the bleats of goats ambling forlornly up and down looking for food. The sound of a dog's frenzied yapping rose above the cacophony of other animals and cursing men.

'Stay, or I shoot!' For all that she spoke in a lower tone, Jack could not mistake Anne's voice. She was with Paddy and Jim, all with pistols trained on a young man who had broken free from the group of mariners under guard to run after the small dog.

Paddy placed himself between the whey-faced seaman and his pet, keeping them separated while the mutt nipped Paddy's ankles, trying to return to his master. Jack laughed: let Paddy have his sport. He turned back to Captain... van den something. He pulled up a box and sat, gesturing to the captain to do the same as if they were at Charlotte's or Betsy's watering hole with the whole afternoon and evening stretching before them.

Dick ambled over, a demijohn of brandy in his hand and two drinking vessels. 'Found this in the cabin, Calico. Might help the conversation along.'

Jack poured some for himself and for the Dutch captain, whose name still eluded him.

'We'll leave you enough supplies to get to the next port. So... what did you get for your parcel of slaves?' The Dutchman leant forward and rested his head in his hands. Jack prodded his shins. 'What coin, Captain? And where're you keeping it?'

The Dutch captain raised angry eyes, looking disinclined to share either a drink or information. Jack gave him a further prod. 'See your fine young fellow over there? The one with the dog...'

'No harm. You promised no harm!'

'But Paddy hasn't the sweetest of tempers.' Jack leant forward. 'Tells me he killed his dear old ma back in Ireland.' Paddy had told Jack this story; whether he was blagging or for real he couldn't be sure, though he wouldn't put it past him.

Sam now joined in the sport with the dog. He scooped up the mutt and dangled it over the side by its hind legs taunting the seaman, saying, 'Woof woof!' while Paddy kept the desperate fellow at arms' length. Just as Paddy let the fellow go and he raced to rescue his dog, Sam flung the animal out to sea. Shit! Jack thought.

'B-b-bastard!' The whey-faced seaman thumped Sam's chest; Sam punched him in the gut; Jim yelled at Sam, 'What'ya do that for? It was his pet!'

Jack jumped to his feet. 'Dick! See to it!' As soon as he was satisfied Dick was sorting out the fracas, he turned back to the captain. 'So, where were we?' But before they could resume their discussion Dick shouted.

'Calico!' Dick had the dog-loving seaman by his arm and was leading him forward. 'English he is. Carpenter. We can use him. Yup, we can use him.'

'Ah.' This got Jack's attention. 'What's your name?'

'F-F-Francis B-B-B-Bates.' Whether Francis had a stutter or was terrified Jack couldn't tell, but that aside, he had expertise they sorely lacked. The *Curlew* needed work done, and they'd been getting by with the inadequate skills of one of his crew – and God forbid if they ever needed to call on his competence as a surgeon. Jack was delighted with this find. 'Excellent! You're coming with us, Francis.' He slapped the fellow on the shoulder.

'N-n-no! P-p-please, I beg you!' Even more colour drained from the fellow's sallow face.

Captain van den Oetelaar – Jack remembered his name now – stood and faced him.

'Leave him be. You'll not force any of my men to join you.'

Jack's eyes narrowed. 'Sit down, Captain. We're inviting him to join us – aren't we, Francis?' He smiled at the fellow. 'Can't leave an Englishman on a foreign ship; he wouldn't be safe.' He laughed at his own feeble joke then turned back to the captain.

'We'll take what we want – including your men. Dick!' He turned to his old comrade. 'Check out the rest of the crew – some of them may wish to join us in any case. If they've a cooper on board we'll take him too. Let's get this done.' Dick nodded and set off towards the merchant crew still under guard.

'Jim! Jim!' Jack yelled, and the lad rushed forward, eager to please.

'Captain?'

'Take others with you – help Francis bring up all his tools.' He pushed Francis away. 'Go! Hurry!'

Jack assessed progress. Roundwood logs were being hauled from the hold; handy for masts and spars, should anything get damaged. He needed to press on.

'Paddy! Will!' He beckoned them.

'Now, Captain.' Jack turned back to the distraught Dutchman witnessing his livelihood being destroyed. 'Your coin, if you'll be so kind. Your cabin?'

The captain shook his head, no longer looking inclined to be either kind or obliging. In one swift move Paddy deftly sliced the tip of the Dutchman's ear off. He yelped in pain and raised a hand to the bleeding wound.

'Next time be quicker.' Paddy put away his knife, cocked his pistol and looked as if he meant to use it. Jack knocked it aside. 'Keep your powder for another time. Killing a man should mean something.' Jack turned back to the captain.

'Lead on, show my men where your money is: Paddy, Will. When you're done bring me what you find. He and I can tally the coin with what's in the ledger.'

Jack knew Paddy would winkle out anything of value that might be hidden, and he had deliberately sent Anne with him, as she would get more of a thrill from lifting this rather than the mundane but valuable things they were offloading. As far as he could tell, Anne hadn't quite accepted that his two cruises with Jennings lifting the Spanish treasure were exceptional cases. He had tried to wear down her insistence on joining him by talking about the reality of it all, and still she didn't quite take in what he said. She clearly had her own reasons for being here, but he hadn't quite fathomed them.

'Tom!' Jack yelled to his crew member in charge of the guns and ammunition. 'What's the powder situation?'

Jack looked with satisfaction at the organised chaos around him. Like a pack of wild beasts that might only succeed in catching prey once every several days, this prize would feed his pack for a good while. They would celebrate later. They had food and drink enough, and for him at least, sex might be on the menu. He hoped Anne would find her way to his cabin tonight. This would round off the day nicely.

35

Anne had celebrated with the rest of them deep into the night before making her way unobserved to Jack's cabin. Now, naked and astride Jack on his bed, Anne let herself go.

Jack pressed his hand over her mouth. 'Shush – you'll wake the devil from his sleep. Worse, you'll wake the crew.'

Anne nipped his finger, he yelped, and she laughingly urged him to shush. All her pent-up energy had been released through a long bout of drinking and fucking and now she was spent, her brain as soft as sheep's wool. She should get to a hammock before she fell asleep by Jack's side. She kissed him, pulled on her shirt without rebinding her breasts – that could wait – and pulled on her trousers. Cautiously she opened the cabin door, peered into the dark and stepped out.

Hoarse singing and laughing of carousing men reluctant to call it a night drifted down. They, along with the watchmen, were the only ones awake. Creaking timbers and soft thuds of waves against the hull were comforting sounds, and snoring men guided her towards the sleeping quarters.

A man separated from the shadows, his hands propelling her backwards pinning her to the bulkhead. 'Been watching you.'

Who was this? She could barely see, but the figure looming over her was huge and stank of rum. He leant closer, whispering, 'This is why he has a pretty boy on board.'

She tried to wriggle free, but his hands were clamped against her shoulders.

'What're you on about?' She tried to laugh it off. She could handle this, would offer to share a drink. The man tightened his grip, the weight of his body against her, the stiff hairs of his beard brushing her cheek as he whispered, 'A sin – sodomy.'

She had him now: Rye, a man she had barely spoken with; had taken no interest in and assumed had none in her.

'Do you like it, hmm? Does it feel good – what Calico does?' His soft words were menacing.

'Get off, you drunk idiot.' She tried to push him away, but his weight crushed her ribs and she could scarcely breathe. All her weapons had been thrown back in their storage box while she feasted and partied. Still, she was confident she could deal with this man and more than anything she wanted to avoid a scene.

'What the cap'n enjoys, the rest of us can too. So, what does he like, eh?'

Rye spun her around to face the wall and pinned her, feet barely touching the floor, one cheek pressed into the rough wood, breath knocked from her.

'Don't bother telling me. I'll find out m'self.'

A calloused tarry hand covered her mouth while his other hand wrenched down her trousers. She tried to twist away but it was impossible to move and her cries for help were muffled. The full weight of his body pressed against her and his powerful fist connected with the side of her skull, jerking her head sideways.

She struggled for breath; his hand clamped over her mouth and nose. Fresh pain shot through her as she felt the skin of her anus ripping. She gasped. This wasn't as it was meant to be, thrust against a wall, skewered by a reeking drunken seaman's cock. As her body rocked back and forth memories of the first time she had been raped flooded back. She had sworn it would not happen again, and yet here she was, little more than a carcass for this disgusting man to poke. During the past days she'd listened to men joking about others buggering the hogs and goats kept in the hold. Maybe they did. Maybe men could take pleasure in such a thing. Right now, she was little more than a sow being defiled.

Tears spilt down her cheeks as Rye pumped away, emptying himself into her. She was dizzy, hurting, fully awake and thinking ahead. One thing was certain: she would have her revenge. Suddenly she was free, her body sliding to the floor, and she could hear Noah's voice, soft and silken: 'I could slice you – but I'll leave you to the cap'n.'

In the dark she could just make out Rye's head snapped back and the blade of Noah's knife at his exposed throat as he complained loudly, 'What do you care if I fuck Calico's cabin boy? You want him too? Take him. I'm done.'

'Fool. All of you with sand in your eyes.' Noah spoke scornfully before turning to her. 'You all right?'

'Yes...' She managed a hoarse whisper. 'Thank you.'

Noah scoffed. 'I ain't done this for you. Now, very slow. Move, dog.' Noah pushed Rye forward, the blade of his knife against his neck.

She would not be sleeping for the remainder of the night – and neither now would Jack.

At dawn, out on deck, Anne stared at her assailant from her left eye. A dark bruise covered the right side of her face and the swelling had forced that eye shut.

Rye stood between four men, head bowed, shirtless, arms bound behind, ankles shackled, looking as sick as a dog knowing it would be whipped. And he did expect a flogging: the cat-o'-nine-tails lay ready and cord to bind him. She had not an ounce of sympathy for him and would take her turn wielding the whip on his bare back.

Every man had been pushed from his hammock or kicked awake from wherever he had fallen into a drunken doze. One by one men staggered up from below, mumbling and curious. The deck had become crowded, not just with men but with goats tethered to the railings, and jumbled-up goods and tackle taken off the Dutch vessel; everyone had been too intent celebrating to bother clearing up. All the crew were to witness this punishment; the only exemptions were the helmsman and lookout. Jack stood rigid, his face set. He had barely spoken to her since she and Noah had burst into his cabin a few hours earlier; he had offered little sympathy, just saying to clean herself up and he'd deal with it.

'Everyone here?' Jack asked, and Dick nodded.

Jack walked to where she stood, and without looking at her, grasped her shoulder and led her back to stand by his side. He took a moment to compose himself.

'We have rules, and this man' – he pointed to Rye – 'will be punished for striking another.' Her face provided ample evidence. 'As captain it's my duty to uphold our articles.' Jack hesitated, let go of her shoulder and took a step forward. 'But there's more to say, and, so help me, something more I need to do – as I swore I would long ago.'

All eyes were on Jack, waiting and puzzled, and Anne was wary.

'Before that you all need to know something.' His gaze encompassed the men gathered in front of him and came to rest on her. Anne's heart thudded. Surely he wouldn't betray her. She would be put ashore and that would be the end of it after barely a week. Jack gripped her shoulder again and took a deep breath. 'Will's not—'

'Jack, no!' Anne twisted out of his grasp.

'Shut up. Shut your damn mouth!'

This was to her! Jack was yelling at her! Anne opened her mouth to argue, then felt the tip of George's cutlass in her back. What was happening? Was she guilty? Would they turn on her? Jack grasped her shoulder again and spun her back to the crew.

'Perhaps I was wrong. If you think so, vote against me – I can't stop you.'

'About time you spoke. 'Bout time, I reckon.' Dick nodded at Jack.

'Did I ask your opinion?' Jack wheeled around to face his quartermaster.

'He's right, Calico, and you know it.' George's grating voice came from behind.

'This is not for you to say!' Anne yelled at Jack.

'Hold your tongue. If you can't I'll have you removed. I'm captain and I will speak.'

'Goddamn, Jack!'

Anne twisted out of Jack's grip. In a frenzy she tore at her shirt, ripping the fastening at her throat. She had not rebound her breasts after her visit to Jack's cabin the night before and now stood defiantly before the company of gawping men, her breasts exposed for them all to see.

'There. Don't tell me you've never seen these before!' Anne stood naked for a moment before pulling her shirt up to cover herself. She had made her point.

Around her men reacted: 'Fucking hell!' 'Jesus Christ!'

'Nobody dares touch her.' Jack was taken off guard. They all were.

Anne could hear their condemnation as they cursed and shouted in protest. 'Knew something was odd. Fuckin' women!' Paddy spoke, but others shouted equally loudly. 'We couldn't've got away with it – it's not right!' 'Christ! What the hell's she doing here?'

'You know they're right, Jack. Give 'em time to consider things. Give 'em time and let them think on it.' Dick offered his counsel.

Rye, the muscles on his neck taut, appealed, 'Let me loose! I've done nothin' wrong – you know it. It's that bastard who's broken the rules bringing that whore on board.'

Jack shook his head as if to clear his brain. 'We don't have an article forbidding women on board. It says, "Any man who meddles with a prudent woman without her consent shall be put to death."' Jack glared back at Rye. 'Well, we have a woman here and she has been meddled with and I will punish you!'

'Deceitful son of a bitch!' Rye tried to charge Jack, but his shackles and the men guarding him kept him back, though they looked uncertain about whether or not to let him go.

Men whispered and shuffled. This was beyond anyone's experience – no one knew what to do. Jack gave a new order.

'Tie him up. Remove his trousers.'

Rye howled in protest and fear. All the men stared at Jack in confusion.

'I promised long ago to cut off the balls of any man who touches her. She is not the ship's whore.' Jack withdrew his knife and turned to Paddy and Thomas. Anne could sense their hesitation to follow orders. The muscles in Jack's neck bulged as he yelled again. 'Do it! My fucking orders! Tie him up! Not that way – I don't want to see his back, I want his balls.'

Jack's command could barely be heard above the protests of the crew and the outraged cries from Rye, a man now truly fearful of what was to come.

'Stop him! He has no right! Will you stand by? Fucking cowards! I was drunk, so help me. Which one of you hasn't poked a whore when you had the chance? I fucked her in the arse! So what? So fucking what? Deceitful bitch!'

A sow! A sow! A sow to poke. That was what she had been reduced to. Anne shoved Jack forward from the small of his back, 'Do it, Jack! Do it!'

'Bind him! Bind him tight!' Jack bellowed.

More of the crew hesitantly joined Paddy and Thomas, grasping the thrashing, shrieking man resisting all attempts to wind and bind him.

Jack, knife drawn, approached the immobilised man, but others in the crew were moving forward as if to restrain him. No! No, this must not happen. The beast must be punished, and she had come prepared.

Swiftly Anne moved to a better position, reached for the loaded pistol tucked in her trousers, raised it and with the only eye that could see, took aim and fired. Her shot whistled past Jack and hit Rye in his chest. The sound of the shot startled everyone: the dying sailor as blood seeped out, and the dozens of men who glared with unveiled hostility at her. She was trembling.

'I'm not a whore – not a sow to be poked – or whatever else you animals get up to!'

Hisses emitted from narrow-eyed men as they turned from her to Jack and then to each other. A rumble grew, like thunder rolling in. Then a different sound: steel against steel; cutlass edges scraped against knife blades as men edged forward. Jack drew his cutlass, George and Dick did the same, and before her two opposing groups fronted up. Would there be a mutiny? Had she caused this? Would they turn on her next?

She rushed between the two groups.

'Stop! Listen!' She would be heard, even if she died in the process. 'He deserved what he got.' She jerked her head towards the slumped body of Rye. 'I'd do the same to any man who touched me without my say-so.'

If this was meant to calm the situation she had misjudged it; her words antagonised them further and fresh curses filled the air. Jack pushed her aside. She expected a knife hurled in her direction – or Jack's.

'Wait! Wait!' Anne flung her arms wide and willed the men to pause and back off. She looked into their faces, many with sunken cheeks, pock-marked skin and broken teeth, all of them desperate to survive, to find a place for themselves in this world. She took a steadying breath.

'I'm working – doing everything each of you is doing. Why shouldn't I be here?' Her voice sounded firm, though inside she was quaking.

George's words spat in her ear: 'This'll not win you friends, Mrs Bonny. You're responsible for breaking up the whole fucking company.'

'Lower your weapons. It's done with.' Jack slowly and deliberately sheathed his cutlass. 'I saw no other way to have her aboard. She wants a part of this life, and I want her here with me. It's unusual – perhaps never happened before.' Jack rubbed his forehead. 'Vote as you must, both for me to continue as captain and to accept her in the company. Or not. Let her have her say, that's all I ask. You'll find me in my cabin – while it's still my cabin.'

Jack walked away, head bowed.

'Right then, c'mon now, put yer weapons down.' Dick was coaxing. 'Jack's always been fair, yer know that, so think long and hard before yer vote. Yep, I know he was wrong, but me and George were in on it, so we share some blame. No secrets and all that. Jack's 'specially fond of her.'

Fond of her! Fond of her! It sounded like she was Jack's lap dog. Fury poured from Anne's mouth – from her soul.

'This isn't just about Jack and me. This is about your life – the life I want to be part of, and why shouldn't I? Forget I'm a woman. I haven't asked favours. I hand ropes, reef sails, clean the shitty heads, take my turn at the helm with the rest of you.'

Anne appealed to some whose names she knew: Francis, the carpenter forced to sign articles, looked too dumbfounded to say anything; Sam, the burly rigger, looked as if he would rape her himself given half a chance. Her gaze moved swiftly to Paddy's face, only to see a deep frown creasing his forehead and his piercing blue eyes glaring angrily at her as if he had been personally cheated. And Noah? Why did he look so hostile? She turned to George, but the sharp angles of his cheeks and narrowed eyes and mouth gave her no comfort. No, not flinty old George. Dick then? For all his brawn he was a little soft in the brain, no doubt a legacy of his days as a prize fighter. He'd go to the ends of the earth for Jack, but even he looked at her and shook his head. Her gaze darted away from Davy's mutilated face, his good eye glowering back at her. Thomas, perhaps? He'd been transported to the Indies for some petty crime before he turned pirate. She'd had a laugh with him the past week. Jim? Surely young Jim would understand. She sought his face, scarred deeply by oily spots, but he looked terrified by the very sight of her. Could she count on no friends amongst them?

Dick nodded to her. 'We'll come to some agreement, lass, and put you ashore somewhere safe. Go down and wait with Jack while the company votes. Yep, I'd go on down to Jack if I were you.'

She jumped on an upturned box to give herself a platform to make her case and reeled round to take in the entire crew.

'All of you have your reasons for being here, and no one cares; no one asks about your past life. So why shouldn't I be here alongside Jack and all of you? What does it matter I'm a woman, if I'm prepared to fight and die by your side?'

Hostile faces stared stonily back at her.

'You heard. Go down to Calico. Give him a comfort fuck before you leave – he might need it.' Sam's scornful words caused a ripple of laughter. She swung to face him.

'Is that all you can think of? You just think I'm Jack's woman? You saw me shoot Rye just now – and I'll do it again. I'll do it again if any man thinks he's better than me because he's stronger or has a cock between his thighs he wants to use against me. If any of you dare do what Rye did, you'd best kill me afterwards rather than let me go, because I'll come after you. I'm a good shot, even with one eye.'

The faces staring back were not yielding to her arguments.

'I can chase down prizes and fight alongside you, and I'm willing to work hard and share your life. What more can you want of anybody – man or woman?' The faces remained unyielding. 'I'll stay as Will if you think it's easier – stay in these seaman's clothes. Why should it matter?'

George reached up, pulling her off the box. 'They've heard enough, Mrs Bon—'

'Don't you dare call me that again. Don't you dare!'

She was furious at their narrow-minded views. Furious they could not share her view on how things could be and accept her as part of their gang. She stared at the gathered men, feeling drained and exhausted. There was nothing more she could think of to say.

36

During the past hours it had crossed his mind more than once that Anne was more trouble than she was worth. Jack had fleetingly wondered if she had encouraged Rye, but Noah's story tallied with hers. He felt furious – at his own jealousy and with her for shooting Rye. It was his job to mete out punishment and she had undermined his authority.

By leaving Anne to face his company Jack had given her rope, and he would soon find out if she had hanged herself or saved her skin. Bringing her on board had been a massive gamble. He had a great deal to lose: his position as captain, possibly the *Curlew* and his whole livelihood – or maybe he would lose Anne if they voted to keep him but rejected her. Had she turned his head as Dick – or was it George – had once implied?

Jack reached for the demijohn of brandy from the Dutch captain's stock, the large glass vessel protected with a sturdy wicker casing and handle. He took a slug, then another. He barely glanced up when Anne arrived and settled on the chair across from him. Silently they passed the brandy back and forth.

Jack had never known a vote to take so long. By now he reckoned the sun must be fully overhead, and what was more he was starving. Despite his nerves he needed food in his belly.

'Come in and let's hear it.' He responded to the knock and rose unsteadily to greet Dick and George, trying to read their faces. 'Let's have it. Do I still have a vessel to my name?'

'There's good news and bad news.' George helped himself to the brandy.

'The men had a lot to say Calico – yep, a great deal to say. We could've all been gone – all four of us. None of them took a fancy to our trickery... I'll have some of that.' Dick grabbed the demijohn from George and drank deeply.

'Get on with it!' Jack slammed one fist into the palm of the other, longing to punch someone.

George leant his knuckles on the table, ignoring Anne, looking directly at him. 'In the end it was a close vote, Calico, but the *Curlew*'s still yours.'

Jack sank back into his chair.

'And me?' Anne spoke flatly. 'Am I the bad news?' Her good eye, glazed by exhaustion and brandy in a face puffy and purple, turned to George.

George didn't look at her but kept his eyes on the drinking vessel. 'In a way, yes, she's the bad news.'

Jack's heart sank. Having Anne aboard was too much to hope for, then.

George turned to Anne. 'You and Jack – it gets in the way – causes trouble – and this stupid idea of yours was bound to fail.'

'That wasn't the main thing, George. Be fair. That wasn't the thing worrying the men most.' Dick spoke out. 'In the end, they didn't really care that she's your woman, Jack.'

George laughed harshly. 'That's a fact. No one else is keen to have her! Calico, the vote for you to remain as captain was soon decided. It's her that's the problem.'

Anne leapt to her feet, fists clenched, looking like she'd like to attack George. 'You've never accepted me. You think I get in the way of your men's life together.'

Jack wished there could be peace between them. 'Let's have the rest of it. Tell us what happened. Do we understand the men won't accept her in the company? Is that the bad news? Spit it out.'

'No, Calico, not as bad as that.' Dick smiled.

What could this mean? Jack glanced at Anne, but her eye was fixed on Dick.

'She can stay.' George's words came out reluctantly as if they were stuck in his throat, and he turned to Anne. 'And for the record, just so you know, Mrs Bonny – or Anne or Will or whatever the hell you want to call yourself – I voted for you to stay too.'

'Anne can stay!' Jack felt enormous relief, enormous gratitude to his two friends who had negotiated this. He slapped George and Dick on the shoulders, then he frowned. 'You said there was bad news…'

Dick cleared his throat. 'Look, Calico, the men don't much like what happened to Rye, to put it mildly. What she did wasn't right, y' know that. Everyone has to keep to the rules, and they don't want you sticking up for her. Yep, that's about the long and short of it.'

'I don't need protecting. No favours,' Anne snarled at George.

'Not you! Some of them want protecting from you and your hot temper.' George glared at her. 'The bad news is – and you listen – you listen well, my fine lady. You have their promise not to meddle with you – and you make damn sure you don't do anything to rouse them. Know what I mean? If you cause, or if anyone even suspects you've caused, another episode like this, then you're off the *Curlew*. First opportunity.'

Jack nodded. This seemed fair to him, and would keep both her and the men in line.

'That's not quite the end of it, though – not quite, George.' Dick prodded George to continue.

George stared directly at Anne. 'If you fly off the handle again and kill or injure anyone else, you'll be marooned – dropped off on the first uninhabited island we come to, and it will be my pleasure to row you out.' He leered at her. 'You've proved you're a good shot. Well, your life may depend on it, while your powder supply lasts.'

Anne snarled. 'Is that it? You'll never have a reason to put me ashore on some goddamn island.' She pushed her chair back, stumbled the few steps to his bed, flopped down and was asleep the moment she hit the mattress.

Jack longed to sleep as well, but he had work to do and so did his crew. His mind began to churn. Dick had records to keep on the division of loot; Howie, the bosun, had inventories to update; George had plundered charts and ship's instruments to sort out; Tom needed to record the ammunition and weapons brought aboard, and everything needed storing and securing.

Jack nodded to both his companions as they headed out. He glanced back at Anne sprawled face down on his bed, and on an impulse reached out to hold George back.

'Find out when Anne's next watch duty is – let's hope it's not for a while. No favours, mind. If she's due out now, I'm ordering you, as second in command, to personally come down to wake her – she'll love you for it.'

George's face took on the shape of pure horror. Laughter bubbled up in Jack's throat from deep in his belly and exploded with a roar; all the tension of the past night came with it. A tight band that had been squashing his ribs fell away and he could breathe again.

37

MILE BY MILE THE *SEA HAWK* WAS GAINING ON ITS quarry.

'Can't be sure, boys, but looks to me she must belong to one of 'em. If I were a betting man, I'd say its Rackham's outfit. Fits the description and she's none too keen to let us catch up to share a cup of hot chocolate.' Price peered through his spyglass towards the vessel's stern, well ahead off their starboard bow. 'She means to outrun us, but we'll not let this little beauty go. Think of the prize, boys. Just think of the prize!' His undulating Welsh voice sang his encouragement.

Mary squinted at the distant vessel rising in and out of view with the swell. So, Rackham then. Maybe. She'd be happier if it was Vane, but money was money. They'd been randomly cruising for twelve weeks and Mary was spoiling for a fight.

Before long James joined the group clustered around Captain Price.

'Captain, if it is Rackham, how do you rate our chances?'

'Expect we're carrying heavier guns, but we'll be outnumbered, so best pound them into submission. Better that than trying to board.' Price turned to James. 'So what are our chances? Are you a betting man, Bonny? It's against my religious beliefs to gamble, my father would turn in his grave, bless his soul, so I leave it to others.' He looked amused. 'Well, what d'you say?'

'I say this is one we'll win, Cap'n. Definitely one we'll win. We have to.'

Price looked around at his gathered men. 'Do you all share Bonny's view? Are you ready to fight and pocket your prize?'

Mary punched her fist into the air joining the chorus of rousing, "Aye"s.

Captain Price had a way of drawing them together to work as a team. She liked this about him. He was a good man at heart, not like some of the bastards she'd had the misfortune to be commanded by, like Vane, who would as soon sacrifice all their men if it would save their own skin.

'Cap'n!' the lookout shouted down. 'Their flag! They're raising their flag!'

Mary elbowed her way forward, peering over the shoulders of two tall seamen who'd beaten her to a better place. She could just make out a black smudge of colour high on the mast as the vessel crested a wave. Her heart raced. On the quarterdeck Captain Price raised his spyglass for a closer inspection.

'Hah! Rackham it is, then! Well, well, I must say, I didn't expect to bump into him.' Price sounded smug. 'He's trying to scare us, but it'll take more than a skull and crossed swords to do that. Coward that he is, he's trying to outrun us, but if it's a fight he wants we'll grant his wish.' Price lowered his spyglass and surveyed the expectant faces of his crew.

'God's on our side, no doubt of it. Those men do the devil's work and they'll not be rewarded on earth or in heaven. And for those of you who put their faith elsewhere, then luck's on our side today. If that's still not enough to keep your spirits up, think of the governor's reward!' He raised his arms high. 'Are you ready, boys?'

Mary punched the air again, joining the cries of, 'Aye, Captain!' echoing around the deck.

Captain Price, feet apart, hands on hips, bellowed the commands she had been longing to hear. 'Clear for engaging. To your quarters. First team to fire gets an extra ration of ale tonight. To your quarters!'

Mary roared with the rest of them and sped down the ladder to the lower deck where hammocks were already stowed, gun deck cleared and hatches on both sides being opened. She hurried to the iron carriage gun on the larboard side which she was assigned to, with James and the rest of their team. When she had come aboard she had anticipated Captain Price would assign her a role as a topman, but once he knew she'd seen naval combat his response was unequivocal.

'No, no, Read. We're with a bunch of raw recruits, so I need your steady head at a gun. That's where I want you and that's where you'll be.' Captain Price had leant forward confidentially. 'Many of these men haven't fired anything more than muskets – some not even that.'

If Captain Price felt any anxiety he hadn't shown it, and she supposed his faith in God overcame any shortcomings of his crew. But she reflected that while he wasn't fussed about scrupulously swabbed decks, they kept their small arms clean, swords sharpened and had practised their drill over and over. They couldn't afford to waste ammunition during these exercises, so this would be their first time firing round shot, grape shot, iron bars and all manner of metal projectiles.

Organised chaos. It was the same before every battle. Mary ignored the noise, methodically checking everything was in order for her part in what was to come. Her eyes rested briefly on one fellow making the sign of the cross and mumbling a prayer, while others nervously checked and rechecked their weapons. When she had been a foot soldier in Flanders, prior to battle, she would find a quiet place and smoke her pipe to calm her nerves. Now, on the gun deck, amongst the gunpowder cartridges set far back from the guns, her pipe would have to wait.

She paused, arms dangling at her sides, breathed deeply and glanced to where James checked ropes threaded through their gun carriage. If there was justice in the world then James deserved his day. Let him be the one to take Rackham down for stealing his wife.

They were closing in: updated positions and orders were relayed down, and replies shouted up. The intention was to manoeuvre alongside and be first with a broadside to take advantage of their superior gunpower – if indeed they had it...

'They're turning! Rackham's coming around first! To your bracing stations!'

Hearing shouted orders to brace yards and ease the *Sea Hawk's* sheets, Mary longed to be up in the open, climbing out to adjust top sails, instead of huddled below with sweating, anxious men with little idea of what was happening out there.

'Positions, men! Go! Go!' Mary's gun captain barked. She stepped deftly out of the way as men took up thick ropes either side of their gun. They had practised for this moment, and she hoped no one panicked or blundered in the precise sequencing of the drill. 'Two, six, heave! Two, six, heave!' Hand over hand, men hauled their gun carriage into position.

As the *Sea Hawk* began to swing into position, the vessel tilted.

Without talking, the fellow next to Mary brushed past her in the tight space, dipped a long-handled swab in a bucket of water and thrust it down the gun muzzle. Others of her team pushed the wrapped powder charge into the dampened muzzle, hefted and loaded a round shot, thrusting loose oakum after it. Her turn next.

She leant out through their gunport, the rolling of the *Sea Hawk* dipping her to within a yard of the water. As she stretched out with her long-handled rammer the *Curlew* gradually swung into view. Her heart sank; for all Captain Price's hopes of lining up first, this was not to be.

'They're before us! They're in place!' Her voice joined others out on deck urging more speed. She thrust her implement down the muzzle, ramming the charge and shot right to the end of the barrel. Before she could pull herself back, a cry rang out as a fellow at the next gunport collapsed, his face dripping with blood. She dived back inside.

Puffs of smoke from across the water confirmed a volley of musket shots searching for targets through their open gunports, on deck, the helmsman and aloft. Mary heard the sharp retort of their own shooters and prayed that their aim was as true as that of Rackham's men.

Mary's team heaved their gun back into position and her gun captain lit the fuse. She turned away, crouched and covered her ears as a blast penetrated the air. Smoke filled her eyes and nostrils as the gun recoiled to the length of its restraints. Mary had a fleeting moment of satisfaction as she noted theirs was the first to fire from the *Sea Hawk*. She peered out anxiously to see if it had been effective, but drifting smoke obscured her view.

The hull of the *Sea Hawk* shuddered as a blast from the *Curlew* found its mark, followed by screams and curses.

'Larboard bow – above the waterline! Two men down!'

She knew the vessel itself would be safe – it was hard to sink any ship – but wooden splinters would have exploded outwards, penetrating soft flesh and muscle to the bone; by the sound of it, some of her shipmates were suffering.

A second blast from the *Curlew* was followed by a crack of timber and high-pitched screams. A spar must have gone, taking sail with it, along with one or more of their men. She didn't know where she would rather be now: out in the open or trapped below in the claustrophobic gun deck fast filling with smoke, ear-splitting booms of fired guns and cries of injured men.

Rammer in hand, Mary waited for her command. This was her job, this was what she had to do, and she hoped the smoke might shield her from sharpshooters. She reached out, rammed and yelled, 'Rammer done!' and ducked back as the gun muzzle rolled further out.

Again and again she performed her task while her gun captain chose his shot and fired at their target: sometimes round shot to the *Curlew's* hull, or bars and chain shot at the mast, spars and sail. It was a matter of his judgement when to fire, to catch the *Curlew* as it rose or fell with the swell.

Mary could barely see through the smoke and sweat dripped into her eyes. Shouted commands fought to be heard against the thrump of guns till her head felt ready to explode. She did not know what was happening in the overall scheme of things, but just did her job. She was the rammer for her gun. This was all she had to think about.

A massive blast flung her backwards. Moments later she found herself pinioned to the deck under something heavy, unable to move and gasping for air. She tried to focus, eyes swivelling. Men were stumbling over her and past her: they seemed to be shouting, but she couldn't hear for the ringing in her ears.

The enormity of it began to sink in.

The impact of the shot – directly through their gunport – had shattered the hull along with their gun, sending shards of wood and iron throughout the deck and leaving men badly injured and dead. Warm blood seeped through her clothes, but she could not tell if it was hers or from bodies on top of her.

She became aware of a lightening sensation in her chest as men came to her aid, pulling bodies away. She gasped for breath, filling her lungs with smoky air, whispering, 'Thanks,' to nameless faces scurrying past. Her right shoulder. She knew now she had been wounded, and could see her ripped shirt and torn bloodied flesh. But was this all? Could she stand? Walk?

Why were her feet soaking and cold? She was confused. No – not blood. Seawater was rising, already at her knees. The *Sea Hawk* was listing. The natural roll of the vessel and an untimely wave had been enough to breach the waterline. Vessels rarely sank, but the *Sea Hawk* was going down.

Mary's brain cleared. No seaman had been helping lift bodies off her – the bodies pinning her down had rolled off with the tilt of the vessel. No man near her was in the least bit interested in her welfare as each of them scrambled to escape. Each man for himself.

With her good arm she struggled to pull her legs clear from a tangle of rope, splintered wood and sharp shards of metal. She felt a surge of anger and pity when she saw James had been one of the broken men holding her down but could not tell if he was alive or dead and didn't stay to find out. Pulling herself onto her knees she clutched a fixture, resisting the suck of the sea pouring in, and dodged out of the way of loose ammunition, boxes and buckets sliding across the tilting deck. Rising unsteadily to her feet, she found her legs could function; nothing appeared broken. A fellow, left leg twisted at an unnatural angle and right hand blown away, reached out to her, pleading to be saved. She could not and would not try. Not now.

'Cease fire! Cease fire! We surrender!' someone was shouting across to Rackham on the hailer above the clamour of panicking men.

'What does it matter now? We're done for.' The bitter words were dragged from Mary's throat as she fought her way out of the listing vessel.

Distant cheers from pirates aboard Rackham's vessel reached Mary, while around her on the listing *Sea Hawk*, men desperate not to drown clambered over obstacles impeding their escape. The devil was on the winning side. So much for Price's trust in God and Bonny's in good luck.

On the tilting deck Mary shut her mind to the chaos around her and focused on surviving. Swirling water lapped at the broken wooden island she was marooned on. Her heart raced. Water held more terror for her than anything in the world. Like many seamen she could not swim. Yards and yards of sail spread out over the sea, dragging the listing *Sea Hawk* closer to its watery grave. Panicking men pushed and shoved, their instinct to survive strong. In the water men clung to broken planks, boxes and ship's tackle, anything buoyant.

She flung her arms wide, hollered, leapt as far as she could, kicking her feet, willing the air to give her purchase, her eyes fixed on a piece of floating timber she meant to cling to. The water swallowed her, sucking her further and further down. Looking up, she kicked and kicked.

Spluttering and gasping, Mary broke the surface, stretched out her left hand and grasped hold of the plank. It was barely big enough to keep her afloat. A hand grasped her ankle and she instinctively kicked out and clung more fiercely to the piece of broken wood keeping her in this world. She could not save anyone else, and she doubted she could save herself. Furiously kicking her legs, she propelled herself away from the sinking *Sea Hawk*. From a distance she watched her vessel being sucked down until it disappeared neatly and without fuss.

With her head just above water, Mary clung to life in the vastness of the Caribbean Sea, her left arm wrapped around the plank while blood seeped from her aching right shoulder staining the water a muddy red. Men, both alive and dead, floated nearby along with all manner of wreckage. A bleating goat paddled desperately looking for purchase for its hooves; barrels and ship's goods bobbed up and down. Captain Price's hat floated past – the last sign she saw of him. How long could she cling to her float? How long before sharks arrived?

She watched a boat being lowered from the *Curlew* and focused on its steady progress as rowers drew near. She would choose life over death, even though it meant pitching in with a bunch of pirates again.

38

ANNE GRIPPED THE LEEWARD RAIL, LEANT OVER AND spewed up the half-digested meal she had willed to stay down. Next time – if there were to be a next time – she'd be sure not to fill her belly with greasy meat so close to engagement.

The past hour had been more terrifying than anything she had experienced or imagined. The noise and smell had been overwhelming as they fought the *Sea Hawk*. She had missed being hit by inches, and the fellow working next to her had an arm blasted away at the shoulder. She had gagged at the sight, watching in amazement as in a daze he picked up his severed limb, sat down and died. His would be one of several bodies to be thrown overboard. No soldier forgets his first battle, and she was now a battle-hardened member of Jack's pack.

Vivid orange shafts of light from the setting sun added further drama to the carnage. Mingled with pleas from drowning men, Anne could hear Paddy in the rescue boat. 'Join us or drown. What's it to be?' From the howls, and the clout from Paddy's raised oar, the man had not been decisive enough, and Paddy left him to his fate, rowing on to the next man. 'Don't waste m' time now. What's it to be? In or out?'

One after the other, bedraggled and injured seamen from the *Sea Hawk* climbed up from the rescue boat. Some had not been injured and could manage, but others were in a bad way.

'Here, grab my hand.' Anne reached over to haul the exhausted men aboard. One seemed to be missing half his face and she was surprised Paddy had bothered to rescue him; another was all but naked, trousers blasted away, thighs scorched and blistered; another had a deep gash on his right shoulder so she grabbed his left hand, clutched the belt around his trousers and heaved him up. Paddy rowed off to rescue others.

With everyone aboard, Anne stood with her own crew as Jack, with George and Dick by his side, addressed the newcomers.

'You're under my command; your choice. You need to know who I am, as well as George and Dick, and mind what they say as much as me.' Jack gestured to both men. 'They'll tell you who's who in the company. Dick's going to read our articles and you're going to sign them. That's all I have to say right now. Oh, one more thing.' He cocked his head in her direction. 'We've a woman in our company. And just to let you know, I'll cut off the balls of any of you who muck with her.' And with this brusque introduction Jack walked off.

Later that evening Anne went to Jack's cabin as the last of the new men hurried past her, having signed ship's articles.

'You'd best hear this from me.' Jack looked serious.

Anne slumped into a chair, too tired to think what he might have to say, or to try and interpret his look.

'Sweetheart…' He paused and Anne stiffened, unsure what was to come. 'James was on board…'

'James?' Anne hadn't thought of him in a good while. Right now she could barely conjure up his face. 'He's dead?'

'He was working one of the guns…'

Anne absorbed the news, discomfited by the thought that her own actions might have contributed to his death. She didn't ask how much Jack knew of his manner of dying. That would be too much. 'Foolish man for coming after us. I never wished him harm; you know that.'

Jack nodded, rummaged around the cupboard bringing back a half-full bottle of rum.

Anne sighed. 'What a foolish thing to do. He should've stayed working for Mr Harmon. He wasn't cut out to be a pirate hunter.'

'Nope. Nor a pirate.' Jack squeezed her hand and raised the bottle. 'To James.' He passed the bottle to her.

'James.' She took a slug. One more person connected to her, dead. One more reason to live for the moment.

Anne sat in silence, sharing the bottle with Jack, just as she had when waiting to hear whether or not she had a future on the *Curlew*, but now she contemplated her past. She felt genuinely sorry James's life had ended in this way, but he should have stayed home.

By the time the bottle was finished, so too was her grieving for James.

Next morning everyone was cleaning and repairing. Francis, with helpers, shaped a log to replace a damaged spar; men wielding big needles and strong thread methodically patched and repaired torn sails. Anne dipped her broom into a bucket of seawater, scrubbing and scrubbing. She found herself working side by side with Jim, who seemed to have overcome his objections to her; further along, one of the newcomers was on his knees scrubbing: a small brush easier to manage than one with a long handle. He appeared to be struggling, his right shoulder giving him pain. Anne frowned. There was something about him, and she recalled he'd taken more than a passing interest in her after Jack had introduced her – if you could call it an introduction. As she carried on swabbing, the new fellow stood, walked to where Dick was smoking and stared longingly at his pipe.

'A fellow 'baccy appreciator.' Dick smiled. 'Well, you fellows have been through the mill, and I'll not hold it against you now you've joined us. I've a spare pipe – give it you later – and some 'baccy if you want. Not my best Virginian, but I can cut you some from my other cone. Here, have a pull.' Dick offered the new man his pipe, which he accepted with a nod, inhaling deeply.

Yes, Anne considered, she liked this man's face – it looked trustworthy. He might be someone to get to know. She sighed and looked at the expanse of deck to scrub.

Astern, Paddy rolled out an empty cask, making room near Francis. She guessed what Paddy was up to as he whistled a tune, flipped the cask lid upside down to expose the scratched lines on the underside, and from his pocket took out some counters. Lots of them enjoyed playing nine men's morris. Jack allowed gaming as long as the bets were small exchanges or tokens, not involving money or share of prizes either real or yet to be gained.

Paddy called the fellow with the injured arm. 'Oi! You there! Fancy a game?'

'Later.' The newcomer gestured to his waiting bucket.

'Ah, go on, I'll answer for ye. With that shoulder of yours, we can make an allowance just for today. C'mon now, give us a game.' He pulled up boxes to sit on. 'Best of seven.'

The two of them set about playing and by the sound of Paddy's profanities – 'Jesus, Mary and Joseph' – it sounded it wasn't going his way. 'Jesus fucking Christ, wish I'd left you scrubbing the decks. When're you going to lose?' Paddy looked distraught at his run of bad luck. His fellow player shrugged. 'Not yet, it seems. My bucket's waiting...'

Anne laughed at the exchange and watched Paddy stand, kick his box in irritation, make his way to the new fellow's bucket and send it flying with another kick.

The new man made his way over to where Francis had hewed the raw log into shape with an adze and was now carefully chiselling off wafer thin curls of wood.

'Good work.' The man ran his hand over the smooth wood.

Francis smiled shyly. 'C-c-can you sm-smell it? Fresh-planed w-wood? Love it. Just rather not b-be doing it here...'

'What's y'name?'

'F-F-Frank.'

Anne only knew him as Francis, yet here he was revealing his familiar name on his first meeting with a stranger.

'Mark.' The new fellow offered his name in return.

Yes, Anne looked forward to getting to know Mark.

39

In the weeks since they had destroyed the *Sea Hawk* Jack had often chuckled, imagining Rogers's frustration. His mind had conjured all manner of scenarios of how the news reached Rogers's ears. There had been some fun with Howie, striding the deck with an improvised walking cane, pretending to limp and doing a fine impersonation of the governor's West Country burr and carefully enunciated speech, damning them all as rogues deserving to be hanged. Then Paddy had dropped his trousers and let rip a massive fart. 'Here's in your face, Governor Rogers!'

Yes, they'd had their fun, but however the news might have been imparted to Rogers, Jack knew this would not be the end of it. The *Sea Hawk* had not prevailed, but Jack had been alarmed to find the price on his head. They were being hunted and he meant to stay ahead of the game.

'Get the second mains'l... Now!'

Jack's bellowed command was relayed back to men struggling to stay on their feet. They first loosened the heavy gaff and fought to bundle a new reef in the foot of the sail till only half the area of canvas caught the wind. Any more and it would be in danger of ripping to shreds or capsizing them. Holding a steady course was the devil's job with wind gusts of at least fifty knots and rising.

The *Curlew* was driven onto a crest of the mountainous swell before pitching into a trough with a massive *whoomph*. They were being pounded, and the sounds of sea, wind, sails and groaning timbers were something every landlubber should experience. Terrifying. Exhilarating. Jack was in the midst of it all – right where he belonged.

They had a block and tackle attached to the helm, and Jack weighed in to help two helmsmen pulling hard on the windward side, fighting to keep control. Jack's hair whipped about his face and spray broke over him as George and he shouted above the storm, deciding which sails to leave up and which to take down.

Clinging to the rails, George made his way to midship, yelled instructions, and within seconds Sam, Mark and others were on the dizzying journey climbing the ratlines of the pitching vessel. Jack had done it numerous times – what seaman hadn't? Still, Jack admired the topmen who worked in atrocious conditions like this. Providence had shone on them when he found that Mark was one such man.

His crew had shown their resolve first against the *Sea Hawk* – a paltry show of strength – and now against the wind, a far deadlier foe. Men above clung to the top yard, and their feet cautiously worked their way out on the ropes, while on deck Anne was behind Noah in a chain working the lines for the sails being hauled in and lashed. All of them fighting to keep their balance on the pitching vessel.

When the storm abated, leaving the *Curlew* mildly rolling, Davy risked firing up the galley stove. Men who had been injured in the battle with the *Sea Hawk* and couldn't work the ship had been allocated to cooking duties under Davy. Jack headed below in anticipation that the past weeks' practice had improved their culinary skills and together they had conjured up something better than Davy's normal fare. With Paddy's feet threatening to step on his hands in his rush to fill his stomach, Jack jumped off the ladder onto the 'tween deck, looking forward to a hot meal.

He accepted a bowl from the steaming pot, then Davy dolloped a scoop into Paddy's bowl. 'Jesus! Is this the best you can do, after what we've been through? All I can see are globs of fat. What the hell is it anyway?' Paddy had to complain – he usually did – and Davy, as always, justified – or didn't bother to justify – his miserable cooking efforts. 'If you don't want it, leave it. See if I care.'

Jack's body sagged in disappointment as he joined Dick and others in the crew he wanted to get to know better. When Anne arrived he automatically made space for her next to him, but after filling her bowl she made her way to sit with Mark, Noah and Frank. Jack's attention was drawn from his own group to Anne's.

Noah nodded to Anne as she sat. 'Mark's been telling me about himself. Tell Anne.'

Mark scowled. 'I'm not starting over again.'

'Did I ask?' Anne sounded prickly.

'F-f-fought against the F-French, he did. Not m-much good with guns m-m-myself.'

Frank was good at his work, but Jack found it hard going holding a conversation, always wanting to complete his sentences.

'Sounds a cold place, up north.' This from Noah. 'But I'd like to feel snow one day, just to see what it's like.'

Jack thought this unlikely, but was pleased to be able to provide Noah with a home – if you could call this company a home. Perhaps Noah might find himself a free man some day and feel snowflakes drifting around him. Who knew what fate had in store for any of them?

As Jack mused on this, Noah and Frank finished their meals and drifted away, leaving Anne and Mark alone. Jack watched Mark unwind a filthy rag from around his hand – he must have cut himself during the storm – and Anne seized the opportunity to take Mark's hand to check his wound. At least that's how it looked to Jack. He stiffened. He hadn't been imagining things. Anne had been taking more than a casual interest in this fellow, and unless he was mistaken he'd seen Mark stare candidly at Anne when he thought she wasn't looking. Now, Mark withdrew his hand sharply, and there was no hint of any dalliance. Sitting with his own group Jack could hear Dick droning on with some long-winded story as he strained to hear Anne and Mark. Jack locked eyes with Mark for a split second and he just made out Mark saying, 'Calico's watching. Why's that, d'you reckon?' Anne shrugged and turned to frown at him.

Enough. Jack beckoned and made a space next to him and Anne picked up her unfinished meal and joined him.

'Taking a keen interest in a small scratch. Didn't know you had such compassion. I must remember.'

Anne narrowed her eyes and spoke softly. 'Don't start. I'm not fool enough to make trouble, you know that.'

'And I won't stand for any nonsense… and you know that.'

'I keep company rules, don't I? Besides, most of the time I forget I'm a woman.'

Jack had to laugh. Fair enough. 'Keep thinking like a man then, my sweet, except when you're with me.' He traced a line up her thigh to her crotch with his hand, and she slapped it away sharply. 'Leave off. This isn't the place.'

She was right. They had agreed they would keep their intimacies for the privacy of his cabin. She was right about the other thing too: he should trust her not to fool around.

Jack became aware of a small commotion by the hatch ladder. Frank had been sent spinning and by the look of Sam's out-thrust leg the cause was obvious. Sam was a bruiser and he had asked Dick to keep an eye on him. Frank got to his feet and looked ready to confront Sam, so Jack rose to intervene. But before he could take a step Mark had deftly steered Frank aside saying, 'Frank – there's something I want to ask.'

He shared a smile with Anne at this smooth intervention. Mark had skills other than being a good topman. Jack patted Anne's shoulder and burped as the grease of Davy's damn stew rose in his gullet.

40

Mary dabbed the corner of Frank's weeping eye with her scarf. She had been sharpening tools for him, while he sat astride his carpenter's bench chiselling a new sail block, and a small splinter had flown up. It was nothing much, and her gesture meant nothing, but it was annoying Sam had witnessed it.

'Ah, poor Frankie. Still missing your little d-d-doggie!' Sam snuffled, and Frank jerked back out of her reach.

Frank had told her about Sam tossing his dog overboard and she had looked surprised and nodded in sympathy. In truth she had heard versions of the tale from others, no doubt more elaborate with each retelling. Why they took pleasure in taunting Frank was beyond her. Weren't these stupid men aware that Frank was probably the single most indispensable member of their crew? Sam continued snuffling and boo-hooing, and Frank deftly stepped off his work bench, his face pink and his freshly sharpened chisel clenched in his fist.

'Oh, planning on giving me a shave, are ya? Got m' own razor.' Sam did not look too worried by Frank's array of carpentry tools. 'When're you going to fight like a real man? Even Davy used to be a fighter before his accident. But you...'

Sam raised his fist as if to strike. Frank ducked and Sam chortled. Frank, face flushed, gripped the sharp chisel.

'I've had a g-gutful! I'll take you on any d-day!'

Mary reached out. 'Frank. Stop this!'

Sam roared with laughter, watching the slender carpenter dance towards him, chisel outstretched.

'A gutful, eh? Can you shoot straight, Frankie?' Sam's face took on a mean look. 'Can you shoot at all?'

Mary held her breath as Sam continued, 'Know what it feels like to have yer flesh ripped open?'

'Shut up, Sam. That's enough!' Mary willed Sam to back off.

Before she could decide what to do, Frank had dropped his chisel and launched himself at Sam. Frank was so light he almost bounced off the bulky man and within seconds Sam had wrestled him to the ground. Mary yelled and leapt in to hold back Sam's right arm; fist clenched ready to slam down onto Frank's head. Others were gathering, attracted by the hollering, and Dick was soon at their side.

'No fighting on board.' Dick hauled Sam away. 'I don't know what this is all about, and I don't much care. But while I'm quartermaster I'm stickin' to the rules. Yep. No fighting on board. Sort out your differences on shore.'

Sam and Frank were back on their feet. This need not escalate. Mary stepped forward.

'A misunderstanding. Nothing to sort out.'

Frank roughly pulled her aside. 'Yes! There is s-s-something to sort.' Frank glared wildly at Sam and all the gathered men. She sighed. Clearly he felt he had something to prove.

'He's keen!' Sam laughed and looked incredulous.

'Really? You really want to go ahead with this? Want to fight him?' Dick frowned, clearly puzzled why anyone in their right mind would take on Sam. But Frank could not back down with so many of the crew watching.

Mary tried again, tugging at Frank's sleeve. 'Frank!'

Frank swung around, his eyes pleading with her to understand.

Dick shrugged. 'Well then, if I were you, I'd get some practice in. Yep, definitely get some practice in. Next time we're ashore y'can both sort out your differences. In the meantime, keep out of each other's way. Calico Jack's not going to be best pleased.'

Dick walked away shaking his head, shoving Sam and others ahead of him. Mary appealed to Frank.

'Are you crazy?'

'I k-know one end of a g-gun f-f-from another.'

'Sweet Jesus! You don't stand a chance. Go and talk to Dick… to Calico. Don't do this wild thing!'

Any bravado Frank was nurturing evaporated. Mary grabbed his shirt in both hands. 'Frank. Listen. It's not too late. Sam's just bored, doesn't want to be seen as a coward…'

He pushed her aside and looked at her, his face stunned but determined. 'Wh-what do I have to d-do? What will happen? What do I need to know?'

Were all men such idiots? Even Frank? He was a decent man, a kind man, someone who used his brains, someone she could have a conversation with, someone she wanted to befriend. But the way things were heading, he'd be dead inside a week.

Four days later, perched precariously on the tops'l footrope, Mary made sure she was working next to Sam. Neither of them was in the least bit troubled by the motion of the *Curlew* as they kept up a steady rhythm, hand over hand, gathering the sail and lashing it tightly. She judged when Sam's balance was most vulnerable, deliberately lost her footing, and with a yelp, dropped her weight into the hefty man, clinging to the yard at the last split second.

'What the fuck? You almost had me over!' Sam clutched a rope.

She muttered, 'Sorry,' and turned back to her work. She smiled grimly to herself: almost but not quite. The movement of the *Curlew* had favoured Sam, sending his body leaning into the safety of the wooden arm of the vessel. Sam gripped her shirt with one hand as they both clung to the yard swaying back and forth.

'Nothin' more to say for yourself?' Sam looked more puzzled than angry.

Mary knocked his hand away. 'If your belly was smaller you'd take up less space.'

Sam peered quizzically at her. 'And I had you down as a quiet one.' He leaned close. 'Some years ago, I was up high with a lad who was being a fucking nuisance.' He looked down at the deck far below. 'Should've heard the sound of his skull splitting. Am-az-ing!'

The men working with them on the yard fell silent as they waited for this to be over – wherever it was heading.

'You threatening me, Sam? You threatening to tip me off?'

'Nah! Not my way of clearing up business. Not usually, let's say. Looks to be your way, though. Looks like y' want to save your friend having to face me.' Sam's laughter was harsh. 'Looking forward to it.'

'Frank can fight his own fight. But I'll take you on.'

Sam leered at her. 'You're keen to meet your maker. I'll have great pleasure seeing you off after I've gutted your frien—'

'Before. You and I fight first. Or don't you fancy your chances?'

'I fancy m' chances all right.' Sam smirked, looking at the nearby men. 'Hear that! I'm going to be busy.'

She lashed her section of the sail, working silently side by side with Sam as if nothing had happened, all the while her mind racing.

41

'GODDAMN, DICK! IT'S YOUR ROLE TO KEEP THE PEACE and sort out arguments. Worse still, it seems we're about to lose our carpenter!'

Jack's fury was justified. These were petty issues – the kind of squabbles he'd had with his brother when they'd been forced to stay inside waiting for the rain to pass so they could roam the streets again. His and Hal's idea of sorting out differences was to throw themselves into a spontaneous wrestling and boxing bout. Jack had never heard of men prepared to die for such pathetic reasons.

Anne begged him. 'Stop them, Jack. Sam'll slaughter them both. Is this what you want? Frank's valuable.'

'Think I don't know?' He was annoyed by her sudden interest in the well-being of their carpenter. 'Seems to think his manhood requires him to stand up to Sam, but he won't be standing for long. Sam's blade will slice through him like butter.'

'And Mark – what about him?' Anne glared.

'What about him?' Jack was less concerned about his fate, but he sensed this was where Anne's interest lay. Mark was a good enough seaman, but after the incident aloft with Sam he was watching this new man. He couldn't put his finger on the reason, but he didn't quite trust him and was inclined to agree with Sam's version. But why Mark would care to stick up for Frank was a mystery. Perhaps it would be a blessing if Sam dispatched Mark too. Jack didn't particularly like Sam, but he was straightforward, and he knew for a fact Anne had not the slightest interest in him.

Jack convened a meeting with Dick, Sam, Frank and Mark. Surely he could get them to see sense. He said his bit and Dick weighed in, but Frank was sulky, in a do-or-die frame of mind. Sam seemed bemused he suddenly had two fights on his hands but wouldn't back down from either. And Mark? How and why he had got himself involved still puzzled Jack. The man stood sullenly before him and kept his eyes lowered. As the men were leaving his cabin after this unsuccessful attempt at reconciliation, Jack's mind turned to what immediate repairs were needed. Best make the most of Frank's talents while he remained in this life.

Five days later the *Curlew* dropped anchor in an isolated bay. They packed into the ship's boat: Jack, Dick, the three silent men about to fight, along with Anne, who had insisted on coming. And Paddy, to keep hold of weapons until the fights began.

Jack's heart filled with the beauty of the place: cries of birds in the forest and at sea, soft waves lapping the beach, dragging back shells and pebbles. He tutted in exasperation at the foolishness of this enterprise and tried a final time.

'C'mon, men. See sense. Two out of the three of you won't get to see another day. That's the truth of the matter.'

'Maybe only one of us.' Mark stared accusingly.

In Jack's mind the future was already mapped out: the boat trip back to the *Curlew* lighter of both Frank and Mark.

'True enough,' he conceded, 'but we chose this life, so we could be—'

'Ch-chose?' Frank spoke bitterly.

Jack raised his arms in resignation. Dick gestured to Sam and Mark to draw near.

'Right then, you two – let's get on with it. These are the rules you're going to follow, so listen up: I'll not stand for any cheatin' or I'll kill you myself, with Paddy as m' back up...'

Frank looked green around the gills and seemed to be edging towards the trees. Jack wouldn't be surprised if he legged it into the forest, so, hand on the hilt of his cutlass, he casually walked over to him.

'Watch and learn, Frank. Hope you got some practice in.'

He and Frank watched silently as Dick measured out fifteen paces and marked a circle in the sand: the duelling arena. Frank groaned as Sam and Mark strapped on cutlasses, tucked knives into belts and loaded pistols. Jack shook his head. His carpenter had been a fool to let himself be riled by the likes of Sam. Well, he was about to witness a fight to the death and had time to contemplate what was in store for himself. Idiots, the lot of them.

'Anne!' Jack shouted. She was hovering near Mark, and he wanted her out of harm's way; the edge of the trees seemed a safe position from where to witness the fight. Out in the bay, his entire company had gathered at the rails of the *Curlew* to watch. To his knowledge none of them had bothered to wager on the outcome and Dick had hesitatingly requested Mark return his pipe, to which Mark had responded with a curt, 'I'm not dead yet.'

Mark and Sam commenced a cautious dance, circling each other at a distance, eyes locked, as if unsure what steps to make, what kind of fight this would be and who would take the lead. Both had pistols cocked, lowered to the ground, with a cutlass in the other hand. Curses flew from Sam's mouth and he formed his face into a terrifying mask.

Mark remained silent, watchful. Jack fell silent too. All of them, Dick, Anne, Paddy and Frank, were barely breathing, waiting to see who would strike first. He heard Dick's whispered, 'Come on… come on,' willing the tension to break.

Neither man was in a hurry to use his shot. Mark had increased his speed, trotting around the arena as if he were a horse on display, forcing Sam to keep pace or turn and fire. Mark paused, danced from foot to foot, swivelled and began circling in the other direction, all the while keeping an eye on Sam. Jack couldn't see the point; it just seemed to be some sort of delaying tactic.

Sam had had enough. He aimed his pistol, discharged his shot, tossed the pistol aside and charged with a bellow, changing his cutlass to his right hand.

Mark dropped to a squat. Had he been hit? Jack couldn't tell. Anne's shrieks of, 'Fire! Fire!' pierced his ears.

Mark didn't need Anne's advice. In a split second he'd raised his pistol and fired.

Hah! Jack expelled a breath, and at the same moment both Anne and Mark bellowed in distress.

The pistol had not fired! For whatever reason, fate was not being kind to the seaman he had so recently rescued, and Jack felt a twinge of sympathy. Mark dropped the pistol, swapped his cutlass to his right hand and sprang aside as his attacker bore down. The encounter wouldn't last long.

Anne shrieked, 'Get him, Mark!', her nails digging into his arm. Given half a chance she would pitch into the battle.

The two men faced each other just beyond cutting distance, cutlass blades upwards, shielding their faces, making small testing moves with their wrists. They gripped their knives in their left hands, blades pointing forward. Sam flicked his right wrist, his blade drawing back, and sliced diagonally towards Mark's right shoulder. Mark pivoted his shoulder back, his knife blocking, then lunged forward, meaning to strike Sam's left flank with his own cutlass – but Sam's knife arm was too quick.

Steel on steel, the two men were at each other with wide slicing and guarding actions, hilts up and hilts down.

Jack had witnessed many fights and taken part in many others, so he watched dispassionately and wondered how long before Sam prevailed. He had weight and height advantage, and the slighter man was no match for the force behind his blade. But Mark was nimble, placing his feet carefully, knees bent. Jack watched his body stretch to the right to avoid a blow to his left shoulder, regaining his balance immediately. As cutlasses clashed in front of their faces, Sam's forearm thrust against Mark's arm, propelling him back. Mark stumbled and almost lost his balance. Almost. He stepped back out of range, his body sagging, as Sam stepped forward. This would be it then. The fight had lasted at least a minute; now Sam would end it.

Mark tossed his cutlass in the air, blade upwards, swapped his knife to his right hand before catching the hilt of his cutlass in his left. It had been done in a second. Jack's eyes widened in admiration. This brought a new dynamic to the fight, something Sam would have to adjust to.

Jack stepped forward, drawn in by Mark's strategy. He had never seen a man equally comfortable left and right-handed. Now Mark wielded his cutlass in his left hand he seemed more assured, more powerful. Jack took another step closer, and without thinking he began shouting encouragement along with Anne.

'Good work! Watch your right flank!' Jack had no right, and no reason, to show such bias, but Dick and Paddy couldn't hold back either and they too shouted encouragement to the underdog. The fighters' faces were dripping with sweat, but still no strike.

Mark darted past Sam's left side, slicing his cutlass down to Sam's shoulder. Sam parried with his knife. As Mark moved past Sam he jerked his left elbow back, slicing his cutlass into Sam's flank.

The bellow from Sam told them the cut had hurt, but how much they could not say. Whatever the case, Sam was not slowing down. Again they were at each other. Sam thrust out his boot and caught Mark in the groin with a resounding thud. Jack flinched, imagining the force would surely rupture Mark's balls.

Mark staggered back then dived, guarding Sam's cutlass and knife with two swift swings and plunging his knife into Sam's belly. He looked intent on gutting the man. Sam dropped his cutlass, swayed back and forth, and sank to his knees, his face registering shock.

Mark stood over him panting and trembling. 'You son of a whore! You dog! That's right – hold your guts in.'

While Jack absorbed this unexpected outcome, Anne darted past and grasped Mark's arm, her eyes wild. She shook him until he lifted his head and his exhausted gaze met the intensity of hers. 'Teach me! I want to fight like you!'

Mark shrugged her off and turned away.

'I want to learn how to do this!' Anne persisted, but Mark ignored her.

Jack remembered another time when Anne had shown such admiration and enthusiasm, such tenacity, and perhaps a touch of hero worship. Then his own prowess at swordplay had been the chief attraction, and he himself the object of her desires. Now Anne trailed after Mark as he staggered to the water's edge, kicked off his shoes and immersed his body in the sea as if to cleanse himself of what he had done. Oh well, the man deserved respect, and Jack meant to practise one or two of the nifty moves he had witnessed.

His mind turned to practical matters. Best get digging. Sam was as good as dead and would be cold by the time the hole was deep enough.

'Calico!' Jack turned to Dick. 'Now we're here, how about we heave down? The *Curlew* could do with her belly scratched and it would take Frank's mind off all of this – give him something manly to do, if you know what I mean. Yep, it would be a good thing all around.'

'Good idea. Wait till high tide, then beach her.'

The *Curlew* needed careening and Jack was grateful he still had his carpenter. He shielded his eyes and turned back towards the treeline where he had left Frank under Paddy's guard. Jack smirked. No fear of Frank making a run for it. He had keeled over in a faint and Paddy's boot was nudging him in the ribs to bring him to.

42

Rain struck the deck and Mary welcomed it. All of them did. Near her, men stripped naked, letting the driving rain wash grimy bodies as they pummelled rank-smelling clothes in buckets of fresh water; others laid out salt-stiffened garments to soak up fresh water; the most indifferent carried on with their tasks fully clothed, letting the rain do what it might to freshen them.

Pail in hand, Mary made her way to the lowest reaches of the *Curlew*. Taking a candle from her pocket, she struck a light with her flintlock before removing her jacket and shirt, unbinding her breasts and setting about washing with a piece of soap she had been saving. She washed her face as best she could, leaving smudges of tar on her cheeks by way of disguise, and lowered her hair into the pail. Sponging her body of salt and grime, she felt she was cleansing her soul of Sam's blood. A week had passed but she wasn't over it. It had rattled her badly.

She had planned to dispatch Sam with a well-aimed shot at close quarters. When that failed she had expected Sam's blade to make quick work of her, and bitterly regretted taking on Frank's fight. She liked Frank, that was part of the reason; but for the most part she could not bear to see men bullied till they lost confidence in themselves. She had witnessed men cowering at the time of battle, incapable of fighting because they had come to believe what their tormentors said about them. They all relied on each other, and this company needed Frank to believe in himself.

With soaking hair hanging around her face, Mary became aware of a widening chink of light and glanced up to see the hatch opening and legs reaching down, rung by rung. She hurriedly reached for her shirt and turned her back but before she could dress she heard a thud beside her.

'What are you doing down here?' Anne sounded genuinely surprised.

Damn the woman! Anne had been on her tail for days, practising some move she had seen Mary execute when dispatching Sam; pestering her to teach her some fighting tricks. This was the word she used: tricks, which annoyed Mary. The skills she had absorbed on the battlefield were strategies to keep herself alive, not some stupid parlour game. More than once she had brushed Anne aside like a persistent fly. 'I'm busy, another time.' Or, 'Go practise with Paddy, or ask Calico.'

In the confines of the orlop deck Mary was trapped. She pressed her shirt to her chest and moved further into the shadows, her back to Anne. This couldn't be a coincidence. Though to be fair, she imagined this lowest deck would be the only place Anne too could freely wash and slosh about without male prying eyes, as people were always in and out of Jack's cabin. Or was she being too generous?

Over her shoulder she saw Anne beginning to remove her jacket.

'You're done?' Anne was matter of fact.

Surely the woman didn't mean to strip in front of her. Mary hastily leant towards the candle and blew it out.

'I'm heading up.'

'You could've left it for me.' Anne's voice was plaintive.

In the gloom, Mary fumbled to pull on her shirt, find the arms of her jacket and stuff the binding cloth into her pocket. This woman of Jack's was trouble. She'd heard the story about Rye, over and over, and seen for herself how wary the men were about overstepping the mark – any mark – with Anne Bonny. She felt boxed in, and vulnerable to whatever flights of fancy the younger woman took.

'Stop following me. Leave me be!' Mary's anger boiled over. 'I don't want you around. I've heard about what happened to Rye, and I know what Jack'll do if he thinks we're up to something – so why put me in harm's way?'

'No! No.' Anne sounded surprised. 'Why would I want to harm you?'

'How would it look if someone came down and saw us? Tell me! I don't seek out trouble, so leave me alone.'

Mary barged past Anne and sprang up the steps, Anne's voice behind her. 'How did I know you were here? What were you doing anyway? No need for you to wash in private.'

She had momentarily felt refreshed but now this new worry pressed in on her. She could not hope to hide her disguise from Anne much longer. Was the woman blind?

For a day or two Anne kept her distance. Mary kept to herself, fretting about what to do, then she picked her moment. Anne was at the helm with Jack by her side giving instructions. Mary waited till Jack took over and as Anne walked away she fell into step with her, speaking softly.

'I've been thinking about the other day. You beginning to take your clothes off and—'

'What? I did not!' Anne looked startled.

'Been thinking about it.' Mary blocked Anne's path and stared intensely at her. Anne looked uncomfortable and glanced back at Jack. His eyes were on them, but he couldn't leave the helm; there was no one around to take over from him.

'I could've been put in danger because of you.' Mary jerked her head in Jack's direction. 'Calico's not a fool.'

Anne tried to sidestep. 'Can't you let it go?'

Mary shook her head. 'Something to show you. Come.' She motioned Anne to follow, passing seamen going about their business, and headed down to Jack's cabin.

Anne hesitated. 'In here?'

Mary pushed her through the door, closing it behind them. 'This is what you want, isn't it? A quiet place, away from others.'

'Sweet Jesus, no! What's got into you?' Anne placed her hand on the latch.

'No!' Mary grabbed Anne's wrist, twisting the younger woman to face her. She calmly placed Anne's hand on her belly and slid it down inside her trousers. She was giving away her long-held secret to this woman she didn't quite trust.

Anne jerked her thigh upwards to knee her in the groin. 'What are you doing? Are you crazy! I'll not be part of this, and Jack'll cut off your balls!' Anne sucked in her breath. 'Oh my God! My God!' Anne pulled her hand out and stumbled back.

'And while you're about it, you can thank God I'm not a man. I don't like careless people – they get others killed. You should think about what you do.'

'Don't preach at me! I'm not careless!'

'Glad to hear you say so. And one more thing – don't you tell a living soul. Not Calico Jack, not anyone.'

Anne's face registered shock. 'Who are you? What's your name?'

She hesitated. 'I don't think the company'll want a second woman on board, so best not say.'

'I'll keep your secret. Promise.'

She doubted it. Anne would surely talk with Calico when they lay together at night.

'Best remain as things are until I can find a safe place to go ashore.'

'Come on, what's your name?' Anne appealed, and Mary summoned her courage to reveal a little more of herself. Speaking her name was difficult.

'Mary.' It came out as a whisper.

'Mary... Mary... That was my mother's name.' Anne smiled, leant over and kissed her lightly on the lips. 'We can be friends. That's all I've wanted.'

Mary recoiled. Friends with Anne? Man or woman, Mary sought companions who were steady and trustworthy and would have her back at the time of battle.

'How in hell's name did you get into this life? How did you become so good at... at... everything?' Anne's eyes sparkled.

'Another time. Best get out of here before Calico Jack comes looking.'

'Jack'll not be getting your balls, we can be sure of that!'

Anne shrieked with laughter as she bounded out. Mary watched her go. Could she trust this flighty young woman to hold her tongue?

43

ABOVE, OUT ON DECK, JACK COULD HEAR THE PARTY gathering pace with drumming feet and clapping hands. Howie, who had entertained them, mimicking Rogers, had a fine voice, and was leading them in a song with a catchy chorus which everyone rowdily joined in.

'With a hey down, ho down, derry derry down, Among the leaves so green-o.'

Someone had a fiddle, accompanying Howie. Every company needed musicians to keep spirits up, whether fighting for king and country or keeping bored sea rovers from making mischief. A singalong was definitely overdue.

Cleaning and repairing the *Curlew* had been a strenuous job, hauling her ashore on the high tide by fixing ropes to the top halyard and the stoutest tree they could find near the beach and winching the vessel foot by foot out of the water. They'd propped her first to one side then the other, burning and scraping the hull free of barnacles and weed, with Frank kept busy replacing planks rotten with worm and all the rest of them caulking, tarring and slapping on a thick coating of tallow, oil and brimstone.

Jack had first needed to persuade the men to come ashore. They weren't keen on spending time on the beach with Sam buried not far off. George in particular had had a view on it.

'I'll not set foot on the place till he's moved. No one wants to know they've a dead man beneath their feet, it'll bring bad luck.' So Jack had ordered Sam's body dug out of the sand and reburied in the forest.

Following the careening, back at sea, George had been troubled by a shark following them for a day or so. 'Who next, Calico? Who'll be next to die?'

'George! Since when were you so easily spooked? I'll not hold with such nonsense and have the men unsettled!' Jack was as superstitious as most mariners, but George's excesses annoyed him.

Yes, a party was definitely in order and Jack longed to join his company. He and George were poring over charts spread out on the cabin table. As always, George had taken the noon sight with his quadrant and navigational instruments to work out their latitude. It was not so easy now they were in open sea out of sight of land and could no longer refer to their coastal charts or spot high landmarks. They believed they were off course, but could not be sure, and if so, by how much.

'She's putting a hex on the cruise. She's a Jonah. I told you she'd bring bad luck.' George's face set into a stubborn frown.

'You can't blame Anne. Admit it. You might've made an error.'

George's scowl deepened at the insult to his navigational skills. They wanted to stay well clear of Bahamian waters as they cruised north towards the Florida Gulf, just as they were giving wide berth to all British-controlled colonies further south. All governors seemed hell bent on destroying the way of life Jack held dear.

'I'm never wrong,' George growled, 'leastways, not until now. We've run out the log line and calculated the knots, allowed for winds and currents and for the cleaned hull. Still it's possible we're drifting a little eastward. I'll adjust course.' George gathered his instruments as Jack rolled up the chart and headed up to the main deck.

Time to party.

Tom Bourne was proving a dab hand with the fiddle. Tom and Howie had known each other for years so they should have a good repertoire of tunes between them. Jack slapped Tom's back as he passed, helped himself to a generous ladle of rum and joined in the song Howie had moved on to. All of them knew the chorus of 'The Mermaid'.

'*Oh the ocean waves may roll, And the stormy winds may blow, While we poor sailors go skipping aloft, And the land lubbers lie down below, below, below, And the land lubbers lie down below.*'

Howie carried on singing the verses, acting the part of different characters and everyone rallied with the chorus.

'Another! Sing another!'

Howie struck up 'In Praise of the Pudding'. Jack remembered his mother singing it: a song that had been doing the rounds of London pubs for many years. He hummed along, laughed at Howie's rendition of the ribald song, and helped himself to another drink.

Skipping up and down drunkenly, Paddy appealed, 'Strike up a jig, Tom, if you've got one in ye. I feel a dance comin' on.'

Moments later others had joined him, or were finding partners, arms around waists and shoulders of other men, all intent on enjoying themselves. Noah was dancing, his head thrown back, a broad grin lighting up his face, hips twisting and weaving with elbows and knees all angles. Jack supposed this must be some long-remembered dance from his homeland – somewhere in West Africa. The stomping dance was strangely beautiful among the galumphing English, Irish and Scottish men jigging up and down the deck. Jack tried to copy Noah's intricate movements, bending his knees and sticking his bum out. But why dance by himself when he had his own woman on board? This was too good an opportunity to miss.

'Come on, sweetheart, let's show them a thing or two.'

With an arm around Anne's waist, Jack negotiated a path along the crowded deck and realised this was the first time he'd ever danced with her. He couldn't believe it. He looked at her animated face, laughingly telling him what a lousy dancer he was when he got too rough. It felt wonderful to have her in his arms. He lifted her off the ground and swung her around as she shrieked in delight.

'Ah, Anne! If I shut my eyes I can imagine you dressed in that fancy blue gown. Remember that day at Charlotte's?'

'How could I forget?'

He nuzzled his face into her hair. 'And I can pretend you smell as sweet as then with perfume, instead…'

Jack regretted the words the moment they were out of his mouth. He felt her flinch, and supposed he deserved her tart, 'And what of you?'

He tried to make a joke. 'You don't love me enough to wash my clothes.'

'Hah!' Her look was stinging. He flinched. That had been the wrong thing to say too, even in jest. No woman likes to be told she smells, and of course he didn't expect her to wash for him. He swung her around on the spot, trying to recapture the party mood.

'But do you, Anne?'

'Do I what?'

'Love me?' He planted a kiss full on her lips, grinning at her.

'Don't do that. Not here!' Anne squirmed out of his grasp. 'You've spoilt things.' She turned away.

Clearly it was not the moment to be sentimental, but she might have offered some friendly words. Never mind, he wouldn't let this spoil his day; he had the camaraderie of his men. Jack shouted, 'Rum! More rum!' And Davy? Where the hell was the man? 'Davy! More meat and bread to soak up the booze. Take others down with you to help. Quick as you can.'

Jack reached for another drink. If Anne didn't want to dance or show affection, the cask of rum would not refuse him.

Damn Jack! Why did he have to kiss her in front of everyone? Anne scowled, annoyed with him for spoiling a chance to dance together. Out of the corner of her eye, Anne had seen George witness the kiss, and caught his scornful glare. It wasn't her fault! She felt she was always being accused of behaving recklessly. She yearned to be one of the men and made sure she didn't stand out. She wanted to be as strong as them, as good as they were at fighting. She didn't want them thinking of her as a woman, but as a comrade. An equal. Now with everyone partying and in high spirits they'd surely miss the company of women. Jack was the one being reckless.

Anne glowered at Howie as he started another song full of innuendo. The first verse was about a miller whose maid opened the sack; the next a baker kneading his maid, and by the time he got to verse five with the weaver shooting his shuttle at his maid Anne had had enough. 'Howie! Give us another song!'

Her suggestion was met by howls of protest by others and a decisive, 'Only halfway through,' from Howie. He continued, with the men laughing raucously and fooling about acting out the scenes. There was Paddy on his knees, his face thrust in Jim's crotch, as Howie sang a verse about the blacksmith and his maid blowing the bellows. Yes, damn Jack – this wasn't the time or place to provoke anyone to lustfulness that might put her at risk.

Anne turned away from the carousing men and strode towards Mary – or Mark, as she always remembered to call her – where she leant on a rail, a bottle of rum in her hand.

'See?' Anne grabbed the bottle. 'You saw Jack just now. It was a stupid thing to do. I know I can be impulsive sometimes, but I'm not reckless.' She took a swig.

'Is that a sorry then? You want to say sorry?'

Anne did not believe she had put Mary at any risk by trying to befriend her.

'I'm not going to apologise. Why should I?'

Mary gave a snort of laughter. This was progress. Mary was always so serious, and now, with a chance to join in and party, she was keeping away. This wouldn't do.

Tom retuned his fiddle, saying, 'This hornpipe's one from my home town, Portsmouth, the devil take the dismal place.' He began playing a cheerful tune that had Anne jiggling up and down, reminding her of her dance lesson with her family. She tugged Mary's arm.

'C'mon now. Let's join them.'

Mary pulled away. 'No. Not for me – I don't dance.'

'Anyone can. I'm a good dancer, it might surprise you to know. C'mon!' She hummed along with the catchy hornpipe.

'No. I'd feel lumpen and foolish.'

'Nonsense. It's easy – follow me. Just don't stand on my feet like Jack did.'

Mary resisted, but Anne meant to have her way. 'You're drawing attention to yourself by not dancing. Everyone's enjoying themselves. Come!'

Anne set off, her arm around Mary's waist, forcing her to keep pace galloping along the deck away from the gathered men.

'No need to look down – your feet know what to do.' She remembered the advice from her own first lesson. Mary looked up and smiled. Actually smiled! Anne hopped from foot to foot laughing gleefully. 'You see, it's fun.'

Before Anne could turn her dancing partner around, she felt a grip on her shoulders and was violently thrust away. She stumbled back, barely keeping to her feet, as Jack, smelling of drink, his face stormy, loomed over Mary.

'You know I'll not stand for this!' Jack grabbed Mary's knotted neck scarf in his hand and began to throttle her.

'Jack. It's not as you think!' Anne grabbed his arm. Mary's face was turning red. 'No! Stop! Tell him, Mark!' But Mary wasn't in any position to talk.

'I'll not be made a fool of in front of my men.' Jack twisted the scarf.

'Jack!' Anne screeched now, audible above the fiddle and rowdy singing and laughter. 'You're the one being a fool!'

Anne leaped onto Jack's back, gripping his waist between her thighs, grabbed a hank of hair and screeched in his ear, 'Stop! Stop!' She clawed at his hands to loosen his grip, and when this failed to achieve anything she bit down hard on the soft tip of his nearest ear.

'Shit!' Jack boxed her on the head, propelling her backwards.

'Need help, Cap'n?' 'What the fuck's goin' on?' Paddy and Dick were pulling Mary and Jack apart. Within seconds George was on the spot, his gimlet eyes piercing her own. Anne leapt to her feet.

'You're wrong. This is not my doing. Jack started it! You tell them, Mark!'

Jack glared. 'Something's going on. Let's have it.'

Paddy moved closer to Mary. 'What're ye hiding?'

Mary raised her eyes and looked in turn at the gathered faces. 'It's time, I suppose – should tell you…'

Anne sighed in relief as Mary cleared her throat.

'Always worked hard…In the navy and army, then—'

'What's this got to do with anything?' Anne was beside herself.

Mary folded her arms. 'Being a man protected me from—'

'Understand you there. Used to be a prize fighter m'self—'

'Shut up, Dick!' Anne willed Mary to get on with it.

'For the last time. What the hell's going on?' Jack thrust Dick out of the way and stood in front of Mary, his knife to her throat.

Mary twisted her head to look at Anne. 'You tell them, go on, you're busting to say. I don't care.'

'She's a woman!' Anne shrieked. 'There, I've said it. She's a woman, with breasts to prove it!'

Stunned silence met her statement, then everyone began talking at once.

'You sure?' Dick looked perplexed. 'I saw you kill Sam!'

'He – I mean *she* f-f-fought for me!' Frank looked stunned.

Paddy's hand reached between Mary's legs. She flinched but remained still as he groped. 'Nothin' down here, Cap'n! Nothin' you can take your knife to!'

'The devil take all women! I'll not stand for it, Calico. Double bad luck. She's going – first chance we get!' George snarled at this new female threat.

Anne's heart sank. She could do without him weighing in and influencing Jack or any of the others with his poisonous views.

'She's not going anywhere. I want her to stay.' Anne spoke forcefully.

Mary came out of her daze. 'It's not about what you want. I don't need you speaking up for me – I can look after myself.' Her gaze moved to Jack. 'I suppose you want to know why?'

Jack shook his head as if to shake the remainder of the booze from his brain, but instead of questioning Mary he dabbed his bleeding ear and turned to Anne.

'How long have you known? Why didn't you tell me?'

'Couldn't. I promised Mary—'

'Mary!' Cries rang out. 'Mary, mother of fucking Jesus!'

'Well, I'll tell you this for nothin', and I think I'm speaking for the lot of us.' Paddy gestured to the gathered men. 'I didn't come close to guessing. While this one here' – he cocked his head towards Anne – 'only lasted as long as she did in disguise 'cos we were too busy to bother looking at what was in front of our noses. And to be honest I also thought Calico had brought a cabin boy on board – just as Rye did. But you?' Paddy's gaze rested on Mary and he gave a soft whistle.

The shock of revelation was followed by a grudging admiration Anne shared. She could easily see how Mary hid her sex. She wore her hat tilted at a low angle shading her face; her jawline was strong and stained a tarry black. A scarf hid the lack of an Adam's apple around her thick neck. Her arms were steely, and stronger than many of the men on board. As to her breasts, they were barely noticeable, bound tight to her muscular chest below broad shoulders. Her trousers and jacket were large and loose-fitting, and she walked with the gait of a sailor, arms dangling from her sides. This woman who had lived for so long in a man's world had fooled the lot of them. Anne watched as men continued to poke and peer, exclaim and curse at this latest problem.

'Enough!' Jack took command. 'Whatever your story – and we'll hear it later – you can't stay on board.'

Mary smiled. 'Fine. Put me ashore somewhere we agree to.'

'And m-me!' Frank looked desperate. 'We were both forced to s-s-sign articles. If you let her go, you have to l-let me go too!'

'Well, Calico, he has a point. Yep, he has a point.' Dick nodded and frowned. 'Then again, anyone who signed articles stays with us – no exceptions. There's something to puzzle over.'

'She's going ashore, if I have my way!' George spoke forcefully, and a handful of men offered "Aye"s.

Anne's heart raced as she turned to Mary. 'No! You must stay! Where would you go anyway? What would you do?' She had an inkling this rootless woman didn't have any fixed plan and could not for the life of her imagine Mary contentedly living on shore opening a shop. Anne grasped Mary's jacket. 'You're made for a life at sea. You belong here!'

'Well…' Mary hesitated. 'I wouldn't mind staying for a while. This company's not like Vane's, and the way I see it, this life's as good as another.' Mary glared at the surrounding faces. 'But I'll not be fooled with, I want to make that clear.'

Mary had such a masculine air about her Anne doubted if any of the men would have any such lustful thoughts.

'Two women.' Jack scratched his chin. 'Two women in a rover's company. Never heard of such a thing.'

'But, Cap'n.' Noah spoke softly. 'This life's for anyone… Yes?'

'True… True. I've spoken such words, though I may come to regret it.' Jack managed a tight smile. 'Vote on it. Get on and vote on whether you accept her – Mary – whatever your other name is.'

'Read. Mary Read.'

'That much was true then.' He turned to the company. 'So vote on it and let me know your decision.'

Anne grabbed Jack's arm. 'We'll not vote. There's nothing to vote on. Mary's a member of the company, just as I am.'

'Hold your tongue.'

'No. We'll not vote, I tell you!' Before she could stop herself she stamped her foot, the way she had behaved as a child when she didn't get her own way. 'We don't need to vote. Mary's not broken ship's articles. She stays!'

'Told you I don't need you to speak for me, so shut up!' Mary was riled.

Anne wanted to let this woman know she wished to be her friend; they could both find a place amongst the men. 'But I only want to help, I only want to—'

'I don't care what *you* want.'

Mary stood legs astride and without any passion addressed them all.

'I meant to hunt you down, maybe kill you if it came to it, and claim my share of the prize. Instead you saved me, and I owe you. That's the way things have worked out. You've seen I can fight and hold my own, and y'know I'll shin up to the top in a gale to fix sails. I do anything that's needed and expect the same of everyone else.' Mary paused and spoke flatly. 'If you'll have me, I'd like to stay.'

Jack stepped up to Mary's side. 'This is, um, you might say, unusual.' He laughed uneasily. 'But she can stay as far as I'm concerned.'

'And me!' Anne could not hold back. 'I say she stays!'

'Bossy Bonny thinks she's in charge.' George sniggered.

Anne turned on George, her hands planted on her hips. 'I hear you've got us lost. You're the navigator – you're supposed to know.' She crowed enjoying his discomfort. 'No vote. It's done. We're here to stay – both of us.'

Anne heard George's muffled grumble. 'Thinks she's the bloody captain.'

Jack spoke firmly. 'I'm in command, not her. But let's agree – there'll be no vote. If any of you want out we'll put you off somewhere. We're low on provisions, so time ashore is no bad thing.' Jack turned to George. 'You're staying, I hope?'

George spat. 'I'll not let ladies spoil our lives together.'

'I'm no damned lady,' Mary said forcefully.

'Agree with you there.' Jack's admiration was clear. 'And you?' He turned to Anne. 'You're no damn lady either, biting my fucking ear!'

'Don't make a fuss – it's just a nick. You should have stopped when I told you to.' Anne thrust out her chin.

George's voice rose. 'Told you to? Told you to? Hear that Calico – the way she's talking to you?'

Jack brushed him aside. 'Right – party's over. Clean up and sober up; you never know what's ahead. We've crows to pluck… Two damned women! Hah!' Jack looked bemused by the situation he found himself in. 'We'll have stories to tell our children. If we live long enough.'

'Don't say such things.' Anne hated it when Jack sowed doubts into her mind. Of course, they'd survive. Why on earth wouldn't they? She linked arms with Jack, and pulling Mary towards her, tucked her other arm into hers. Standing between her man and the woman she hoped would become her friend, a broad grin lit up her face as she yelled.

'You heard Jack. Let's pluck crows!'

44

Captain Price's failed venture had infuriated Woodes: a waste of good men and the *Sea Hawk* when armed seaworthy vessels were a rarity. Rackham had shown himself to be no better than Vane, and deserved to swing with those sailing with him, man or woman. But while Price had failed, Woodes had plans of his own.

Standing on Nassau's beach, the harbour long since cleared of burnt-out hulks and sunken ships, Woodes gazed at the *Venture* riding at anchor. His heart was gladdened by the industry: sawing and hammering; levering and hoisting a cannon on board; fixing rigging. All manner of preparation. The *Venture* was his enterprise.

'Sir!' Woodes turned to the approaching man, the shipwright he had engaged, and accepting the paper he proffered. He studied the page, his eye drawn from the left, itemising goods, to the right-hand column with costs, his attention moving swiftly to the heavily underlined total sum at the bottom.

He frowned. 'Your revised calculations and costings...?'

'Yes, sir, and all of it is necessary. I've done my best to economise, reusing timbers and salvaging what we can. Look over it at your leisure, but I need a decision from you before we continue.' The man hesitated. 'And there'll be more to come.'

Specialist equipment was difficult to source in Nassau, and dearly bought.

'Get what you need.' The shipwright hesitated again, clearly trying to find the right words, so Woodes found them for him. 'I'll pay for it in advance.' The shipwright saluted and walked away.

Woodes's debts were rising as surely as the sun rose each day.

'Sir! Captain Rogers! How are you?'

'Mr Harmon.' Woodes responded to Harmon's hail. The man was overseeing his own group of men who were rolling barrels and carrying boxes to a boat, obviously about to set out in the *William*.

Woodes made his way across to the merchant. There was a meeting of minds between them and he enjoyed his conversations with Harmon. Neither could abide laziness, and Harmon was, in his own robust way, a man of honour. If only the colony had a hundred more such men.

Harmon pumped his hand. 'I see we're both preparing. Good luck with your cruise, sir. Bring them in, I say! A few more of Blackbeard's ilk should do the trick. Perhaps if you bag Vane and Rackham, it won't be just the crew of the *Venture* who earn a pretty prize. Should do nicely for you too.' He winked.

Woodes face was blank. He didn't know what the man was leading to. Harmon leant in, speaking confidentially.

'There's a rumour about... Talk of a knighthood. After all, Jamaica has Sir Nicholas Lawes as governor. I and many others believe you deserve the same recognition! Why not? You're doing all that's humanly possible.'

Woodes found himself drawing back, repelled by such loose talk.

'I truly don't expect any such honour – I'm merely doing my duty. If you have heard anything from London, anything at all, you are in a more honoured position than I am. For the moment at least.'

'Oh, come, come, sir. You're too modest.'

Woodes changed the subject. 'And, where are you heading?'

'Virginia and Carolina. We'll be off shortly – tomorrow morning's tide – carrying sugar and salt, for the main. We'll be back with provisions and news in a matter of weeks.'

'Will you carry a letter for me if I get onto it today?' Woodes would not let this opportunity pass. Harmon could deliver it to Charles Town, where another vessel would take the accumulated bags of mail on to London.

'My pleasure.'

'And how is Mrs Harmon?' Woodes remembered to enquire. 'How is the Ladies' Guild progressing? Church matters, our scheme for sending young women to Carolina. Any idea?' Woodes received reports every so often, but Mrs Harmon had not been to see him in recent months, and the last time he had bumped into Sarah Walker he had been distracted by another matter and forgot to ask.

'You'll have to ask her yourself, sir. I don't enquire – don't have an interest in such things. The ladies like to meet and sew and gossip, I know that much; and my good wife is fond of bending my ear about tittle-tattle. I must say, with the lovely Mrs Bonny having departed these shores, there is a great deal less gossip reaching my ears.' Harmon laughed then his face dropped. 'A great shame about James Bonny, though – I had a lot of time for him.'

'Yes, I'm sorry too. But there you are, he was set on it, and it wasn't for me to interfere. We'll see if the *Venture* has more luck.'

'Indeed. It is only because the *William* is so quick that I have no fear of any of those scum. Let any of them try to take me on and I'll lead them a merry dance, I assure you.'

Harmon's pride in the *William* was justified. Woodes promised to have a letter with him by the evening and turned to leave.

'Captain Rogers! Perhaps send a message to Mrs Harmon yourself. She'll be delighted to know you're thinking of her. Notwithstanding the little incident with Mrs Bonny, she's keen for another party – or *soirée*, as she tells me is the correct term. Just giving you fair warning.'

Fair warning indeed – he owed the man for this piece of intelligence – but Woodes couldn't resist teasing. 'A *soirée*? Do you think we should adopt foreign habits? The French have been our enemy until quite recently, after all.'

Harmon's face coloured. 'No offence intended, I'm sure my wife… Ah… Ah…' Harmon chuckled. 'You had me for a moment!'

'As we enjoy French brandy we can't be hypocrites and turn our backs on the better things that nation has to offer the world. I'm sure we can rise to whatever occasion the ladies see fit. Good day, Mr Harmon, and safe voyage.'

Woodes did not mean to contact Mrs Harmon – he had quite enough on his plate without having to dodge attempts to snare him into hosting another social gathering. A *soirée* indeed!

Stepping into his office, Woodes tried to rid his mind of Harmon's loose talk. A knighthood? Could there be such plans afoot in London's corridors of power? Were there people in the right places ready to champion him and put in a good word? If he had any vanity, and every man did, it was that those who mattered to him respected and valued his skills as a mariner and leader of men. But talk of a knighthood? Somehow this did not square with the evidence before him.

He settled to write his letter, ending, 'most obedient and humble servant.' Earlier letters he had signed, 'I am, with your utmost ambition and zeal, your Lordship's most obedient and humble servant.' For the most part this was still true – he still had ambition and zeal – but accepted he was jaded. This Bahamian project was exhausting him and his pocket.

45

As dawn broke Mary tended the men lying under a makeshift canvas awning. Howie wouldn't be entertaining them with amusing songs or sentimental ballads any time soon, nor, more importantly, carrying out his duties as bosun: keeping an eye on supply stores and undertaking daily inspections of sails and rigging. All his deck activities had been delegated, including to her. Tom wouldn't be picking up his fiddle for a while, nor doing his duties. He was in charge of guns and ammunition: sifting gunpowder to keep it dry, oiling the great guns to keep them rust-free, and making sure all the company kept their weapons in good repair. His work had been shared out too, and they were fast running out of able-bodied men to manage the *Curlew*. Calico Jack had changed the watch cycle from three to two so there was barely time to sleep. She stooped and lifted the head of one restless mumbling man, helping him sip from a ladle of water.

'How many now? How's it looking?' At Dick's voice, Mary straightened, removing the scarf covering her nose and mouth.

'None dead, but he doesn't look too good.' Mary gently prodded Jim with the toe of her shoe.

'Poor lad. Got a soft spot for the youngsters.' Dick shook his head.

Jim's face was shining with sweat and his teeth were chattering despite the blanket wrapped around him. Mary could definitely smell what she had earlier suspected: he had soiled himself. Someone else could sort him out.

All fourteen men lying out on deck were in a bad way, stricken with flux and fever. This had happened suddenly and within days they were dropping like flies. Mary had seen it so often in her years at sea or in the army camps in Flanders. Everyone said bad air must be to blame for it, but neither she nor any man or woman understood how or why it happened. The day before Mary had helped fumigate. She'd sloshed down the lower deck with buckets of vinegar and water while others carried pans of burning brimstone till she could barely breathe for the smoke and stench.

'Four more below – come down with it overnight. Yep, four more.' Dick shook his head and Mary sighed; the fumigation had not worked. 'I'll get 'em brought out here. Calico won't like this. If there's one thing he can't abide its rampant fever on board. I'd best go and report to him.' Dick turned to go.

'Leave him, he only went down a short while ago.' Calico Jack had been up and down during the night, issuing new orders and counting the sick. She was lucky – they all were – to have Calico as their commander. Apart from the one time he had lost his temper and gone for her, you knew where you were with him, and during the past few days she'd witnessed him looking out for his men.

'You're taking over, I hope?' Mary grabbed the sleeve of a passing seaman and thrust the pail of none-too-fresh drinking water into his hands. His reluctance was clear, and she couldn't blame him – none of them wanted to be close to the ill, possibly dying men – but everyone had to take a turn, and if she fell ill she'd want someone to tend to her. On a reflex, she reached out and tapped the *Curlew*'s wooden rail.

Before she slept she had work to do, checking the top yards and all their associated rigging for chafing and wear. The last thing she wanted if she had to shin up a ratline or out along a yard was to have a rope give way. As well as allowing for daily wear and tear, she suspected some amongst the crew had supported Sam's assertion that she'd almost pushed him off the rigging, and someone might take it into their head to take revenge and cut through a rope. While aloft, if she found any wooden components to be cracked or weakened, she would report these to Frank. Teamwork. Their lives depended on each playing his part.

Mary calculated at least two turns of the sand glass must have passed by the time she made her way to her hammock for a quick sleep before the bell announced her next watch.

'Mark... um... Mary.' She turned in the dim light of the 'tween deck to see Calico Jack's strained face. 'It's Anne – she's in a bad way.'

'Take her up on deck – that'll be best.'

'I'll not move her out with the men... Come.'

Mary longed to drop into her hammock, but instead she followed Calico to his cabin where Anne lay on his bed, her face beaded with sweat, her body shaking.

'You want me to look after her?'

Jack nodded. 'I'll have your watch rotas rearranged.' He dashed out the door.

Mary pulled up a chair and glowered at Anne. Here she was doing all the usual work expected of her, on top of duties the sick men should be responsible for, and now, just because she was a woman, she suddenly had an extra unwanted responsibility thrust upon her. Weren't they all supposed to be treated the same? In a recent conversation with Anne, Anne had blithely said, 'Oh no. I'm not given any favours! I'm part of the company on the same terms as everyone else.'

As Mary gazed at Anne her resentment rose. Didn't Anne have the comfort of Calico's bed? No doubt Calico shared all manner of important things with her he didn't mention to the rest of the company, and who knew what ideas this woman put into his brain, whispering into his ear? Now Calico was giving Anne special treatment, and she, Mary, had to nurse her. She was tired, and for a moment she even wished Anne dead. She sighed. She had no choice but to get on with it.

In the coming days she spent a great deal of time in Calico's cabin caring for Anne. The ship's bell sounded the watches; someone brought her news – who had died, who was recovering; she heard raised voices as orders were given and the rush of activity as they altered course to avoid a confrontation.

Where Calico Jack slept was of no concern to her – any hammock would do for the time being. When Mary needed to sleep she wrapped herself in a blanket and lay on the floor. The rest of the time she cared for Anne: bathing her face; wiping her teeth and gums with a rag; clambering on the bed so Anne could lean against her body to sit and drink; assisting Anne off the bed and supporting her as she squatted over the bucket groaning and expelling a flow of stinking runny shit. Then of course she had to throw the putrid liquid overboard on the leeward aft side and swill the bucket.

During the spells when Anne was not in a feverish sleep, they talked. Conversations moved on from her own gruff enquiries – 'How are you? You want anything?' or Anne's plaintive, 'Water,' or a desperate, 'Quick, the bucket!' – to longer exchanges.

Mary was dozing when Anne asked, 'Why did you fight for Frank?'

'Because.' Mary jolted awake. She hadn't been ready for this question. She glanced at Anne to see her lying quite still, eyes closed but her brain obviously busy.

'But why risk your life?' A crease deepened between Anne's brows as she grappled with this puzzle. Mary, stumbling to find the words, began to explain what it meant to be comrades, what it meant to look out for those you needed to look out for you. It was difficult to explain so she ended by saying simply, 'Besides, I like Frank.'

'You want to share his hammock?'

Must everything come down to sex? She didn't answer.

Anne told her a little about her life growing up: the horse she had loved; her marriage to James: 'A man of little ambition, but I'm sorry he's dead.' Mary let that pass and instead talked about her own fighting days. Anne was quiet and attentive, only interjecting with more questions until Mary found she had told Anne about her marriage and her dead child – things she had not divulged to anyone.

'Enough talk now.' Mary wrung out a rag, sat on the edge of the cabin bed and gently bathed Anne's face, her freckles standing out sharply against her waxy skin. Even ill, there was an openness about Anne's face as she lay there, trusting Mary to care for her. There was not one part of this ill woman's body she didn't touch while tending her, and as she gently stroked the hair away from her face she realised she did not want Anne to die after all.

Leaving Anne sleeping, she softly closed the cabin door behind her. Mary filled her stomach and drank her fill, cut some tobacco, and stood at the rail, savouring the taste of smoke in her throat and the salty sea air in her nostrils. Later, returning to Anne, she paused outside the cabin door, placed a pail of fresh water down and softly lifted the latch. She drew back at the sound of Calico's voice. Instantly she knew she had no place here, but she hesitated, and in that moment of indecisiveness became rooted to the spot listening to his drunken rambling.

'You've no idea what you mean to me. Know that? You never want to hear such things... Well, so help me... if y'can hear me... I'll say it... I love you. You hear? You hear me, you crazy bitch?'

Mary heard him glugging from a bottle and his deep expulsion of breath.

'Don't slip away. I don't mean to feed you to the sharks. This is no way to die. You hear? You hold on... I want you here with me.'

She heard the break in his voice and the sound of the bottle crashing to the floor. Softly, she closed the cabin door and moved away. This was not her business. She sought out her hammock and dropped into it. Someone would shake her awake when she was needed, and she hoped it wouldn't be any time soon.

46

'Who the fuck's wanting our company?' Jack wearily raised his spyglass and squinted at the persistent vessel that had been trailing them for hours. She was flying the Union Jack but none of them had the slightest idea who might be on board. She was not a fighting frigate, but she was no merchant vessel either.

He had rarely felt so exhausted, barely sleeping the past week, and he couldn't remember when he'd last eaten. Half the company were puking, shitting and shivering, making it difficult to raise enough men to crew the *Curlew*; it was out of the question to muster a fighting force. Dick had been the latest to take to his hammock, a bucket by his side. Jack couldn't spare any fit man to assist the sick, so the stench in the lower deck was enough to turn a strong man's stomach.

'One thing's certain, Calico – we're back in home waters, I'm happy to say.'

George's reference to the Bahamas as "home" was not meant with any irony, as nowhere else had a claim on his heart.

Jack didn't share his view, but he too was happy to be here. He knew these islands' coasts and shallow seas as intimately as George.

Earlier in the day the lookout had spied a sail approaching from the south-west as they steered towards a long line of cays and shoals extending north-west from Long Island. If they could reach there they would be safe.

'Could Rogers be having another go?' When she had tacked Jack had made out her name, the *Venture*, and could see she was armed. 'If we keep them off till sunset we've a good chance of giving them the slip overnight.'

George was an excellent master, and if he couldn't guide the *Curlew* to safety in the narrow passages they were heading towards, no one could. This was where nerves came into it, and Jack hoped the commander of the chase vessel wouldn't have the stomach for it. One false calculation and they'd join the wrecks of many others who'd sailed this way.

All able hands were on deck, responding to commands as they tacked slowly towards their destination. With so few men it took longer to fix sails or adjust yards, and with each slow turn when sails rippled and billowed the *Curlew* was losing ground. Worse, despite their recent careening, she had sprung a leak. Frank had done what he could to caulk it, but Jack had to divert teams of men he could ill afford to take turns at the exhausting work of continuous pumping.

Jack glanced at Mary making her way aloft. He had got used to having a second woman aboard. She was the hardest-working member of his crew bar none, and now he realised he didn't have a rival to Anne's heart he welcomed her wholeheartedly.

'Drop the mains'l,' George shouted.

This was the dangerous moment, cutting speed as they approached shallow waters to manoeuvre their vessel carefully without ploughing into a reef. They were vulnerable, as the *Venture* was less than two hundred yards behind.

A resounding boom reverberated, and smoke rose from one of the *Venture's* bow swivel guns. While it didn't have the reach to do damage it confirmed her business: she was a pirate hunter.

'Paddy! Make ready and fire!' Jack rushed to join the group rapidly preparing their own chase swivel. With master gunner Tom ill in his hammock, Paddy was in charge of guns.

Paddy lit the fuse and moments later their own missile headed towards the *Venture*.

The *Venture*, easing closer, fired her second bow swivel, and a whizz of hot jagged metal shot past Jack's head shredding a jib. Perhaps if the *Venture* had known they were so low on manpower they would have aimed at the crew and not the rigging and canvas. Jack could afford to lose a sail, but not more men.

As Paddy and his makeshift team reloaded their single stern swivel, the *Venture* swung around ready for a broadside, while yard by yard the *Curlew* made her way forward.

Within minutes the *Venture's* starboard guns were out and a volley of fire enclosed the vessel in a pall of smoke. Jack ducked – they all did. He wasn't ashamed to do this; he was no naval captain, having to stand his ground. The *Venture's* big guns did their work, pummelling the *Curlew's* retreating stern. Shattered splinters of wood shot up and Jack heard Paddy's howl of pain and saw him grasp his bloodied forehead. 'Fuckers! You fuckers!'

Jack scoured the sails and rigging. Sails ripped, and one of the aft spars smashed. And what of Mary and the others? There – safe on the foremast.

'Stand firm! They've shot their bolts!' Jack shouted comforting words.

And it was true; in the minutes it took the *Venture* to reload and release another barrage, the *Curlew* had extended her range yard by yard, easing her way through a narrow passage between two low-lying cays. Noah was at the bowsprit, a lead line extended, reporting the depth and changing colour of the water.

As George piloted the *Curlew* through the shallow narrow passage towards open water on the eastern side of the string of isles, Jack watched the *Venture* turn and begin to sail northward, keeping to the western side, where she would look for a wider channel and follow them through.

Frank approached carrying a heavy bag of tools. 'What first, C-Cap'n? What'll you have me do?'

Jack noticed Frank's stammer had all but disappeared as he answered, 'Aft spar.' Frank grabbed two seamen and instructed them to bring timber up from below and began laying out his tools.

Paddy's hollering and cursing showed he wasn't in danger of dying any time soon, so Jack need not worry about him. Who else? Jack hurried around the deck, checking his men.

Noah appeared to be in one piece and grinned at him. 'Not our time. I'll see snow yet.' Jack grinned back. 'I'm sure of it!' Highly unlikely even if they all lived for twenty more years; Jack had no plans to sail to cold climates.

The shredded aft mains'l needed removing, so Jack began climbing the aft mast ratlines to join a group already at work on it.

'Jack? What's happening?' He looked down at Anne gazing up at him, her face almost as pale as the unbleached blanket she clutched tightly around her. He dropped back to deck and embraced her. 'Too tough to die, heh? No shark would have a chance biting through your hide.' He grinned in relief.

Anne rested her head on his chest, asking vaguely, 'What's happening? Who's firing?'

'You missed some fireworks, but we're fine.'

He ruffled her hair, kissed her clammy cheek and leapt back onto the rigging. As he began to climb, dizziness overcame him, and he clung to the ratlines, swaying like a landlubber, before starting off again. He had work to do.

'Cap'n? Captain – you all right?' He felt the steadying hand of someone behind him. He paused as a fresh wave of dizziness overcame him, and he barely had the strength to hold on.

'Calico?' Mary scuttled down, towards him. 'He's ill. Help him down.'

Jack shrugged off the hands reaching to support him. He wasn't feverish, and his gut was fine. 'No... No... I'm tired. That's all.'

'Jack?' He looked down at Anne staring up at him, her face etched with concern.

'Anne, tell Davy to get a hot meal ready. Food and sleep will sort me out.'

'Likely be porridge again, Cap'n; meat's gone.'

This was unwelcome news.

Jack shook off his fatigue, then, hand over hand, continued up. From this height in the dusk, he could make out the sails of the *Venture* stalking them from the far side of the cays. He calculated they wouldn't risk sailing through any channel. Meanwhile he needed to make the most of the fading light to get the *Curlew* sorted.

Under cover of darkness with all lights doused, the *Curlew* veered north-east towards Eleuthera. Here they meant to find a hidden bay to make repairs, replenish supplies and allow the sick to recuperate. Time ashore was a welcome prospect even under the nose of Rogers and his spies.

'You know, George, it's time to ditch the *Curlew*. I can't afford to be sentimental about her.'

George looked surprised. 'Never thought I'd hear that from you.'

'We need a swift vessel – one that neither Rogers nor any damned pirate hunter is looking out for.'

'Fair enough.' George grunted and headed away.

Jack dismissed the helmsman and took over. He wanted to be here, standing under the stars with the gentle flap of canvas and waves lapping against the hull, for what might be one of his last nights aboard his much-loved vessel. He would stay awake for this.

'You want company?' Anne slipped her hand into the crook of his arm and nuzzled close.

Jack adjusted the blanket wrapped around her and kissed the top of her head.'Always.'

47

THEY FOUND THEMSELVES SHARING THE ELEUTHERA beach with a colony of seals. The animals raised wary heads but didn't move as Anne, with others from the crew, cautiously approached, muskets raised. They picked off several of the docile creatures, sending the rest into a panic, flippers propelling them rapidly across the sand, back to the sea in search of a quieter haven.

At one end of the beach they set up a fire with a cauldron in which Davy boiled down blubber for lamp oil. The reek of slaughtered animals littering the beach, seals and turtles both, combined with the acrid smell of boiling oil, wafted towards other fires at the opposite end of the beach. Here meat roasted and soup boiled in equally massive quantities to feed ravenous men.

While the *Curlew*, anchored in its hidden north-east cove, might not be visible to anyone sailing nearby, they had not endeared themselves to the locals. En route, sailing up the coast of Eleuthera, they had waylaid two small trading vessels and helped themselves to supplies. Anne, still unwell, had been a passive witness to those sea raids, but in the past days, while others sawed, chiselled and planed planks of wood to repair the *Curlew*, she had undertaken land raids, lightening farmers' herds by a beast or two. None of the settlers on the island dared confront them, and by the time word got through to Rogers of their whereabouts they'd be back on the high seas hunting down a replacement for the *Curlew*.

For two days men had toiled under Frank's instructions, making the *Curlew* fit to sail; now with that work done, and with their supply of alcohol exhausted, the men were parched.

Paddy, his head heavily bandaged, rounded up loitering men. 'C'mon, move. I need fire in my belly and my firestick rubbed… And you, m' lad' – Paddy slapped Jim on the shoulder – 'you're going to come back a man or my name's not Patrick Carty!'

Jim grinned sheepishly as the men whooped and cheered. He had bounced back quickly from his illness, and the others intended to oversee this rite of passage.

Anne waved them off as they walked along the beach and disappeared into the forest. Jack and George were among the group, along with Frank and Mary, heads close together in conversation. Despite what Mary had said about Frank, Anne didn't believe her. Surely the two of them would find somewhere private to enjoy each other. She expected Jack back before dark – she had insisted. The paths would be too dangerous to negotiate, and she wasn't having him staying away overnight.

Along with other convalescing crew members whose constitutions weren't yet strong enough for booze or sex, Anne filled her day as best she could. She loathed not being well enough to participate fully in life, and, more seriously, not being strong enough to defend herself. An afternoon downpour kept her huddled under her makeshift canvas shelter, the kind hundreds of men had made for themselves on Nassau's beach. Waiting for the rain to stop, she sharpened her cutlass and knife, oiled her pistol and prepared cartridges.

Noah, though healthy, was avoiding unknown company, spending his days watchful and as nervous as a wild horse. He emerged at sunset after hiding out in the forest all day and squatted by her side at the cooking fire.

'Has Calico said? We sailing tomorrow?' He was edgy and looked disappointed at the shake of her head and brief, 'Not sure.' Noah grabbed some food and water and headed back to the cover of the trees.

She had come to accept Noah and had learnt a little of his past – as much as he cared to share about his enslavement. When she asked why he owed Jack he said, 'W's hiding in marshes, runnin'. Calico come huntin' waterfowl ... said to go with him...' Anne had wondered what stories, what past lives, her father's slaves had. At the time she had not given it the slightest thought. Why would she? None of the families she'd known ever talked about their blacks, other than who was the laziest and would be sold on, how many had given birth or died.

Settling by the fire, Anne listened to Howie singing. As she tossed a chewed bone over her shoulder, she remembered her disdain for the camped-out pirates on Nassau beach. She had become indifferent to the dirt and chaos of her own life and now acknowledged she was no better than those men. When Howie's song ended, Dick began reminiscing about his pugilist days.

'Set up my booth in Margate – a fine summer day. By afternoon I'd seen off five challengers – yep, five. By then my purse was full. Well, this butcher came forward, a big brute of a fella, and I thought, oi, oi, he's going to give me a run for m' money. You should've seen the crowd, yelling and wagering. Well, we went for it. What a fuckin' fight! Couldn't see no more for the blood in m' eyes, knuckles flayed, but we were both standing, still throwing punches. Yep, some fight – neither of us could knock the other out. Went on and on, it did – just stood there and bashed each other. Ah, them were the days!'

Dick paused, eyes glazed, remembering his youthful self. 'Fifteen, yep, fifteen rounds later, we looked at each other and I thought, sod it. That was the only time I've divided a purse – only time in m' life I've not been knocked out or knocked the other fella out. Thirty-seven times I done it. Thirty-seven fuckin' times!'

This brawny, thick-headed man was proud of his record and the men around the fire showed their appreciation, repeating, 'Thirty-seven times!'

'Mary's way's best.' Anne spoke out. 'The way she fought Sam – using her brain instead. Got to be the best way.'

Dick snorted. 'I'm talking bare fist to bare fist. Raw skin and bone. Man to man, without weapons. That's fighting for ya. If Mary wants to fight me with her fists, you'd soon see who'd win!'

Anne kicked her heel in the sand. It wasn't worth arguing. She knew both Jack and Mary were better fighters, tactical, and this was what she admired. She desperately wanted to get strong enough to practise with her own weapons, as her life might depend on it.

As night fell, crew members drifted back to camp. She looked up when she heard Mary's voice. 'Wasn't going to risk leaving him.' Mary staggered into camp, arm linked in Jack's; he mumbled, 'Said I'd be back. Don't need another bloody woman telling me what to do!' Jack plopped down on the sand, dragging Mary down with him.

'Where's Frank. You left him there?' Anne was curious.

'Dunno… Having fun… Back soon.' Mary feebly raised an arm.

And Frank arrived back soon enough. She saw a lantern bobbing along the beach announcing the arrival of a handful more cheerful men, and before long Frank fell into a comfortable drunken slumber, his head resting on Mary's lap, her hand casually stroking his hair.

Anne smiled: this was her family. She had a momentary pang, thinking about her father and Billy – and Richard – wondering how they were, then dismissed them. She was reminded of groups of monkeys she'd seen grooming each other, picking lice from their fur, casually mounting for a quick fuck, or sleeping in a jumble of furry bodies. She picked her way over sprawled legs to where Jack lay and curled on her side with her back into his stomach, drawing his arm over her. She was just where she wanted to be, and contentedly drifted to sleep with Dick droning on about his glory days.

Gunshots! Shouts! Jack pushed her aside and was instantly on his feet. Others around the embers were scurrying for cutlasses and knives discarded the night before. Alert, they stared at the track leading into the forest, waiting to see who might emerge into the grey light of dawn.

First Jim raced onto the beach, Paddy close on his heels, sprinting as if their lives depended on it. A handful more from the *Curlew* darted out from the tree cover and, chasing them, a dozen or more unknown men and boys.

'Kill them – I'll answer for you!' 'Get them!' 'Get them!' The pursuers were shouting and brandishing pistols, swords and pitchforks.

Anne instinctively bunched closer to her own hastily gathering group, drawing Paddy and Jim into their fold, and faced the irate locals now advancing at a cautious walking pace.

'Stop! Wait. I'm captain here.' Jack, one hand on his cutlass, raised his free arm. 'What's this about?'

A breathless man stepped forward his pistol trained on Jack. Anne wasn't going to stand for this! She levelled her own pistol. 'You pull the trigger and I'll blow your face away!'

Her opponent was taken off guard and hesitated. She had long ago stopped disguising her voice, though she always wore seaman's clothes. The local man eyed her suspiciously, then his eyes flicked back to Jack. 'You got a woman with you?'

'Two.' Jack cocked his head towards Mary. 'And they're both excellent shots. Put down your weapons. I don't want anyone dead – me in particular. What d' you want?'

'We want you gone.' The leader lowered his pistol. 'We've got two of your men and we want these two.' He pointed to Paddy and Jim, Jim's face turning a sickly green.

Paddy appealed to both sides. 'It got a little out of hand. High spirits, that's all, Cap'n. To be fair, it wasn't Jim's fault.'

'Got two of our men?' Jack frowned at the local man, then turned to Paddy. 'What do you mean, not Jim's fault?'

'Told ye – just enjoying ourselves.'

A local man with a bruised and bloodied face stepped forward from the group and confronted them. 'Abigail's a good girl, my youngest, just celebrated her fourteenth birthday...' He faltered. 'I don't care for what you done to her. What Christian man—'

'Fourteen, ye say?' Paddy looked shocked.

'You fucked this man's daughter?' Anne glared at Jim's guilt-stricken face and she turned her pistol on him, tempted to shoot.

'He wasn't the first or the last – we nabbed two of your others. Round the bastards up.'

Anne looked around, trying to calculate who was missing. Jim's whispered, 'Chris and Robbie,' was the answer. Two seamen in their twenties – men you wouldn't think twice about.

Jack beckoned the hostile group forward. 'Let's work something out. Our men you're holding. I'll pay for their night's lodgings and we'll be gone by midday.'

The leader shook his head. 'Too late. We're sending them to Nassau for Governor Rogers to deal with.'

A silence fell, and Anne watched Jack's face, calculating if this might be negotiated. The local man read Jack's thoughts.

'Fact is, they've left already.'

The story unfolded. Heavy drinking had been followed by a brawl with local men, glasses smashed and tables broken. Paddy had been determined to find a whore for Jim but had no success. This sparsely populated backwater of poor farmers did not cater for a hoard of carousing seamen. Drunk and desperate, the pirates had hit on the wrong girl, the tavern owner's daughter, plying her with drink and compliments.

Anne's heart pounded. Poor Abigail! It had been several years since her own rape in the Carolina forest, and this brought the terror of that encounter to the front of her mind. She turned to Paddy and Jim. 'Any fool knows the difference between a whore doing it for money and a young girl minding her own business!'

Paddy sounded defensive. 'There're many who go whoring young. How were we to know?'

'But… But… I didn't! …Couldn't!' Jim spluttered.

'What?' Paddy turned on him. 'After all the effort I made!'

Paddy turned back at Abigail's father. 'Look, mister, sorry for your troubles. We meant no harm. I'll pay for your broken stuff – can't offer more.'

The local men huddled together, whispering. Before long the leaders from the island sat with Jack and Paddy and thrashed out a deal, itemising broken glass and crockery and arguing replacement costs. As the bargaining proceeded, Anne could feel herself getting angrier but dared not intervene, so she sought out Mary.

'Listen to them. Just listen. What of the girl? What about Abigail?'

Mary sighed. 'Nothing much changes – it's a man's world and I just try to fit in. Don't get me wrong, I don't like it any more than you do, but then I don't like men much – not generally speaking.'

'But this girl!'

'You can rest easy about her. She's seventeen if she's a day. And as to being a good girl, it depends who you ask.'

Anne frowned, wondering why Mary hadn't spoken up. Mary sensed her unspoken question. 'Look, it's not my business. I kept an eye on Jack – thought I'd do that for you. He looked inclined to settle down for the night and I figured he might regret it.' Mary raised an eyebrow. 'You know what men're like – shut their minds like a trapdoor if it suits them. And as to Paddy – he can stew a while longer. Let him give over some of the booty he's collected. These local men'll be happy with that, and more than happy to see the back of us.'

Mary kicked over the ashes of the fire with her shoe. 'Let's get out of here.'

Anne looked in fresh admiration at this woman striding around the beach in her seaman's outfit, dismantling her canvas shelter, doing what needed to be done before any of the men had thought to organise a thing. Not a thing. If Mary didn't like men very much, she trusted Mary could grow to like her.

48

'WELL, CALICO, WHAT'S IT TO BE, THEN? I NEED TO SET a course.' George picked up a bundle of charts and unrolled them. 'Still want to continue north to the Carolinas?'

As others prepared to hoist the anchor, Jack conferred with Anne, George and Dick in his cabin. His priority was a new vessel, something swift, with enough guns to get them started on a new cruise. Carolina's coastline, with its abundant inlets, offered perfect opportunities to hide and pounce on passing shipping. That was the plan... had been the plan. A new idea popped into his head.

'Forget Carolina. We're going to Nassau. At least I am.' Jack spoke decisively.

'Nassau? You out of your mind?' George scowled.

'Jack?' Anne looked puzzled. 'What on earth are you talking about?'

'Where are we likely to find a decent-sized vessel anywhere near here? The only place is Nassau. We could waylay a vessel arriving or departing, but we're unlikely to be lucky with the timing. I say we ditch the *Curlew*; I hide out on New Providence and steal a vessel from the harbour.'

This plan was met by silence for a moment or two.

'You're putting your head in a noose. I'll not be a part of this!' George choked.

'Right under Rogers's nose. What's got into you? We can't go back there!' Anne rose from her chair, glowering. 'Anyhow, we've spent days and days restocking—'

'You're not going – I said, I'm going. I'll round up a crew there and meet you later.'

'Oh no!' Anne thumped his arm. 'I'm not being dumped on some island not knowing where the hell you are, or if you're alive or dead. I've done it once, and not again. Where you go, I go. You're not leaving me behind!'

Jack was momentarily surprised and flattered by her passion. He wasn't sure if this was for him or the life he helped her have. 'I don't want to worry about you getting caught. You're not well, and—'

'I am! Really, I'm fine!'

Jack looked at her slender body; she barely had the strength to defend herself. He soundlessly mouthed, 'No!'

'Well, you two can do what you want, but I'll not set foot on the place, Calico. Nope. Not even for you and old times.' Dick sighed.

'I don't want you there with me. We're too well known – all of us. It'll be impossible enough for me. We'll agree a place to meet.'

'I'll come, if it helps You can't do this alone.' George spoke reluctantly, and Jack shook his head.

'No, not you either. I need faces that aren't known to Rogers or anyone.'

'Take Mary, then. And Frank. He'll do it if she tells him to.' Anne spoke with conviction.

'Mary?' It was on the tip of his tongue to add, 'She's a woman,' but he bit that back as it didn't matter in the slightest. However, there was one drawback. 'Rogers recruited her – she's known to him and others.'

'He met her once – in seaman's clothes. She can dress as a woman, can't she? Someone can find her a dress to wear – I don't expect she has one with her. I bet she'll come with us. I'd trust her with my life, so let's take Mary.'

'With me – not us. You're not coming.' He didn't want Anne getting caught but equally felt she might be a liability. It would be enough to keep himself hidden, without her to worry about. But he knew he'd lost the argument by the determined look on her face: the tilt of her chin, lips pressed together... Jack sighed. 'Damn!'

They set sail around the northern tip of Eleuthera, drove the *Curlew* onto a deserted beach and took away what they could carry. The locals were welcome to salvage the rest; he could offer that much. Some of the company were going their own way; others, including George and Dick, had agreed to rendezvous at Great Abaco.

'God bless the good fishermen of Eleuthera.' Jack's thanks were genuine as he untied the single-mast fishing smack they were stealing, and with Mary, Frank and Anne aboard, he set sail under cover of darkness. Nearby two other stolen fishing boats headed out, and two canoes whose rowers would hug the coast and trade up to bigger vessels.

Of all the idiotic schemes, Jack found himself sailing towards the quiet southern coast of New Providence Island. To all intents and purposes, for anyone sailing nearby, they looked like an innocent group of fisher-folk heading out from Eleuthera.

He expected to firm up plans as they sailed between the two islands, but his brain remained blank. Anne sat shivering, wrapped in a blanket, perhaps having some sort of a relapse, and his other companions were sullen. Mary chewed tobacco, avoiding any conversation, and Frank busied himself improving pieces of tackle not to his satisfaction. This irritated Jack and he snapped, 'Stop fiddling, man. Why bother? We're ditching the blasted boat as soon as we arrive!' Frank reluctantly put it down, then didn't know what to do with himself until Jack thrust the piece of wood back in his hands again.

They bickered, all short-tempered and getting under each other's feet in the confines of the small boat. Mary snapped at him, 'Empty the damn bucket yourself – why do you expect me to?' So he had emptied Anne's foul bucket and didn't ask Mary again. Another time he laughed loudly at what he thought Anne meant as a joke. She had been describing the kind of vessel to steal: 'Something like the *Benjamin*.'

'Like the *Benjamin*? Hah! We should be so lucky! You'll have to lower your expectations, sweetheart!'

'Don't you dare laugh at me!' Anne punched him none too lightly on the shoulder. 'Why shouldn't we have a vessel like that?'

Hornigold's flagship had been magnificent: packed with guns and could carry two hundred men. He dared not say he was unlikely to rise so high; dared not suggest he believed those days were over for all rovers.

As they neared their destination, Mary broke one of her many silences. 'You got a plan yet, Calico? Something to share?' Mary kept her gaze directed away, but Frank turned hopeful eyes on him.

The time hadn't been wasted. He had been thinking, discarding first one idea then another as unworkable or too risky. He needed intelligence: what vessels were in harbour, which were about to leave or expected. Could he hide on the island when he was so well known? And crucially, was there someone he could trust? Ideas swirled through his head. He stalled.

'Got to get Anne settled somewhere safe. Get her back to good health.' He looked tenderly towards Anne.

'I tell you, don't fuss, Jack! I'm not dying. And since when have you put my needs above your own or those of the company?'

Jack was taken aback but let it pass. He would avoid another squabble.

Mary frowned. 'And after? What then?'

'Well…' Into the blank space of his brain, an image formed. A woman's face came to mind. Jack smiled with relief. He turned to Frank. 'First thing – sort out a dress for your wife to wear. Something plain, no frills or flounces.'

'M-my wife?' Frank looked bemused.

'Yes, Mary: your wife.' Mary tapped her pipe on the rail as she considered this sudden change in status, and Jack rushed on. 'There's a woman who runs one of the waterside taverns: Charlotte. She knows me. She'll help us.' As soon as he'd said that, he was unsure. Had he paid his last bill? She'd been nagging him and refusing to serve any more drink or food until he had cleared his debt, and he had left in rather a hurry. Still, surely she wouldn't hold it against him. Would she? This slender thread of hope was all he had.

'Yes, Charlotte. Good idea!' Anne smiled with relief.

They ran the smack onto the sandy beach and sent Frank off on his errands. Jack hid with Anne and Mary, waiting for his return. Skulking in woodland seemed a cowardly thing to be doing, but better safe than sorry. By nightfall they were beginning to worry Frank had been rounded up and were whispering whether to take to the boat again, when they heard a soft whistle.

'Calico… Ch-Ch-Charlotte said to give you this m-message. M-made me repeat it, to make sure I got it right.' Frank took a breath, looked unhappy and did his best to imitate Charlotte's tone.

'"You tell that s-s-sea dog, that son of a whore—"'

'What?' This was not promising.

'S-sorry, Captain, she made me promise I'd s-say it word for word.' Frank tried again. '"You tell the son of a whore I don't owe him n-nothin'! Nothin'! Why would I want to s-s-s-stick my head out and make trouble for m'self? I'll not lift a finger!"'

Jack felt his heart contract as Frank continued, his stutter suddenly troubling him.

'She p-poked me in the chest. Said you deserved to be caught and strung up. Said you were a crazy man showing up here and she had no sympathy for your p-p-predicament.'

Jack felt sick.

'"You tell him I'll not lift a finger to help him—"'

'Shit!'

'"—b-but I'll help her. I'll help Anne."'

Anne bounded forward and embraced Frank. 'Of course she'll help. I never doubted it!'

'She gave me this.' Frank tossed a folded piece of fabric to Mary, who shook it out, revealing a shapeless brown dress.

Mary held it up against her body and nodded. 'It'll do.'

'Bless the woman!' Jack grinned with relief.

49

Mary tugged at her ill-fitting dress, far too tight across the shoulders and the hemline too short, revealing scuffed, well-worn sea shoes. No one had thought of getting her daintier footwear, and she could have done with a pretty scarf draped across her sunburnt chest. But her attire was the least of her concerns.

Standing at the Nassau waterfront with Frank, Mary could not ignore what was blindingly obvious: the *Delicia*, stationed exactly as she had been when Mary set sail with Captain Price on the *Sea Hawk*, the old warship keeping unwanted guests from coming in, and more to the point, leaving. Mary knew powerful guns would be in position, ready to roll out behind closed gunports. On deck, three armed soldiers casually leant on the rail.

'Why in God's name did Jack believe them? And why did I?' She should have known better and couldn't just blame Jack.

'S-seems they w-were wrong... And it was dark when I came here last night. D-didn't see her. What'll we d-do?' Frank looked forlorn.

Some days earlier, at the Eleuthera tavern before things had turned sour, Jack had bought rounds of drinks for the local men and plied them for news. What news from Europe? North American colonies? Jamaica? Jack's questions had circled in closer and closer. And what was Rogers up to? How many vessels did he have on patrol? This had been when one of the Eleuthera men had confirmed the *Venture* was Rogers's vessel, his only one on patrol; and stated "for a fact" the *Delicia* was unseaworthy, saying, 'She's riddled with worm and last I heard she'd sunk in the harbour.'

Those men at the tavern had been wrong, and Mary wondered if their estimation of number of troops dead of fever was incorrect too.

'Let's move on.' Mary didn't want to draw attention to themselves so tucked her hand into the crook of Frank's arm and strolled along the waterfront. They eyed the merchant and fishing vessels riding at anchor; admired the state of the fort before casually enquiring how many cannons were fitted and how safe the community was; stopped to chat with a merchant opening his shop, displaying baskets of fruit and vegetables at the entrance, with casks of grain and all manner of household goods inside.

'I'm th-thinking of setting up a chandler's supply, if trade warrants it. I'd value your opinion.' Mary was impressed. Without even trying, Frank sounded unsure of himself.

'Business is steady enough.' The merchant paused, eyeing them both up and down. 'You new here?'

Frank spun the tale they had practised: they'd just arrived from Eleuthera, where they've given up trying to make a go of farming. The merchant, holding a wicker basket full of corn cobs, jerked his head. 'The warehouse over there's empty – fellow died, and his wife left for wherever it was she'd come from.'

'And living in Nassau: would we be safe?' Mary hid one calloused hand in the crook of Frank's arm and the other in the folds of her dress. With her sunburnt neck and ruddy face, she was not sure she could manage to appear demure, but the merchant seemed uninterested in the sturdy woman before him.

'Well, ma'am, life's not so bad. The Spanish haven't been back, and Governor Rogers has the militia on patrol day and night, which gives us comfort. And as you see, the *Delicia's* always manned. Really there's no need to concern yourself.'

The man turned to his wife, who was setting up a punch stall at their doorstep. 'We're content enough, aren't we?' She assured them of the fact and asked if she could tempt them to a drink and her home baking. Mary refused politely, thanked them, and she and Frank walked over to the boarded-up warehouse, pretending to inspect it before turning to survey the gaudily painted taverns dotting the waterfront.

'Which one's Charlotte's?'

'The p-pink one.'

Outside the bright pink tavern, Mary watched two girls with low-cut bodices leaning against the wall. Even at this time of the morning trade was brisk with seamen disappearing inside, and Mary didn't see anyone coming out. This would be a good place to pick up news, but it was not a place a self-respecting woman would enter.

'I think I'll sit and have a glass of punch with that woman after all. You go into Charlotte's. In fact, that's no place for any husband of mine to frequent either. We'll both take a glass of punch.'

She linked arms with Frank and led him firmly away, shortening her stride, making a conscious effort to walk in a more refined way. Their task was to learn what they could of the vessels in harbour. Which was the fleetest? What was expected in or about to head out? Charlotte's would be an ideal place to gain such intelligence, but they'd have to wait for Charlotte to visit them.

The night before, Frank had followed Charlotte's instructions and led them all to an abandoned shack a mile or so from Nassau, and this was where she and Frank returned following their excursion to the waterfront. Ridding herself of the constricting dress, Mary put on her seaman's clothes; these were her true skin, reflecting the person she had become.

For the remainder of the day and into the evening, all four of them waited in the shuttered hovel. A soft knock at the door alerted them and Charlotte slipped in.

'You can put aside your damn weapons for a start.' Charlotte put down a bag and removed a dark cloak as Mary and Jack put aside their cutlasses and Anne lowered her pistol.

Mary took in the woman they were pinning their hopes on, this brothel owner with small hard eyes like blackcurrants in her leathery face. Charlotte looked her up and down too. 'Don't expect the dress fitted you too well.' Her gaze turned to Calico. 'Didn't expect I'd be seeing you again – how are ya? No, don't tell me – don't care – haven't got time.' She turned to Anne. 'What you see in this red-legged son of a whore beats me. But who am I to say?' Charlotte crossed to Anne and the two women hugged.

'Thanks, Charlotte.' Anne grinned.

'Appreciate your help and I'll pay for your troubles.' Calico smiled broadly, which earned him a scowl from their visitor.

'Don't try and charm me! And yes, I've reminded myself of what you still owe. But let's not worry right now. Thing is, you can't stay any longer – you all need to leave. Tonight.'

Tonight? This was a blow. How could they?

Charlotte continued, 'Those men of yours Rogers locked up have been gabbing, plus complaints from the good folk of Eleuthera have reached these shores. Word is, Calico Jack has two women in his crew, and' – Charlotte turned to Frank – 'a carpenter on board, a fella with a stutter.' She pressed her lips tight together. 'It hasn't gone unnoticed.'

Mary's eyes met Frank's. How could such a small thing prove to be their downfall? And what had Rogers been doing to Robbie and Chris that they would reveal so much? They began to talk over each other, desperate to come up with a plan.

'Hush now!' Charlotte interrupted. 'I've being asking around. The best vessel for you is the *William*.'

'The *William*! Mr Harmon's pride and joy. I know it.' Anne was animated.

'It's in the harbour?' Jack asked.

Charlotte nodded. 'Leaving tomorrow – no time to waste.'

Mary had noted a well-kept sloop in the harbour. This must be the *William*. She didn't want to dampen spirits, but she spoke up. 'I don't see how we can get past the *Delicia*.'

Charlotte shrugged. 'Not my problem, but let's see if this helps.' She opened her bag, rummaged around, unfolded a razor and soap, and looked sideways at Calico. 'A change of appearance might help, and those red legs of yours are a giveaway. Wear these overtop.' She tossed him a large pair of dark seaman's trousers.

Charlotte set about giving Calico a clean shave while Anne wielded shears, hacking away at his long hair. Despite Charlotte's brusque manner, it was obvious she had a tender spot for Calico. As she worked the soap into a lather, tilted his head back and scraped her razor under his chin, nicking him for the second time, he grumbled, 'Why not just cut my damned throat while you're at it?' She retorted, 'I just might do that if you don't shut your mouth – ungrateful son of a whore!' and deliberately nicked him again and chuckled as he cursed her.

More surprising to Mary was the bond between Charlotte and Anne. The two women spoke quietly together, sharing stories about Charlotte's girls. As Anne sympathised about news of one girl who'd died in childbirth and another of fever, Mary glimpsed a more tender side to her.

A plan was forming, and Charlotte would play her part. She thumped Calico's chest in parting. 'Pay me next time you drop by – I'm keeping a tally.'

First Anne and Calico slipped away, then she and Frank followed, all of them in their sea clothes, hats low over their eyes, with Anne wearing Charlotte's cloak. A nearly full moon illuminated the land and Governor Rogers's people had been diligent, clearing and cutting back trees. Armed as they were with sheathed cutlasses, pistols and knives, no one meeting them could doubt their purpose. Mary hadn't bothered to concoct a cover story. If she was challenged she would fight to kill, as they all would. People rarely ventured out at night into the interior of the island, but Nassau was a different matter. Pulling Frank close, Mary flattened herself into the shadows afforded by a shuttered building at the top end of town, and cautiously peered out towards the harbour, assessing what lay between them and their prize: the *William*.

The waterfront was busy with late-night revellers drinking at the taverns and on the beach. In the moonlight and the glow of three beach fires, Mary could see armed redcoats patrolling. She counted eight, and these were just the ones in view.

Hearing a soft whistle, she turned to see Calico emerge from the shadows motioning to retreat out of town. When she judged it safe she edged along the building, and with Frank behind her, set off at a trot.

'Hey there! Stop!'

She glanced back to see two advancing redcoats hollering as if to wake the dead. Frank bolted, and she charged after him. 'Stop, I say!' A shot rang out. Frank yelped, and she flinched in expectation of a burning pain but felt nothing. Legs pounding and arms pumping, she asked, 'You hit?' Frank managed a strangled, 'D-don't think so!'

A second shot came from behind, but off to their side. She heard a cry and glanced back to see one of the redcoats drop to his knees and the other drawing his sword. Calico and Anne emerged onto the path behind the soldiers, weapons drawn, with Mary and Frank ahead.

'Stop! Wait! Who are you? What are you about? Tell me, in the name of the law!' the soldier bellowed.

'Shut your damn mouth!' Calico spoke softly but sounded as jumpy as she was feeling.

'You're English!' The redcoat relaxed. 'Thought you were the Spanish come back.'

'Put your weapon down.' Calico approached cautiously.

'What're you up to? What're you doing out?' The man backed off the path so he could watch them all. Staring hard at Calico she saw a flicker of recognition then his gaze rested on Anne. 'I've seen you before. Governor Rogers's party... Mrs Bonny?'

'What of it?' Anne's response was surly. The redcoat's eyes swivelled back to Calico, and he spoke softly. 'And you – I know who you are...'

All of them were alert, watching, unsure what to do, how to resolve this situation and silence the moaning redcoat slumped on the track.

'Can't set you free.' Calico shook his head. The redcoat began to breathe hard, raising his sword arm, backing away. Step by step, with weapons drawn, they closed in on him.

Calico kept talking calmly to the man. 'Don't want to kill you. Do as I say and drop your weapon. Do it. Drop it!'

The redcoat did not look inclined to trust any of them, and Mary could not blame him with three cutlass tips raised to his face and one pistol levelled.

'Damn you! Do as Jack says!' Anne's patience was wearing thin.

The man lowered his sword, appealing to Anne. 'Mrs Bonny?'

Calico kicked away his sword and spoke hurriedly. 'Mary, Frank, deal with the other one. And you,' he motioned to the unarmed redcoat, 'unbuckle your belt. Hurry!'

As Calico and Anne pushed the redcoat off the path, she and Frank turned to the wounded soldier.

'W-what about th-this one? What did Calico m-mean, deal with him?' Frank looked at the groaning man trying to staunch the flow of blood from under his knee.

'You shot at us first!' Mary felt justified in reminding the soldier of this fact. Even in his pain he looked surprised and whispered, 'Please... you're English, aren't you? You're on our side... I've a wife and kids... Have mercy!'

'We're not going to kill you.' Mary removed her scarf and knotted it tightly around the man's shin. 'It'll have to do for now.' She and Frank dragged the hobbling man to join his companion. Sitting the men back to back around a tree, they lashed their wrists together with their own belts, bound scarves across their mouths and left them to be found in the morning.

Whichever way Mary looked at it, she was a marked woman; all four of them were, once these men had been discovered. She hoped the injured one didn't die of loss of blood: that would mark them as killers.

'Let's head to our beach, Jack. There's more cover, and we can work back along the coast towards town.' Anne's eyes looked wild – with fever, fear or excitement Mary couldn't tell, and what "our beach" meant, she didn't ask.

'This way.' Calico set off, skirting the edge of town, and the rest of them followed.

50

Tonight of all nights! Woodes was irritated by the raucous celebration going on at the waterfront, creating more noise than usual. Would he have competition for an audience? Would he be heard above the drunken singing?

As Jeremy arranged chairs, Mrs Walker and Mrs Harmon set out glasses around a large punchbowl and delicacies on intricately patterned paper doilies. Woodes turned down their offer of a glass; he needed to keep his wits sharp.

A week earlier Mrs Walker had returned the account of his pioneering expedition: *A Cruising Voyage Round the World.*

'My dear Captain Rogers, you've been hiding your light for far too long. Many people have only a vague idea about your past. Of course I knew you had commanded a fleet and understood something of the discoveries and hardships involved. But my goodness, so many stories… Please, let me organise an evening talk. Will you consider it?'

'That's kind of you, ma'am. I enjoy writing but I'm not one to speak from the stage with flourishes of an arm here or there – I wouldn't relish it. I fear it would make for a dull evening.'

'Not at all. I assure you, not a bit of it! And Thomas thinks the same.'

While he had managed to ward off Mrs Harmon's insistent requests to host another dance, he was won over by Mrs Walker's warmth and genuine interest in his past exploits and allowed her to organise this event at the council room.

He watched with satisfaction and relief as men and women arrived and gathered around the punchbowl, and by the time his audience of two dozen or so were ushered to their seats they looked relaxed and receptive. At the lectern his book waited for him, pages marked in readiness.

As he got into his stride, he found he enjoyed reliving his adventures on the high seas and could indeed play to the gallery. Everyone loved the story of Selkirk, the marooned man they had rescued after four years of solitude on Juan Fernandez island, and he told them how, back in London, his friend Daniel Defoe had sucked him dry of stories about the man, and now Defoe's book, *Robinson Crusoe*, was proving a runaway success. Questions shot out to him from curious listeners.

Woodes skirted over the battle in which he had lost his own brother – he did not wish to dwell on it – but for the first time he recounted the story of his battle with the Spanish galleon, and how he had received his injuries. He looked out at the rows of attentive faces in front of him, with just the rustle of the ladies' fans creating some breeze in the stifling heat. Closing his book, he smiled at the applause. He had enjoyed his moment in the limelight, however modest.

'Such escapades, and such a dull life here by comparison.' Mr Harmon was by his side pumping his hand as the audience milled around the rapidly emptying punchbowl.

Mrs Harmon joined them. 'Ah, my goodness, Captain Rogers – I cannot think why your wife would let you out of her sight. Indeed, I would have thought you would be only too pleased to put your feet up and stay at home. You surely deserved a rest, rather than head away to sort out our little community.'

These comments, spoken lightly, struck Woodes forcibly and his smile was a little tighter than he meant. "Rest" and "home" were clearly not great attractions to his restless soul.

Mrs Walker's hand touched his arm. 'Captain Rogers, Thomas and I are taking a stroll to the waterfront before retiring. Will you join us?'

'And we'll join your party if we may!' Mr Harmon beamed at them.

So, this was their beach.

Mary caught Calico's eye. 'Best I go ahead, and you come with me.'

'I'll not be left – I can fight!' Anne hissed.

'You stay with Frank. I want Calico with me – we're the best fighters if it comes to it. Calico?' Mary looked at him for confirmation. He nodded and turned to Anne and Frank.

'She's right. Follow us and keep your distance.'

'Damn it, Jack. I don't need protecting!'

'Shut up!' And with these words Calico set off, Mary at his heels with Anne's frustrated curses in her ear.

Mary kept pace with Calico's loping strides as they covered the distance back towards Nassau. They ducked behind a boat, ideal for their purpose to row out to the *William*, as were two others beached nearby, but all of them were within view of revellers on the beach and the noisy waterfront taverns. And redcoats. There were still eight patrolling, muskets slung over shoulders and swords at their sides. In the distance Mary watched Charlotte step outside her tavern, jug of ale in one hand, a clutch of tankards in another, calling out to soldiers to join her. Two soldiers paused, chatted to her, refused her offer, then moved on.

'You'd think they'd be tempted by a drink at least. Rogers has got them under his thumb, blast the man.' Calico's disappointment matched her own.

Charlotte had told them of her special offer: 'Free drinks and pokes for Rogers's boys in red – for the first and last time.'

Mary turned to face the harbour, hoping to find some comfort, some miracle to show a clear means of reaching the *William*. She could just make out the *William*'s mast among the many others dotting the harbour, and she judged it no more than thirty yards from the *Delicia*. In the shadows behind her, Anne and Frank waited for the signal to move forward.

'Follow me,' Mary whispered to Calico as she dropped to the ground.

As stealthily as they could, she and Calico crawled along the beach, sliding on their stomachs, digging in their elbows and knees, inching forward as she had in Flanders on night patrol. Flotsam and jetsam provided cover above the waterline: a large driftwood log planed smooth by the action of the sea; old planks of ship's timber; a broken barrel; tangled fishing nets; an abandoned shelter of ripped canvas – any object to provide shadow to merge with.

Cautiously they moved from cover to cover, whistling for the others to follow. Jack tapped her foot. They froze as two soldiers stopped just ahead of them, in no hurry to turn back towards town. They were so close she could hear their conversation. Mary's hand slid to the hilt of her knife, and beside her she felt the slight shift in Calico's weight as he did the same. The soldiers turned and strolled back along the beach, stopping at each of the three fires to chat to the men sitting around them.

With Calico by her side Mary continued edging forward, vacating their last hiding spot for Frank and Anne. A beached boat with the bottom long since rotted away provided a welcome shelter. Calico motioned Anne and Frank forward. From that cover they peered out at the three fires burning on the beach. The nearest had burnt low, with ten or more men lolling or slumbering around it, while around the other two men were singing loudly as if to drown out the competition.

'Which one?' Calico looked at her.

Mary played over Charlotte's words in her mind. 'They'll have a sing-song going. It's the closest I can get you to the water. Just say, "Charlotte sent ya," or something like that.' Many of the men on the beach would be only too happy to turn them over to Rogers, but Charlotte had assured them they could trust these hand-picked men.

'I bet it's the middle group,' Anne suggested, 'the bunch singing "The Ballad of Captain Kidd". They've been singing that song over and over, probably wondering where we are.'

Calico grunted. 'Charlotte knows I hate that miserable song. For all their bragging, Kidd and his men ended at the gallows. I should know, I witnessed it when I was a kid. I wouldn't put it past Charlotte – a joke—'

'Or a w-w-warning!' Frank had barely opened his mouth since they left the shack, and Mary was irritated he had no more encouraging words.

None of the redcoats were patrolling the eastern end of the waterfront where they were skulking.

'I'm going alone.' Mary spoke decisively.

Calico countered, 'Oh no, I'm not having that. I'll go!'

She shook her head. 'Has to be me.'

'Hurry, Mary! Take this!' Anne slipped the cloak off, slung it over Mary's shoulders and pushed her forward. 'Go!'

With three cocked pistols covering her and with her hat pulled low, Mary staggered along the beach in what she hoped was a fair impersonation of one more drunken seaman. She gathered the cloak tightly around her. Perhaps she might try shivering and pretend to be ill? Apart from impersonating a man, play-acting was not something she was familiar with.

Only one of the men at the first fire took the slightest notice of her, drunkenly dipping his head by way of salutation, so she staggered on. Approaching the middle fire, she became aware of the men watching her as they kept on singing. There was nothing for it. Swaying on her feet, she mumbled, 'Charlotte wants you.' The group of men eyed her and all but one kept singing. She held her breath, half expecting the reply, 'What the hell does she want with me?' Instead the man looked beyond her shoulder, saying, 'Just you?' With relief Mary knew these were the ones. The man reached up and tugged at her leg to sit, and as she joined the group one of the others slunk away. One arrived, one departed.

'Where's Calico Jack?' The man looked cautiously at her and Mary jerked her head. 'With two others.' The man nodded to the other group of men singing around the third fire a little further along. 'When we wouldn't let those bastards join us they decided to make their own entertainment. Good job you found us first. Get singing.'

'What?' Mary frowned.

'You've the sourest face I've seen tonight – try and look as if you're enjoying yourself. Sing!'

At this command Mary tried to unlock the muscles in her throat, and in a croaky voice joined the roistering chorus.

First Anne, then Frank and finally Calico joined her, as one by one three others drifted away from their group.

The remaining men all wanted a piece of Calico, clapping him on the back, wishing the "old bastard" good luck. He was their man! One of the last of the gang leaders. They sang louder than ever, delighted that here was Calico Jack, once again hanging out on the beach with them "right under Rogers's fucking nose". They didn't seem in any hurry to break up the party, and Mary worried Calico might be tempted to settle in, so she kicked his leg. 'What next?'

'Last-minute provisions to be taken out. Mr Harmon's orders.' Anne looked pleased with her suggestion. They hastily debated such a scenario but dismissed it in favour of Calico's idea.

'Charlotte's generosity extends to our friends on the *Delicia*. Let's take them something to drink – and a girl. Tell Charlotte to add it to my bill.'

Two of the local men hurried up to Charlotte's, and they reappeared, each carrying a demijohn of brandy with one of Charlotte's girls at their side. They headed to one of the beached boats. No one had any idea who the boat belonged to, and they hoped the owner wasn't nearby. As they pushed it out, Mary recognised the voice behind her as one of the patrolling redcoats. She kept her head down, and with Calico, back bent, continued to push the boat out from shore.

'Charlotte's gifts for your friends on guard – for when they're off duty.' The girl from Charlotte's laughingly indicated herself and the demijohns of brandy already stowed in the boat. With gentlemanly manners the redcoat lifted the girl into the boat, and Mary and Jack began rowing away from shore as the local men engaged the redcoat in conversation drawing him away from the water's edge.

Even shorn of his beard anyone with half a brain would recognise Calico. As he protested they pushed him down and Charlotte's girl spread her skirt on top of him. It was not the escape he had in mind, but Anne told him to shut his mouth and stay still.

Mary dug her oar into the water, with Frank on the opposite oar and Anne with her pistol cocked.

'Kiss me! Give me a cuddle!' Charlotte's girl looked at Anne. So Anne stepped over Jack and cuddled up to the girl, spread her cloak over her legs to give Jack extra cover and gave her ardent attention to the giggling girl. At this time of night they were the only boat in the harbour; fishermen or others who had genuine business in the water were long ashore.

They rowed alongside the *Delicia's* hull; Charlotte's girl, laughing loudly, called up to the watching guards. 'Be with you shortly, boys. Charlotte's celebrating, don't ask me why, all I know is I'm coming to you. Me and the brandy both!'

'We're on duty, my lovely. Would like to accept, but—'

'No rush, I've got all night. First him, anyway.' The girl prodded Anne; but only her back and the top of her hat were visible to those above. 'I'll be back later. When you're off duty. Make sure you wait for me!' She waved and blew kisses.

Mary rowed on. If they got away, it wasn't just Charlotte they owed thanks to. Mary was impressed by the girl's ready wits, and the men on shore were like actors born to the stage. She rowed steadily between anchored vessels, towards the western side of the harbour, towards the *William* hidden among masts.

'M-Mary!' Frank broke the silence. 'I'm thinking of staying...'

'What?' This took her by surprise. 'You'd leave us?'

'I'll never p-pay you back for saving my life... but I've paid you back some. Being here and all. I'm prepared to make my case to the g-g-governor. Take my chance...'

Before Mary could reply Calico's arm, knife in hand, emerged from under the folds of the cloak, soon followed by his head and body.

'You think I'm leaving our carpenter behind? You're coming willingly or I'll drop you over the side.' Frank stopped rowing, forcing Mary to do the same or they'd row in a circle. 'Quick, man, I've no time for this!' Calico's knife was at Frank's throat, and they all knew this was no idle threat. Frank let out a sob and silently picked up his oar again. They were in this together. No turning back.

The *William* identified itself with its freshly painted white lettering against a dark background. All was silent on board. Without a ripple they manoeuvred their boat to the stern anchor cable. With the delicacy of a cat settling onto a cushion, Calico gently transferred his weight to the underside of the cable and waited for the movement of the *William* to settle. Clinging on with hands and knees, he made his way up. Within minutes Anne climbed aboard, followed by Frank, and last of all Mary pushed herself off from the boat. Charlotte's girl took up both oars and gently set off.

Calico had his knife out, sawing through the anchor rope as she and Anne, cutlasses and pistols ready, tiptoed below. They opened the cabin door, revealing two sleeping men.

Anne raised her pistol. 'Make a noise and I'll blow your brains out.'

Both men jolted awake.

'Shhh. Quiet now. Nice and slow.'

Mr Harmon's men sat up and cursed.

'Cuss us if you want, it's all the same to us, just don't budge or yell.' Anne spoke for them both.

The *William* was beginning to move, and Mary prayed the outgoing tide would be strong enough to allow them to drift out of the harbour before it turned, and daylight was upon them. She could sense the two men weighing them up, wondering if they should rush them. With her cutlass held firmly in her left hand, Mary withdrew her knife with her right hand and locked eyes with one of the men.

'Just two women – what are the odds? That's what you're thinking, isn't it?'

A lively company of ten or more processed through town towards the waterfront. Woodes loved the evenings. At the height of the day the scorching sun could be unbearable at this time of the year, but with summer ending and the hurricane season not yet on them, they could enjoy a comfortable night under a luminous moon.

Woodes tutted, seeing three fires burning on the beach and drunken carousing along the waterfront. Tonight was worse than he had seen for some time. 'Shall we walk to the fort?' Woodes's mind was never far from his duties. He could show his party their newly installed cannon, and check the militia were all present. It didn't harm to turn up unexpectedly from time to time and take them off guard. Ever since an aborted Spanish attack, he had increased patrols with many men recruited into the militia: able-bodied, less able-bodied and elderly.

As they reached the stout doors leading into the fort, his mind turned to the two men held prisoner inside, and as if to read his thoughts, Thomas Walker enquired, 'Any fresh information?'

Woodes shook his head. 'Ordinary men caught up with Rackham's enterprise hung out to dry. Flogging, bread and water rations haven't told us much, nor has any amount of questioning or inducement.'

'A pity.' Walker looked thoughtful. 'Will you let them go?'

Fairfax, his Chief Justice, had urged the council that they should be released, as there was not enough evidence against them to prove they had been pirating. What was more,

Woodes could ill afford to send them back to London bound in irons and under guard.

'Another day or two in irons to let them search their souls, then I think we must release them.'

Woodes had been disappointed that the two men from Rackham's crew had provided such scant information, and so far the *Venture* had failed to capture any pirates. The trail had gone cold on Rackham, but he understood the company included two women, Bonny and another. This intrigued him, and he wondered whether he and Fairfax would have the strength of character to condemn the women to death should he oversee their trial.

Woodes led the way up the stairs to the open roof of the fort. The soldiers on duty had spotted their party arriving and spruced themselves up, buttoning jackets and buckling swords; they were ready for him. He acknowledged their salutes and ushered his party towards the newest addition to their arsenal, an eighteen-pounder he had imported from Virginia, explaining the range of shot if arced at different degrees. He had commanded his audience's attention during his talk, but he was losing them now. They drifted away, chatting in small groups, Mr Harmon bragging about what he hoped to gain on his next commercial venture. Woodes listened with half an ear. He approved of Harmon's enterprising spirit, though he did not think it right to talk about profit.

'I swear he loves the *William* more than he loves me and can't wait to be off in the morning.'

Mrs Harmon's words were met by protests: 'Oh, no, no, dear!'

Woodes was just returning to the subject of the cannon's range when Harmon interrupted. 'What the devil... The *William*'s adrift.'

'Nonsense.' Mrs Harmon spoke firmly. 'You're imagining it.'

'I am not! I know where I left it anchored. Look!'

Woodes and the others followed the direction of Harmon's outstretched arm. In the moonlight Woodes could just make out a vessel drifting slowly, passing them. He frowned and turned to his officer on duty.

'Hand me your spyglass – let's see what's going on. And where's our hailer?' Both were quickly located, and Mr Harmon snatched the hailer and bellowed.

'What ho on the *William*! Can you hear me? Ho there!'

They all gathered at the battlements, leaning out to scour the water, trying to pick out the *William* and decide if the vessel was indeed drifting. Woodes had the spyglass to his eye but it was too dark to be useful. With his naked eye he could just make out two figures on board but could not be sure. By his side Harmon was becoming agitated and stood on tiptoes to extend his reach a little as he bellowed, 'Ho there on the *William*! Answer me if you will!'

This time Mr Harmon was rewarded with an answer from across the water. 'The cable broke... And the grappling iron won't hold.'

Mr Harmon tutted in displeasure and was about to reply when the fellow on board the *William* spoke again. 'We're fixing it. Don't worry!'

'Is that you, Evan?' Mr Harmon sounded cautious.

'Yes, sir.'

'For heaven's sake! Get on with it, man, we're heading out tomorrow! Bring her back in!' Mr Harmon turned away from the water, his anger palpable. 'How could this have happened? I've just invested in new rope and cordage. It cost me a pretty penny, I can tell you.'

'Better to have found it wanting in the quiet of our harbour rather than finding it doesn't hold when you really need it.' Woodes offered words of comfort, though this was a serious matter for any mariner.

'Hmm.' Mr Harmon did not look consoled. 'I'll have to check it over tomorrow, which will hold us up. Damn that chandler – excuse my language, ladies – he's sold me a pup! I bought it in Virginia, and I'm not even heading there to toss it back in his face.'

'Come, dear.' Mrs Harmon tugged his arm. 'Watching won't make it happen any quicker – your men know what they're doing; it will soon be under control. Better go home for a good night's sleep and head out early. Come.'

51

'WHAT HO ON THE WILLIAM! CAN YOU HEAR ME! HO there!'

Anne's eyes had widened, recognising Mr Harmon's voice. Why was he out so late?

Hurriedly she and Mary locked one of Harmon's men in the cabin and pushed the other out on deck, a pistol in the small of his back. Keeping out of sight, she prompted his strained conversation with Mr Harmon through their own hailer.

'Go on.' Anne prodded him. 'Tell him, you're fixing it and not to worry... Go on, hurry up!' She prodded him again with her pistol. After that stilted conversation she handed the man, Evan, over to Frank and hoped he had the guts to shoot him if required.

As Mary cast gaskets off the gaff-rigged mainsail, Anne set about hauling the gaff up the mast. The *William*, with its single raked mast, was rigged quite differently from the *Curlew* and there was much to learn. As the mainsail began to flog, Anne hauled on the other halyard to raise and tighten the peak of the canvas, smiling in relief as the sail filled, caught the wind, and she sensed the *William's* swift response.

They were just beyond the harbour entrance, Hog Island close by. The sound of a splash and Frank's startled intake of breath took the smile off Anne's face. She spun around to see Evan swimming strongly towards Hog Island, his white shirt glowing in the dark.

'Damn you!' She kicked one of his discarded shoes and took aim with her pistol.

'Don't!' Jack's urgent shout joined Mary's. 'The sound'll carry! Leave him to his fate. Tide's against him, but if he makes it to shore it'll be some time before he's back in Nassau.'

Anne watched Evan strike for shore, then looked beyond him to the remains of two men hanging in gibbets on Hog Island, remembering the day nearly two years earlier, when she had witnessed Rogers execute them. She shuddered and moved to stand by Jack. He contemplated the sight himself, and with his hand on the helm, spoke softly.

'One by one the old gang are disappearing. Blackbeard's head ended up separated from his body.' Jack was silent for a moment. 'Not sure which way I'd rather go.' He looked out at the dangling corpses flickering in the light of a nearby brazier.

'Jack!' She pulled away from him, but his arm gripped her tightly and he spoke urgently.

'These times can't last.'

'Nonsense!' She did not want to have this conversation, not now when they were barely out of danger – barely out of Nassau harbour.

'It's true. If you care to look about you, you see changes. Everywhere changes. Things cleaned up, tightened up, and I don't just mean the filth and remnants of camps on the beaches. I mean rules. Rules and regulations. More damned laws, and more of them being enforced rather than ignored. You can be sure this means more of us are being hunted down.' Jack sounded bitter.

'Not us, though. They'll never catch us!' Anne meant it. They ruled. They would not be overcome.

Jack indicated the debris bobbing around the hull on the outgoing tide. 'See them?' He pointed to a branch of bedraggled hibiscus flowers caught up with other tropical foliage washing in the tide. 'If it comes to it, I'd like some on my grave. Prom—'

'Stop this talk!' she snapped, twisting away from his arm. 'You're as strong as an ox and the best fighter around. You and Mary both!' How dare Jack talk like this. She did not want to think about death and dying. This was their life and it would go on and on: she and Jack living free, doing as they wished. 'Why, we've barely got started!'

Jack touched her hair, pushing a strand behind her ear. His touch triggered a memory: tucking one of those vivid red hibiscus flowers behind her ear when she had set off to track him down at Charlotte's. He must be remembering that as well. It seemed a world ago, the girl – the young woman – she had been. Jack turned her face to make her look at him.

'If we're wise, Anne, we'll know when to throw it in. Decide when we've taken enough to get by and find somewhere to live quietly. I get double shares as captain; I can put money enough away for both of us for some time to come.'

Giving up the roving life had to happen – but not now: at some distant future she didn't wish to consider. No doubt she'd end up with a parcel of snotty-nosed children around her knees; this always seemed to be the consequence of loving a man, and it wasn't fair.

Above the mainsail the stars shone brightly in the clear sky, and she was alert to the beauty of the moment. She could see Mary moving upwards to the top yard and working her way along, releasing gaskets for the top sail.

They had done it! They had escaped! She was jubilant and couldn't help but jump up and down in victory.

Frank brought Harmon's second man up from the cabin, and Anne took a wide stance, her pistol trained on him.

'I'm not intending to shoot – not unless I have to. You want to join your friend? He's gone.' Anne jerked her head starboard.

The man looked uneasy. He couldn't be sure if Evan had been thrown overboard or jumped. He turned to Mary as she sprung off the ratlines. 'You promised we'd be put ashore. I've been a damned fool to believe what any of you say.' He stared at them all in turn, body tense and alert.

Jack eyed Harmon's man. 'You crewed the *William* before?' The man nodded, and Jack smiled. 'You'll know how to sail her to best advantage then.'

The man nodded again. 'Could say so.'

'What's your name?'

'John.'

Jack paused. 'Right, John. This is how it's going to be. You help us, and we'll keep our promise. I guarantee you dry land at our first stop – unless you cause trouble, in which case you'll have a watery end. On the other hand, you might decide to join us.'

John scoffed but held his tongue.

Hammering on his door woke Woodes, and he threw on a loose silk dressing gown he would never normally wear to receive visitors. Mr Harmon burst in, face a dangerous shade of purple, almost incoherent with rage and grief.

'They've taken her! They've got her!'

For a moment Woodes supposed something terrible had happened to Mrs Harmon.

'The audacity of the man! Rackham! Right under our noses. You've got to bring them in. String 'em up! All of them! My sweet *William*...'

Mr Harmon sank into the nearest chair, head in his hands, and Woodes understood the *William* had been stolen. One of Harmon's men had escaped and Woodes questioned the merchant about the whereabouts of the second man on board. Harmon looked vague, his thoughts entirely on his vessel and his lost enterprise.

Self-loathing filled Woodes. While he had been vaingloriously recounting his past to an attentive audience, this fresh outrage had taken place. He knew himself to be a private man, a serious man, but the previous evening he had allowed himself to be distracted from his duties, and afterwards he had not questioned what he saw happening in the harbour.

'I'll alert the American colonies and send dispatches to Jamaica and Barbados. If Rackham and the rest of them fetch up in their jurisdictions, I'll request they're sent back to me. I would like the satisfaction of stringing them up myself. I've dug into my own pockets deeply enough to rid the Bahamas of these wretches, and I won't flinch at going further into debt to see justice done.'

At that moment Woodes knew he would have no hesitation, no hesitation at all, in seeing both Mrs Bonny and the other woman dangle from the end of a rope. And Rackham, of course; this went without saying. The world would be better off without any of them.

52

AFTER A DAY ANNE STOPPED WATCHING JOHN, NO longer alert to his every sneeze or sudden movement in case he jumped her and grabbed her weapons, satisfied he posed no danger. He was a rigger and knew everything there was to know about setting up the lines.

The *William* was in top condition, with new cordage, well-maintained sails and tackle, a good array of ship's instruments, and best of all, Mr Harmon's idea of provisioning had been to provide, at least for himself, food and drink fit for high society. She found her appetite returning.

After taking her turn at the helm, Anne rifled through the food stores, helped herself to brandy and flopped down on deck in the warmth of the afternoon sun. With her hat covering her face and the sounds of sails and the wash of the sea against the hull, she felt utterly content. Mary was napping, Frank was at the helm and Jack sat with John, their conversation floating in and out of her tired brain. Jack talked enthusiastically about his philosophy of roving, and she could tell John was listening by his frequent interruptions and questions. Raising her head, she called, 'Jack! Fancy a fuck?' Jack broke off mid-sentence.

'Here?' John sounded alarmed, clearly unsure of what passed as normal behaviour in this outfit.

Within seconds Jack was at her side, extending his hand and bowing with exaggerated gallantry. 'How can I refuse such an invitation, Mrs Bonny? May I escort you to your boudoir?'

A laugh exploded from her; it was good to feel well again. Jack pulled her to her feet, and they headed to Harmon's cabin: their cabin, their bed.

Lying entwined with Jack in a sticky, sweaty tangle Anne was happier than she could ever remember feeling. Their passion for each other was well matched and didn't need words.

Anne's high spirits were infectious, all of them laughing and joking. By the time they neared their rendezvous on Great Abaco, John Fenwick had decided he would join them to put Calico's philosophy to the test. Jack shook hands, sealing the bargain.

'Every mother's son seems to be called John; we're overrun with the bastards, Johns and Thomases both. Choose another name before I give you one. John Davies is called Davy, John Howell's Howie. How about Fenwick?'

Anne looked at John Fenwick with his broad freckled face, bushy sandy hair, and strong calloused hands. 'Fen?'

John considered. 'I'll settle for that – been called worse. Fen then.'

As they neared Little Harbour on the eastern coast of Great Abaco, men stood on the beach, waving shirts above their heads. Anne rummaged for Harmon's Union Jack and tried waving the heavy emblem about her head, whooping and yelling to the men on shore, then tossed the flag overboard.

'Hey!' Jack reprimanded her. 'That could've been useful!'

Too late. She did not want this symbol of British authority on board, and watched the flag spreading out as the *William* drifted past. Among the valuable items they'd kept from the *Curlew* was Jack's black flag with the skull and crossed cutlasses. Anne trusted George had kept it safe, and soon it would grace the *William*'s mast.

George and Dick were first on board, clasping hands with Jack, then Dick pulled Jack to his chest and looked like he didn't mean to let him go. Paddy, Noah, Jim, Howie, Tom Bourn and Thomas Earl were there too, and Davy. All of them wanted to find out everything there was to know about their new home, checking out her four fixed guns, calculating the tonnage and assessing her speed.

The world was open to them, and Anne couldn't have been happier. She linked arms with Mary as they gathered around Jack, who beamed at them all.

'A small company, but a good size for the *William* – and we can always pick up more men and bring more guns aboard.'

'So, what's the plan, Jack?' George looked enthusiastic and ready to follow Jack to the end of the earth.

'Set course for Eleuthera.'

George scowled. 'Surely safer places.'

'We'd have to be damned unlucky to be picked up in Bahamian waters – they won't be looking for us here.' Jack sounded confident. 'I've no idea if those fools at the tavern had really heard the *Delicia* had sunk or if they lied to trap us. Whatever the case, they need to pay for their false information. And as for shipping our men across to Rogers to be whipped like dogs – I can't let that pass.'

Just off north-east Eleuthera they attacked a fishing boat, followed soon after by another. Cruising south along the chain of tiny islets they found a third boat, then another.

Firing above the heads of those on board they cursed and yelled, brandishing their weapons. Chiefly it was their black flag flying from the mast of the *William* that put fear into the hearts of their quarry.

The first five boats didn't resist; all the men and women on board, sullen, silent and cowed, watched them steal their catch for the day, their fishing tackle and all manner of useful items on board.

One fisherman clutched Anne's arm. 'I saved a damn long time for this. How am I to feed my wife and kids?' She shrugged him off. She did not want to know his story.

The sixth fishing boat resisted. It was a bigger boat and the men on board fancied their chances, daring to exchange fire and making a run for the shallows, a small sail assisting the four men rowing with all their might.

After a brief chase, when the fishermen were on board the *William*, Paddy boiled with indignation.

'Let's burn the boat. Don't leave it for them – they don't deserve it!'

'Tempting.' Jack frowned at the fisherman. 'What's it to be, fellas?'

One of the fishermen spoke for them all. 'Come on! Leave us the boat, won't you? What've we done to you?' Another said belligerently, 'Pick on something your own size.'

Anne didn't recognise any faces as those who had confronted them on the beach, but even so, Jack was right to punish the entire community. She dropped down into the fishing boat and began to rummage around, tossing anything taking her fancy into the growing pile ready for loading onto the *William*, but they left the boat intact. She felt good about this small act of kindness.

Rounding the tip of Harbour Island, the southernmost islet of the chain, they spotted another fishing boat approaching.

'One more. Seven's a lucky number. One more!' Jack urged them on. So once again they fired in warning, set up an unholy hollering and attacked the terrified fishermen. She was getting good at this. It was easy to scare people as part of Jack's pack. She recalled the times she had scoffed at attacks on fishing boats and canoes, thinking them small fry and unworthy prizes, but she had learnt better: it was what kept them going day to day.

The *William's* deck became a chaotic jumble of tangled nets and tackle, tarry ropes, fish stowed in baskets or twitching in tangled nets, and turtles alive and dead. The smell of sea creatures mingled with sweating men.

Following their escape from Nassau, they had sailed in glorious weather with just four companions on a pristine *William*; those few precious days were already feeling like a dream. Now, looking around the crowded stinking deck, she knew things would never be like that again, just as she could never be the woman she had once been.

She looked at Mary leaning over the rails of the *William*, hauling fishing nets up from the boat below: face sunburnt, hair loose, shirt sweaty and in disarray, and the outline of her unbound breasts under her shirt for anyone to see. Suspecting she herself looked as dishevelled as her friend, Anne took a moment to tuck in her shirt and look at her rough hands with their broken nails and calloused palms. Little by little she had changed.

'Where to? Where next?' Jack touched her shoulder.

She grinned and shrugged. It didn't matter as long as they took prizes every so often. She felt safe in this small wooden world. This was her family, with all their squabbles and bickering, and Jack was her man.

53

MARY ENJOYED GAMING WITH PADDY. HE HAD A temper, but as often as not it was a charade, and he could be good company. Mary rattled the dice in her cupped hands and cast them. While the game was light-hearted, their conversation had turned serious.

'Hanging's no great hardship as far as I'm concerned. If we didn't have that threat hanging over us—'

'Hanging over us! You're a joker, and you didn't know it!' Paddy reached over and boxed her on the shoulder. Mary grunted; she hadn't intended the pun and continued with her train of thought.

'The way I see it, if it weren't for hanging, every cowardly fellow would turn pirate infecting the seas, and no merchant ship would venture out. Where would that leave us? Too many rovers and nothing to chase down – we'd starve to death.' This was her logic. This was the life she had been sucked into, so she applied herself to it fully, just as she'd knuckled down to life as a soldier or a sailor.

Everybody had to survive, and pirating had become her trade.

'Ah, ye can't mean it.' Paddy calculated the score. 'I mean about hanging. No fellow wants to strangle in front of a crowd of jeering onlookers, there's no glory in that.'

'Death'll get us all in the end, so best not worry how and live our lives as we want. You're not a coward, Paddy?'

'Sure I'm not. You don't need to ask!'

'Well then, best not dwell on the future.' She frowned when she saw the roll of her dice and Paddy crowed. 'Got ye this time, ye old witch!'

She cocked her head, conceding defeat. 'You can strike off one of the tasks you owe me.'

Mary stood and stretched. This game of hazard had ended, but there would be more gaming. Fen had produced a worn pack of cards, "my lucky ones", he told them, which he expertly shuffled and encouraged the men to gamble all manner of things. She'd underestimated Fen and ended up doing a double rota of watch duty, which was no hardship. Another time she and Anne partnered Calico and George, with Anne shrieking at every trick she won, thumping down her card and crowing to the losing men, 'You fopdoodles! Got ya!' They kept stakes low and often bid tasks, following company articles: no gaming with anything above a piece of eight.

Mary looked over to where Noah was yet again cleaning the heads, reaching over the side of the *William* and scrubbing caked-on shit with a hard-bristled broom, swilling it with a bucket of water. She'd taught Noah how to play blackjack, but he needed to improve.

Gaming filled the hours, and there had been plenty of hours to fill during the four weeks they'd cruised the north Caribbean Sea or skulked in small coves waiting their chances to pounce. Day and night, someone would be aloft watching for sails: those to avoid and those to chase.

None of them could face fish right now. They'd eaten fish, every which way: fried, stewed and even raw soaked in lemons. This last experiment had earned Davy curses and complaints: 'I'll only eat this stuff if I'm marooned and have no choice.' 'Call this Christian food?' Piles of rotting fish and rank-smelling turtles were thrown overboard. The sea boiled with a feeding frenzy of squawking seabirds diving to feast and fish shooting up from below. They'd taken far too much fish from the boats off Eleuthera, but Calico Jack had been thorough in his revenge.

They had cruised south towards Cuba, once risking going ashore with rolls of pillaged cotton, linen and wool to exchange for food supplies. Apart from cloth, the merchant vessel had yielded two swivel guns to add to the *William*'s fixed guns, along with boxes of powder and ammunition. Now they were cruising along the north coast of Hispaniola.

Mary prepared her tobacco and pipe. Leisurely but alert summed up the past few weeks. Anne had been practising with her cutlass with anyone she could find, dancing on her toes, stabbing and slicing. She even volunteered to go aloft to change sails, racing up the rigging to build up strength. The woman bounded with energy and could hardly keep still.

As Mary savoured the tobacco smoke, she became aware of Paddy rustling up the crew for some sport, so she turned away, not wanting to be drawn in. She valued time to herself on this crowded vessel, and the crew had come to recognise the sign: if she was smoking by the bow boom, they knew to leave her be.

A cask was rolled out, prised open, with the would-be sportsmen gathered around guzzling the beer, bragging about which of them was stronger, quicker, fitter. They jostled and shoved, dividing into two teams.

'I'll not go with you, ya fat bastard – you'll slow us down!' Tom propelled his friend Howie to the other group, while Paddy called out in dismay to Jim, 'Traitor! Come over to our side. I'll have your bollocks for this!'

Mary straddled the bowsprit as others cleared the decks. When Anne yelled to her to join in, she shook her head. 'I'll be judge, so no cheating!'

Noah's face peered down from the lookout, looking none too happy to miss this sport.

'Noah!' She whistled. 'Come on down – I'll take over.'

He needed no encouragement, and as he scampered down she set off up. She enjoyed being aloft; it was the only place to be truly by herself. High above the deck, she kept one eye out for sails, the other watching the sport unfolding below.

First a race. Paddy and Noah set off, Paddy with Anne clinging on to his back, walloping his backside as if he were a horse, shrieking into his ear to urge him on, while Frank clung to Noah. With two circuits of the small deck completed, Anne leapt off, slapped Jim's hand, and Jim raced up the starboard ratlines while Fen shinnied up the larboard.

'C'mon, Jim! Don't let him catch you!' Mary shouted her encouragement, adding to the cacophony as the men raced to touch the button at the top of the mast then race back down to slap hands with another of their teammates.

Screams of, 'Mary! Y' can see they're cheating! Punish them!'

Dick tossed Davy off his back, complaining, 'You're fucking strangling me!' and clambered onto Davy's back, but there was no way Davy, with only one functioning arm, could carry a man the size of Dick.

Mary laughed and laughed at their foolishness, happy to see the sport, but just as happy not to take part. She pressed herself out of Calico's way as he scuttled up on the crow's nest then onwards and up beyond her to touch the button. Despite the drink in his belly he never looked in danger of falling. Always the drink, but Calico knew when to stop. But Anne? She watched Anne tip back her head and guzzle. Anne caught her eye and waved, and, mug in hand, clumsily clambered up the ratline to join her. Mary hauled her over the futtocks and Anne landed belly first on the platform, her mug still full and held high.

Mary took a sip, handing it back. 'Go easy, eh?'

'Sweet Jesus, don't you start.' Anne got to her feet. 'Jack's just said the same. We can have a little fun, can't we?'

'No harm.' Mary knew better than to pick a fight with Anne in this mood, so she turned back to scour the horizon.

'Look at them. Look at them all.' Anne tugged at her sleeve, indicating the men below.

'I'm looking. Why?'

Anne leant in confidentially. 'You could have any of them. I always thought you and Frank…'

Mary looked down at her companions, who, growing tired of their sport, were settling down to drink and argue about which team had won. She ignored their shouted appeals: 'Mary! Mary! We need you!' 'Come and sort us out!'

Anne pressed her. 'You could…'

There had been a time she'd considered sharing Frank's hammock but was content to be his friend. There had been one occasion… Mary turned her face away, aware she was blushing… when she and Fen were both drunk, but she'd found she hadn't enjoyed it and they'd both agreed that would be the end of it. In truth, she didn't fancy being intimate with

ANNA M HOLMES

any of them and none of them ever looked upon her with any desire.

'I'm done with men.' There, she'd said it. She hadn't been sure until this moment, but now pushed to articulate her thoughts, she knew it for certain.

'Really?' Anne frowned. 'You're missing so much. Having sex is fun.'

Mary knew Calico cared deeply for Anne and no longer hid his feelings. His hand might touch Anne with a brief caress, or an endearing word might slip from his mouth. She could not recall hearing Anne speaking words of love to Calico. But what did she know about what went on in private between the two of them? And there had been plenty such occasions. Anne and Calico had been at it like rabbits, their yelps reaching the rest of them from the cabin. The crew teased Calico, saying, 'You've got two minutes before you're needed: don't waste them.' Or, 'Cap'n, you're looking tired.' It was all good-natured. And just as none of the men showed any lustful interest in her, neither did they show any interest in Anne beyond a brotherly comradeship. Any concerns about having women on board had disappeared long ago.

Anne again prompted her with a querulous, 'Truthfully? Not even with Frank?'

She shook her head, reiterating, 'I'm done with them.' Anne leant over and kissed her lightly on the cheek. 'You're a strange one.'

The drink Anne had successfully kept in her belly would no longer be contained. In one neat motion Anne leant over the rail and vomited. Some puke must have landed on men below judging from their curses, but a good deal splattered back on Anne.

'That'll teach you!' Mary's tone was tart, but she hid her smile. This drunken woman wiping her wet hands on the back of her trousers was her friend – her first real friend. She turned back to scour the horizon for sails.

Next morning Mary woke to cries. 'A sail! A sail! Ahead off portside.'

A week had passed since their last encounter and everyone was bored. Chasing became addictive, just like gaming. Soon the well-drilled routine began: guns and small arms prepared; decks cleared. She and Fen waited for George's orders, ready to hurry aloft to set top sails. Soon the *William*, with all sails set, would be primed to chase, or flee. She waited and watched, and with every mile gained, learnt more about their prey.

The chase was on! Mary raced up the ratlines.

Much closer now, with Paddy, Tom, Noah and Anne on the bow swivel gun, they fired ahead of the bow of what appeared to be a trading sloop. It made a token attempt to ward them off, first returning fire and changing direction, but it had no chance against them and before long they boarded. As Jack began his parley with the captain Mary began sorting through the cargo and searching for coin. Using her axe, she smashed panelling in the cabin, fingers reaching in, prying into nooks and crannies. She became aware of movement behind her and spun around to find one of the merchant crew glaring at her.

'Do you have to destroy the fucking place? You'll not find anything here.'

She grunted and turned back to her task, but the man rushed her, so she swung the back of her axe towards his shoulder. He ducked, warding off the blunt blow with a raised arm. Did she hear a bone crack? Certainly she heard his scream.

'Should've kept out of my way.' And with this brief apology she turned back to her task. She had her job to do. When she had searched thoroughly, she went out on deck to hear Calico say, 'We'll take her. George'll take over.'

The sloop's captain groaned. He appealed to them as God-fearing Englishmen on the same side. They always did, all of them coming up with the same arguments, and she was indifferent to it. She rounded up the merchant crew and watched as one by one the eight men clambered down into the longboat they had been towing. She had a slight pang of regret watching the seaman she had injured negotiate the ladder with one hand.

'You're all healthy and strong – you'll make the coast in no time if you put your backs to it.' Calico cheerfully farewelled the crew. 'Get rowing!'

With long hours of toil ahead crewing two vessels with little sleep possible, they first celebrated. Jack had allowed this. 'A quick one,' as he put it, inviting all manner of jests.

Sitting on the deck of the *William* with Calico in command and a drink by her side, Mary could hear men singing from the captured sloop George was commanding. She hummed along tunelessly.

'Come on now,' Anne shouted to everyone within hearing. 'We can do better than them.' Anne pulled her to her feet. 'Come on, Mary, give it all you've got. Us against them!'

The two of them jumped on to the rigging, four men alongside, and all six bellowed the chorus, joining the distant voices from the captured vessel. They sang one song, then another and another; sang until they were hoarse, choruses lagging till any semblance of order fell apart. Then they traded insults with their mates across the water, calling them all the names they could think of and some they imagined.

'I challenge someone to a song – just me against any of ye bastards!' Paddy shouted across from the captured vessel.

'You're on. We're putting up our best fighter!' Anne choked with laughter. 'Mary!'

'All right! Mary, ye old witch! You and me then!' Paddy challenged her.

She glared at Anne. Anything but this humiliation. She clamped her lips tight.

'What d'ya say, Mary? Are you too much a coward to take me on?' Paddy goaded her. 'The others can vote which of us is the winner. C'mon. How about it?'

A cry of, 'Ma–ry! Ma–ry!' set up from across the water.

Anne was laughing hysterically and bellowed back to Paddy. 'She'll do it, you cock-eyed bastard. You don't know what you're up against. You know what she's like – keeps her weapons hidden, then blasts you away! You wait!'

Mary steeled herself – she would rather duel than duet. She was not a great conversationalist, let alone singer. The outcome was a foregone conclusion; she'd heard Paddy singing on many occasions. Anne was digging her in the ribs, urging her on, and the men whispered, 'Go on, Mary – we'll not let that Irish cock beat you!'

'All right then.' She yelled across the intervening stretch of sea, 'You're on, you Irish knucklehead, but I pick the song!'

She racked her brain, trying to conjure up the words of a song – any song – then she remembered an old broadsheet ballad requiring drinks to be fetched and drained throughout. This would do.

'Have you got booze on hand, Paddy? You're going to need it. We have to drink and no cheating. Paddy's men? You listening? Make sure he downs a mug after each verse!'

A chorus of assurance reached her from the stolen vessel. She smiled. Maybe, just maybe she could hold her own, as this had many verses. She doubted she could remember half the words, but looking around at her companions festooned around the rigging she was happy to see Howie. He could be guaranteed to help her out. Paddy sounded well into his cups and she might just outdrink him and still hold a tune of sorts. This contest mightn't be about the sweetest voice, but who could last longest.

'Are you ready?' she bellowed across to Paddy, then whispered a plea to the men around her. 'Help me out.' She filled her lungs, her rasping voice searching for each note.

'*Be merry my hearts, and call for your quarts, and let no liquor be lacking. We have gold in store, we purpose to roar...*'

She finished the first verse.

'Was that you, Mary, or a foghorn? Just askin.' Paddy could barely get his words out between spluttering hoots of laughter.

'Save your breath, you... you... fopdoodle!' Anne shrieked her favourite insult of the moment, setting them all off, bodies quivering in drunken laughter.

Never in her worst nightmares could she have imagined such a display, and yet she found she was enjoying herself. She need not hide anything from her companions any longer. And she had asked for help. That hadn't been too difficult either.

54

On the *Curlew* Jack had commanded fifty or more. Many had drifted away to other lives or other companies, some searching for Vane. Mary had told him Vane was intent on making a nest in the Spanish Main, and rumours were circulating that he was doing well for himself with a growing fleet. Jack tried to quell pangs of envy. What did he care? He was doing well enough, and the *William* was proving very much to his liking. He knew if he wanted to fill the boots of Jennings, or Hornigold, he needed to expand his operation. If that was what he wanted; but he wasn't sure he did.

All this was on Jack's mind as they skirted Cuba cruising eastward along the north coast of Saint Dominique, the French-owned western side of Hispaniola.

'They're getting too damned fancy for the likes of us, so we won't be putting in here.' Jack's view of Saint Dominique was shared by his crew. Before the French had taken control, the sparsely occupied north coast had provided many pirates with bases. Those days were long over, and this territory fell into Jack's category of things tightening up.

The *William*, in convoy with their captured sloop, cruised from Hispaniola to the Spanish side of the divided island and across to Puerto Rico. Here they sold their prize for a pathetic amount to a merchant who didn't ask questions and didn't speak much English. Still, they were keen on having coin in their pockets, and in the circumstances they couldn't hold out for a better deal.

At the Dutch-owned southern territory of the tiny isle of St Martins they stocked up on supplies and took on fresh water. They weren't fools, these Dutch – they knew where the goods Jack offered to trade had come from, and he could not talk up the price. Still, they swapped bales of tobacco and linens for things they needed, and all of it expensive on the tiny Dutch outpost. Well-fed men were more content than those on rations.

There had been arguments the past weeks, as was bound to happen. One day Dick had come to him, dragging Noah and Fen in his wake.

'These two, Calico – and you don't need to look at me like that, I know it's my job to sort out squabbles, yep, I know that, and I'd like to bang their skulls together.'

Dick threw an old woollen jacket down at his feet.

Noah appealed, 'Cap'n. I found it. I want it – you know why.'

'It makes sense I have it, Calico – I think it's fair,' Fen countered.

Clothes and personal items counted as pillage, not loot to be carefully recorded and shared, so pillage was important to the men. Jack had seen crews on captured vessels stripped naked; he drew the line there, but clothes not on a man's back were another matter. He picked up the well-worn garment, nodding first to Noah to have his say, his mind blank as to why he should know the reason Noah wanted the thing.

'If I go north, where it's cold.'

Ah, yes, Noah's wish to touch snow. Well, there were worse reasons to covet a patched-up woollen jacket with frayed elbows. 'And you?' Jack turned to Fen, who looked at him squarely.

'I'm heading home to Whitby after this cruise, so it'll come in handy. I've made up my mind it's the right thing to do – to leave before worse things happen. You can't object if I take my share and leave when this cruise is over?'

He had wondered about Fen testing the water, as he'd put it. And no, he couldn't object. It was Fen's life to do as he wanted.

He tossed the jacket to Noah. 'Finders keepers.'

This was true enough, but more than anything Jack wanted Noah to hold on to his dream. Every one of them needed something to hope for. He had ideas of establishing a home for himself and Anne. He imagined a brightly painted Spanish-style house they could use as a base, but never got beyond this fanciful vision. Anyway, first he needed to put plenty away in his coffers.

Cruising south nearing the Venezuela coast, they searched for a quiet inlet on a small island in the Little Antilles, as the men needed to let off steam. For three days they'd battled gale-force winds and were tired and out of sorts. Once ashore Jack helped manoeuvre a large driftwood stump into a prominent position, then drew a line in the sand with his shoe.

'Axes only, best of three, and a bottle of rum for the winner.'

They practised hurling their axes at the stump, aiming to strike it soundly, the blade cleaving the wood. This kept everyone entertained; Dick emerged the winner, grinning from ear to ear. 'Remember this moment, lads and lasses. Don't muck with me!'

Jack hadn't known Dick still had the brawn and eye for this difficult task. Most of them, him included, had totally missed the target more than once, some on all three occasions.

Their search for water yielded small, mosquito-infested pools, which would have to do, so they refilled water barrels, hunted unsuccessfully for wild hogs, then settled for shooting birds in the wooded interior. Good target practice, though they were wary of encountering snakes, and more comfortable back at the coast where they shot waterfowl, herons and oyster catchers, and captured hawksbills and green turtles until Davy decided his stores were full. Over the following days plucked feathers flew and flesh was smoked, roasted or boiled.

Where next? Always the question.

Neither he nor George was keen on turning away from the Caribbean. He had no interest in intercepting a slaver on the middle passage. The prizes Jack wanted were merchant ships on the northward leg of their journey from the Caribbean to Europe, or small coastal traders plying the Americas. These were all lower risk, and more useful rewards than human cargo. All part of his philosophy of successful roving.

They turned the *William* into Caribbean water, heading for the isolated northern coast of Jamaica. Very few troubled to visit the north, but the sea routes could be busy and the bays popular for fishing. En route they found themselves tailing a Spanish galleon with two outrider gun vessels. All the company took a keen interest in this small convoy. She had most likely left Panama, in which case she'd be carrying minerals: silver, gold and copper from Colombian mines.

Anne took the spyglass and peered out. 'Jack, how would you approach taking her?'

He'd been having fun thinking the same thing, pondering scenarios.

'A straightforward chase and attack would be out of the question. We'd have to decide on some ploy, some tactics. We could use our Spanish flag, of course—'

'Might that work? How?' Anne gripped his arm.

'Jack!' He heard George's sharp reprimand. 'Don't let that woman addle your brains!'

'Fuck you!' Anne yelled at George. 'I was only asking how it might be done.'

'I know. I know.' Jack calmed Anne's ruffled feathers. 'Anyway, I'm not fool enough to lead a suicide attack. I value my life even if some crazy bastards on board mightn't value theirs – or mine, for that matter. For a start we don't have either the gunpower or the manpower to take on these beasts, but we can have fun considering the possibilities, can't we? One thing we can all be certain of—' He paused as Anne looked at him, eager to hear what the one thing was. 'If they thought we were a threat we'd have been blasted from the water long ago. They're content to leave us trailing in their wake, because let's face it, we're no more than a flea on a hog's back. The thing we have going for us is our speed, and it's more likely to be put to good use if we have to make a run for it!'

He laughed as Anne screwed up her face, repeating, 'A flea on a hog's back, Hah!' Jack suspected she still harboured romantic notions about roving and turning away from a challenge was not in her nature. He chucked her under the chin. 'But don't let us stop you, sweetheart. If you come up with a plan with an odds-on chance of taking her, then let us know and I'll put it to the company!'

Anne thumped him on the shoulder. 'And fuck you too, Jack Rackham!' She stalked off. Well, he supposed he deserved it.

The Spanish galleon with her convoy continued sailing north-west while the *William* veered to the north-east, tacking against a strong northerly, between Jamaica and Hispaniola. With Jamaica twenty or so miles off, they turned to cruise westward along the British island's northern coast.

Through his spyglass Jack watched the distant vessel. At George's commands more sails were set, and within a short time Jack had the schooner firmly in view.

'Are you for her, men?' He received the reply he expected, and immediately everyone prepared for the chase: top sails set, his black flag raised, and within an hour they had intercepted their prey, firing their swivel across her bow and aiming muskets high above those on deck. The vessel hove to; theirs for the picking. Jack raised his hailer and yelled across the water as the *William* glided forward into position ready for boarding.

'Captain Jack Rackham. And you are?'

Shortly after came the reply: 'Thomas Spenlow – commander. I beg you to show mercy to me and my crew.'

'Prepare for us to come aboard. Expect no trouble from us unless you resist.' Jack had no wish to harass these mariners more than necessary.

Mr Spenlow was a weaselly-looking man Jack took an instant dislike to. He kept the crew locked up deep in the orlop and Spenlow in his cabin while they offloaded rolls of tobacco and sacks of dried peppers along with ship's stores and other useful things. Two days later Jack opened the cabin door to find Spenlow sitting with his hands dangling between his knees. 'You're free to go. All yours again!'

During Spenlow's long, anxious wait he would have been alert to the sounds of heavy items being dragged or rolled across the deck; to raised voices arguing over the best way to shift something; to every grunt and groan as they took the strain, lifting and heaving goods. Spenlow stood and watched him cagily. Time in his own company would have allowed terrible thoughts to chase around and around his head.

'Your men are safe, if that's what you're wondering. Maybe a little hungry and thirsty, that's all. Go!'

Spenlow let out a breath of relief and bounded past. Jack paused, considering the wisdom of releasing them. They'd had long arguments about what to do with the captured vessel and the men sailing her.

'Hell, Jack, we can't let them go – not here!' Anne had been furious.

'I know, I know! Where're they going to head to with an empty hold? Back to Kingston, that's where. I've no doubt.'

'Then don't do it! Let's take the vessel with us – take them all with us for now. Let them go later!'

'The vessel's old and too big for us. She'll hold us back.' George was adamant he did not want the added burden.

'And the trouble of keeping their crew under guard and fed rations. Yep – bound to be trouble. Who knows how long we'd have to keep 'em with us? Best get rid of 'em now – though it's risky if—'

'Not "if", Dick; "when"? How long have we got in these waters once they raise the alarm?' This was the burning question for Jack.

'Then don't do it!' Anne remained adamant. 'Put it to a vote.'

They had voted, albeit reluctantly, to let Spenlow and his crew sail their tub away.

Jack figured he had three more days before they needed to be clear of Jamaican waters, but he was full of confidence in the *William's* abilities to show a clean pair of heels if they had to flee.

The following day they chased down another merchant sloop.

'Can't let this one go, Calico – it bears my name. Got to be lucky for us,' Mary pointed out. The vessel was the *Mary*.

So the rigmarole started over again. The chase; preparation of weapons, ammunition and powder; Jack's hail across to the master, a man answering to the name of Thomas Dillon. George bringing the *William* alongside, just so, and remaining on board with a handful of others. The company drill was well oiled. Jack noticed men choosing to team up with the same companions. Howie and Tom Bourn assessed stores and weapons; Noah and Jim helped Frank pick over the ship's tackle; Anne, Mary and Fen teamed up, checking sails and cordage; Davy and Dick calculated cargo and stores. Paddy liked to be the one to round up those on board, blaspheming and cursing and puffing out his chest to "put the fear of the devil into Christian souls", as he put it. While Jack questioned the captain in his cabin, Dick oversaw the systematic searching and stripping of the vessel.

Repetition. They were getting good at this. Jack was cock-a-hoop, and all of them were elated, he and his entire hunting pack.

Soon after, cruising past a bay, Mary spotted three fishing canoes. Jack considered the wind direction; for a change it was coming off the land in this normally leeward location. He yelled his instructions to take in the jibs and trice their mainsail, and left Mary and Anne to take a lead on this one. Both women were leaning over the rail, hair tied back by scarves, pistols in one hand, axes in the other, yelling and cursing the fishermen and women below them. Jack smiled, listening to Anne's threats.

'Put up your oars! Don't you dare think of rowing away. Don't think of it. We'll fucking kill you. That'll stop you going against us. Don't doubt either of us will kill you!'

Jack didn't doubt Anne meant it, and he sincerely hoped those aboard the canoes heeded. He knew Anne would shoot. Or Mary. Before long turtles and tackle smothered the deck.

'And your oars. Hand them up.' Mary reached over to grab them, and Jack watched, amused, as a rower attempted to manoeuvre the heavy hollowed-out canoe, paddling Indian style with just the aid of one oar. It would take them a while to get back to shore.

They continued cruising, restless and searching, always restless and searching.

By midday they'd come to a long shallow bay where they found more canoes with men catching turtles. The *William* had enough turtles... but the men? Jack could see the strength in their arms as they powered away back to shore and cupped his hands, yelling, 'Wait! Come aboard! Share a drink!'

'Jack, you sure?' Anne was puzzled.

'We can show hospitality, can't we? Some news would be welcome, and fresh company. Who knows, we may tempt some to join us.'

The fishermen had reached shore with canoes pulled up, but they didn't rush into the woods. This was promising. Jack was about to hail them again but flinched at an unexpected boom. Smoke rose from the stern swivel gun where Anne had joined Paddy, both of them leaping up and down and waving to the men on shore.

'Paddy, you reckless idiot! What kind of welcome is that?'

The men on shore didn't think it much of a welcome either and had taken to the trees, but a catch of young fit men was worth waiting for.

'Let's drop anchor. Calm some nerves. Show we mean no harm.'

Sails were furled, anchor dropped and shortly after a dozen or so fishermen began to emerge from the trees.

'C'mon over! Join us!' Jack yelled, waving a bottle in the air. On shore the men whispered together. Jack continued with his efforts. 'C'mon! We have enough fucking turtles – just want your news and company.' He turned to Tom. 'Get out your fiddle, play them a tune.'

Within minutes Tom had struck up a jig or some such thing, and Jack began a courtship dance, angling his elbows and knees, sticking out his backside and jigging up and down.

Again, the men's heads came together as they conferred, and to his delight they pushed their canoes out. 'Yes!' Jack punched the air. Soon the canoes were tied midship, and Jack appraised the men being handed on board. They were young and looked healthy, hopefully weren't married, and might be up for an adventure. He smiled and looked as inviting as he could.

'What'll you have to drink? And let's have your news…' He had a better idea – he could lay on the entertainment a bit thicker to make their company life look more inviting. 'Howie! How about a song?'

Into his fifth drink, Jack knew they couldn't wait long, but he was learning things: chiefly that Governor Lawes had commissioned ten vessels to seek out pirates. This unsettled him, especially as he had quizzed the masters of both merchant vessels he had just taken, and they had both shrugged and said they had no idea about Lawes's capacity.

'Ten? Are you certain?' Jack pushed the fishermen on this fact. Yes, they were certain, but no, the fishermen had no idea where they were being deployed. Jack grunted. Lawes's spending power clearly outstripped Rogers's. He reached for another bottle. They should get moving. Soon...

'So, how's the fishing life working out for you all?' He asked the question, frowned in sympathy, learning they were just scraping by, and casually mentioned how much money each of his crew could expect from this cruise. Some were warming to his conversation – warming to the idea of joining them. Others were getting restless, standing, ready to leave. He needed a little more time, then he'd have them.

The glorious taste of rum in his throat drew a sigh of contentment. He glanced fondly at Anne where she leant against a rail, laughing with Mary. A leisurely fuck would round off the afternoon nicely. Later.

Anne's body stiffened. 'A sail! East point. A sail!'

He rose to his feet unsteadily. Too bad, this would be one prize they'd have to let pass; they weren't ready. He burped.

'Jack!' Anne's shriek jerked him to his senses, and his clouded eyes saw what was gliding into view a mile out to sea beyond the eastern point of the bay: a square-rigged two-masted snow, a beast of a vessel, easily weighing ninety tons, and well-armed. Very well-armed.

His body propelled into action before his brain realised it. 'Cut the fucking anchor cable! To ship's oars! Go!'

55

'OUTTA MY WAY!' DICK HURTLED PAST, HEAD THRUST forward, a jutting elbow catching Anne under her ribs. His eyes bulging, axe clasped in both hands high above his head, Dick brought the blade down with a roar, cleanly severing the thick anchor rope. Leaving the axe head embedded in the wood he charged off, sending men flying like skittles. It had taken no more than seconds. Precious seconds. There was no time.

Move… 'Move!' Anne's command was to herself.

'Loose the canoes!' George's order reached her through a fog. She was nearest, but it seemed to take an age, her fingers clumsy, to release first one then a second hitch knot. Two bodies launched past, leaping over the rails; the fishermen, half-swimming, half-drowning, thrashed out towards their canoes, their lifelines drifting away.

Over top of the din, Jack's command: 'New men on board. Ship's oars. Row, or get the fuck off!'

Everyone yelling and tripping over legs in a hurry to be somewhere, do something.

Listen to Jack. Listen! A string of bellowed commands issued from his mouth: 'Set the mains'l! Set the fucking tops'l!'

Howie's voice: 'Heave ho... Heave ho...' measuring the rowers' strokes as the long oars dipped and pulled, dipped and pulled, men straining to get the *William* moving while the sails were set.

Anne shoved past a group of terrified fishermen still clutching mugs of whatever amber liquid they'd been enjoying. Dropping to a crouch at Dick's side, she braced her feet and unhitched the tricing line, releasing the mainsail from its pleated, bunched-up position.

Above, Mary almost danced along the topsail footrope, one arm supporting her, with Fen close behind and Noah sliding out along the opposing top yard. Mary cast off a gasket, her feet sliding back, reaching over to untie the next. At Mary's shout, 'Let fall!' the topsail dropped, loosely gathered to the yard. 'Sheet home!'

'Ease clews. Haul away the sheets!' Jack's voice.

Anne let go one rope, picked up another and, hand over hand they pulled in unison, straining to set the topsail. Her hands worked deftly, winding her line around a belay pin and rapidly coiling remaining rope. A fresh command to brace the top yard. Hurry. Don't talk. Save your breath. She squeezed into the line of men to uncoil the larboard halyard rope. 'Two, six, HEAVE!'

She heaved, dizzy, panicking, trying to focus on Jack's commands as Mary and others with her dropped the main course.

She glanced at the armed vessel. It was bigger than she'd first thought.

The helmsman eased the *William* forward. She had little faith in God, but at this moment, she would have promised her soul. Within seconds the mainsail responded, sagging canvas rippling, flapping, becoming taut.

What next? The headsails. Fresh commands to set the jib and stays'l.

The *William* was moving but Anne swore it wasn't water beneath them; it felt thick and syrupy, dragging them back.

As Anne kicked abandoned oars out of the way she glanced at the powerful, fully rigged vessel further out to sea, already adjusting the set of its sails and turning a little away from the bay. It had no intention of coming closer to land, but it also didn't mean to sail on beyond them. She imagined the captain would have his spyglass out, watching them.

Jack grabbed the collar of a fisherman making himself small, his back pressed into a nook. 'Know it?'

'The *Tyger* – one of Governor Lawes's privateers – seen it in Kingston.'

Anne hissed. If this was the best news these damn fishermen had for them it was unwelcome.

Jack continued. 'Commander?'

'No idea.' The panicking man grabbed Jack's arm as he turned away. 'Wait! Put us ashore!'

'Swim!' Jack wrenched himself loose and hurried to George standing by the helmsman.

Anne turned to the tangle of ropes and began coiling them out of the way. A tug on her shirt forced her to focus on the person at her side, shaking her. She frowned at the persistent fisherman, face pale, voice squeaky. 'You can't mean to keep us on board! Let us off?'

'Jump. Swim ashore for all I care!'

'Can't swim!' The young man's face – he was no older than herself – had the terrified look of a trapped deer or a cornered hare. She had no time for this man, no time to feel sympathy for his predicament. 'Go below – just get out of our way if you're not going to help.' She pushed him aside.

Taking a deep, steadying breath, she looked into the early evening sky, sun hovering above the horizon.

The *Tyger*, no more than four hundred yards away, was aligning herself broadside, still sailing on, larboard gunports open. Shortly the *William* would need to intersect the point where they would be perfectly lined up with her guns; they had no choice. She willed the *William* to pick up speed, to be free of the bay and into the open sea.

At the first blast Anne flinched and dropped to a crouch. In quick succession a second, third and fourth boom of the *Tyger's* great guns cut through the air, followed by the sound of ripping canvas, splintered wood and thuds of iron bars and chains falling near her. Yells and curses filled the air. Their main course had been shredded, jib sails ripped, rigging dangled.

'Mary?' Anne shrieked, frantic eyes raking the yards through the damaged sail. Mary was not there – none of them were aloft. Then she spotted Mary on deck. 'Thank God!' Anne berated herself as a hypocrite, knowing the only time God entered her thoughts was when she was in trouble, and she doubted God had much interest in a woman like her.

She pushed her way to where Mary stared stony-faced at the damaged rigging. 'Difficult to get aloft. Not impossible, but...'

As Fen and Mary tested their feet step by step, making their way up the damaged lines, curses and fresh commands filled the air. Focus! She needed to heed Tom, their master gunner. She was ready to work her gun, but first she needed a moment with Jack. Just a moment of his time.

'Jack?'

'What is it?' He was by the helmsman and didn't spare her a look but continued staring at the small cresting waves ahead. Away from shore the sea had become choppier, and Jack was alert to every change, to the smallest of gusts, while moment by moment the helmsman was fractionally adjusting the *William*'s line.

'Jack?' She hardly knew what she wanted to say to him, but she wanted a quick smile and a comforting, 'We'll be fine!' This would be enough to soothe her. Instead his face was set hard as he calculated the best way to coax maximum speed from the damaged *William*. His eyes flickered to her and he snapped, 'Tom called you, didn't he? Get to your station!'

She turned to go. 'Anne! Chances are you'll need your cutlass before the night's over – or earlier.'

Trip after trip, she eased past bodies rushing up or down the 'tween deck ladder. She carried up gunpowder, arranged an array of ammunition by the three portside guns and the stern swivel. She would be with Paddy and the rest of their team.

Above the cacophony Mary yelled down to George from where she precariously balanced on broken ropewalk, the strands ahead of her dangling and useless. Fen straddled the yard, inching his way out to reach down for the broken lines. It would take hours to fix these – hours they didn't have. The shredded course was tearing more and more, interfering with the other sails, but they couldn't furl it.

'If you're going to die, don't do it falling! Work on the jibs then get down where you're needed!' George yelled up to Mary, then turned to Frank, who was preparing to re-thread new cordage through a replacement block.

'W-w-we can fix this line. Just need m-m-more men.' Frank's hands shook as much as his quavering voice.

George spoke quietly. '"More men" are more than we've got. Put that aside, Frank – use your tackle to move the bow swivel astern.'

George caught Anne's eye. He looked like he wanted to say something, and she steeled herself to hear some such nonsense about women bringing bad luck, but he just pressed his lips together, shook his head and walked away to join Jack.

'Bastard!' she yelled after him, not sure why she said it, but he didn't seem to be acting with urgency.

At Dick's call for assistance she rushed forward to help dismantle and lift the bow swivel gun. With a rope secured around its barrel, they hauled the heavy metal cannon along the deck, to where Frank fixed a block and tackle at the stern, ready to hoist it in position. They should never have anchored. Had this been Jack's idea? She couldn't remember.

Two stern swivels faced the *Tyger*'s bow swivel guns. The privateer was closing in, less than two hundred yards astern. Anne could just make out a Union Jack, with a small white square patch sewn in the centre, flying from the *Tyger*'s mast, the patch possibly some symbol to mark them as privateers. Damn the King! She had never managed to get beyond an image of a pompous monarch in full regalia, sitting on a throne in a stone castle in a damp and dismal land. All the stories she'd heard about the kings or queens of England were bad ones: her father's tales of Irish repression or his rants about trade regulations in Carolina. And Governor Rogers's face came into her mind. Damn his soul too!

As the distance shortened she could see troops on deck. Grimly she realised there were many men aboard the *Tyger* and these men would be fighting fit.

The *William*'s ragged sails were tinged with gold as the sun sank below the horizon ahead, making them a perfect target, but the *Tyger* held fire. Shortly it would be dark; they might escape yet. She held on to this slender thread as she gazed back at the bigger, stronger vessel closing in. On board the *William* a silence had fallen.

She made her way to Jack again, his spyglass raised, watching the *Tyger*.

'Can we lose her tonight? Any chance?' She tried to keep her voice calm.

Jack lowered his spyglass, his eyes no longer clouded by drink, but there was a new look in his eyes, a look she had never seen before: resignation. 'Doubt it.'

She moved closer to him, feeling the comfort of his presence. They watched their pursuer gain ground; about a hundred yards astern now and easily within musket range for their best shooters.

'Strike your flag and show the King of England's colours!' A clear, amplified voice reached them from the *Tyger*: the captain laying down his gauntlet.

'The hell we will.' Jack spoke softly. 'Haven't even got the damn thing, even if we wanted to.' He managed a feeble grin, knowing she'd tossed Harmon's flag away.

The voice persisted. 'Raise the King's colours and we'll hold off. Answer me if you will!'

'Let's answer with a fucking blast!' Paddy was agitated, hopping from foot to foot.

'Do it, Jack! Why wait?' Anne pressed him, as anxious as Paddy to make a move.

'Here's why not.' Jack was measured. 'They're carrying two twelve-pounders at the bow, as far as I can tell, against our three-pounders, which may prick them a little but that's all. It'll be dark soon – the less they see the better.'

Jack turned and spoke to the silent company. 'Do we hold off and hope for the best under cover of dark? Your say, men?'

Muted "aye"s and a reluctant "if you think it's best" followed. It was as if the stuffing had been knocked out of them. They were as soft and floppy as Nancy's cherished cloth doll. This would not do!

'No. Strike now! I say we strike!' Anne yelled, desperate to do something, but looking around at the gathered sullen faces, she knew she would be outvoted.

Mary touched her shoulder. 'We're working on things. If we can refit the tops'l we'll be back in business. Bide your time and keep a cool head.'

Mary's brief smile gave her comfort. Anne watched her friend's sturdy body make its way up the damaged ratlines to join Frank and Fen working on the rigging. Anne took a deep breath. She would trust the *William* could be brought back to full sail. She would believe this to be possible, just as she would trust Captain Barnet to hold fire a little longer.

The sun dipped below the horizon and Anne longed to be encased in darkness, a blanket shielding them just a little.

Again, the amplified voice: 'Captain Rackham, I believe? Captain Barnet here. Raise the British colours immediately and we'll not attack.'

'Jack. Fire!' she pleaded.

Jack turned to look at his crew repairing the rigging. 'Every man to the guns… weapons ready! Prepare to engage!'

Anne raced to her station. She was on Paddy's team, the winning team, he always told her when they had target practice, competing against each other to see which team could fire and reload the quickest. As often as not they were the quickest, spurred on by Paddy's threats of cutting off bollocks and other such inducements. Right now they needed to be the winning team; nothing else would do.

Out of the corner of her eye, as she hurried to reposition ammunition and powder she'd brought up earlier, she noticed George cross his chest. The small gesture irritated her. Since when had he become religious? Damn him! They would fight. They would blast the *Tyger* from the water.

'Jim!' Anne glanced at him as he prepared the ramming rod. 'I'll do your next night watch if we win. Promise!' He managed a bitter smile.

'Bollocks to that!' Paddy joined her. 'I'll do it and throw in my best jacket – don't want to wear it for the hangman.' They managed some jokes, promising each other clothes or hats or whatever else they owned that another man coveted.

Again, the voice from across the water: 'Your final warning. Show the King's colours!'

Through the hailer, Jack shouted, 'We'll not wear any colours but our own!'

She joined the cheers. That's what they needed: rousing talk to lift their spirits.

In the last glow of the sun's rays they hoisted their black flag to where it jammed halfway up the tangled rigging, the white skull and crossed swords refusing to flutter and display. In the past the *William* had looked magnificent with their emblem flying from the highest point, but now it was a sorry sight. Anne sucked in her breath as she realised she had allowed herself to think of the past.

A thunderous blast rocked the *William*, throwing Anne off her feet. Her cries, mingled with those around her, were made insignificant by the sickening crack of timbers. Above, in time slowed down, she watched their splintered mast separating, bringing with it the gaff along with wreckage of their mainsail. And people. Bodies were hurtling down, landing with thuds among the wreckage of rigging and sails.

She threw herself sideways as a wooden spar crashed to the deck; for a moment she was stunned, floundering under weighty canvas and yards and yards of tangled rope. She scrambled to her feet and checked her body. Even if she had been injured she doubted she would have felt anything.

The helmsman: 'Can't fuckin' steer!' Thomas: 'Over here! Can't move!' Jim's wail: 'We're done for!' Jack: 'Prepare your small arms!'

Among the curses, shrieks and commands, Mary's wail pierced Anne's brain, and like a hatchling in a crowded colony of shrill squawking seabirds, Anne fought her way to reach her, scrambling over the mess, hauling aside ripped canvas. She found Mary squatting, heaving on the broken spar to push it aside. Mary was alive! Relief flooded over her, then she absorbed what was before her.

Frank was pinned beneath, blood seeping from his head colouring the surrounding sailcloth a crimson red, eyes glazed and unseeing. She and Mary locked eyes. Anne could not tell if Mary was afraid; if so, she was hiding it, and this gave her courage. 'You'll fight, Mary?'

Mary gave her a withering look as she stood and adjusted her pistol braces. 'I'll fight and condemn any man who won't. Where's my cutlass?' She started rummaging.

'Fire on the bastards! Pepper the deck!'

Jack! The sound of his voice giving this command filled her heart. He was safe. But of course he was safe. She had never doubted it, not for a moment.

The *Tyger* was no more than fifty yards behind their stern.

Anne fumbled for a pistol held by ribbons across her shoulder. She, who was always such a good shooter, wasted first one shot then the other, her hands shaking badly. Only those with muskets had any chance of being in range of their targets. She should have held fire, as now she had to spend precious time reloading, and her fingers were stubbornly slow. If any of them managed to hit an intended target on the *Tyger*, it would be a miracle, with the *William* lurching uncontrollably at the mercy of the waves and all of them tripping over each other. A miracle? She frowned and berated herself. Her fate was in her own hands, not God's.

Return shots from the *Tyger* whistled past. At a cry her head whipped up, but it was too dark to see. Was it Howie? Yes, Howie stumbled forward holding his chest. Frank dead, now Howie wounded: two men out of action. She was counting.

Dick's voice... Listen to his commands. They shoved, hauled and pushed the shattered boom attached to useless canvas and tangled cordage over one side then the other – anything to delay the inevitable and make boarding more difficult for their attackers.

'Anne! Anne!' She turned at Jack's urgent call and looked at his craggy face, his eyes hard. 'Get below – no need to be out here.'

'I'm not a coward. We fight together, you and I!'

'I don't see—'

'Save your breath. I'll not leave the deck!'

He nodded, raising his voice. 'Listen! All of you, listen!' He bellowed till he had the company's attention. 'This is it – not the way we wanted, but there's still hope! We're outnumbered, but Barnet's men are fighting to take a cut of prize money – the money on our heads. We're fighting to live! Nothing like it to put fire in your belly. We can do it!'

Jack looked like he believed it, and she believed him.

'Hah!' George grunted, and swigged from a bottle of rum which he passed to the man standing next to him.

'Sober up, you fool! This is no time to drink!' Anne grabbed the bottle and flung it overboard.

A tight smile stretched George's lips. 'Now's definitely the time to drink. I recommend it. Enjoy it while you can!' He turned to Jack. 'Sorry, Calico. Sorry, mate – our luck's run out. Sorry about...' He waved his arms indicating everything: their predicament, their lives together, everything he might be sorry to leave behind. 'I'm going below to get rat-arsed, with an invitation to anyone to join me.'

'Below!' Fresh outrage filled her heart. 'To hide with the fishermen? Damn any of you who turn your backs now!'

George was scornful. 'The game's up, and I mean to drink as much as I can as fast as I can.' George turned to the hatch.

'Jack!' Anne appealed. 'Stop them. Make them fight!' She glanced back to where the *Tyger* glided towards their stern, with possibly two dozen armed men preparing to board from midship despite the entanglement of timber and sails.

'Each man for himself. That's the way of it.' Jack planted a hard kiss on her lips and pushed her aside. He withdrew his cutlass. 'Go below! Please. For me.'

'Shut up, Jack.'

'And I'm staying with you, Calico! Yep, I'm staying till the end, and that's not looking too good!' Dick planted his feet wide in front of them, as if to put himself between Jack and this new danger.

A nudge of the two hulls bumping and the sound of grappling hooks catching on wood.

A shot followed by a shriek from somewhere below. Anne was momentarily confused, unsure what was happening until Mary shouted. 'Whoever I hit, I'm glad of it! Cowards, all of you. I'm fighting to the last and I defy any man not joining me!' Mary stood, pistol pointing down through the open hatch at their own men. 'I've no time for you.' She kicked the hatch closed.

Again, Captain Barnet issued his order to surrender.

Never! Never! No king of England or his lackey would tell her what to do!

Shoes thudded on the deck. Their deck. How many men? This fast-moving tide threatened to drown her. She raised her pistol and fired randomly into the men surging forward. A soldier yowled. One down! No time to reload. Anne withdrew her cutlass.

It was crowded, as Jack had said it would be. She barely had elbow room, but enough, and she was alert to the superiority of her curved cutlass compared to the short military swords of her opponents. She meant to inflict as much damage as she could.

Smoke and the smell of gunpowder filled her nostrils. Someone was shooting. More men shooting. Whose men? Jack's men? Barnet's men? She couldn't tell. Her eyes were locked on the soldier advancing towards her, sword in hand. Anne widened her stance and willed every muscle in her body to be strong and up to this moment.

'A woman?' Her opponent paused momentarily before his blade met hers.

The force of the blow took her unawares and she almost lost her grip. All her practice fighting, long ago with Richard, then Jack and Mary, had not prepared her for this. Her more skilled opponents had held back their strength when fighting her to give her a chance. This man was immediately on to her again and would maim or kill her.

The edge of her blade deflected the next thrust. She twisted her wrist and sliced down, her grunt of exertion matching her opponent's grunt of pain as he dropped his sword. She would not kill him, just stop him. Stop this tide of men.

'That's him! That's Calico Jack. Know him by his colours!'

Even in the dark Jack's trademark trousers would set him apart. Out of the corner of her eye she was aware of soldiers swarming around Jack, his cutlass cutting arcs through the air.

'Keep them off, Jack!' Anne screeched. Every fibre of her body focused on saving her life. This life. She raged, slicing and stabbing at whoever got in her way. She would stop them. She would stop all of them.

How long had this been going on? She could not be sure, but it could be no more than a minute or two, and her strength was giving out. Blood soaked her shirt – her own blood or others' she could not tell. If she was injured she felt no pain. Her head swivelled. What was happening? Were they winning? Even this she could not tell, but the deck seemed to be emptying. Her companions: where were they?

And Jack? Surely not! Jack stood; head bowed; cutlass dangling from his hand.

'Fight, damn you, Jack! D'you want to swing? Fight, God damn you!'

His cutlass clattered to the deck and one of Barnet's men disarmed him of pistols and knife. This could not be!

Mary's voice, cursing and bellowing. She was alive. Mary was alive!

Slipping on the blood-slicked deck, Anne inched towards Mary. A solid wall of men confronted her, each with raised swords and cocked pistols.

'Put down your weapons!'

Sweat stung her eyes and dripped off her nose as she glared at the men through strands of sodden hair falling over her face. She had become a she-devil, hair unbound and tangled, teeth bared and panting, dragging in long, jagged intakes of air, never getting enough to fill her lungs.

She was trapped, not by some imagined entanglement of marriage to a Carolinian planter, but snared like an animal, its leg crushed in a jagged-toothed metal trap. If she could not cut herself free she would die. The life she had yearned for spiralling ever outwards was instead spinning inwards at terrifying speed. She fought to fill her lungs.

They were talking to her, these men, but Anne couldn't hear their words for the ringing in her ears; she could only see their mouths working. The tip of a sword nudged her cutlass away and she felt a hard pistol barrel to her temple. She lowered her cutlass, loosened her grip on the hilt, letting it drop to the ground, and a hand reached out and disarmed her of her knife. Looking at the cutlass at her feet, she mourned its passing. Strong fingers gripped her shoulder and her right arm was wrenched behind her.

Mary stood panting by her side, jacket and shirt in tatters, face gleaming with sweat. Their eyes met, and they stared silently at each other.

And Jack? She turned to see him, disarmed and surrounded by soldiers, pistols pointing at his head. Fury filled her and she yelled, 'What of your promise? You should've fought till your last breath!'

Twisting away from her captives Anne barged across to Jack. Hysterically she kicked his cutlass abandoned on the ground. 'You can use that thing better than most!'

'It's over. I'm sor—'

'Idiot! You idiot!' She pummelled his chest and kicked his shins.

'Anne, it's over. Understand? No point killing more men.'

'You could've got us out. We could've done it!'

'It's over. This is the end of it. I'm—'

'Over?' The words she did not want to acknowledge came as a whisper. 'End?'

Her legs could not support her. She dropped to her knees, a low bellow forcing itself up through her throat. The pain of childbirth was nothing to this. These sounds coming from somewhere deep inside her were those of mourning, and she could not stop. This loss was too much. Losing Jack was too much.

'Anne.' She felt his hand on her head, the briefest of touches, before it was snatched away, and she was yanked upright. She swayed, brain and body exhausted.

Cords cut into her wrists as they were bound tightly behind her back, just as Jack's were lashed. She raised her eyes to meet his and all they could do was stare at each other, trying to communicate everything they felt.

'So, Captain Rackham then? John Rackham?'

Anne focused on the uniformed figure of Captain Barnet, glorying in his successful catch. Jack nodded, and Barnet smiled brightly. 'We heard your gunfire. A lucky day for us!'

The damn man was crowing. Anne worked a gob of spit in her mouth, meaning to project it in his direction, but instead she swallowed it. 'The gun!' This was the gun Paddy fired. That she helped fire. Jack merely smiled – a small smile without blame.

'Captain Barnet.' The man stood to attention. 'I have a commission from Sir Nicolas Lawes, Governor of Jamaica.' His voice, full of authority, carried beyond Jack and her, to reach Mary and those skulking below deck. Captain Barnet continued, getting the formalities out of the way. 'In the name of King George, I have the honour of arresting you, all of you' – he stressed the words and she felt his eyes on her – 'and escorting you back to Sir Nicholas, into his custody.'

Jack merely nodded and continued to hold her gaze. She tried to keep her eyes on his, but they flickered away.

Captain Barnet seemed to think more was required of him, or more needed to be said. 'No doubt Governor Lawes will find accommodation for your large party, until such time as he prepares a trial – a fair trial, of course – and we'll see what the outcome is.'

Captain Barnet was smirking, it seemed to Anne, holding back the cock-a-doodle crows he longed to shout. The crows of the victor over the vanquished. Anne had always been the one to leap jauntily aboard a prize. Had been...

She could not look at Jack. They all should have fought more. Longer. Harder.

'Get your hands off me.' Mary shrugged off a soldier attempting to manhandle her. She squared her shoulders, scowled at him and positioned her own hands behind her back, then nodded for him to get on with the job.

Man by man, Jack's company – her company – were escorted up from below deck, all of them numb and dumb, all of them diminished in size. Even Dick, that old prize fighter, looked like a shadow of himself, though he tried to stand tall, his chest lifted high.

'Fucking bastards!' At the end of the day, it seemed Paddy had only words to fight with.

'You should have fought harder too!' Her voice breaking, Anne yelled across to Paddy and all of those who had drifted away below deck, more fearful of the uncertainty of death in hand-to-hand combat than the certainty of a hangman's noose. 'You should've fought to the end, Paddy!' Her contempt cut as deep as any sword.

Paddy looked up and gave the slightest of shrugs, as if puzzled himself about how things had turned out. 'Lost this one, Anne. Maybe Governor Lawes will accept the shirt off my back.'

There'd be no more bargaining extra chores or duties, no more banter about someone's run of good luck at a card game.

And Noah? There he stood, jaw dropped to his chest, shuffling and submissive like the slave he had been. So much for his dream of freedom.

The fishermen were jabbering and gesturing, begging to be listened to. 'Ask the others! Ask them! We just came on board for a drink. It's the honest truth, I swear by God. Listen, please listen!'

Captain Barnet waved them aside. 'The judge can do the listening. He'll decide.'

Captain Barnet left his men to get on with the job of sorting out his unexpected human cargo, cautiously dividing Jack's crew into groups of three or four, nervously watching over their charges, arguing the best way to get them across to the *Tyger*. It was only when George growled, 'How the fuck are you going to do that?' that Barnet's men rebound their captives' hands in front of them so they could grab on to something as they clambered over. Some wag, Fen, she thought, mumbled, 'I wouldn't invite you men to organise a party at a brothel.' This drew a chuckle from some who still had energy for it.

They took Jack over first. Anne watched him being bundled unceremoniously over the rail, looking ungainly as he struggled, hands bound, to reach across the netting dividing the rocking vessels.

There was something important she needed to say to Jack. Another time. Later.

PART FOUR

1720 – 1721

To the Devil

To the execution dock I must go, I must go,
Now to execution dock I must go,
To execution dock, while many thousands flock,
But I must bear the shock, and must die.

My name is Captain Kidd, as I sailed, as I sailed,
My name is Captain Kidd, as I sailed,
My name is Captain Kidd, God's laws I did forbid,
And most wickedly I did, as I sailed.

TRADITIONAL SONG, FINAL VERSE AND CHORUS

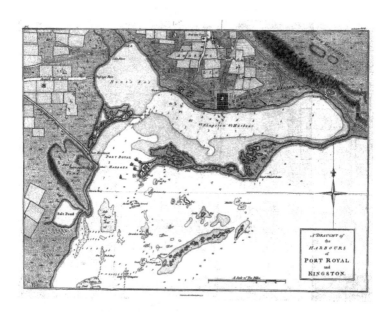

Kingston, Jamaica

56

JACK FOUND HIMSELF SHACKLED DEEP IN THE BOWELS
of the *Tyger* with the rest of his men and the terrified
fishermen, everyone's piss adding to the stink of bilge water.
There was no dignity in this. Anne and Mary were locked
up elsewhere. He begged Captain Barnet to let him visit
Anne but was met with a decisive, 'No favours, Rackham.
I'm not granting you access to a woman – that wouldn't be
right, or fair to the other men.' The fool! Did Barnet think
he wanted to fuck her? Did he think she was the company's
whore? Idiot! Jack just wanted to see her, comfort her and
talk. He explained as much, but Barnet wasn't having any
of it.

At a west Jamaican cove, transferring from the *Tyger*, Jack
began to panic. Where was Anne? He needed to see her.
Soldiers with bayonets fixed to muskets watched him clamber
out of the boat with a group of his men, then herded them up
the beach, saying, 'Shift your carcasses, while you still can.'

Craning his head back he could see another boat: Anne with Mary and some of the fishermen. He watched her climb out and was relieved to see she had no obvious injury. He had not been sure back on the *William*; there had been too much going on.

Jack made his way to Captain Barnet and plastered on the best smile he could. 'A word with the lady – if you don't mind.'

'All right, Rackham. Fair enough. I'll give you a minute.' Barnet nodded to his soldiers to allow him to pass back to the shore. Jack pushed his way through a group of damn fishermen who always seemed to get in the way and hurried towards Anne, who was pulling against the restraining arms of a soldier, trying to reach him.

'Jack! How are—'

'I tried to see you… Bloody Barnet wouldn't—'

'Did you? Oh…' She frowned.

What did she mean? Did she doubt he'd tried hard enough? Was she indifferent to whether he tried or not? He was afraid to ask. His heart was bursting with all the things he wanted to say, but this wasn't the place to begin an intimate conversation and the words wouldn't form themselves. He cleared his throat. 'You all right?' His question was hardly adequate.

Anne nodded. 'Jack… I—' She bit her lip. Unusually, she too seemed at a loss for words.

Soldiers or no soldiers, he needed to be closer, needed to touch her. He longed to hold her in his arms, crush her tight. That was out of the question with their damned wrists bound in front. But he could raise his arms; could touch her cheek; could bend forward and kiss her… It was a deep kiss, a kiss to show he wanted his soul to pass to hers.

Too soon he was pulled away and each of them mumbled, 'Bye,' as if they'd see each other the next day and pick up where they had left off. Too soon he was marched to Major James:

a brusque man who was very clear about his mission as he addressed them all.

'Every effort will be taken to deliver you to Sir Nicholas Lawes, preferably alive, but if any one of you wishes to test the resolve of either me or my men, be my guest. They've orders to shoot should any of you attempt escape.' He turned to his mounted soldiers. 'Load them up, let's get on the road.'

Jack jolted along in an old cart in company with Dick, George and Howie across the plains, valleys and lowland hills towards Spanish Town. The other men, and Anne and Mary, followed in procession. He tried not to think about Anne. She would certainly die, and this thought crippled his brain.

A man needs to occupy his mind with something, and now big decisions had been wrested from his control, small things became magnified, elevated to significance. Jack spent hours concocting elaborate means to win battles against flies and mosquitoes and designing ingenious ways to keep the sun off his blistering face, his hat long gone. These were the only battles he faced now. Nothing was in his control.

And water. This was another preoccupation; there was never enough of it.

'Oi, you!' George shouted to the nearest guard on horseback. 'I'm spitting foam my mouth's so dry. Any chance of ale? Rum? Anything?'

The man sniggered. 'In your dreams. Not even for us. The horses are good for another five miles. You'll get water then – maybe even something to eat.' The soldier kicked his horse into a trot, and George scowled, sinking into himself.

This was the pecking order: horses, soldiers, prisoners.

None of them had ever been as sober in their adult lives.

'Something to look forward to at the gallows, heh? We'll be offered a drink to see us on our way.' Jack said aloud what all of them must have been thinking at some time or other. They fell silent, with only the plodding of horses' hooves and crunching of cartwheels to fill their ears. And Howie's moans. Always the damn man's moans and groans, his wound festering and his singing days behind him.

While Jack was forced to be idle, signs of industry were all around him. Sugar plantations stretched in all directions along the plains. Hundreds of black slaves along with shabbily dressed white men and women laboured in cane fields, loading ox carts with cut cane.

He passed donkey carts transporting cane to nearby mills, and pairs of horses pulling carts laden with hogsheads of processed sugar. These would be bound for warehouses at Kingston port. Every so often he caught sight of long low plantation houses, single-storey to withstand the hurricanes, the houses becoming grander the nearer they got to Spanish Town.

Jack was glimpsing aspects of an industry through which rich men became richer on the backs of slaves; an industry that had sustained his stealing from sea merchants and selling on the black market. Sugar. Sugar had been a staple of the cargoes he had plundered. Had. His sober brain appreciated this was behind him.

As the procession of carts loaded with prisoners trundled through Spanish Town Jack was aware of people lining the street, gawping and jeering. He gazed over their heads, preferring to look at the buildings, but found little to admire; so much of the earlier, more ornate, Spanish architecture having been destroyed by the victorious English. He imagined the house he had fancied living in with Anne, allowing the colourful concoction to fill his restless mind as they rumbled towards the prison gates.

From the brilliant afternoon sunlight Jack found himself pushed into a gloomy cell along with Dick, George and Jim. As the cell door slammed shut Jack paused. He rubbed his chafed wrists, now unbound, and closed his eyes, orientating himself to the darkness and steeling himself to endure the foul smells of his temporary lodging.

'So, you red-arsed cocksucker, they caught up with ya.'

Jack's eyes shot open. He knew this voice. His eyes darted in the direction of the speaker, and through the gloom the only other occupant of the cell materialised. An emaciated man with long matted hair sat on a heap of flattened straw, his back to the wall, an arm resting nonchalantly on a bent knee.

'Vane?' Jack was completely taken by surprise; he had not expected to see him ever again. 'Vane! How long have you been here?'

'Can't say… Months… Fucking months.'

Vane struggled to his feet and Jack could see how ill he was. Jack sucked his teeth. He felt pity for the man who would share his own fate, pity tinged with a guilty pleasure that it wasn't just he, Jack Rackham, who had lost the game. He had been envious of Vane, imagining him acquiring a large fleet and becoming king of the Caribbean rovers. Just the other day, when a flock of parrots flew squawking overhead, his mind had turned to Vane, wondering of his fate. Jack stared at the miserable-looking wretch before him, a shadow of his former self.

'Vane!' Jack repeated his name, to assure himself it was really him. As Jack embraced Vane he could feel decay permeating the man. 'Months? Why so long?' Jack couldn't see the point of keeping a man mouldering away. He hoped he would be dispatched soon. He felt Vane's thin shoulders shrug.

'Can't say. Finding witnesses? Seeing how long they can keep me alive? Who the fuck knows? No one tells me anything.'

Vane grinned, his face close to Jack's. 'I've not had company for months – started talking to the fucking rats.' Laughter caught in his throat, followed by a dry racking cough.

'What's your story then? Tell us your story.' Dick thrust out his hand. 'Dick. You'll remember me from the *Ranger*. You'll not hold it against me for voting for Jack? And you'll remember George...'

Jack glanced around the squalid cell, deciding where to stake his claim to space. Not near the corner buzzing with flies, where shit mixed with piss-soaked straw; the smell pervaded the entire cell and he hoped, with four more men here, the guards would clear it out. How to deal with rats would be something else to occupy his mind. Other men, Lawes particularly, would have his hands full organising his Admiralty Court, getting everything in order. Other men, not him.

'Yes, Vane, what's your story?' Jack was genuinely curious as to what had brought him down.

'How much time ya got?'

Jack pursed his lips. 'Not going anywhere just yet, so take your time.'

Vane grinned and they settled themselves, leaning on the walls.

'We were cruising the Main, everything going well for us when a fucking hurricane came out of nowhere. Couldn't hold the vessel. Monster waves like you've never seen. Smashed to pieces on a reef. Everything gone... men... vessel... And what's more, the fucking island was deserted.'

This story was grabbing their attention. Good. Anything to fill the hours; fill his head. Jack watched Jim leaning in, fascinated by Vane's story of survival and ultimately of bad luck. They all kept the story going with prompts of, 'What next?' 'And then what?'

For all that Jack had detested Vane, he knew there was only one possible end to both their stories. And what of other sea rovers? If he and Vane couldn't make it, then who could?

Vane got to the part of his story where he'd been rescued and taken on board a vessel, and he became quiet. Jack prompted him. 'And? What happened then?'

'I was spotted, that's what happened. Spotted by a fellow I'd met before and didn't know was on board. But he knew me and knew I wasn't a fucking castaway; some stray they'd taken pity on.' Vane sighed as the men murmured their condolences, then he looked at Jack. 'And what's your story?'

Jack waved his hand at Dick. Let him begin, and the rest could chip in. He shuffled restlessly around the room, then brought his attention back to Dick's story. 'Stop. That's enough! Enough about how Barnet nabbed us. We've plenty of better stories.' Jack turned to Vane. 'You remember when we were with Jennings out at the Spanish wrecks? Those were the days, heh?'

Vane chuckled. Vane, the man Jack disliked so heartily, suddenly felt like his best mate. Someone he shared a past with – a past disappearing quicker than he cared to think about. Yes, keep the stories going. They'd had a lot of good times, and if they didn't reminisce now, then when?

'A bit of baccy would go down a treat...' Dick sounded forlorn.

'Nah. Booze. Definitely!' This was George's wish. 'Should've emptied the *William*'s supplies down my gullet while I had the chance.'

'Jim?' Jack called to the lad, sagging against the wall.

'Cap'n?' Jack was touched Jim still conferred the title on him.

'Remember at Eleuthera – the girl at the tavern?' This got Jim smiling and George chuckling.

'What's that about?' Vane was curious.

Keep the stories going – remember the good times. And Anne? Remember the good times with Anne. In a way Jack knew it was simpler being with men now. Nothing about being with Anne was ever easy, and he felt too much grief over what would happen next to think about her. Almost anything else was easier for him than to let his mind drift back to her, and he didn't care to share his thoughts with his cellmates. Tender words and raw emotions were not for the likes of them.

During the days Jack sought small things to occupy his mind, but nights were no better. He paced till he could no longer stand.

Sleep was sporadic, and when it came vivid dreams filled his brain. Once he woke with a cry, tearful, after imagining his mother's head in a noose. When he'd shaken this image away his waking brain introduced a fresh one: Anne standing at the gallows, a noose placed roughly around her neck. He shuddered and pushed this all-too-real picture out of his mind.

A memory flooded back. He had been ten at the time: 1701, just after May Day festivities.

'C'mon. Down to the docks. Let's have a jolly time – just the three of us. Promised I'd take you, didn't I? Quick, before your ma gets home and puts a stop to it.'

Jack and his brother Hal had kept pace with their father, zigzagging through the narrow east London streets all the way to the wharves, where they'd found themselves pushing and jostling with others gathered on the quayside. Many onlookers, hoping for a better view, were crammed onto small boats on the Thames.

Above the hubbub Jack heard drumming. He peered over men's shoulders and between their hats. His father, a tall, broad-shouldered man, had a better viewpoint as he watched the horse-drawn wagons approach from the Marshalsea prison.

'Ah, there he is! The man himself, with the fancy hat. Just about missed him.'

They were at Wapping Docks to witness Captain Kidd and seven of his men executed.

Neither Jack nor Hal were small boys, but their father hoisted each of them on his back in turn. From here Jack watched snippets of the drama playing out on the tidal banks of the Thames. His father kept up a running commentary, so whichever boy couldn't see could still participate. Gripping his father's back with his knees, Jack witnessed the condemned men lined up with nooses around their necks, and before he was ready – unquestionably before the men were ready – they were shoved off the platform, legs jerking in an ungainly dance of death. Everyone cheered, but he had felt discomfited.

As they walked home along Wapping Dock, passing men and women raking the muddy banks of the Thames for cockles, Jack's eyes were drawn back to the dead men swaying in the breeze.

He, Hal and his father stopped at a stall selling cockles and whelks and chatted to others who were filling their bellies. Some people they knew, others became friends for the moment, united by the excitement of the day.

'We've had our fun, boys, but just remember this day. I'm not one to tell you what to do with your lives, but just remember this day – that's all I'll say.' His father had tossed more cockles into his mouth, chewed and paused. 'No, one more thing. Whatever it is you do, don't get caught. That's got to be the chief lesson of the day. If you're going to gamble, be a winner, not a loser.' He threw back his head and roared with laughter, choking and spluttering and spitting out half-chewed cockles.

57

With every swing of the man's arm the ceremonial silver oar glinted, catching the morning sun. Jack found it distracting, so he lowered his head, making sure he put one foot evenly in front of the other.

The prison courtyard echoed. How could two drummers create such a commotion? Every tootle of the fifer's 'Dead March in Saul' pierced his ears, but he couldn't ignore the music that played for the five of them in the column: George, Dick, Davy and Howie, with him at the rear.

About thirty steps to reach the prison gate. His chest felt tight, bound as surely as a cooper encircled a barrel with a metal band. He knew which cell Anne was in; he'd found out that much. He would shout his love, his sorrow and regret that she would soon follow him. He counted the iron barred windows to his left.

'Godspeed.'

Anne! Jack's heart pounded; his mouth dry.

George reacted: 'We go to the devil if he'll take us.'

Then Dick: 'And good luck to you, lass!'

Jack took a breath to shout, but Anne was quicker. She was always quicker.

'And you!'

His head jerked up. He could see her fingers clutching the bars, her face illuminated.

'If you'd fought like a man you wouldn't have to die like a dog!'

He felt kicked, winded, could not find any words, only stretch dry lips into a tight smile.

One... two... three more steps and he had missed his chance; time had moved too quickly. He knew she didn't mean it. Not really. She was distraught, and it was just her way. Damn! This was not the parting he had imagined. He put Anne out of his mind, needing to think of himself and prepare for what was to come.

Out through the gates now. The fife and drums were no longer so overwhelming in the open public space, drowned out by the noise of the gathered crowd. He looked them over. A lot of people had turned out.

Ahead was a platform with five gallows, thick rope nooses hanging heavily, unmoving in the still air. Ahead were Governor Lawes and his cronies, men of his council, men he'd seen in court the day before. And Lawes's Marshal and armed guards – plenty of those. And harnessed horses, patiently waiting, reins held firmly.

One step in front of the other. He needed a drink to help him get through this thing.

Ahead was the prison chaplain, Bible in hand. He was glad of the man's presence, his simple black cassock standing out plainly against the colour and pomp of the military uniforms. The man had visited them daily, and while George seemed to have turned his back on God, Jack found comfort in the chaplain's words. If the afterlife was all he had to look forward to, then why not?

Another fifty steps or so. Jack became aware of people pressing in. He could smell their odours, could feel the heat of their bodies, their faces a blur, mouths working, but he had no idea if they were jeering or offering words of comfort. It was strange; he'd not experienced anything like it.

Perhaps twenty steps now. He ran his tongue over parched lips and kept his head erect.

He had arrived.

Sturdy hogsheads, put to a different purpose from transporting sugar, supported a wooden platform with a ladder resting against it. Everything looked solid. Nothing was likely to give way till Lawes gave the order.

Ah! The man Jack most wanted at this moment. A large glass of rum was pressed into his hands, wrists bound. Jack gulped it down and held his empty glass out. He tried to steady his hands and attempt to speak. The words would not come but he nodded his thanks to the man. Rum had never tasted so delicious. The liquid heated his throat, hit his stomach and fired up his brain.

He found his voice. 'Thank you.'

Up the ladder, steady as she goes; Jack kept his eyes on the chaplain. Which gallows to go to? Did it matter? What did he have to do? He wanted to do it right. Someone helped him find his spot, one of the militias guiding him under his noose, guiding his head through the noose, which settled heavily on his shoulders.

He thanked this man too, grateful for his help.

Now he was standing on his spot in the middle, George and Dick either side of him, and Davey and Howie at the two furthermost gallows. He relaxed. This would be all right. He could do it. He turned and nodded swiftly to George to his left, and Dick to his right. Yes, he could relax now, he was with his old mates. There was a comfort in going together.

'I'll not go with m' shoes on! Someone can make good use of them. Yep, I'm done with 'em! May they bring you better luck.' Dick levered off his old cracked leather shoes, kicking first one then the other high in the air above the crowd. People jumped, arms stretching up to reach for a souvenir to take home. Dick had done his best to spruce himself up, begging for ribbons to tie around his hefty calf muscles. Dick was ready for his last fight, and Jack shared a smile with him and turned to George.

George had resigned himself to this long ago. He hadn't cared about sprucing himself up or shaving. He was right, of course, but for Jack it mattered how he presented himself at the end.

He'd done the best he could to be tidy. Tidy: a funny word. Jack chuckled, saying it softly to himself.

His gaze moved beyond George to Davy, scratching the dry, flaky skin on his face and neck that so often afflicted him. 'Stop itching, you mangy dog. Stand tall!' Davy's bound hands dropped as if scalded. Jack was gathering strength by the moment.

Nearly time.

Howie softly began singing 'The Keeper'. Jack was delighted Howie had one final song in him after all. He and his men would make a show for the Spanish Town folk who'd turned out to see them. Howie's voice was no longer strong, but what he could no longer manage in volume he made up in speed and set off at a cracking pace. Jack had last heard this song when he had been in his cabin, longing to join the party out on deck. Finally he could join in.

'Jackie Boy. Master. Sing ye well. Very well. Hey down, ho down derry down, among the leaves so green-o. To m' hey down, to m' ho down, hey down, derry down—'

Singing loosened his tight chest and Jack found he could breathe again. Still breathe. Howie sang two verses, his voice gaining in strength with all the crowd joining in the chorus, before the Marshal put an end to it, earning him curses from the crowd. Jack leant forward, caught Howie's eye and mouthed, 'Thank you.' There'd been quite a few thank yous to say today.

Someone was talking to him, asking if he had any final words. Final words? He should try – it was expected. Jack looked out at the crowd and focused on the faces before him.

'Well, we all come to this, one way or the other. Mine's been a life no worse than many—'

'Aye, but you got caught!' some wag amongst the spectators called out, and Jack found himself laughing. Hadn't his father warned him?

'True enough.' He couldn't think what else to say.

A woman called out, 'Calico Jack! It's me. I'm here!'

Who was "me"? He scoured the crowd and spotted her in the front, waving a scarf above her head. Betsy from the Dew Drop Inn, his favourite watering hole in the whole world. Ah, Betsy! His heart leapt. He was so happy to see her plump figure and friendly face. Stupidly and unreasonably happy to see her. Yes, she'd muscled her way to the front all right. Her truncheon, hanging from her belt, would have whacked some legs to get in the best spot.

He shouted, 'So what's brought you here today? Must be important to take you away from business.'

'Told you I'd come, Calico, if the day ever came. Told you!'

He remembered now – remembered why he felt so happy to see her. Ridiculously happy. It all came flooding back. He appraised her body and was glad her sturdy arms looked as strong as ever and she had put on more weight since he'd last seen her. He nodded to her, choking with emotion as he shouted, 'Thank you!' There! He had said those words again. They were good words to end a life with. No more words were necessary.

Very nearly time.

He closed his eyes and opened his ears to the chaplain's prayer.'The Lord is my shepherd: I shall not want. He maketh me to lie down in green pastures…'

Jack was remembering green pastures all right: green pastures of Kent. Precious memories of summers hop picking with his father, mother, Hal and sisters. Lush green pastures… beautiful. He let his mind drift, imagining green fields and the gentle warmth of an English summer's day.

He opened his eyes, listening to the prayer continue: '…I will fear no evil; for thou art with me…'

He felt the soft cotton of his scarf protecting his neck from the rough hemp rope.

He heard the chaplain's soothing voice.

He smelled sweet fresh air.

He saw the horses' rumps whipped and harnesses yanked.

He heard the grinding sound of wood on wood as the hogsheads were hauled clear.

He felt the earth tipping.

He felt his throat constricting, his scarf no longer any protection.

He felt space beneath his feet.

He heard a buzzing in his ears.

He felt warm liquid trickling down his legs.

He heard his own choking.

He felt himself performing his last ungainly dance.

He saw Betsy's face below him, her eyes on his, right there where she'd promised to be.

He felt her arms gathering his jerking ankles to her ample bosom.

He was filled with gratitude. Hanging on to his struggling feet, Betsy added her weight to his, gave a mighty roar and pulled with all her strength. His brain exploded with the sound of his neck snapping, and unimaginable colours, before darkness claimed him.

58

THE SAND IN THE HOURGLASS HAD EMPTIED FOR THE men in the crew. They'd been tried together and executed over two days. All hangings were the same, and Mary didn't want to upset Anne needlessly by dwelling on it. It had taken courage to question their jailer about Calico. Clearly fascinated, he described what happened after Calico had been cut down.

'Seen hangings before – natural, given m' job – but it was the first time I've seen this being done, to be honest. They had a tub of tar and big brushes handy, then began slopping the stuff all over his body till bit by bit even his red trousers disappeared under the goo.'

'Where is he?' Anne whispered; her face chalky white.

'He's to be taken to Deadman's Cay. He'll make quite a spectacle out there, hanging in his iron cage.'

Anne swayed unsteadily and Mary rushed to help her sit on the floor. With her head in her hands Anne keened. 'I said the wrong words. Not what I wanted to say... I never told Jack. I should've told him.'

'Too late now. You should've said what you wanted while you had the chance.' Mary knew these words were not comforting, but they were truthful. Anne had missed the opportunity to say the thing pressing on her mind, something which would have given solace to Calico, and Mary didn't admire her for it. She'd considered Anne's relationship with Calico had not been her business, and to be fair Anne hadn't opened up to her – not till after Calico had been strung up.

For the next week she and Anne waited in their cell, despondent and dazed.

Mary scrutinised Anne. Her undyed calico dress, faded to a muddy grey, far too short for her long legs and baggy at the waist, did nothing to enhance her womanly attributes. Mary was glad she had decided to stick to her seaman's clothes. A seaman was who she was, and no amount of trying to make her "look womanly for the judge and jury", as their kind-hearted visitor had suggested, could persuade her otherwise. Anne had little choice in the matter, as her jacket had been lost and her shirt ripped beyond repair. Anne managed a joke with their prison visitor, saying, 'Don't you think I'll look womanly enough for all of them if I let my shirt fall open?' The poor woman averted her eyes and blushed as Anne exposed a breast.

The flustered woman had continued, 'Please accept my gifts. You may reconsider what you wear before the trial, and I hope you both take comfort from the Lord's good words.' Her gentle eyes appealed to them both. Mary accepted her parcel of old dresses, a small piece of soap and a Bible.

Following the brief visit Anne picked over the dresses disdainfully. 'Bet she just wanted to gawp at us up close. Bet you even now she's rushing out to gossip about the women pirates she met, boasting about how close she got and telling every damn detail.'

Mary believed the visit and gifts were a genuine act of kindness – maybe the last they would receive.

The prison door creaked open. Two armed guards stood behind their jailer ready to escort them to the Admiralty Court.

'Remember what we talked about – what we agreed?' Anne spoke hurriedly.

Yes, she remembered. They'd had long discussions about it, and she was still considering.

While Mary had defended their devout prison visitor's motives, the spectators pressing into the Court House were definitely here to gawp and enjoy themselves as they jostled for seats. She spotted one woman peeling an orange and another a hard-boiled egg. Mary could feel their eyes on her and hear their whispers. She stood a little taller and looked straight ahead.

Governor Lawes – Sir Nicholas Lawes – presided. Mary studied him closely. He was older than she'd anticipated by a good ten years, and wore a long wig, with a crisp white cravat around his throat and a richly embroidered jacket. Some men become avuncular with age, but she did not think this would be the case with him. He sat behind his broad desk, shuffling through a sheaf of papers, glasses perched on the end of his nose, leaning towards a colleague for a quick consultation, occasionally glancing up at her and Anne. He looked ready to get on with things.

A dozen respectable-looking men, two wearing the uniforms of naval captains, sat on benches to Governor Lawes's side: his commissioners. Mary studied their solemn faces and decided they looked ready to get on with the day, as was she. There was no point in hanging around.

Hanging around! She caught herself remembering Paddy's jest: 'You're a joker and you didn't know it.' She grunted. There would be few things to amuse her now.

A gavel beat a rhythm on the desk and the hubbub in the room dropped to a murmur. Mary stood looking straight in front of her and disciplined herself to stay still.

The clerk read the King's Commission: 'George, by the Grace of God, of Great Britain, France and Ireland, King, defender of the faith...' On and on, making sure the court records were correct and Sir Nicholas's authority was stated clearly, and reading out the names of each man of the Council. The clerk droned on, referring to the Act of Parliament to do with suppressing piracy. And still more. Outlining their right to examine witnesses under oath; their right to pass sentence, and sentence of death. On and on. Mary feared that the opening proceedings was taking so long she might struggle to retain her discipline – afraid her body might sag, and she meant to stay erect, shoulders back, head high and meet her fate squarely.

The spectators were also becoming restless, and the earlier quiet of the court had given way to shuffling feet, rustling fans, and whispers. Somewhere in the audience – and it was an audience – she heard a mumbled, 'Get on with it,' and a small ripple of laughter. But the clerk hadn't finished. Mary perked up at his words: 'And lastly...'

'...we do direct, empower and require you, the said Commissioners, to proceed, act, adjudge and determine, in all things according to the powers, authorities and directions of the recited Act...'

It had become hot and stuffy. She could feel sweat gathering under her armpits and in the small of her back and her body slumping. She dug her nails into the flesh of her hands: a small pain to divert her.

She and Anne were brought to stand before the governor. The clerk took a sip of water, and again his monotonous voice droned on, reading the charges against them, the whole thing long-winded and detailed.

'On the third day of September upon the high sea in a certain place distant about two miles from Harbour Island, did piratically, feloniously and in a hostile manner, attack, engage and take seven fishing boats, then did attack and assault certain fishermen, putting them in corporeal fear for their lives. Then did steal fish and fishing tackle to the value of ten pounds.'

She glanced at Anne. In her memory those men hadn't been in fear of their lives. She frowned. Or had they?

The legal words continued to unwind from the clerk's mouth. 'On the fifth day of October...'

Who cared what day? Neither she nor Anne could remember what date they took the prize off the Hispaniola coast, though in fairness the master and crew of the vessel would probably remember. Mary became uncomfortable hearing the story – her story – put in different words. Words telling of mariners in "corporeal fear of their lives" saying Calico's crew "piratically and feloniously did steal the two said merchant sloops".

What had taken weeks of cruising suddenly all piled up together: these charges and more charges.

'On the nineteenth day of October off the Jamaican coast...'

She heard a gasp as spectators learnt they'd shot at Thomas Spenlow and his mariners. She frowned. Yes, they'd shot across the vessel's bow. So what? No one had been killed. Why make such a fuss? She nodded at the estimation of twenty pounds' loss to Spenlow: fair enough.

'On the twentieth day of October...'

Mary concentrated on the charge being read. This would be Dillon's sloop, and the man had assessed his losses at three hundred pounds. She raised an eyebrow: Dillon was pushing his luck for compensation.

The way their cruise was being presented to court, it sounded like a frenzy of looting and barbarity, but it had been nothing of the kind; it had taken place over many weeks. Sea rovers getting by in the world. She again studied Governor Lawes: his face was impassive as he listened intently, watching them all, occasionally writing a note or two.

Then came the pleas to the charges, and of course she and Anne pleaded not guilty. This was expected of them; it made it harder for the court to prove their case. Why not? She had little confidence she would win this game any more than Calico and the other men had won theirs, but she'd play her hand as long as she could.

Now for the witnesses. She heard a Dorothy Thomas called, and turned to watch a small, pinched-faced woman in her thirties walk determinedly forward to the bench, place her hand on the Bible and swear her oath. Had they met this woman? Mary frowned.

Dorothy told her story, vividly and in detail, gesturing at both her and to Anne, recounting the seamen's clothes they'd worn and the weapons they brandished at her. Mary glanced at Anne trying to recall, then a vague memory of the woman emerged. She'd been wearing a sun bonnet, paddling furiously away from them in her fishing canoe off the Jamaican coast; not fast enough, so they'd caught her and stripped her of her goods. Mary was forced to confront this woman, who she knew would be hard-working, eking out a living on land and sea, but at the time of their encounter Mary had come out on top. Now Dorothy was taking enormous pleasure in being on the winning side.

Thomas Spenlow was called to tell his story. This took a while, and everyone looked hot and tired. The clerk whispered to Governor Lawes, but he shook his head and gave directions to continue.

'The court calls Thomas Dillon.'

Dillon made sure he included Anne and Mary, saying determinedly, 'Yes – they were both profligate, cursing and swearing a lot, and ready to do anything asked of them.'

Governor Lawes looked first to her then to Anne. 'Have you any witnesses you wish to call in your defence?'

Mary shook her head, as did Anne. What else could they do? Of course they didn't have any bloody witnesses.

Governor Lawes pressed them. 'Please answer for our records.'

She and Anne both said, 'No,' loudly and watched the scribe record this.

'Have you questions you wish to ask? It is your right.'

She shook her head again and answered, 'No.' She and Anne had somehow become docile creatures and allowed themselves to be led out while the court deliberated.

At least four turns of an hourglass passed. Two hours: half a watch duty. Mary paced back and forth, longing to smoke her pipe, longing for this to be over. She did not want to talk with Anne, she'd seen enough of her in the past week, and right now she was content with silence. The court door opened. The commissioners were ready with their verdict.

The heaviness of the atmosphere in court struck her. The air felt oppressive, threatening a thunderstorm, tempting her to look upwards and breathe deeply for a moment or two. All faces were on her and Anne: grave faces, looking as if they themselves faced death. She twitched. Get on with it. Say the words. And as if in response to her unspoken command, Governor Lawes wasted no time saying they had been found guilty of all charges.

'Do you have anything to say, anything to offer us, why the sentence of death should not be passed upon you?' His unflinching gaze moved from her to Anne.

She glanced at Anne, who had begun to fidget. Anne took a breath to speak, but clamped her mouth shut. Mary nodded. This was the way it would be then: they would die together.

Mary shook her head, and she and Anne both mumbled, 'Nothing to say.'

Governor Lawes took a moment and, reluctantly it seemed to her, pronounced their sentence in a long, roundabout way she felt to be unnecessary.

'Mary Read, and Anne Bonny, you are to go from here to the place from whence you came, and from there to the place of execution, where you shall be hanged by the neck till you are dead. And may God in his infinite mercy be merciful to both your souls.'

Mary gazed levelly back at Governor Lawes.

'I am with child! I am quick with child!' Anne spoke hurriedly, the words bursting from her.

Why she'd waited till this moment Mary could not say, but she was glad of it. She was glad Anne had spoken. Behind her she could hear gasps.

'Mary... Tell them! Tell them.' She felt Anne's elbow jabbing her in the ribs. Insisting. 'Mary!'

So she said it, her heart beating fast, blood rushing to her face: 'I'm also with child.'

This was the thing she and Anne had talked over endlessly in recent days. Anne was carrying Calico's child – no doubt about it. They'd calculated, by her missed monthly bleeding and her tender swollen breasts, Anne must be at least two months gone.

But she herself? It was possible her one fuck with Fen had begun a child. Her monthly bleeding was overdue, but this had happened before in battle campaigns. She hated to think the court might believe her a coward, that she was lying to avoid the noose. But at the same time, didn't a small living thing that might be inside her, a small thing growing into a baby – didn't this child deserve to live? This had been the topic of her endless arguments with Anne this past week, and her gnawing debate within herself.

Governor Lawes looked steadily at them; lips pressed together. He too might be wondering if they were lying and cowardly. He too might wonder why they hadn't spoken earlier. One of the commissioners, the one Mary had pinned as the most legally minded, sprang to his feet and whispered in the governor's ear. The governor nodded.

'Well, this is a turnabout and we must ascertain the facts of the matter. This is an Admiralty Court, and we have no authority to kill an innocent child – or two children, as the case may be.'

Governor Lawes skewered first Anne then Mary with his sharp eyes. 'Mary Read and Anne Bonny – a stay of execution is granted while your conditions are considered.' He turned to the guards. 'Take the prisoners away.'

Governor Lawes rose, collected his papers and turned to speak with his commissioners. His business with them was done for today.

59

'Sir! I think you'll enjoy this.' Jeremy held out a letter, its seal broken.

Woodes cautiously enquired, 'What is it?'

Correspondence to do with the responsibilities of governing he had authorised Jeremy to open and sift through, deciding what could wait and only bothering him with urgent matters. Such letters were rarely accompanied by the word *enjoy*. Might this be another of Jeremy's jokes? Jeremy had become more and more confident, interrupting him to share gossip and trivial matters. Stories Jeremy found amusing were usually about drunken or foolhardy disputes, or stupid people risking encounters with crocodiles or snakes and coming off the worse for it.

This time Jeremy was not giggling but bubbling with excitement. 'Read it, sir. I beg you. It's from Sir Nicholas.'

Woodes absorbed the words on the page. And he did enjoy what he read; it astonished him.

Jeremy grinned. 'We'll have to tell Mr Harmon the *William* was outrun. He won't be pleased to hear that.'

'Lawes doesn't go into detail, but I agree: no doubt Mr Harmon has lost his vessel.'

Woodes reread the short letter. 'Governor Lawes is having quite a time of it. It's a wonder he has space enough to hold all his visitors.'

'Temporary visitors. Didn't need feeding for long.'

'True, though the women are still being fed and watered from what he says.'

Both Bonny and Read had pleaded their bellies: lewd women, both of them, about to bring fatherless children into the world.

'The carpenters will be busy. How many trees? How many gallows?' Jeremy frowned, mentally calculating.

Woodes and his council had pondered such things: had considered the industry needed to support an influx of pirate prisoners. It was a costly and complex business, involving a great many logistical and legal considerations. Prisoners were expensive to keep: their own provisioning plus their guards. And there were legal costs. Rogues though they were, they were owed a fair trial, and London demanded correct legal procedure and record-keeping.

Woodes was surprised at his own relief. For so long he had wanted the satisfaction of stringing up Rackham, and Vane, and any of the pirates refusing to be dislodged. Clearing the seas of this menace had driven him. Yet now, reading Lawes's letter, he was grateful it wasn't he who had to bear the cost. He had played his part well enough, but the end game would be in Lawes's hands – no bad thing, as Jamaica's overall economy could handle it, while Woodes's bills were being rejected right, left and centre. His health was deteriorating, his money long gone, and London officials continued to ignore him.

Woodes turned to Jeremy with tired eyes. 'You know, I feel in need of sea air. A change.'

'I'll call a meeting of the council. If not this evening, then first thing tomorrow.'

As Woodes watched Jeremy bound out of the door, he was astounded by the young man's energy when he himself felt bone tired. Perhaps a sea voyage to South Carolina might help? He could leave Fairfax in charge and escape this oppressive heat for a short while.

Several weeks later Woodes was back in Nassau, but still exhausted and beginning to doubt his own sanity.

'You did what? Did I hear you correctly? Is this some jest?' Thomas Walker looked as if he didn't know whether to laugh or not.

Woodes had been debriefing his council on political matters – things he'd found out while in Charles Town. He'd learnt changes had been put in place for the co-partnership of the Bahamas without him being aware of it. This news shocked him. He'd been telling his council he had written to London asserting that he did not deserve such treatment. The men around his table, Walker, Fairfax and the rest, sighed and nodded, mumbling, 'Par for the course.'

Woodes talked of constitutional changes taking place in South Carolina and the ensuing riots and disturbances.

'I hope you kept yourself safe, Rogers, and didn't get caught up in things. It sounds an unsettling time to have visited.' Walker's comments were no more than a platitude; he knew Woodes would have kept well away from any rabble. But this wasn't quite the case. Not quite.

Woodes took a steadying breath before saying, 'By the way, you may care to know I bumped into Captain Hildesley. Unfortunately we fell out. And, well, the truth of the matter is I challenged him to a duel.'

This had made them all sit up and stare at him slack-mouthed and Walker enquired, 'Is this some jest?'

'It is a fact. I lost my temper and we duelled. One thing led to another and we found ourselves going at it – though in the end we both came away with just a scratch or two.'

Fairfax nodded. 'Unfinished business then. But I'm surprised your passions were riding so high after all this time.'

'I surprised myself.' Woodes could acknowledge this. He'd last seen Captain Hildesley in Nassau harbour on the *Flamborough* at the time of a failed Spanish attack several months earlier, when Jose Cornejo had arrived at the harbour bar with a flotilla of heavily armed vessels. Throughout Nassau windows had been shuttered, doors barred and valuables hidden wherever their owners thought safest. Throughout the night they had feared they would be invaded, the town torched and Woodes had expected to be taken prisoner.

In Charles Town he found himself jabbing his finger at Hildesley, berating the man. 'You left us to our fate. Left us, knowing we needed you. Refused my orders to remain!'

Hildesley, his face flushed with indignation, retorted, 'Your orders! Damn you, man. I do not take, nor have I ever taken orders from you! I needed to get back to my station at South Carolina.'

'My position was clear. My task was to protect His Majesty's territory, and the people living—'

'You overreached your position!'

'Captain Hildesley. Any man who truly serves his country would not have left us to our fate – would not have quibbled about such a thing. Not then. Not now. Not ever!' Then Woodes threw his worst insult at him: 'Your action in leaving us was not honourable!'

'Honourable! How dare you!' Hildesley almost spat the words. 'You have presided over those far-flung patches of earth, as if their loss would make the slightest difference to His Majesty. They are not significant to anyone but yourself. You flatter yourself if you think anyone gives a damn about their fate!'

Hildesley turned away as if to dismiss him, but Woodes would not let this slight go by.

'No, sir, you shall not leave before I have satisfaction from you!'

All the injustices of the past years had risen to the surface and losing his temper with Hildesley was not something Woodes was proud of. Despite all the years he had commanded men on his long and arduous voyages, keeping a cool head, keeping the peace, damping down hot-headed fools, yet in Charles Town he became one of those men, hot-headed and raving. Might he be losing his sense of proportion?

Now, back in Nassau, Woodes looked at the astonished faces gathered around his dining-room table, none of them any longer concerned with political matters or threats of new wars with Spain; they were only interested in hearing about his duel.

When he had finished his story, he felt Walker's eyes on him.

'I, more than any man here, know how this life, the role you have been playing and continue to play mightily, can suck you dry. How this climate can sap you of energy. We managed well enough without you for several weeks while you were in Charles Town. Fairfax is more than capable of holding the fort. Perhaps you need a longer break… Why not go home, enjoy an English spring? Stay for a while.' Walker smiled invitingly.

Should he venture so far? He frowned, considering it.

'No one has done their duty as tirelessly and persistently as you,' Walker stated firmly, receiving a, 'Hear, hear,' and thumps on the table. 'You've done what you came to do. You've got rid of the pirates.'

'Damn it. This sounds like an obituary!' Woodes felt alarmed, but the faces and voices of all his council were sympathetic and supportive.

Spring in England, then. The thought of fresh air and a mild climate appealed. His body and mind needed a rest, and a long voyage home and sea air would do him good.

Home, though? Did he consider England home now? What did home mean? He looked forward to visiting Bristol, and seeing his two children in particular, but he had invested too much of himself in this Bahamian project to consider it completed. He meant to return.

60

ANNE WAS LEARNING TO ACCEPT JACK'S DEATH. SHE missed lying next to him at night, and the daily exchange of small talk; little things she wanted to tell him bubbled to her lips. She missed hearing his voice, and the way he threw his head back when he laughed. She missed the intimacy of sex. She missed Jack.

Rage overcame her, and at first she would pound the prison wall till her fists were raw and she'd fall down exhausted. Those occasions were becoming fewer.

'Stop your bloody ranting,' Mary might say, or simply, 'Let it go – just let it go.'

Gradually her heart seemed to beat less painfully. She felt calmer for longer periods, learning to get through each day and night in the confines of their cell, learning to be patient, accepting that some days were bound to be worse than others.

Her baby quickened inside her, fluttering movements refusing to be ignored. Each day she had time to learn about it, resting her hand on her swelling belly, feeling the smallest of motions, wondering about its watery world. She had never speculated about such things with her past two pregnancies – but she had never been so idle as now.

She accepted the fact that a baby would come into her life again. Mary teased her. 'Must've been conceived after we left Nassau, when you and Calico were fucking like rabbits. That's what comes of having fun.'

Anne smiled, remembering all that was best about her time with Jack. Even so she wasn't sure if she could love any baby and spoke of her doubts to Mary.

Mary grunted. 'By the time this little one's born you might actually want it – might learn to like it. Love it even. It's Calico's baby, after all.'

One night, as she and Mary lay on their straw pallet waiting for sleep to come, she haltingly told Mary of the baby she had left behind – abandoned – and told her of her lie to Jack, saying the baby had died. As she found the courage to tell Mary, her tears flowed: tears of shame and regret. At Mary's prompting, 'Why, Anne? Why would you do such a thing?', she tried to explain how badly she'd wanted to join Jack at sea, and her fear that a baby would shackle her. Babies always did this. Mary reached out a hand to touch her, saying, 'Let it go, Anne, nothing you can do now.' She lay awake for hours, listening to Mary's even breath as she slept, gradually allowing her own breath to quieten and synchronise.

Another day Mary turned to her out of the blue, saying, 'You should've told Calico, y' know that, don't you?' Anne began to bridle, but Mary stopped her with a gruff, 'Hey now. Hey, it's me, remember? I'll not put up with your nonsense.'

Anne turned her head, wanting to push away the truth Mary forced her to confront. As if this hadn't been constantly on her mind!

Yes, she could've told Jack she was with child. Should have. This would have comforted him, knowing she'd likely get a stay of execution, and a bit of him would live on into the future. He would have loved to learn this. Yet at the time she could not bring herself to acknowledge this pregnancy, to accept that Jack would not be there. Could not bear to think of what would happen to him. All this weighed heavily.

Yes, she should've told Jack, about the child left behind and the one to come. Going over this in her mind had kept her awake for nights on end. She had meant to shout out to him as he was marched under guard to the gallows; had practised saying the words, 'Jack! I'm with child!' Instead she had flung cruel words at him. She deeply regretted it, but at the time she could not contain her anger: anger at his leaving her; anger he had not proven big enough to fight the world. There remained a hard part in her heart that had still not forgiven him, and even after his execution she had been dry-eyed.

Jack was dead and she missed him mightily.

All the men from their crew were long gone. The day after Jack's execution she and Mary had yelled their farewells through the cell window to Paddy, Noah, Fen, Jim and the others.

The fishermen who'd joined them for a drink were dead too. Nine innocent men hanged.

'Poor bastards – poor damned bastards!' Mary had stared in shock when their jailer brought this news along with their evening meal. The court had found the fishermen guilty just because they'd helped row the *William* to get them out of a tight spot. Anne had been aghast. She stared at Mary, both silently acknowledging that this news didn't bode well for either of them.

Vane had been dispatched; this stood to reason, and Anne was glad of it. She knew his body had been put on display near

Jack's at the harbour entrance and didn't like this one bit. Jack deserved better company.

Anne learnt to live with uncertainty.

Gnawing away at her was what would happen to Mary. She was not with child, and they had no idea if or when she would be called back to court for Governor Lawes to end her stay of execution. Each time they heard the key in the door, they waited to see if this would be the day. But each time the door opened it was to bring in a meal or take out slops.

Mary managed to jest, 'The Admiralty Court's a bit busy right now – perhaps they haven't got time for me.'

So they passed another day and another week amusing themselves with games of cards and dice as they waited for the next thing to happen.

And she herself?

'Mary, do you think they're waiting for me to have the baby? Perhaps they'll take us both out together? Perhaps we'll get hanged together, side by side?'

'Maybe. That wouldn't be too bad, would it – you and me together at the end?' Mary frowned. 'Best not think about it too much.'

But she did think about it, and while they lived, hope remained.

'Perhaps when we get out – if we get out – we can start something together – I don't know – some sort of trading business – some sort of—'

'Stop this!' Mary's spoke sharply. 'I know where my life's heading – it's just a matter of when. That's it. This is my fate.'

'We don't know that. We don't know for sure.'

And they didn't know anything – didn't know a damn thing about the outside world.

Days and weeks went by.

Another thing Anne was learning: caring for Mary. This was easy in itself, but the thought of losing her weighed heavily. This was Mary's second bout of fever since they'd been in jail, and Mary couldn't understand it. 'I'm never ill – don't know what the matter is.' But despite her protests it was Anne's turn to nurse her friend.

Mary lay shivering and sweating on the straw-filled pallet they shared. Anne dipped a cloth into the bucket of water at her side, wrung it out and gently bathed her face. A small smile spread on Mary's face. 'I did this for you, y'know...'

'I remember.'

'Not everything. You don't remember everything.' Mary spoke softly.

'What?' Anne dipped the rag back into the bucket.

'What I heard Calico say, when he was with you.'

'He never nursed me. Hardly visited. You were the one who was there.'

'No, he came. Said stuff.'

'What?' Anne paused; not sure what Mary was talking about.

'That he loved you and so on – all of that.'

Was Mary's mind wandering? Jack never once talked about love to her, never used those words. Nor she to him, for that matter. She frowned, thinking back. She remembered Jack asking her if she loved him when they were dancing on deck. But he had just been fooling around, and she had been annoyed because he'd kissed her in front of the men, so had pushed him away. Thinking about this made her feel uncomfortable – made her shiver. Her frown deepened.

Love was a difficult word and Anne didn't like to use it, not even to Calico; and she didn't encourage him to get sentimental with her. Love? She associated the word with loss. You gave your heart only to have the thing you cherished snatched from you, so best not give it in the first place.

'What d'you mean?' Anne asked again, curious.

'Calico was distraught – I heard him; he was weeping—'

'Weeping? For me?'

'Who else, you damn fool!'

Anne dropped the rag into the bucket, her hands shaking. Had he really loved her so deeply? Was she so blind? She thought it was she who needed him, anxious she would get turfed out of the gang and out of his life.

Mary raised a hand and squeezed hers, her eyes flickering open then closing.

'Stupid damn woman. Course it's possible to love you.'

Anne looked at Mary's work-hard hand with its thick, capable fingers resting lightly on her own. Anne kept very still, feeling the touch of Mary's hand on her own.

'And you?' Anne's words were no more than a whisper.

'Love's a funny thing – there's all sorts in the world.' Mary opened her eyes and looked directly at her. Anne met her gaze steadily.

She was a slow learner, such a slow learner. She gently stroked Mary's hand resting lightly on hers and lay down next to her friend, listening to Mary's laboured breath.

'You're free to go, Mrs Bonny... Mrs Bonny? Hear what I said?'

Anne woke with a start. She hadn't heard the jailer jangling his keys and pushing open the squeaky door. The sounds and smells of the place were so familiar that she slept solidly now. She awkwardly levered herself into a sitting position and looked stupidly at the man swinging his bunch of keys.

'Said you can go.'

'Go? Go where?' Anne was confused. Was she being taken back to court?

'Anywhere you bloody well please. Whaddo I care?' This jailer, a man called Toby, whose belly overhung his trousers and who wheezed every time he spoke, stared at her, his face as stupid as hers probably looked.

'What's happening?' Mary rubbed her eyes. Despite her fever, Anne trusted her brain would make sense of this.

The jailer smirked. 'Seems it's your lucky day, Mrs Bonny. Seems you've got a daddy who loves you.'

'Daddy? My father?' Anne was confused. 'What's he got to do with anything?'

Toby rubbed his thumb and forefinger together. 'Not all of m' charges're so lucky. Seems the gov'ner received a letter and a tidy sum of money for the good of the poor of the parish. Toby rolled his eyes. 'Seems the gov'ner reconsidered things – your having a baby and all.' Toby jangled his keys. 'Get out before he changes his mind – that's what I'd do.'

Mary sat up with difficulty. 'Go, Anne. Don't think. Just go!'

But her feet were leaden. After all these months, raging and longing to flee, the moment had come, but she couldn't just bolt through the door.

'Time... Time, Toby, give me some time.'

'Time?' Toby stared at her uncomprehendingly.

'We need some moments to say goodbye.' Mary found the right words. 'Leave us a while.'

Toby shook his head, mumbling that he thought they'd had quite enough time inside. Still he heeded Mary and lumbered out, shutting the door.

Anne faced Mary, suddenly awkward. What to say? What to say when you find you are the lucky one, and have to leave your friend to her fate – and this fate a known outcome?

'Go! Go and don't you dare come back! You hear me?'

'But, Mary—'

'But, Mary, what?' Mary stared fiercely at her. 'But, Mary, I can't leave you? Is that what you mean? Don't be stupid. I've said often enough this was a game we played and took our chances. Haven't I said that? Haven't I?' Mary found the energy to thump her in the chest, pushing her off balance.

'Yes, Mary.'

'Well then, go.' Mary shouted. 'Toby! We're done!'

'But, Mary...' Anne could feel the panic rising in her. She couldn't just leave – it was unthinkable. 'I'll come back and visit tomorrow. I'll stay around and visit.'

'Don't you dare!' Mary shouted. 'I'll refuse to see you. Go... Go far away. Go. I don't want to see you!' Mary turned her head and bellowed. 'Toby! Get your fat arse back here!'

Anne heard the keys in the lock turn, the lock grind open. She leant forward and hugged Mary as close as her belly allowed. For long, long seconds they clung together. Mary drew back and planted a firm kiss on her lips and, with equal firmness, pushed her away.

Anne took a steadying breath. 'Goodbye, Mary.' She would not see this woman again.

Mary nodded and grunted. 'Don't look back. Just don't look back.'

She walked out and didn't look back.

For three days Anne walked. Streets near the jail, Spanish Town, roads of the parish, walking in ever greater circles, allowing her mind to settle. She had a pouch of money from her father, but if there had been an accompanying letter it hadn't been passed to her. Anne circled until she felt ready to set off along a straight road.

In Kingston Anne waited for news from Spanish Town and finally, two months later, the news she had been dreading arrived. Fever claimed Mary in the end, not the noose, and Anne was grateful for it.

Anne's face and heart were hard from all her experiences. Even her belly had grown hard, and she would feel a rounded rump or an elbow or foot dig into her ribs, reminding her of her child's presence.

Time to leave this place.

'Where shall we go, baby?' She stroked her belly. She had taken to talking to her unborn child; was even beginning to look forward to its arrival and had decided on a name: Mary or John. No question about that.

Anne fingered the leather pouch of coins: enough for a sea voyage, or maybe two.

'But first, baby, there's something we've got to do.'

EPILOGUE

DEADMAN'S CAY, APRIL 1721

ANNE HAD WAITED WEEKS TO GAIN THE MENTAL strength to face this, only to find her journey delayed by lashing rain and high winds. Today was the day.

'You sure I can't take you all the way? I'm strong for m' age and the wind's dropped.' The boy's eyes were fixed on her swollen belly. He might be thinking of her condition but more likely he was hoping for an extra penny.

Anne shook her head. 'Just the boat.'

She left the boy at the jetties at the tip of the Palisadoes, the thin peninsula leading from Kingston to Port Royal harbour entrance. Rearranging herself, she took up the oars. This would be a short journey and one she needed to do alone.

The boy yelled after her. 'Bring Daddy's boat back!'

She rowed steadily away from the jetty, twisting her head every so often to keep her course straight. First she had to pass Gun Cay, where Vane's body hung in irons on the shallow sandy islet: in death the man finally proving useful to her.

'Halfway there, baby.' She glanced at Vane's body to get her bearings and rowed on.

She had told the boy she could manage, but it was hard going, the distance greater than she'd anticipated. Twice she stopped and sat bobbing in the small waves, gathering her strength before picking up the oars and rowing on.

Dragging the small boat onto the sandy islet, barely reaching above the waterline, she kept her eyes averted and reached into the boat to retrieve her basket.

'Ready, baby?' Talking aloud helped.

Even if the baby was ready, she was not. She stood facing the open sea, easing her aching back, breathing in the sea smells, feeling the sun and wind on her face and listening to the screech of gulls. She allowed these familiar sounds and smells to calm her, only then becoming attuned to a new sound, so slight she was barely aware of it: a dry creaking of iron rubbing against iron.

'Ready.' She stroked her belly and raised her eyes to look squarely at what she had come to see: Jack's body embraced in thick iron bands dangling from a gibbet.

She had imagined this moment for so long, dreading how he would look five months after his execution, and dreading how she would cope. She stared at this rotting body. She only knew it was Jack because she'd been told he and Vane were on display for everyone to see as they entered the harbour. But she could not see Jack – could only see a tarry body in ragged clothes, skin almost picked clean.

'Well, baby, that's that. It wasn't so bad. No need to stay.'

She wanted to be gone from this place. She didn't need to be here after all. But she waited. No point in rushing back.

She looked again at the body swinging gently in the wind encased in its protective cage, exploring it with her eyes. Then curiosity got the better of her. Reaching out, she tentatively touched a shoe. Was this Jack's? She could not be certain; all seamen's shoes looked alike. Her finger traced the side of the tar-encrusted shoe to where it stuck to the heel and ankle bones. She reached higher, exploring a shin, and flinched, realising she was touching bone, the skin and muscle rotted by sun and stripped by birds. But it could be any man. Tarry ragged trousers flapped above the knees. She fingered the ragged fabric between thumb and forefinger it as if it were a piece of cloth for sale at market. She breathed in relief. This had been easier than she had dared hope.

A small gust caught a ragged edge of fabric. It fluttered, and she glimpsed the underside: distinctive red calico. She recoiled. Jack! Oh yes, this was Jack!

Without warning a hurricane force storm overcame her, completely, utterly. Never in her life had she experienced such a thing. Sobs convulsed her till she could no longer stand. Snot streamed from her nose. She clasped her arms around her belly, hugging herself, aware there was no one left on earth to comfort her, apart from herself.

She had not cried when Jack had been executed, nor when Mary died; now she sobbed and sobbed, rocking and keening as she mourned for them all: Jack, Mary, Paddy, Noah and all the men who had been her family – her life. Most particularly she mourned for Jack: her man.

'Jack?' She spoke his name softly, tentatively. She'd grown used to speaking to her yet-to-be-born baby, because – who knew – it might be able to hear her. She doubted talking to Jack's corpse was any use, but it felt good, nevertheless.

'Jack – I'm so sorry...' A whisper. 'I miss you. I miss you, damn it... Damn you, Jack, I miss you so much...' Words tumbled out. Tears and words needed to flow.

The sun had long passed the midday mark, but she did not rush. The boy would have to wait for his dad's boat.

Sitting on this tiny islet under Jack's body, Anne began to understand that this thing called love could only be truly understood in its absence, and she knew without a doubt that she had loved Jack and been loved by him, and by Mary in her strange way. But it was too late to talk to Jack, and she had no intention of whispering words of love to this corpse dangling by her. Too late to get sentimental.

'Right, baby.' Anne lumbered to her feet and picked up her basket. 'Almost time.'

Opening the basket, she took out a handful of red hibiscus flowers, their vibrant petals beginning to wilt. She judged the direction of the wind, tossed the flowers high and watched the breeze catch them, lifting them on an eddy before the flowers dropped to settle on the water. She repeated the gesture with another handful and a third.

'There, Jack, I've kept my promise. Hope you know it, and they give you comfort.'

Time to go now. The boy, or most likely his father, would be wanting his boat back. Anne wasn't sure the father knew it had been taken.

Still she waited. 'Where next, baby? Where shall we go?'

She should return to Great Abaco and search for her abandoned boy and claim him if she found him alive. Yes, she must do this. And then? Maybe return to South Carolina to have her child. Her father might agree to meet her in Charles Town, if his shame wasn't so great that he refused to see her. Perhaps he might even allow her to stay at the plantation for a while, as it was the only place she could call home. She couldn't be sure of any of it. She was damaged goods, and for all she knew her father might have risen in society and wouldn't want the likes of her around. And then what?

She cupped her hands in front of her mouth, blowing gently as her small boat bobbed out to the extent of her outstretched arms.

ACKNOWLEDGEMENTS

No NOVEL SPRINGS READY FORMED. IT HAS BEEN A long journey from my initial fascination with Anne and Mary to the story in print today. Philip Holmes advised on nautical aspects and we hope things are ship-shape.

With grateful thanks to my first readers for their feedback and encouragement:

Vivienne Hamblin, Jane Scroxton, and my partner Hubert Kwisthout, for reading more than one draft; Diana Štainerová, Jo Holmes and Nona Shepphard; my invaluable Slack Writers' group, with particular thanks to Karmen Špiljak, Katie John, Andreina Cordani, Lidija Hilje and Cara Finigan.

I am indebted to Lynne Patrick for line editing.

Anna M Holmes
Website: annamholmes.com
Facebook: Anna M Holmes Writer

BLIND EYE

Anna M Holmes

**An environmental thriller published by
The Book Guild autumn 2021.**

Cockroaches, rats, humans. All of them pests. And forget rats
and roaches, it's humans that are destroying the planet. Linda
took a breath to still her shaking hands then opened the web
portal and began.

DAE.org/Blogs/Linda

Just imagine, it's hot, sticky, can't wait to hop in a shower
and you could kill for a cool beer. Maybe you're
thinking this trip was a bad idea and you should've
stayed home. I had one of those moments earlier.

The day started well. We were in the forest when I

heard thrashing in the top branches, looked up, and there she was: Mom with a baby clinging onto her tummy, swinging to the next tree. Awesome. Take a look at this **video**. See how caring she is? You can't help but feel the connection between our species. But that's it for the cute bit. I want to tell you what happened later when we saw a different mom and babe. She was clutching a branch on a solitary tree and keeping hold of her little one. Long story short: Mom fell from a great height, missed the darned net they were trying to catch her in, and it took a long time for her to die. These guys were trying to save her, move her to a protected area. Huh! Sickening to witness.

Linda winced, recalling the thud of that massive orange bundle of fur connecting with the hard earth. Goddamn humans! If she had known then what she knew now, she wondered whether she would have had kids. But she loved her two – both decent human beings – and she was getting used to being a grandma. Not a hands-on granny, but her daughter understood. Whatever time she had left was going to count. Linda interlocked her fingers, cracked her knuckles, and continued.

If you've a strong stomach, click on this **link.** The babe you see survived. Another one for the sanctuary. Let's stop shit like this happening!

To find out what Direct Action for the Earth is doing to save our planet and how to get involved, go to our **Campaigns**. Check out our **Membership** schemes and don't log off till you've clicked through to **Donations.**

She dispatched her latest blog post into cyberspace.

*

Ben pedalled steadily, dodging traffic on Westminster Bridge and along Millbank. London's toxic air probably cancelled out the benefits, but cycling was a matter of principle. He secured his bike, checked there was no chain oil on his good chinos, raked his fingers through his hair and headed towards the Department for International Trade's Whitehall office.

After he passed security, he made his way deeper into the functional part of government. He knew the way, but he followed a junior staffer to the second secretary's office where she knocked and showed him in.

'Mr Ahearn, Doctor Fletcher's here.'

Connor Ahearn looked up from whatever he was working at on his laptop. 'Thank you, Grace. Good to see you, Ben. Thanks for coming.' He stood, a welcoming grin on his face. 'How've you been?'

'Fine.' Ben nodded noncommittally as they shook hands, and settled into a chair across the desk. So it was to be just the two of them then. That informal.